# WARLORD
## FURY OF THE GOD-MACHINE

*Discover the war machines of the Imperium in*

IMPERATOR: WRATH OF THE OMNISSIAH
A novel by Gav Thorpe

• **IMPERIAL KNIGHTS** •
By Andy Clark

Book 1: KINGSBLADE
Book 2: KNIGHTSBLADE

KNIGHTS OF THE IMPERIUM
A novella by Graham McNeill

TITANICUS
A novel by Dan Abnett

TITAN
A graphic novel by Dan Abnett and Anthony Williams

*From the Horus Heresy*

MECHANICUM
A novel by Graham McNeill

TALLARN: IRONCLAD
A novel by John French

THE BINARY SUCCESSION
An audio drama by David Annandale

HONOUR TO THE DEAD
An audio drama by Gav Thorpe

IRON CORPSES
An audio drama by David Annandale

*Tales of the Adeptus Mechanicus*

• **THE MARS TRILOGY** •
By Graham McNeill

Book 1: PRIESTS OF MARS
Book 2: LORDS OF MARS
Book 3: GODS OF MARS

• **ADEPTUS MECHANICUS** •
By Rob Sanders

Book 1: SKITARIUS
Book 2: TECH-PRIEST

# WARHAMMER 40,000

# WARLORD
## FURY OF THE GOD-MACHINE

### DAVID ANNANDALE

BLACK LIBRARY

*For Margaux, and the odysseys of summer.*

**A BLACK LIBRARY PUBLICATION**

First published in 2017.
This edition published in Great Britain in 2018 by
Black Library,
Games Workshop Ltd.,
Willow Road,
Nottingham, NG7 2WS, UK.

10 9 8 7 6 5 4 3 2 1

Produced by Games Workshop in Nottingham.
Cover illustration by Akim Kaliberda.

Warlord: Fury of the God-Machine © Copyright Games Workshop Limited 2018. Warlord: Fury of the God-Machine, GW, Games Workshop, Black Library, The Horus Heresy, The Horus Heresy Eye logo, Space Marine, 40K, Warhammer, Warhammer 40,000, the 'Aquila' Double-headed Eagle logo, and all associated logos, illustrations, images, names, creatures, races, vehicles, locations, weapons, characters, and the distinctive likenesses thereof, are either ® or TM, and/or © Games Workshop Limited, variably registered around the world. All Rights Reserved.

A CIP record for this book is available from the British Library.

ISBN 13: 978 1 78496 682 9

No part of this publication may be reproduced, stored in a retrieval system, or transmitted in any form or by any means, electronic, mechanical, photocopying, recording or otherwise, without the prior permission of the publishers.

This is a work of fiction. All the characters and events portrayed in this book are fictional, and any resemblance to real people or incidents is purely coincidental.

See Black Library on the internet at

# blacklibrary.com

Find out more about Games Workshop
and the world of Warhammer 40,000 at

# games-workshop.com

Printed and bound by CPI Group (UK) Ltd, Croydon, CR0 4YY

It is the 41st millennium. For more than a hundred centuries the Emperor has sat immobile on the Golden Throne of Earth. He is the Master of Mankind by the will of the gods, and master of a million worlds by the might of His inexhaustible armies. He is a rotting carcass writhing invisibly with power from the Dark Age of Technology. He is the Carrion Lord of the Imperium for whom a thousand souls are sacrificed every day, so that He may never truly die.

Yet even in His deathless state, the Emperor continues His eternal vigilance. Mighty battlefleets cross the daemon-infested miasma of the warp, the only route between distant stars, their way lit by the Astronomican, the psychic manifestation of the Emperor's will. Vast armies give battle in His name on uncounted worlds. Greatest amongst His soldiers are the Adeptus Astartes, the Space Marines, bioengineered super-warriors. Their comrades in arms are legion: the Astra Militarum and countless planetary defence forces, the ever-vigilant Inquisition and the tech-priests of the Adeptus Mechanicus to name only a few. But for all their multitudes, they are barely enough to hold off the ever-present threat from aliens, heretics, mutants – and worse.

To be a man in such times is to be one amongst untold billions. It is to live in the cruellest and most bloody regime imaginable. These are the tales of those times. Forget the power of technology and science, for so much has been forgotten, never to be re-learned. Forget the promise of progress and understanding, for in the grim dark future there is only war. There is no peace amongst the stars, only an eternity of carnage and slaughter, and the laughter of thirsting gods.

## CHAPTER 1

# DUTY AND PRIDE

*Does he really believe this is almost over?* Ferantha Krezoc thought. *He can't. He isn't stupid and he isn't mad. He has to know better.*

*But he's proud,* she reminded herself.

Cursing the blindness of Adrel Syagrius, the princeps senioris of the Warlord Titan *Gloria Vastator* lashed out. The Belicosa-pattern volcano cannon of the god-machine's right arm burned trenches through the enemy. Las so powerful it could melt armour and fortifications blasted monsters to steam.

Moments later, the trenches filled and the tyranids came on.

The land before Hive Gelon crawled and heaved. Destruction surged towards the walls of the city in waves of terrible life. The land had become a thing of claws and acid, of chitinous armour and swarming, monstrous hunger. There was nothing left of the marshlands that had stretched out before Khania's capital city. Their entire biomass had been consumed, and now the tyranids came to devour the millions of lives within Gelon. The legio of the Pallidus Mor and the 66th Kataran Spears held the line.

While the legio of the Imperial Hunters chased trophies and glory.

The sky over Gelon flashed and burned. In orbit around Khania, an Imperial Navy fleet fought the tyranid bio-ships. Vox-traffic to the surface was fragmentary, transmissions broken up by the fury of ship-to-ship fire and the maelstroms of burning plasma left by the destruction of once-mighty vessels. The signs of the void war reached the combatants on the ground in the form of bright scarlet bursts, silver lightning and clouds that roiled like slow eruptions.

The fifteen Titans of the Pallidus Mor's demi-legio blunted, then tore through, the mass of tyranids. They disrupted the flood while the 66th armoured regiment of the Kataran Spears created a blockade. The latter's tanks had formed up along the ragged line where the industrial wastelands outside Gelon's walls gave way to the sea of mud that had been the marsh. Warhounds loped along the flanks of the tyranid swarm and launched raids into the elements still miles from the front lines. Reavers patrolled the wastes, towering sentinels striding over hills of refuse and through rivers and lakes of toxic effluent. They were the rearguard, mobile annihilators taking down the xenos horrors that got through the Spears.

The Warlords pushed deep into the tyranid assault. Theirs was not a defensive manoeuvre. They were the counter-attack, the storm that had come to purge the tyranids from the face of Khania. They were the immense majesty of righteous war, high peaks that moved across the battlefield, their weapons obliterating the crawling, scuttling, lumbering monsters.

The land heaved, and the Warlords burned it back to the bedrock.

*'Krezoc,'* voxed Toven Rheliax in *Crudelis Mortem*, *'there's an energy spike to the west.'*

In the manifold, Krezoc shifted her focus. *Gloria Vastator* had been incinerating swaths of 'gaunts and warrior bio-forms, easing the pressure on the Spears' blockade and on her secutarii, who were keeping the smaller tyranids from trying to climb the legs of the Titan. Krezoc looked west with the eyes of the auspex array and saw the spike. *Gloria Vastator* was closest to the position, still miles away, where bioenergy readings had surged red.

'Incoming exocrine barrage,' she told her moderati. The tyranids had hit the Pallidus Mor and Imperial Hunters with long-range artillery bioforms when the legios had first walked on Khania. Krezoc and her fellow princeps kept a sharp lookout for another such attack. 'Pre-emptive strike west,' Krezoc said. She fed the coordinates from the manifold to the moderati. Their wills were linked to hers and to *Gloria Vastator*'s machine-spirit, and the Titan turned its weapons to the new targets as if they were an extension of Krezoc's body. On her right, Brennon Grevereign worked the volcano cannon with her. On the left, Agara Vansaak unleashed the Mori quake cannon. On the right shoulder of the carapace, Moderati Minoris Doran Konterus was linked to the Apocalypse missile launchers, while on the left shoulder, Ferrek Haziad kept the Vulcan mega-bolter trained on closer enemies. Missiles, shells and las-beams seared the gloom of the day. The massive recoil of the launchers thrummed through the body of the god-machine. The distant landscape lit up with explosions wide enough to engulf entire hive sectors. The bioenergy spikes vanished from the auspex, the readings overwhelmed by the cataclysm.

From within the firestorm, the barrage of burning bio-plasma arced up. There were large gaps in the attack, but comet flights of destruction soared towards Hive Gelon. And though the Pallidus Mor turned the battlefield into an ocean of flame, the tyranids pushed forwards, their numbers and hunger too great to stop.

'Marshal,' Krezoc voxed, 'any word from the Imperial Hunters?'

*'Nothing new,'* said Eras Balzhan in *Ferrum Salvator*. *'But Marshal Syagrius is aware of the situation.'*

*Perhaps so*, Krezoc thought. Perhaps he even understood it. But his pride wouldn't let him respond as he should. 'He is still reporting bio-titans?' she asked.

*'Yes.'* Balzhan spoke again after a moment, cutting off her curse. *'That is his task, princeps senioris. This is ours. We shall complete it.'*

'So we shall,' she said. The Pallidus Mor's history was a saga of grinding conflicts, not a hymn of battle glory. *Gloria Vastator* fired into the distance again, this time joined by Merys Drahn's *Fatum Messor*. As the western reaches of the battlefield erupted a second time, the bio-plasmic barrage came down. Shouts and reports across numerous vox-channels filtered their way into the manifold, and Krezoc registered the damage done with the edge of her conscious mind. The plasma balls struck a wide area of the wastelands. Kataran tanks exploded and chunks of the hive's walls crumbled beneath the blasts.

*'Close up the formation,'* Balzhan voxed. *'Concentrate on the centre of the mass. Smash the forward advance.'*

Before Krezoc could begin *Gloria Vastator*'s turn, Vansaak warned, 'Harpies!'

A large flight of the winged monsters descended from the flame-ridden clouds. They launched tentacled missiles ahead of them.

'Vulcan,' Krezoc ordered as the view beyond the control chamber's armourglass was filled with wings and the flashes of void shields straining from the electromagnetic shocks of the bio-missiles. The tyranids were attacking with a massive swarm, multiple bioforms striking at once. The Warlord entered its slow turn, spraying massive bolter shells into monsters whose reptilian forms were delirious echoes of humanity's ancient nightmares.

'South,' Grevereign called. 'Large movement to the south.'

There were too many attacks from too many directions. The mega-bolter took down enough harpies to ease some of the shocks to the void shields and for Krezoc to turn a portion of her focus to the new threat. Massive squat shapes shouldered through the cauldron of warrior forms. The auspex spiked again with a surge of bioenergy.

Biovores, Krezoc realised. Another artillery force, a short-range one this time.

There was no chance to hit them first. Before Krezoc and the moderati could bring the weapons to bear, the air of the battlefield was filled with a green gaseous cloud, spore mines making their lethal, floating descent.

Krezoc cursed Syagrius and his pride as she braced for the explosions.

\* \* \*

Harth Deyers dropped into the interior of the Leman Russ *Bastion of Faith* and pulled the turret hatch shut just as the bio-plasma barrage hit. The firestorm swept over the wastelands. A monster roared outside the tank. A hurricane of flame shook the hull. The front of the Leman Russ bucked as it struck an obstacle.

'Are we blind?' Deyers called to his driver.

'No, captain,' Silas Medina answered. The tank levelled off again. 'Just running some xenos into the ground.'

At the controls of the tank's battle cannon, Lehanna Platen said, 'Targets still visible,' and fired. The recoil of the gun was reassurance that they were still in the fight. So was the vibrating shudder of the sponson heavy bolters.

The worst of the storm's roar faded. Deyers slapped a new magazine into his bolt pistol and climbed back up. He trusted Medina and Platen, but he felt useless when he could not see the battle himself. He heaved the hatch back and raised himself into waves of heat. The initial devastating blasts had passed, but the fires still raged. Rivers of promethium had ignited. Ammunition in destroyed vehicles cooked off, setting off secondary explosions across the battered line of the blockade. Some of the tyranid bioforms caught in the barrage blew up as the flammable gases in their bodies ignited. Some of the tall hills of waste metal and rockcrete had melted. The bubbling, industrial lava spread everywhere, swallowing infantry and tyranids. Ahead, another wave of the enemy tide surged forwards. *Bastion of Faith* was near the centre of the Kataran Spears' formation. Cannon and bolter fire was constant along the line to Deyers' left and right. Shells slammed into the chitinous wave. The devastation the Titans were wreaking further ahead had thinned the swarm, and there had been a moment, before the artillery had hit, when Deyers had thought the tanks might hold the enemy, that the wave could be defeated. But there were gaps in the blockade now. The tyranids charged the tanks, and they raced between them too. The cannons did their work, and it was not a sea of the foe that swept into the wastelands.

Even so, the numbers were high.

Deyers opened up with his bolt pistol, punching through the armoured head of a hormagaunt that leapt over the sponson fire. The creature's skull exploded, and its twitching corpse landed across the turret. Deyers fired around the body at more of the bounding horrors. The cannon swivelled right as Platen took aim at a cluster of larger monsters, and the body slipped to the smouldering ground. *Bastion of Faith* had to keep moving now, growling across wreckage and bodies on a short patrol running north to south. There were no longer enough tanks for anything like fixed positions, and any vehicle that was not constantly in motion was a target for the xenos beasts. The vox-traffic snarled with overlapping commands and cries. A hundred yards ahead of *Bastion of Faith* as it made its way north, the Leman Russ *Cardinal Renhorn* was covered in warrior forms. They stabbed into its armour with talons as tall as a man and blasted it with bio-plasmic cannons. The tank's sponson bolters destroyed the monsters that came before their barrels, but there were several of the warriors riding the top of the hull, out of reach of the guns.

'Platen,' Deyers voxed.

'*Already on it, captain,*' she answered, and *Bastion of Faith*'s cannon rose slightly. There were few gunners Deyers had encountered that he would trust to attempt the shot, especially with the Leman Russ in motion. But if Platen thought she could make it, then she had to take it on. *Cardinal Renhorn* was helpless, even as its battle cannon still fired heroically into the rest of the enemy mass. *Bastion of Faith* fired. The shell screamed into the warriors, striking just above *Cardinal Renhorn*'s turret. The explosion ripped the tyranids apart. Jagged, smoking remains fell from the top of the hull.

The freed tank roared forwards, crushing 'gaunts beneath its treads, its weapons sending a torrent of fire into the horde. Then it exploded. The warriors had done their work, rupturing too many critical systems. Its last charge had been a dying stab at a foe that had already killed it. Deyers winced from the glare of the fireball. *Cardinal Renhorn*'s momentum carried the flaming wreckage deeper into the tyranids, adding more of its killers to its pyre. Burning fuel spread the inferno still wider, and then there was yet another gap in the blockade.

In the sky, there was a huge flare. Another ship had met its end. No way to know if that was a Navy victory or not. Deyers choose to believe it was. 'Hope in the skies!' he voxed to the regiment. 'The fire of victory for Khania and for Katara!'

He had to be right. A few days ago, there had been the illusion of triumph. The orbiting bio-ship had been destroyed. The Pallidus Mor and the Imperial Hunters had destroyed an enormous bio-titan, and the remaining tyranids had been pushed back from Gelon. Marshal Syagrius, in overall command of the campaign, had declared the war was almost over.

Then more bio-ships had come. The void war had begun in earnest, and the second wave of the ground war had erupted, more savage than the first. In the first day, there had been more bio-titans. They had since become fewer and were landing in more distant locations, and the Imperial Hunters had moved off in their pursuit. The apparent mercy had been a false one. The waves of smaller bioforms were as ferocious as before, and larger. The marsh was gone, and the tyranids were hungry for the life of Gelon. Deyers felt like he'd been fighting inside the maw of a devouring beast without surcease for months.

He had not. The war was only days old. And the casualties of the Kataran Spears were mounting. The regiment still had fight in it. It was still holding fast for Gelon, but even with the terrifying strength of the Pallidus Mor in the field, Deyers could imagine the destruction of the 66th. And if they fell on Khania, what of Katara?

The home world. In the neighbouring Sevasmos System. As *Bastion of Faith*'s battle cannon fired again, blasting apart a cluster of warrior forms at such short range the heat of the blast cracked Deyers' skin, his last sight of the city of Creontiades flashed before his inner eye. He fought for Gelon and for Khania, but his defence of this world was also in the name of protecting his home. The tyranids were closer to Katara than they had ever come before. He did not know what would be left of Khania by the end of this war. He would die before seeing the same fate reach Katara.

The thought came to him that he very likely would.

Further out on the battlefield, the immensities that were the god-machines shook the earth with the intensity of the fire they directed at the ground. Entire cities would have been razed to the earth by now, but the tyranids kept coming. Flying bioforms swarmed around the heads of the Titans, and the day pulsed with the discharges of clashing energies. Then a green cloud burst across the battlefield, rising high up the legs of the Warlords. Bright orbs floated down.

Deyers saw the new attack only for a moment. Then something exploded from the ground in front of *Bastion of Faith*. Briefings on the enemy forces gave him its name. *Mawloc*. Before the horror of its reality, the name ceased to be a means of classification, an imposition of nomenclature and of control. It became sounds. The hissing roar of a split-jawed maw spreading wide. The clacking chunk-chunk-chunk-chunk of six huge talons jabbing into the armoured flanks of the Leman Russ. The serpentine length towered over the tank, and then the monster lunged down to swallow Deyers.

Hoplite Alpha Venterras recognised the signs of an imminent spore mine attack before the first of the orbs began their descent. So did the rest of his squad assigned to guard *Gloria Vastator*. The Warlord had begun to turn, but now it stopped, its massive legs as immobile as the foundations of the world, as the crew of the god-machine braced for the impact of the barrage. The legs were colossal pillars, dozens of yards in circumference.

<Barrage countermeasures.> Venterras sent the order in binaric. His order was received and obeyed in a fraction of a second, as if every member of the hoplite squad had taken the same initiative at once. Alpha Trigerrix's peltasts moved with equal purpose. Five toe-like supports, each larger than a man, jutted from the base of both of the Warlord's legs. The hoplite and peltast squads of secutarii ducked into the spaces between the supports. The

hoplites raised their mag-inverter shields. Both squads had respected proximity discipline, and their kyropatris field generators amplified each other. The interlocked harmonic fields created a protective sphere around the secutarii squads. The air hummed with holy energy.

The blasts came at every elevation from twenty feet in the air to just above the ground. The spore mines sprayed the dead marshlands with acid and chitinous shrapnel. The sound was jagged and wet, hail in a typhoon. The biovores' assault was huge, spreading over the battlefield as far as Venterras could see. When the orbs in the green cloud exploded, *Gloria Vastator*'s lower void shields flared with the strain of repelling hundreds of blasts in cascading succession, and the shredding kinetic energy of the shrapnel. The shields could not stop the acid. It splashed against the adamantine armour. It rained down on the secutarii. Protected by the base supports from the worst of the corrosive's horizontal flight, the hoplites angled their shields upwards to deflect more of what came from above. Venterras heard the hiss of dissolving metal. Streams ran down the Warlord's leg, scoring the sacred metal. The energy of the kyropatris fields stuttered and spiked from the strain. Rivulets of acid fell upon Venterras' helm and pauldrons, triggering warning runes in his helm's lenses. Cogitators in his armour and his reconstructed body began calculating the rates of damage he could sustain and still act. There was very little organic weakness left in him. Beneath the armour, even those patches on his face and chest that resembled leathered flesh were bioplastic. The readings satisfied him. Despite its ferocity, the attack had failed.

He rose as the blasts lessened. The secutarii had kept the

tyranids from scaling the legs of the Warlord, and now the spore mine explosions had scoured the area. For a few seconds, the illusion of emptiness reigned in a land of lingering fog and bubbling, smoking mud. Tyranids shredded by the shrapnel lay everywhere. They were lesser bioforms, common as insects, no sacrifice at all for the Devourer. In the distance, Venterras heard a terrible grinding. Somewhere, hidden from him by the corrosive gas, a Titan had suffered great injury. Machinery was crying out in anger and in pain. The grinding accompanied a limping rhythm of thuds. With some difficulty, the god-machine was walking. One of the Warhounds, Venterras judged by the speed of the footsteps. It was moving faster than a Reaver, but had been slowed badly, and would be that much more vulnerable to further attacks.

Above Venterras, *Gloria Vastator*'s void shields still flashed arrhythmically as the generators fought to re-establish stability.

The moment of emptiness passed, and a new wave of termagants snarled out of the mist. They raced for the bases of the legs, straight into the secutarii's fire. They were a scuttling horde, their fleshborer forelimbs sending a hail of insects against the defenders. The vermin were tiny, their mandibles fierce. They sought to chew through armour to get at the flesh below, but the greatest mass of them hit the mag-inverter shields of the hoplites' forward line. Half of Venterras' squad hit the termagants with frag launchers while he and the others marched on the tyranids with arc lances at the ready. The fields of the shields repelled the foe's attacks, hurling the bulk of the swarms back. Some of the burrowing vermin made it through the physical and energy barriers, yet there was little flesh for them to eat. Their jaws could eventually damage circuitry and cables, but there was no nourishment for them here. They were an assault on the wrong kind of foe.

Behind the hoplites, the peltasts fired their galvanic casters. Laser-guided projectiles arced overhead and dropped with murderous precision into the tyranid hordes. Bursts of explosive flechettes shredded the termagants, and then the short-range blasts of the hoplites' arc lances ate further into the charge. *Gloria Vastator* walked again, and the secutarii advanced with it.

Yet the field of battle was wide. The secutarii were few. The Pallidus Mor had only a single echelon to defend the entire demi-legio. The enemy's numbers dropped, but they were still legion. The centre of the swarm broke under the secutarii advance, and its flanks circled the feet of the god-machine.

<Climbers,> Hoplite Krightinus warned.

A handful of termagants had leapt onto the left leg when it came down, and they were moving up, clinging fast as it took another step.

<Maintain unit cohesion,> Venterras said. He ran hard for the leg. His omnispex overlaid vectors of speed and angles of approach on his view of the landscape, breaking down his next moves to calculations of physics and efficiency. It projected his path to every target on the leg. This was a war between the purity of the machine and the organic at its most pestilential. It turned every arithmetical breakdown into a sacred act.

Venterras shouldered his shield, mag-locking it to his back as he covered the last few yards to the leg. His arc lance fired a concussive blast ahead of him, hurling bioforms out of his way. The leg came down, shaking the ground. Venterras leapt. He landed on the top of the foot's central toe. He held his arc lance in his right hand and jumped again, seizing a pitted handhold in the leg with his left. Cables contracted. With a movement that would have dislocated a biological arm, he hurled himself upwards. He followed the red-lined path from handhold to handhold. Where there were none, he sent an electrical charge through his palm, magnetising himself to the leg long enough to leap again. He came up fast behind the termagants. They were scrambling towards a service hatch a few yards past the Warlord's knee.

Venterras fired the arc lance. The coruscating energy skimmed the surface of the adamantium. The burning impact was enough to jolt two bioforms free of their grip, and they hurtled to the ground. Three others turned and scrambled back down to attack Venterras. Two more kept climbing.

Three streams of fleshborer vermin blasted against him like sand whipped up in a hurricane. He could not use his shield, and he was too far from the squad for the kyropatris field to link with the others. His lone generator could do little to blunt the attack. Xenos jaws, minuscule but ferocious in strength, ground away at his plate. Venterras launched himself upwards again and stabbed with the arc lance, striking with it instead of firing. He hit one of the termagants directly. The explosion consumed its forelimbs as it fired again. The beast disintegrated in a storm of fire and bioelectricity that swallowed Venterras and the other termagants. Venterras channelled a draining burst of his own power to keep his hold on the leg. Two more tyranids fell.

*Gloria Vastator* took another step. Venterras clung to a

vertical world, and it swung with majestic impassiveness, the movement alone almost enough to shake free the insects fighting on its surface. Venterras climbed again. He moved past the knee, his bionic auditory sense filled with the thunder of enormous pistons. The last two termagants had almost reached the hatchway. Venterras lunged and fired again. The blast jarred the tyranids loose. They fell, cartwheeling as they bounced against the side of the leg. One of them sailed past Venterras and dropped into the void. The other slammed into him. It knocked him back, jerking his magnetised palm from the leg. It scrabbled at him with its claws. They fell in a tangling struggle. The leg sloped away from the vertical as the Warlord took a step, and the combatants slid down the adamantium cliff. Venterras' arc lance became a liability. He could not strike the tyranid with it, he could not use his right hand to arrest his fall, and to release the arc lance would be an unforgivable mark of shame.

The termagant's jaws snapped in his face. The teeth gouged the front of his helm. The wind of their slide shrieked. In another moment, they would fall past the knee and into mid-air.

Venterras fired the arc lance at zero range as the tip struck the Warlord's armour. The blast was point-blank. A ball of lightning lashed at him and the termagant. A galvanic spasm shook the tyranid's limbs, its chitin armour smouldering. The beast lost its grip on Venterras and dropped away. His optics buzzed in and out of focus, warning runes overlapping as the damage to his armour and machined body mounted.

But he was a servant of the Omnissiah, and a secutarii of the Pallidus Mor. Nothing except his complete destruction would prevent him from fighting in the defence of the god-machines of his legio. Though his internal circuits were beginning to misfire, sending micro-tremors down his arms, he sent a powerful energy spike through his left hand once more. His palm smashed against the leg just as he fell past the knee, and the angle of the Warlord's leg returned to the vertical. The yank would have wrenched an organic shoulder from its socket.

Venterras paused long enough to calculate the trajectory of his descent. The pause lasted a fragment of a second. Then he was dropping back down the limb of the colossus, rushing back to the cauldron of the ground war.

'These are poor game,' Adrel Syagrius muttered.

*'Their destruction still burnishes the glory of the Imperial Hunters,'* Princeps Messina Lukretus voxed from the Warlord *Primum Victor*. *'And we are gutting their numbers.'*

The marshal grunted. He kept his attention on the advancing cluster of carnifex bioforms. They were huge specimens. They could have hurled Leman Russ tanks through the air. Against the maniples of Syagrius' demi-legio, though, they were hardly more than an irritant.

They were a greater irritant for not being the targets he sought.

'Sunfury barrage,' Syagrius voxed to the entire demi-legio. 'Banish these vermin from my sight.'

The command was also a warning. Three of the Warlords were equipped with the Sunfury-model plasma annihilator. The simultaneous firing of the full complement of the guns was an event the other Titans had to be ready for, as did the secutarii on the ground. The plasma annihilator was not a precision armament. Its function was total obliteration. Every shot carried risks. Every shot was an enormous drain on a Titan's power plant. And every shot was the act of a wrathful god.

Three shots were the divinity of flame.

*Augustus Secutor*, *Primum Victor* and *Eximius Gladio* fired. Three suns burst upon the carnifex advance. The arc of the horizon flashed with devouring brilliance. A firestorm engulfed the land. Entire cities would have vanished into its maw. The flames rose to the clouds, a towering wall of roiling crimson. The silhouettes of the tyranids disintegrated. Monsters that were the nightmares of full regiments of the Astra Militarum were burned to ash in seconds. The maniples of the Imperial Hunters halted their march until the devastation faded. Before them, the land was a smoking plain of cracked, melted rock.

Syagrius looked at the wasteland he had created. His mood did not improve. The extermination of the bio-titans had been an act of frustration more than a tactical decision. When he had seen the nature of their quarry, he had been unwilling to waste a second longer than necessary on their destruction. The long-range auspex readings of a huge, concentrated biomass had given him false hope yet again.

There had been no hierophants, no true bio-titans since the one that had appeared during the initial tyranid attack. He had taken *Augustus Secutor* into single combat against the hierophant before the gates of Gelon. He had almost lost. Ferantha Krezoc and *Gloria Vastator* had intervened. The Pallidus Mor Warlord had inflicted severe damage on the colossal tyranid. It was true that the mortally wounded monster had seized Krezoc's Titan in a lethal embrace. It was true that Syagrius had fired the shot that had destroyed the hierophant. It was true that, technically, the trophy kill was his. The mark of the victory had been added to the upper torso of *Augustus Secutor*.

Syagrius did not feel any triumph in that outcome. The battle was a canker on his pride. He could not think of it without seeing his errors of judgement. He could not stop reliving the helplessness he had felt in the moments just before the arrival of *Gloria Vastator*, when the hierophant had overwhelmed his god-machine, and he had seen doom reach for him. The memory ate at him, and he could not turn from it. Honour demanded redemption. The only way of lancing the boil was to prove to himself and to others his supremacy as a hunter. He needed more kills on the same scale. He had to crush the spectre of the hierophant. That victory would come only when *Augustus Secutor* stood over the ruins of bio-titan bodies.

The Imperial Hunters had travelled hundreds of miles from Gelon, and exterminated scores of biovores and carnifexes. The promise of greater prey drew Syagrius on, but the promise had been an illusion so far.

'Marshal Balzhan is on the vox,' Rekorus said.

Syagrius glanced down and to the right at the moderati. He had redirected all vox-feeds not originating from within his maniples to Rekorus. He was tired of the endless hectoring of the Pallidus Mor marshal and the insubordination of Krezoc.

Syagrius had assumed supreme command of the Khanian campaign from its inception. He had done so with full justification, due to the larger force fielded by the Imperial Hunters. Balzhan had not protested. Yet he was constantly second-guessing Syagrius' decisions at the strategic and the tactical level. Balzhan concerned himself even with battles at which he had not been present.

Such as the one against the hierophant.

'You used your Sunfury on the enemy?' Balzhan had asked afterwards. He had caught up to Syagrius outside the Mechanicus dry docks of Gelon, where the wounded Titans were being repaired. This was during the false dawn before the coming of the second wave of bio-ships. Skyscraping gantry cranes clustered around the motionless god-machines. Tech-priests, engineers and mono-tasked servitors swarmed over them, healing the bodies of the Titans and soothing their machine-spirits. The air was filled with the sound of industry and ritual chanting.

'Yes, I used it,' Syagrius said.

Balzhan's eyes were bionic, and so impossible to read. His bald head, enclosed by a metal brace, looked like a bronze skull in a cage. 'You felt that was necessary?'

'Are you in the habit of using weaker weapons against more powerful foes?' Syagrius asked, looking down at the squat, wide-shouldered marshal. He intended the contempt in his tone to be all the answer Balzhan would require. It was impossible not to see crude, proletarian stock in the leader of the Pallidus Mor. Syagrius' family was nobility, and traced its service to the Imperial Hunters back millennia.

'I deploy the weapon the moment calls for,' Balzhan said. 'The hierophant's wounds were already severe. It did not require a plasma cannon to finish it off. You put *Gloria Vastator* at risk.'

'My aim was true. I'm surprised, marshal, that you aren't thanking me for having saved Princeps Senioris Krezoc and her Warlord.'

He knew, as he spoke, that he was leaving himself open to the unpleasant reminder that Krezoc had lured the hierophant away from *Augustus Secutor* before launching her attack. The truth was that *Gloria Vastator* had come close to sacrificing itself to save Syagrius' Titan. As he waited for Balzhan to point out his shame, Syagrius tried to think of a satisfying answer. He failed. Balzhan regarded him impassively, and said nothing. The awkward silence stretched out.

Ferantha Krezoc chose that moment to walk by, on her way back from inspecting the work on *Gloria Vastator*. She glanced towards the two marshals. She and Balzhan exchanged slight nods, the understated greeting of old comrades. Her eyes were still organic, but the look she gave Syagrius was as machine-like in its cold neutrality as Balzhan's. She was much taller than her marshal, and perhaps an inch or so taller than Syagrius. She walked with a slight hunch forwards, like a bird of prey on the hunt. Where Balzhan was built like a wall, Krezoc seemed made of cable, a narrow, coiled silhouette in her princeps' greatcoat. Her scalp, like Balzhan's, was clean-shaven. A line of mechadendrite ports ran up the back of her neck to her crown. She was not much younger than Balzhan, and though she moved with the ease granted by juvenat treatments, her face bore the experience of many decades of war. It was a thing of gaunt stone, fractured by deep canyons. Her eyes looked out from their sockets as though from the bottom of wells. They were a blue so pale they were almost white, and were hard as shell casings.

The look she gave Syagrius was just long enough for him to think he felt judgment, but too brief for him to be sure and demand Balzhan call his subordinate to order.

Krezoc was, Syagrius thought, a perfect, grim match for the god-machine she controlled. He glanced up at *Gloria Vastator*. The Warlord, like all the Pallidus Mor Titans, was an engine of death, not of glory. He assumed there was pride in the legio, but it was not the one he knew in the Imperial Hunters. The green, white and red panoply of the Hunters was resplendence itself. What he saw in the Pallidus Mor, though, was a dark embrace of the fatality of war. The bone colour beneath the black of *Gloria Vastator*'s primary armour plates was the shade of an old skeleton. Even the silver trim was cold and pale, turning the glint of sunlight into the shine of ice. Its heraldry showed the same darkness. On the Warlord's right-hand tilt plate, a skull floated in the black void. The left plate was a shield of gold and black, upon which a skeletal arm raised a scythe. Three drops of blood fell below the blade, through the gold. On the banner that hung between the colossal legs, a sun in eclipse glared over golden wings.

Night, shadows, pallor, death. All was death with the Pallidus Mor. Syagrius was not surprised his actions were baffling to the likes of Balzhan and Krezoc. He cursed the fates that had brought him to share a campaign with them.

Krezoc moved on.

'I am sure you did as you saw fit,' Balzhan said dryly.

'Meaning what?'

'Exactly what I said.'

'Our work on Khania is not finished, Marshal Balzhan. Our legios need to continue to work together effectively.'

'I could not agree more,' Balzhan replied. He said no more.

And when the tyranids had come again, Syagrius divided

the efforts of the Titanicus task force. The Pallidus Mor defended Gelon, and the Imperial Hunters took the aggressive role, pursuing the enemy and destroying its largest threats before they could reach the hive. That was the principle behind the strategy – a two-pronged counter to the swarming invasion. This was what Syagrius explained to the princeps of the legios. He admitted to himself that the battle plan served his purposes by putting distance between himself and the grey fatalism of Balzhan's maniples. He had never encountered warriors so deaf to the calls of glory.

But he had not freed himself of the thoughts of that flawed victory over the hierophant, of the judgment of the Pallidus Mor. None of the promising auspex returns had borne fruit. His campaign had been as much of a repetitive grind as the one he had left at Gelon. And the emotionless, remorseless voice of Balzhan kept calling on the vox, *respectfully* requesting his return. At length, he had funnelled those communications to Rekorus so he could ignore them. In particular, he wanted to shut out Krezoc's voice. Her exchanges stopped just short of being cutting, and he could not hear her without feeling the acidic stab of the bad memory.

Balzhan had been trying to reach him now for several hours. Syagrius sighed, resigned. 'Patch him through,' he said to Rekorus.

*'Marshal Syagrius,'* Balzhan said a moment later, *'the tactical situation at Gelon is becoming more serious. This is where the greatest concentration of the enemy is to be found, and it is growing. The presence of the Imperial Hunters is needed.'*

'Are you implying the Pallidus Mor cannot complete its task?'

*'I am saying the realities of this war have changed.'*

Syagrius gritted his teeth. 'Those realities will grow worse if we abandon our hunt. Our roles are clear, marshal. We must both fulfil them if victory is to be ours.'

Krezoc came on the line. *'Is your hunt justifying the effort?'* she asked. *'Have you considered the possibility that you are being lured away?'*

'By a mindless foe?' Syagrius cursed himself for letting his irritation speak for him. He knew better. For all that the tyranids attacked as an all-devouring swarm, that swarm was directed. Every force that had underestimated the tyranids had suffered for doing so.

Krezoc said, *'Will you consider the possibility?'*

Syagrius hesitated. He gazed at the empty, smouldering region ahead of the Imperial Hunters. Krezoc's logic was sound. The fact that the Hunters had found tyranid bioforms in the size and quantity that they had was a bit surprising. The biomass of this region of the continent was significantly less dense and more spread out than what the tyranids hungered for at Gelon. Yet their bio-ships continued to drop more of their monstrosities in the barren hinterlands.

Syagrius sent his consciousness deeper into the manifold. At one with *Augustus Secutor*, he absorbed the incoming auspex readings. The data streamed through his mind like water through fingers. He filtered it for dense clusters, the points of data accumulation that were the echoes of large movements. He found what he was looking for. He was sceptical. At the same time, this was the biggest echo yet. Syagrius and the machine-spirit of the Warlord saw the signs of vast prey thirty miles to the east. The instinct to hunt was overwhelming, princeps and god-machine feeding each other's hunger, fusing them into a single, shared, primordial instinct. It would not be denied. Syagrius had no intention of fighting it.

'The enemy is moving to the east of our position,' he said to Balzhan. The formation of audible speech felt distant from his true self, here in the wash of the power and the hunger of the Titan. 'That is our target. Each legio has its duty. We must see to them.'

'*Marshal,*' Balzhan began, '*Princeps Senioris Krezoc is correct. You are being pulled further and further–*'

Syagrius cut him off. 'Fight well, Pallidus Mor,' he said. 'The Emperor protects.' And he shut down the vox-feed.

There was a greater urgency to his sermon tonight. Confessor Lehrn Ornastas felt the fire in his heart ignite his words. Though he had written notes for the sermon, when the moment came, he ignored them. In the pulpit of the Chapel of Saint Kaspha the Unbending, Ornastas looked out over the congregation and burned with the need, as never before, to give warning. The people were manufactoria serfs and a few lower Administratum bureaucrats. The sectors of Creontiades served by Saint Kaspha's were not wealthy ones. The jewelled spires of the city were a long way from this industrial region. This was as it should be. The dangers Ornastas had seen were in the shadows and grime of the streets. It would be in those same streets that the battle must be fought.

It was his sacred task to warn and to inspire. He must send the cleansing light of fanaticism through the doors of the chapel.

'The might of the Kataran Spears is on Khania,' Ornastas said. 'The salvation of Khania will mean the preservation of Katara. But do not think we have no ramparts to protect, nor battles to fight. Brothers, the heretic is never far. Sisters, I have seen the signs of his foulness.' Ornastas paused. He stared at the anxious eyes looking up at him. The banners hanging from the galleries seemed to move slightly, as if in anticipation of the coming struggle. 'To arms!' Ornastas shouted. 'Do you think yourselves faithful? Do you call yourselves children of the Emperor? Then take up arms! Seek out the heretic! Burn him from his places of concealment! The danger is now! The time of action is upon us!'

He exhorted the congregation for several more minutes. He did not speak for as long as he usually did, and he had made some changes to the order of the service. Nothing that stepped outside the acceptable form of the rite. It was simply that tonight, he needed to end with the sermon. So he preached until the faces in the amber light of the glow-globes were red with fearful anger. Then he let the people go. As they filed out of the chapel, Ornastas listened to the chatter of thousands of voices. He heard the currents of alarm and determination. Good. He wanted to hope he had done enough.

He knew he had not. Unless they encountered slavering cultists in the next few hours, most of the people would lose their fear over the course of the night. Many of them would barely remember the sermon by the next morning.

Ornastas was trying to teach them to read the signs. He didn't think they would be able to. Not until it was too late. He had the insight. He knew what to look for, and even he was flailing about, uncertain as to how to fight.

Ornastas left Saint Kaspha's an hour later. He exited through the small south door. It opened into a warren of alleys that wound between the rockcrete façades of manufactoria and cramped, stinking hab blocks. The sewer gratings overflowed with human waste and the leavings of the forges. The smell was thick as fog. It stung the confessor's lungs and nose. He coughed, his throat filling with gritty phlegm. He took the passageways at random. He had no destination in mind. He was searching. He was hunting. He struck the pavement with the tip of his staff with every step. He was announcing his presence, calling on the darkness to face him or flee.

When had he seen the first signs? He wasn't sure. The awareness had come to him gradually. He was used to seeing the markings on the sides of buildings here. Sometimes they were desperate, illiterate prayers. More often, they were the territorial symbols of the underhive gangs. Their scrawls were meaningless to him, and he had never seen them as more than a background piece of the sector's squalor. Very gradually, Ornastas had become aware of other, more disturbing markings. It took many days before he was sure he was seeing anything wrong. There were stray lines added to other symbols, the hint of something obscene lurking beneath mundane scrawls. Never anything he could identify, never a sign he could point to and say, *This. This is the work of heresy.* Even as his unease grew, he spent sleepless nights doubting whether what he was seeing had any meaning at all.

After the departure of the Kataran 66th, the markings became more frequent. They seemed to be emerging from beneath the overlapping tangles of graffiti. Meaning was pushing its way to the surface. The angles were more aggressive. The lines were sinuous, their lengths trailing off as if they were dropping into an abyss. The makers of the defacing art were becoming more brazen.

This morning, Ornastas had found his certainty. Instinct, or perhaps the guidance of the God-Emperor, had made him stop and look into a darkened recess. It was the doorway to a narrow hab block, barely fifteen feet across, squeezed between two manufactoria. The building had been gutted by fire. Its interior had collapsed. Rubble blocked the way a few yards past the rubbish-strewn entrance. On the left-hand wall, just visible in the gloom, Ornastas had found the harsh angles of a complete rune. Its design made him think of a skull. He could not look at it for more than a few seconds. It hurt his eyes. Something sharp jabbed into his mind. If he did not break off his gaze, he felt the rune might start to glow.

For a moment, he thought he heard, coming from a great distance, beneath the ground or beyond the sky, the tolling of a brass bell.

Now he walked the gloom of the alleys, searching for revelation and an enemy to fight. He had sounded the alarm, but lacked a target for the faithful. He would find it. He would preserve the sanctity of Creontiades.

The lighting in the alleys was poor. The lumen poles were few. Many of their globes were broken. Weak illumination, flickering and red, came from within the manufactoria. Wan glows leaked from the hab windows. Ornastas moved through a night of shifting, pooling shadows. The alleys were almost deserted. Ragged, emaciated figures fled at the sound of his staff. They ran with heads bowed and shoulders hunched in anticipation of punishment. If an ecclesiarch walked among them, they must have been found wanting in some measure.

Ornastas could well believe they were worthy of judgement. Beggars, thieves, the cast-offs of the gangs, they stood condemned by their poverty and desperation. They were undeserving of the Emperor's light, and dwelt in the darkness of their failings. But they were not what he sought.

Knock. Knock. Knock. His staff struck the ground with sharp raps. It bounced off the high, smoke-darkened walls. The echoes ran far ahead of his advance. Ornastas turned a corner, and this alley was completely empty. The walls were blank expanses of rockcrete. Heaps of refuse as high as a man lined both sides of the pavement. The passageway should have been pitch-dark, but Ornastas could see his way forwards, very faintly. A crimson haze, like the promise of a fire to come, hung in the air. It grew stronger as he walked further into the alley. The light was no brighter, but the haze began to hum with tension.

Ornastas stopped. In his peripheral vision, he saw lines glowing red on the walls to his left and right. They disappeared when he faced them directly. He stared straight ahead, and the patterns gradually forced themselves into his consciousness. It was like having a brand slowly burned onto his brain. It hurt. He winced, and his eyes watered. He was standing between two immense iterations of the runes he had seen earlier. The angular skulls towered over him. They were at least fifty feet high.

Ornastas shook his head, trying to push the images away. He was starting to feel as if the walls themselves were thirsty for blood. He shivered, his skin running cold. The danger was much worse than he had thought. Something was eating into the soul of Creontiades, and now he feared he had come to the realisation too late. There was power here, something he dared not try to understand fully. It was lethal, and it was contagious. The psychic pressure of the runes squeezed harder. The haze pulsed with gathering violence.

'The Emperor is my ward, and His vigilance is without rest,' Ornastas intoned. His voice began as a croaking whisper, but as he recited the Psalm of Blessed Intolerance, he spoke louder. Soon he was shouting. 'The Emperor's light is without limit and without mercy. The xenos and the mutant are as ash before its glory. I walk in faith and righteousness, and the heretic burns in my sight!' He was walking again, striking the ground with his staff to punctuate each line of the psalm. His voice boomed with the strength of the prayer. Ornastas marched between the giant runes, and they had no power over him.

Figures burst from the refuse heaps. Their clothing was tattered filth. They came at Ornastas with hands crooked into vicious claws. Their faces were a mass of ritual scars. Some of the wounds still bled, as if in their need for violence, the wretches slashed perpetually at themselves. Their teeth were filed into fangs. Some had no lips, and should not have been capable of speech, but all of them shrieked in a choir of rage.

*'Blood for the Blood God! Skulls for the Skull Throne!'*

Ornastas leapt back a step and swung his staff to the left at the same moment as he depressed a stud in the shaft. The head of the staff was the winged skull of the Emperor, and it flashed with the holy energy of a shock maul. He hit the nearest cultist with the edge of one wing. He smashed the wretch's chest in, and the electrical shock jolted his limbs rigid. The cultist fell, jerking and smouldering. Ornastas took down another with a swing to the right. There were four more, and they were on him now, clawing and biting, trying to pull him to the ground. They were emaciated, as if their fury, unable to find other prey, had consumed their bodies. They were savage, but they were weak. Fuelled with a spiritual disgust, Ornastas kicked the legs out from the cultist clawing at his face, then threw himself back, throwing the others off balance. They tried to pull the staff from his hands. He yanked it free and it hit again. The stench of ozone and burned flesh filled his nostrils as the staff flashed and flashed.

Hands gripped Ornastas' head from behind, jagged fingernails sinking into his forehead. Blood ran into his eyes. The cultist pulled his head back sharply, as if trying to rip it off by brute strength. Ornastas lunged forwards, tearing himself free. The cultist's nails left deep gouges in his flesh. He whirled and struck hard with his staff, bringing it down overhead and burying a wing in the skull of his attacker.

'The Emperor is with me!' Ornastas shouted. 'His light is with me! His judgment is upon you!' He smashed at the cultists as fast as they could grapple with him. He broke arms and legs, then trampled spines with his boots while he held the others at bay with electric shocks. His attacks took on their own frenzy, but he did not lose himself in them. He heard the shrieks of heresy, the howled allegiance to a false god of rage, and he clung fast to his faith.

*The Emperor protects.*

Ornastas swung the staff twice through empty air before he realised the struggle was over. He stumbled away from the bodies, gasping for breath. The cultists were broken and burned, nothing more than fresh refuse in the alley.

Ornastas heard the peals of the brass bell again. The sound was still distant, still beyond a veil, but it was louder, closer. The tolling faded after a few moments.

Ornastas strained his ears. The bell was silent. There was only the muffled, clanking beats of the manufactoria.

Had the crimson haze diminished? He wanted to think so. It had not gone, though, and on the walls, the runes glowered at the edge of sight.

When he had found his breath again, Ornastas examined the bodies. The rags draped around one of the cultists drew his attention. Dirt-encrusted and torn as they were, they also looked familiar. Ornastas knelt over the wretch, looking closely at the markings. They were crude runes, daubed in blood. Beneath the runes, torn and defaced, were other symbols. There was so much filth, so much dried blood, so much hate expended on them that Ornastas had difficulty making them out. At last he did, and he gasped. He saw a fist, and the remnants of scales.

The rags had been a uniform belonging to a trooper of the Adeptus Arbites.

*Stolen?* Ornastas wondered. *Throne, let it be stolen.* The murder of a trooper was a brazen act, like the assault against his person. It was another sign of the danger being worse than he had imagined. *But if it wasn't stolen...* He didn't want to complete the thought. If the wretch was the trooper, then corruption had taken deeper root. And the body was so wasted, so degraded, the clothes barely fit. If this man had been a servant of the Adeptus Arbites, he had fallen some time ago.

Ornastas straightened. He breathed a prayer that somewhere, the body of a missing trooper lay, unmourned until now. He left the alley, heading back towards Saint Kaspha's. He had preparations to make, authorities to warn. The exhortations of the sermon were no longer enough. Spiritual war had come to Khania.

As he turned the corner, putting the alley behind him, he heard the brass bell again. It tolled once, mocking him. It presaged and summoned doom.

## CHAPTER 2

# GLORY

'Magos Tsenzhor,' Syagrius voxed, 'confirm the functionality of the auspex.'

*'There are no anomalies,'* the tech-priest answered. Speaking from the engineering nerve centre deep within the torso of *Augustus Secutor*, Tsenzhor was infuriatingly calm, as if he were beyond the reach of the tides of war.

'The readings are confirmed by the other princeps,' Rekorus said.

'How can they be disappearing?' Syagrius demanded.

The question was rhetorical, but Tsenzhor answered anyway. *'Our extrapolations being unsatisfying and impractical, we must await answers provided by on-site experience. This will not be long in coming. We calculate the distance–'*

'I know,' Syagrius snapped. 'Thank you, Magos Tsenzhor.'

Every mile the Imperial Hunters covered towards the target saw the auspex readings diminish. The biomass was shrinking. The signal was less than a third of its original size.

And now it changed again.

'*Marshal…*' Princeps Lukretus voxed.

'I see it,' Syagrius said. The biomass was moving, heading for the maniples of the Imperial Hunters, and closing fast. Syagrius would have his answers soon. He already knew he would not like them.

He was right. When the silhouettes of the enemy appeared over the horizon, rushing across the stony plain towards the Titans, Syagrius saw nothing larger than carnifexes again.

Another false promise. More prey unworthy of the time it would take to destroy the beasts.

'Marshal,' Rekorus said, 'we are still receiving requests from the Pallidus Mor to reinforce the war effort at Gelon.' The moderati kept his voice carefully neutral.

'I'm sure we are,' said Syagrius. He considered turning back after dealing with the coming wave of tyranids. He could no longer justify chasing a mirage. But something different had happened this time. 'Maintain course for the initial coordinates of the biomass,' he said. 'I want to know what happened.' If the auspexes of the demi-legio had not malfunctioned, then something more *had* been present.

The tyranids arrived, a horde of snarling, clacking monstrosities that would have turned regiments to mulch and cities to ash and bone. Before the god-machines of the Imperial Hunters, they were nothing. In answer to Syagrius' will, flame engulfed the land. Warlords, Reavers and Warhounds marched on the xenos horrors, ponderous machinic steps closing with the clawing, scuttling monstrosities. With plasma and missiles, bolt-rounds and las, the Imperial Hunters scoured the land of tyranids. Majesty confronted the alien abomination, and destroyed it utterly. Syagrius' march forwards did not slow. The Titans passed over the tyranids, as if they weren't there, and when the Titans moved on, the only signs that remained of the invaders were smoking shards of chitinous limbs scattered between the new craters.

Syagrius watched the horizon. The auspex was no longer reading any enemy movement in the vicinity, and it was with his human eyes more than the data stream of the manifold that he took in the landscape and waited for answers. The plain continued for several more miles, growing more arid, its surface scarred by the tyranid advance. It began to rise, becoming more rocky.

He suspected what he was going to find just before the wound in the land became visible. The plain became a wide expanse of rock, the slope became steeper, and then it stopped abruptly. *Augustus Secutor* arrived at the lip of a huge crater. It was misshapen, an ancient impact made larger by the activity of the tyranids. The bowl was deep, the sides high and steep. The crater was empty, as the auspex had indicated.

'Throne,' Syagrius swore.

'I don't understand,' Moderati Trovalis said. 'Where did they go?'

'Look at the walls on the near side,' Syagrius said.

The caves were difficult to make out from this angle. Their entrances looked like shadows in the crevasses of the rock walls. It had taken Syagrius a moment to realise what he was seeing.

*'Marshal,'* said Tsenzhor, *'we are beginning a full scan of the geology of the area.'*

'No need,' Syagrius said. 'We already know what we'll learn.' There was a cave system running west. The prey he had been seeking had gone underground. 'We make for Gelon,' Syagrius announced. 'Forced march.'

He turned his mind to the needs of reaching the hive as quickly as possible. He pushed aside the thought of being too late. He would not dwell upon the ideas of self-doubt, or on errors of judgement.

But as *Augustus Secutor* backed away from the lip of the crater, and began the ponderous steps of its turn, he felt the treacherous gnawing in his chest.

The warning came, and there was nothing they could do.

*'We have word from Marshal Syagrius,'* Balzhan voxed to the demi-legio. *'He warns us that a large concentration of tyranids, with possible bio-titan elements, is making a subterranean approach to Gelon.'*

'What action are the Imperial Hunters taking?' Krezoc asked.

*'They are returning.'*

*About time*, she thought.

Balzhan ordered full auspex scans of the terrain. From Gelon, Lord-Governor Albrecht Fleiser sent all available geologic data of the region streaming to the Pallidus Mor. Krezoc soaked up the new intelligence as it reached the manifold, and it was useless. The records in Gelon were too fragmentary. The marshy sector had been deemed unpromising for mining centuries ago, and ignored since. Their auspex sensors were unable to get any coherent readings from beneath the surface due to the tectonic vibrations set off by the heavy steps of so many Titans, the mass of the tyranid swarms and the explosions of missiles and bioweapons.

*We know they're coming*, Krezoc thought, *and there's nothing we can do about it.*

Nothing except fight. Nothing except burn the ranks of the enemy, and brace for the unavoidable ambush.

In the end, there was no bracing for what came. The eruptions were sudden. The warning from the Imperial Hunters might as well have been no warning at all. It was like trying to prepare for an asteroid strike. The event could not be stopped. Its form could not be anticipated. The earth shuddered and gave violent birth to monsters. Towering claws thrust from the ground, immense spikes that cast long shadows of terror upon the humans below. They folded down, stabbing new wounds into the earth, and heaved arched bodies into sight. One hierophant bio-form after another burst open the battlefield.

A single colossus had almost been the doom of Gelon in the initial attack. *Gloria Vastator* had fought it alone after luring it away from battered *Augustus Secutor*. Krezoc's god-machine was not alone now, but the hierophants kept emerging. Two, then three, then more. Soon there were six of the monsters, immense variants of their type, near matches for the Warlords in size. They disrupted the Pallidus Mor formations with their arrival. They were in front, and they were in the middle of the maniples. Two clambered out of the ground in the wastelands near the hive gates. They shook free of hillsides of refuse and scrambled through the wreckage, lunging after the Reavers. In the wake of the hierophants came the carnifexes, a swarm of giants that fell upon the secutarii and the Kataran Spears.

The two hierophants near the front lines went after the Warhounds. The Titans had been a match for the bioforms present until that moment. They still dwarfed the carnifexes, but the hulking predators went after them in hordes, overwhelming the secutarii squads, hammering the legs of the Warhounds, slowing them down, as the supreme horrors closed in.

The destruction of the first Warhound reverberated through *Gloria Vastator*'s manifold as a long, tearing, multi-layered scream. It was the building howl of ruined metal, out-of-control energy release and auspex feedback. It was also the voices of its crew on the vox. Barked orders became shouts of anger, of desperation, and then shrieks of pain. The end came quickly – too quickly for a weapon thousands of years old, a sacred embodiment of the Imperium's martial history. It was also slow, the agony of mortals and machine spearing through Krezoc's consciousness, inflaming the wrath of *Gloria Vastator*'s machine-spirit. The end was so fast, there was nothing any of the other Titans could do. Their helplessness turned the death into an unendurable torture that went on and on and on.

It ended with a burst of white noise. And that explosion blended into another death-cry.

Two Warhounds lost in the first seconds of the attack.

Chaos swept over the battlefield. Krezoc felt the Pallidus Mor's strategy disintegrate. A collective machine became a tattered web. Mortal crises unfolded on all sides. Her comrades were under threat. But so was she. There was no option except to deal with the immediate threat.

One of the hierophants appeared to *Gloria Vastator*'s rear. It fired its biocannons as soon as it had pulled itself out of the earth. A storm of acid-spewing organisms blasted against the void shields just below the head of the Titan. The flare of shields was blinding. Some of the attack came through, scarring adamantium armour. The Warlord's machine-spirit snarled in anger at the desecration.

Krezoc reined the god-machine in long enough to time her attack. She countered the animalistic charge with discipline, though against instinct. The mega-bolter pounded at the hierophant, chipping away at its armoured legs, but this was not her true attack. *Gloria Vastator*'s great arms rose together, the muzzles of their guns focused on a single point. The volcano and quake cannons fired at once. The force of the simultaneous recoil thrummed through the Warlord's frame like a hymn of power. The power plant took the strain, though the void shields flickered. City-destroying laser and shell struck the head of the hierophant. Shell smashed armour and laser burned through xenos exoskeleton and flesh. The shots tore half the monster's head away. Its enormous mandibles spun off in opposite directions.

The hierophant staggered. It swayed to the left and right, but it did not fall. Huge bioelectric charges flashed along the beast's spine. Its forelimbs flailed, their cannons firing wildly. The tyranid weaved from side to side, legs hammering the ground arrhythmically. If it was dead, the xenos' nervous system did not know it yet. It came on, an uncontrolled juggernaut, but still dangerous. It was approaching fast, and *Gloria Vastator* was too slow to move out of its path.

Apocalypse missiles streamed from its shoulder launcher. The range was insanely close, tantamount to a point-blank explosion. The rockets detonated inside the wound carved out by the cannons. All traces of the tyranid's head vanished. The blasts punched deeper and deeper inside its thorax, blowing the hierophant open from the inside. The armour fragmented outwards. Waves of acid and boiling fluids erupted across the space between the tyranid and the Warlord. The concussions rocked the void shields. The maelstrom of fire and actinic energy filled Krezoc's vision.

'Brace for impact!' she shouted.

The corpse of the tyranid burst through the flame. It had lost one of its legs and it was burning along its entire length. Momentum and the final spasms of its nervous system kept it going, though much of its speed had bled away. It collapsed against *Gloria Vastator*. The burning bio-wreckage hit like a tumbling mountain. It tore itself open around the legs of the Titan, spreading a sea of acid on the ground before it. Krezoc felt the vibration of the hit, but the god-machine stood sovereign and unmoved above the ruin of its foe. Princeps and machine-spirit shared the same fusion of triumph and contempt. There was no dividing line between the emotion of the human and that of the Warlord.

Krezoc trained the mega-bolter on the carnifexes in the near vicinity. She detached herself partly from that attack, turning it over to Moderati Haziad. She looked out over the wider battlefield. No other hierophants had been destroyed yet. The struggles were hard, and everywhere she saw moments of crisis. *Gloria Vastator* was momentarily in a position where it could lend support, but it could not be everywhere at once. *Fatum Messor* and *Crudelis Mortem* were fighting a single hierophant and had the measure of their enemy. The Reavers were doing less well, and though the Warhounds were managing to converge and combine their strengths against the monster, they were still hard-pressed. The demi-legio's vox-traffic burned with the urgency of a war caught in the balance between victory and disaster.

It was when she looked north that Krezoc saw more

than a crisis. She saw a turning point. This was the fulcrum on which the battle would pivot. Two hierophants were attacking *Ferrum Salvator*. They had closed with it on both sides. Balzhan's Warlord could not bring its full force to bear on two fronts. Its armament was similar to *Gloria Vastator*'s, though instead of a mega-bolter, the venerable god-machine's left-shoulder hard point was armed with a plasma blastgun. The Titan's torso pivoted back and forth between the two hierophants. Its fire was constant, but it could not hit either with the concentrated fury that was needed. The hierophants scuttled around and around the Warlord, their biocannons unleashed, a xenos storm pounding the Titan's void shields, straining them past their limit. Both tyranids had been hit. Alien blood coursed down their legs. Fluid bubbled and steamed from rents in their carapaces. But they had not slowed. They circled, advanced, jabbed with claws long as chapel spires and both kept blasting their acid. They were two animals taking down their larger prey. Brute instinct was winning over human battlefield skills.

The entire ambush was a war of gigantic insects, yet Krezoc could feel, now, more acutely than ever, the sense of something larger directing the attacks of the tyranids. It was not an intelligence in any way that she could recognise, yet it was a presence, a shadow, the hint of something beyond human measure and comprehension. Perhaps it was a form of sentience, but if it was, it recognised nothing of the sort in the human animal. There was only prey.

Krezoc turned *Gloria Vastator* to the north. The Titan's great steps seemed too slow. The marshal of the Pallidus Mor was under attack, and his salvation was the priority. Balzhan was her mentor, her former princeps. *Ferrum*

*Salvator* had been where she had served as moderati. She could not let Balzhan fall.

'Marshal,' she voxed, 'hold fast. We are coming.'

The channel crackled as if Balzhan were starting to answer. Krezoc thought she heard strained breathing. Then there was only static.

*Ferrum Salvator* swung to the left, and its quake cannon boomed. The shell smashed into the hierophant's armour just behind its head. The tyranid staggered.

'Target the enemy on the right,' Krezoc told her moderati.

'Acquired,' said Konterus. The Apocalypse missiles were ready now. The big guns were still building up their charge.

'Kill it,' Krezoc ordered. The rockets flew. They arced high, and their descent was true. The upper plating of the hierophant flashed with multiple strikes.

Krezoc hoped the damage already done by *Ferrum Salvator* would make the impact of the missile barrage all the more telling. At the very least, she wanted to pull the hierophant's attention towards *Gloria Vastator*. The principle had worked to save *Augustus Secutor*. Krezoc needed to see the same success now, when the stakes were much higher.

The hierophant ignored the missiles. Perhaps the battles with Balzhan's Warlord had already gone on long enough for the bioform to adapt its defences to the attacks. Perhaps some form of species memory recognised Krezoc's tactic. In the end, the reasons did not matter. The hierophant charged forwards again, reared back, and stabbed both its forelimbs into the back of *Ferrum Salvator*.

The void shields flared a blinding violet and collapsed. At the same moment, the god-machine's volcano cannon fired. It struck the other hierophant in the same wound as the quake shell, and cut the beast in half.

Krezoc felt a surge of hope as her volcano cannon came online and the first hierophant fell in two pieces. But the other monster was still on the back of Balzhan's Warlord, still stabbing through adamantium with its forelimbs, and it was too close for Krezoc to risk a shot. Even a perfect hit would do catastrophic damage to *Ferrum Salvator* while its void shields were down. *Ferrum Salvator* leaned forwards. It leaned too far.

'Throne, no,' Krezoc whispered.

The hierophant stabbed. It fired its biocannons. Acid smoke roiled up from the armour of the god-machine in a black, venomous cloud. The mass of the monster and the ferocity of the attack pushed the Titan past the centre of its gravity.

The unthinkable became the inevitable.

The vox burst into life, and Krezoc heard Balzhan's voice. It was ragged from pain. She could hear the marshal's life bleeding away, and, in the background, the roar of flame and the distant crump of internal explosions. *'The Pallidus Mor is strong,'* Balzhan said. *'Its leader is strong.'*

'Marshal,' Krezoc called, pleading with the fates.

*'The Emperor protects,'* Balzhan whispered.

The vox went dead. With smoke and flame billowing from the gaping wounds in its armour, *Ferrum Salvator* fell with awful grace. A monument crashed to the earth, and the earth trembled with horror. The hierophant scrabbled forwards over the Titan. It fired its biocannons through the back of the god-machine's armour, dissolving the weakened plating still further, then plunged its forelimbs down. They passed through all the way to the Warlord's head. A new explosion shook the Titan.

It was a death throe.

\* \* \*

The response from Confessor Jethen Vilkur was not encouraging.

'You're letting the more primitive elements of your parish get the better of you,' Vilkur said when Ornastas spoke to him from the holo-link in Saint Kaspha's sacristy. The other confessor ministered to the wealthier sector of Creontiades. He moved among the spires of the city. He preached in the Chapel of Human Supremacy. He saw the city's glory and its riches. Vilkur's face was well fed, bordering on bloated. He enjoyed his position and the benefits that came with it, and Ornastas had not expected him to welcome news that warned of upheaval and war. He had hoped Vilkur would listen.

'I was attacked by heretics,' he repeated. 'I have seen runes that–'

'Runes that you cannot produce as evidence,' Vilkur said.

Ornastas stopped himself before he objected. There was nothing he could say that would convince Vilkur of the danger. He stared at the jerking image of the confessor and wondered if Vilkur had been corrupted. No, he decided. The face before him was venal, comfortable, too lazy to have been consumed by the dark passion he had seen in the alley. Vilkur was puffy-eyed from having been dragged out of bed. He was dismissive of Ornastas. He was not a heretic.

*You shame your calling,* Ornastas thought. *Where is your vigilance? This is how we let the evil through. This is how it spreads unnoticed. I am guilty too. At least I recognise that.*

'You are right,' he said, 'I cannot.' There would be no help from Vilkur, and Vilkur was the senior ecclesiarch of the capital, and thus of Katara. He had the ear of Lord-Governor Eukrolas. Ornastas did not. If Vilkur was going to do nothing until events forced him to, the struggle was going to be all the harder. And Ornastas would gain nothing by wasting his time with a blind fool. 'I will not trouble you any further, Confessor Vilkur,' he said, and shut down the holo-link.

He left Saint Kaspha's a short time later. He would have to speak to Eukrolas himself, and he would have to do it in person. It was a few hours before dawn, and he doubted he could browbeat any functionaries of the palace by holo-link to haul the governor out of bed. They were too insulated from the lower streets to be intimidated by the ecclesiarch of that region, particularly if their confessor had dismissed his concerns. He would go to the palace. They would have to eject him bodily to prevent him from speaking to the lord-governor. He did not think their nerve extended that far.

He travelled in a servitor-powered transport. The servitor's lower body had been fused with the forward portion of the vehicle, and its arms extended into the driving mechanisms. Ornastas entered the coordinates of the palace into a data-slate built into a low lectern in the passenger compartment, programming the servitor's directional instincts. The purpose of the transport was to increase his visibility to his flock. The passenger compartment was elevated, its wrought-iron framework holding an armourglass cube. Riding inside, Ornastas would present himself to the streets, engaging in mobile proselytising as vox-speakers broadcast his words to everyone he passed. This time, he said nothing. He sat in silence as the vehicle moved through the dark streets and the night crawled towards dawn. On this journey, he was the one witnessing. He watched the city, vigilant and anxious.

The main thoroughfares of Creontiades were crowded. They always were. The work of the city never ceased. The manufactoria ran from shift to shift, pouring out the material of war, industry and commerce. With hundreds of thousands of citizens always on their way to or from their duties, the marketplaces were always open, as were the tabernae where the people ate to prepare for their shifts, or drank to forget them. The closer Ornastas came to the palace sector, the brighter the streets became. Ahead, the skyline transformed. Soon the manufactoria would give way to the towers of the great trading concerns, and dingy, cramped habs would become glittering sky-needles of luxury.

Even as the lumen standards multiplied, though, there was still darkness. The shadows were deep between the buildings, and along the narrow cross-streets. Even in the centre of the wide avenues, Ornastas could feel the weight of the dark. It was more than the absence of light. It was summoned by a turning away from the Emperor and the calling of something to which he could not give a proper name. It was draped over the city like a veil. Ornastas feared he would not have the strength to tear it. But he gazed into it with determination. He would know the extent of the danger.

It was worse than he thought. In the industrial districts of Creontiades and beyond, the shadows were boiling with heresy. Figures lurked in the recesses of doorways, their features shrouded, their heads turning to watch his passage with hidden, hostile eyes. In narrow alleys, silhouettes contorted. They left Ornastas with the impression of self-mutilation, of people tearing their own faces, transforming themselves into bloody grotesques, the distorted apostles of a monstrous creed. The heresy was even reaching into the light. Brawls were breaking out on the main avenues. The first ones Ornastas saw were fights between individuals. If he had not known better, he might have dismissed them as nothing unusual. Soon, though, he was seeing clusters of combatants, and the fights were savage, gouging affairs. Blood spread on the rockcrete pavement. These were battles to the death. Citizens passed the fights without reacting, and that was a cause for concern in and of itself. Others stopped to watch. Still others joined in. At one intersection, at least a score of citizens were locked in brutal frenzy. It was the beginning of a riot. Enforcers were running towards the fight. Ornastas' transport drove past the struggle before he saw whether the enforcers ended the chaos or became part of it.

Two blocks further on, as the first hints of dawn greyed the sky, the vehicle reached a large marketplace. It took up a wide area on both sides of the avenue. It was even more crowded than Ornastas would have expected. The roar of the people shook the transport's armourglass. The sea of people heaved and frothed, the loud business of the market broken by spreading whirlpools of conflict. The transport had almost reached the westernmost edge of the market when a woman ran out on the right side. She tore across the avenue, leaping over vehicles, and jumped onto Ornastas' servitor. Her clothes were as ragged as those of the cultists he had fought earlier, but though she was wiry, she was not emaciated, as they had been. Whether she was a recent convert or not didn't matter. She was a sign of how brazen the cult was becoming, and how strong. The flesh was gone from the lower half of her face, leaving teeth and musculature in a perpetual snarl of rage. She appeared to have shaved her head with broken glass then carved the skull rune into her forehead. Limp tufts of hair still clung to the sides of her head. It shook and waved with her fast, jerking movements.

She clawed at the armourglass, staring at Ornastas with mad eyes. Her jaw opened and closed, as if she intended to chew her way through the shield. She pounded on the window, howling. Then she turned on the servitor, sinking her teeth into the top of its head.

Ornastas pressed a stud next to the lectern and the forward shield slid down. He struck at the heretic with his staff. She growled and clutched at the winged head. Ornastas jolted her with shocks of electricity, but the attack only increased her fury. Howling, her flesh burning, the cultist held tight to the staff. She yanked with maddened strength, hauling Ornastas out of his seat and halfway out of the passenger compartment. He lay across the framework, unable to rise or find leverage to fight back. He would not let go of the staff. He would not release a sacred symbol to have it defiled by the wretches in the street. He could do nothing except trigger the shocks again and again. The servitor drove on, oblivious to the struggle and to the blood running down its head. The transport bucked up and down. It had run over something. Ornastas heard more furious screams heading his way. He saw rapid movement in the corners of his eyes. More heretics. One had gone under the wheels. In another few moments they would drag him from the transport.

He shocked the heretic again. She finally released the staff. She reared back, shrieking syllables he wished were nonsense, and whose sounds lacerated his mind. He scrabbled back as she pounced. She missed her grab and collided with his head, knocking him backwards. The blow knocked the air from his lungs, but he managed to haul back with the staff and strike forwards, catching the cultist in the chest as she crawled towards him. She jerked from the shock and lost her grip on the canopy. She tumbled off the transport. The rear wheels bounced up a second time.

Breathing hard, Ornastas fed a command for greater speed to the servitor through the lectern. He looked back at the market place as the transport accelerated. The movements of the crowd seemed to be growing more violent before his eyes. The virulent heresy was spreading faster and faster through Creontiades. What had been hidden was now unveiling itself. A block further on, he saw the skull rune splashed across a hab façade in blood.

There was no time left.

He turned back to the nav-slate in the lectern. There were still miles to go before he reached the palace. Too far. He needed an alternative.

The local barracks for the Kataran 66th was a few minutes away. There was only a skeletal force left. He had no doubt any more that this was why the cultists had waited until now to reveal themselves. Nevertheless, the Spears and the Adeptus Arbites were the ones who would mount an armed response to the cultists. There was an enforcer station not too far from here as well, but the uniform Ornastas had found worried him. He did not know how far the heretics might have infiltrated the Arbites. Quick action was needed, too, and if the incipient riots had not yet reached that far, there might be a delay while someone with official jurisdiction was sought. He had to speak to someone who would listen to him.

Before his induction into the Adeptus Ministorum,

Ornastas had served in the 66th. Later, he had returned to his regiment as preacher, marching across the battlefields of numerous worlds with his comrades, wielding the words of the Imperial Creed instead of a lasgun. Since becoming confessor at Saint Kaspha's, he had not lost his ties to the Spears. There was a good chance the officer commanding the reserves would remember him.

Ornastas changed the servitor's programming, redirecting it to the barracks.

Krezoc aimed the volcano cannon high. She would not risk the total destruction of *Ferrum Salvator*. The god-machine must be preserved and reclaimed. And she would not abandon the hope that someone had survived inside.

The laser seared the upper plates of the hierophant's carapace, cutting through armour weakened by the missile barrage. The tyranid hissed, the sound scraping across the battlefield like the surf of a steel ocean. It lunged away from the fallen Warlord, biocannons firing at *Gloria Vastator*. Krezoc advanced head-on towards the monster. Her furious grief was a storm in the manifold. The Titan's machine-spirit responded to her hate. The howl of its war-horn was a cry for vengeance.

The acid streams hit the void shields. 'Full power to the forward shields, magos,' Krezoc voxed to Xura Thezerin. 'We march into the enemy's worst to give it our own.'

'*So ordered,*' Thezerin acknowledged.

'Quake cannon loaded,' Vansaak said.

'Fire,' Krezoc said before Vansaak had finished speaking, word and thought and action coming together. Flaming gases vented from the weapon's arm as the gun launched its shell.

The hierophant had begun an encircling move to the

right. The quake shell hit a forelimb at the upper joint. Chitin exploded. The leg shattered in an explosion of fluid. The hierophant swerved to its wounded side, then limped to the right, still circling, still firing biocannons.

'*Void shields are approaching critical,*' Thezerin warned.

'Thank you, magos,' Krezoc said. 'I am aware of that.' Her lips moved at a remove from her awareness. The bare minimum of her consciousness animated her body. She ranged ahead on the battlefield, her senses projected by the auspex network. She inhabited the vast body of *Gloria Vastator*. She *was* the Warlord, avenging its fallen kin, tracking the movement of the hierophant, ignoring the beast's attack because all that mattered was the immediate and total destruction of the foe. The mega-bolter tracked the hierophant's movements, hammering it with a steady stream of shells. The hierophant was slower. *Gloria Vastator*'s upper frame was able to rotate fast enough to keep up with its awkward, sideways scuttle.

The forwards march of the Warlord ceased. With ground-shaking steps, it changed its orientation, always working to keep its front towards the hierophant. Far below, carnifexes charged the legs. The secutarii met their attack. They could not hope to defeat the monsters. They could slow them down, and that was all Krezoc asked at this moment.

The Apocalypse launcher locked on to the target. The quake cannon loaded another shell. The volcano gun charged up.

'Burn,' Krezoc said.

With a long wail of the war-horn, *Gloria Vastator* unleashed the great storm of its warpower on the hierophant. Quake and bolt shells, las and missiles struck the centre mass of the tyranid. The fireball mushroomed skywards, swallowing the hierophant in a cataclysm of flame. The horizon vanished in the conflagration. Explosions built on explosions. They left a crater in their wake. At its centre lay the curled, jagged remains of the tyranid. The corpse bubbled and smoked. Fragments of limbs were scattered across a land turned to glass.

The thunder of the hierophant's destruction was still rolling over the battlefield when there was another sunburst to the west. The light was terrible in its burning purity. It flashed over the marsh, then faded to the glowering orange of flame. The shock wave followed with a hurricane blast of wind that flattened humans and tyranids on the ground.

Krezoc turned *Gloria Vastator* towards the west, but she already knew what had happened. The light was unmistakeable. It was the death cry of a Titan's reactor going critical. One of the Reavers had fallen to the hierophants.

'Which one?' she asked.

'Superbus Falce,' Thezerin answered after a moment.

The wastelands of Gelon still glowed with a false sunset. Effluent canals and streams had ignited. The firestorm spread over miles. It was difficult to make out the Reavers and hierophants in its midst. They were black shapes within the crimson flame. The sea of fire billowed with their motions. It flashed with muzzle flare and the launch of missiles. It grew stronger, fed by ever more explosions. Its edge drove the Kataran Spears forwards, into carnifexes eager for more prey.

Krezoc began to march towards Gelon. A moment later, a second Reaver died in another reactor blast.

'Manus Mortuis,' Thezerin said.

Krezoc said nothing. She saw the scuttling movement of a hierophant in the flames and sent a missile flight in its direction.

The naming of the dead must stop. Only she knew it would not. No matter how quickly she responded, more comrades would fall on this day.

She accepted two certainties. The Pallidus Mor would suffer more losses. And the Pallidus Mor would triumph. Hardened to the reality, she gave herself up to the march of cold inevitability and took *Gloria Vastator* towards the greater fire.

'It's still on us,' Deyers said. He stared up into the throat of the mawloc. The monster's teeth ground through the plating. The beast's enormous jaws were locked around the sides of the turret. It was trying to eat its way through to the soft prey inside.

'I'm doing what I can,' Medina called. *Bastion of Faith* roared over uneven ground, Medina steering for the hardest jolts. Platen was still pounding at the enemy with the tank's gun, but the shot that mattered most was the one she could not manage.

Deyers' back ached from the fall. He had plunged through the hatch when the monster attacked, narrowly escaping being bitten in half. The serpentine tyranid had seized the Leman Russ. It had been chewing its way through the armour ever since. Medina was trying to jar it loose. Deyers emptied another magazine of bolt shells into the monster's throat. He ducked out of the way as acidic juices poured from the maw and sizzled on the compartment's deck. The pulsing, black-and-pink muscle of the throat was torn with wounds, but the beast would not let go. The stench was overpowering. Deyers breathed through his mouth, and he still felt dizzy from the smell. It was thick as rotting meat, and rich as the interior of an insect hive.

'Carnifexes!' Medina called.

'Where?' Deyers reloaded. Above him, the throat pressed forwards, as if the mawloc would turn itself inside out in its eagerness to devour him.

Medina's answer was drowned out by an explosion that rocked the tank so hard it almost upended it.

'What–' Deyers began.

The wind came, and the fire. The mawloc spasmed. Its jaw clamped down with convulsive strength, and the sides of the turret buckled. Curved teeth the size of Deyers' forearm stabbed through the plating. The mawloc shuddered once, then stopped moving. The interior of the throat blackened. It began to smoke. The tyranid was burning.

The heat inside the tank became intolerable. 'Silas!' Deyers said to Medina, 'Tell me something!'

'A Reaver,' the driver answered, sounding shaken. 'It blew up. There are flames everywhere.'

'Get us out before we cook,' Deyers ordered.

'Yes, captain. That will take us towards the carnifexes.'

Medina's comment did not come from cowardice. It was an observation rooted in realism. If *Bastion of Faith* could coordinate with other tanks, they could challenge the bioforms one at a time. Against a horde, an isolated tank had no chance, and *Bastion of Faith* had been separated from the rest of the formations by the mawloc.

'We'll fight what we have to fight,' Deyers said. 'Find our comrades.' He fired into the tyranid corpse. At last, the bolt shells blew through the carcass, knocking a large portion of it from the turret. Flames roared over the opening, holding Deyers back as he tried to climb up again. The ladder was hot to touch, even through his gloves.

He had to see, though. The moment the worst of the flames receded, he made his way up top. He winced from the heat and turned his back to the furnace in the west. Ahead, his regiment was escaping incineration and rushing towards an army of monsters. The land swarmed with bio-forms of every size. Further out, Titans clashed with xenos colossi. Wherever he looked, he saw a war playing out on a scale that dwarfed the human.

The east was burning, too. *Gloria Vastator* was walking away from the conflagration of its making. The Titan was marching west. Backlit by flames, it was a shadowed vastness the colours of bone and night, hellish light streaming from its weapons. It came closer, crushing tyranids with every step. Its walk was earthquake and thunder, and it brought a new inferno to the east.

'Maintain course,' Deyers shouted to Medina. They would soon join the bulk of the regiment in the struggle against the carnifexes.

*'What is happening, captain?'* Platen asked. She could see her next target but not the wider panorama of the war.

Deyers looked around again at the fury surrounding him before he answered. He was an insect caught in a volcanic eruption. Destruction had reached a paroxysm, and there was no sign of the storm abating. As overwhelmed as his senses were, he could still read patterns. There was a current to the conflict.

'I think we're winning,' he said to Platen.

But if this was the approach to victory, he could not

imagine the pyre of defeat.

Captain Gregor Seth moved from his desk to look out the window. His office was at the top of the central barracks. It was high enough that it had a view over the wall of the base, on the street beyond. 'The reports of violence have been multiplying,' he said to Ornastas. 'I wasn't sure what to think. I didn't imagine it could be as bad as you say.'

'You believe me, though?'

'Of course I do.'

Ornastas breathed more easily. He and Seth knew each other from many campaigns. He'd had every expectation Seth would listen to him. Even so, the fact of the old veteran's belief was a balm to his soul. 'Have you been in contact with the Adeptus Arbites?' he asked.

Seth nodded. 'Just beginning to hear from them when you arrived.' He waved his arm at the city. 'The incidents are widespread, but there's no concentration. It's taken until now to realise this is more than a spike in street violence.' He turned back to Ornastas. 'But this is a cult, you say?'

'I've seen the heretical runes. The adherents bear ritualistic wounds.'

'Then the question is what can we do?'

'What forces are still here?'

'Not enough to mount anything except focused raids and the defence of a very limited number of targets. It would help if we knew what to go after. Does this cult have a leader?'

'If it does, I don't know who it might be.' Ornastas thought for a moment. 'It would help if we could speak to someone in the palace. There might have been some hints they didn't notice until now. Political malcontents...'

*Grasping at straws*, he thought. There was no time to investigate, yet what could be done without a clear sense of the enemy? 'What are you going to do?' he asked, hoping Seth could see his way to some clarity of action.

The captain shrugged, his face drawn, unhappy in his helplessness. 'We'll make a show of force in the streets,' he said. 'We'll have to head for the palace. We...'

Seth trailed off. He met Ornastas' gaze. They both heard it – a roar, coming closer. It sounded like a flash flood, some huge and fast-moving wave rushing through the streets. Ornastas stood up from where he'd been sitting before Seth's desk and joined the captain at the window.

The roar grew louder, closer. The streets in front of the barracks gate filled suddenly with a violent crowd coming from both directions. The mob was ragged, clothing shredded into tattered robes. The faces blended into indistinguishable expressions of rage. The two streams met in front of the gates.

'They're armed,' said Seth.

Ornastas saw the clubs, the blades made of scrap metal. But also the shock mauls and the lasrifles.

Sentries on the wall opened fire on the mob. They might as well have been shooting into a river. The crowd howled and fired back. A massive concentration of las took the individual soldiers down. At the corners of the wall, turrets opened up. They carved swaths through the crowd. Trenches exploded with blood, then filled again as still more heretics pressed in. A few moments later, the entrance exploded. Fire and smoke rose above the wall, obscuring Ornastas' view of the street. The iron gates flew across the mustering ground before the barracks. Troopers were already streaming from the barracks. They formed up and trained their fire on the chaos at the shattered entrance. For a few seconds their steady, disciplined, coordinated fire held back the mob. Then the frenzy and the numbers of the heretics took their toll. Screaming cultists stormed through the gateway. Many fell as soon as they entered the barrack grounds. Many more ran over their corpses, some shooting wildly, others hurling their blades at the troopers, still more charging with nothing but their fury, their hands outstretched to rend the flesh of their prey.

The mob was too great for the troopers to take it down.

'You need tanks,' Ornastas said.

'There's no time,' said Seth.

He was right. The storm had come for the Kataran Spears. His warning had come too late. Everything was too late.

Seth pulled his plasma pistol from its holster and left the window. He and Ornastas moved to the doorway. Seth paused before he opened the door. 'You have to run,' he said.

'What?'

'Don't die here. The fight is already lost.'

'What about you? Aren't you going to fight?'

'I'm going to fight to see you live. You were right. This is heresy of the worst kind. We will need the strength of faith to combat it. This is just the start.'

'So I fear.'

'So run, confessor. Run for the salvation of Katara.'

The Imperial Hunters came at last. With them came the certainty of victory. The proud war-horns of the maniples boomed over the battlefield. The sound penetrated

Krezoc's consciousness, finding her in the maelstrom of smoke and flame. She paid little attention to it. She knew what it meant. It brought her no joy. Instead, she felt only bitterness that this pride should arrive now, so shining and so late, when so much had been lost.

For a moment, at the sound of the horns, she hated Syagrius more than she hated the tyranids. They, at least, fought according to the imperative of the species.

They did not sacrifice their kind for glory.

# CHAPTER 3
# THE FEASTS

Lord-Governor Fleiser's banquet was held in a great hall immediately below his private quarters. The hall took up an entire level of the spire. Its windows presented a circular panorama of Gelon and the land beyond, a grand display to the victors of the world they had saved. The span of armourglass was interrupted only by the gold-filigreed plasteel of supporting columns, and in the north east by the grand entrance, beyond which lay the vestibule and the grav lifts to the rest of the spire. Three long tables took up the centre of the space. An army of serfs moved along their lengths, delivering more than a dozen courses to the assembly. Chandeliers hung from a painted ceiling. The fresco was an allegory, depicting Khania as an armoured saint taking her knee before the Emperor. Her outstretched arms held a bundle of swords, the offering of Khania's industry.

Contingents of each of the armed forces that had come

to Khania sat at the tables. Fleiser was at the head of the central one with the commanders. Syagrius was at his right, and beside him was Admiral Veline Menas of the Imperial Navy. Krezoc sat with Hans Deyers at the lord-governor's left. The rest of the seats were occupied by members of Fleiser's court, alternating between other officers of the Kataran Spears and the Navy. More Khanian nobility and Administratum hierarchs dined with the princeps and moderati of the Imperial Hunters at the right-hand table, and with the Pallidus Mor at the left.

Krezoc mentally congratulated Fleiser on his political acumen. The dining arrangements had been made before the lord-governor had met with her and Syagrius, yet he had had the foresight to put as much distance as possible between the two legios. The wisdom of the separation was clear to everyone in the hall. The Imperial Hunters were celebrating with loud, pointed gusto. The Pallidus Mor ate in almost total silence. The Kataran 66th were subdued too, but the sergeants kept up a steady flow of conversation with their hosts, as if the performance of conviviality would preserve the peace. Krezoc saw the strain on the faces of the Khanians. The evening was not the observance of victory they had expected it to be. They simply wanted it to run its course without incident. Fleiser looked both exhausted and guarded, but he did well to shore up the civility, moving smoothly from one pleasantry to another with all four senior officers. Even the decision to place Syagrius and Menas on the same side of the table seemed the product of careful planning. Krezoc suspected Fleiser and his staff must have carefully gone through personnel data-packets in the process of preparing the reception. The marshal and the admiral were cut of the same aristocratic cloth.

Syagrius was aquiline, the lines of his face sharp enough to draw blood. His age was difficult to guess by sight, but Krezoc had done her reading too. She wanted to know everything she could about the fool whose selfish strategy had precipitated Balzhan's death. Syagrius was younger than she was, but he looked even younger. Juvenat treatments, with a special attention to the aesthetic, had all but erased the lines of age. A single scar ran across his forehead, visible as a faint white line. He wore it like a medal, the lone flaw reminding all who gazed on him that he was a veteran of the battlefield. He had risen through the ranks of the Imperial Hunters quickly, as was the traditional right of his family. The House of Syagrius had an unbroken line of marshals reaching back through centuries of Imperial Hunters history. He spoke with the round, slightly arch tones of the educated noble. He was a man who knew precisely how to converse with his social class and how to demonstrate his superiority effortlessly to everyone else.

Menas was older, more taciturn. Her white hair was as severely cut as Syagrius', and as perfectly in place. Her features were not as sharp, but there was a cold precision to her bearing that implied she tolerated the presence of inferiors only out of painful necessity. She was a fine officer, though. Krezoc could find no fault with her conduct of the void war. The Imperial forces planetside would have been doomed if she had not destroyed the tyranid bio-ships. She had done so, and though the Navy losses had been considerable, they were far from the worst it had suffered against other tyranid attacks of the same scale. The admiral had earned her laurels.

Krezoc chose a moment when Fleiser was occupied with

Syagrius and Menas to turn to Deyers. In sharp contrast to Syagrius, he had many scars. He also had plenty of fresh wounds. They had been treated, but he was clearly a man who had recently seen battle. He looked around the room as if half expecting a bioform to smash its way through the windows. Krezoc suspected he didn't even realise he was doing so. 'Your troops fought well,' she said.

He nodded his thanks. 'They did,' he said, his pride understated and shaded by grief. 'They died well, too.'

'How bad are your losses?'

'Almost half my troops and vehicles.'

'I see.' She looked up and down the table. 'Without implying disrespect to you, captain, where are the senior officers?'

'Dead,' he said. He looked down at his plate and stabbed at the food without eating any. 'General Vargas died when the bio-titans first attacked. The colonels fell during the last charge.'

'They led from the front,' Krezoc said, approving.

'They did.'

'Then I am sorry for their loss, but their legacy is in good hands.'

'Thank you,' said Deyers. 'How badly were you hurt, if you don't mind my asking?'

'Very close to the same degree as your regiment.' Of the twenty god-machines the Pallidus Mor had brought to Khania, twelve remained. *Ferrum Salvator*, two Reavers and five Warlords had fallen to the hierophants. *Killed by pride*, Krezoc thought.

'Khania owes you a great debt,' said Deyers.

'Which it is acknowledging, it would seem.' Krezoc gestured with her fork, indicating the meal. A course of amasec-braised seafood was in the process of being replaced with roast loin of grox. 'The same debt is owed to the Spears.'

'Perhaps.'

Krezoc raised an eyebrow. *'Perhaps?'*

'I'm not selling the sacrifice of my soldiers short,' Deyers explained. 'We were fighting for more than Khania, though. If it fell, Katara would have been next. We answered Khania's call, but if we hadn't fought here, we would have at home. Now we don't have to.'

'So Khania was sacrificed to save Katara.'

Deyers grimaced. 'I wouldn't put it that way to our host.'

'I won't.'

'You understand, though?'

Krezoc nodded. 'The Spears saved two worlds today.'

'So did you.'

'We thought only of one.'

A bright flare through the eastern windows caught Krezoc's eye. She turned her head. The deep rumble of a massive lifter's engines sounded faintly through the hall. Krezoc watched the ship rise slowly. She had been waiting for this launch. Inside the vessel's cavernous hold was the salvaged corpse of *Ferrum Salvator*. Balzhan and his moderati were dead, but some of the crew in the main body of the Warlord had survived. More importantly, the god-machine was whole. Aboard the transport *Nuntius Mortis*, the tech-priests and enginseers of the Pallidus Mor waited to begin the healing process. *Ferrum Salvator* would walk again. Its history was not done yet. A memory of Balzhan would survive with it, Krezoc thought. The lineage of the Warlord's princeps would not end with him. That was cold comfort, but it would have to do.

'You are thinking of your marshal's legacy,' Syagrius said.

Krezoc looked at him, startled. Syagrius' lips were pressed in a thin line. 'I am,' she said warily.

'You are mistaken. He has no legacy. None worth commemorating.'

Beside Krezoc, Deyers held his breath. Conversation at this end of the table ceased. Menas' expression was neutral. Fleiser, though, looked as if he had swallowed an insect. His wide face had turned pale. 'I think…' he began.

'I'm sure you'll explain yourself,' Krezoc said. With a slow, deliberate motion, she placed her knife and fork on her plate.

'The battle of Gelon was a poor showing.' Syagrius turned briefly to Fleiser. 'You have every reason to celebrate the overall success of our campaign, lord-governor,' he said. 'This is despite the shame that covers the land before the gates of this city.'

'I think…' Fleiser tried again, turning grey. No one interrupted him this time. His sentence faded into nothing.

'Shame,' Krezoc repeated. She forced her fingers not to clench into fists.

'That is correct.'

'How?'

'Isn't it obvious?'

At first, Krezoc had thought Syagrius was baiting her for his amusement. She realised now she was wrong. She saw a faint twitch below his left eye. The tendons of his neck stood out. He was not laughing at her. He was furious.

The idea that he had any right to anger made her see red. Through clenched teeth, she said, 'Make yourself clear, marshal.'

'Very well, *princeps*. Marshal Balzhan's strategy was poor.'

'It was the correct one for the foe we were fighting.'

'And when the nature of the foe changed?'

'Our formations turned the tide.'

*Why are you dignifying his remarks like this?* Krezoc asked herself. *Because I want to know. I want to see his logic unfurled. I want to know the truth of this man.*

Syagrius snorted. 'At what cost? It was the duty of the Pallidus Mor to defend Hive Gelon. You failed. Marshal Balzhan failed. Your losses were great. They are regrettable, but they are also of your making. As are our losses.'

So that was it. In the final stages of the battle, the tyranids had managed to bring down one of the Warhounds of the Imperial Hunters, and a Warlord, *Aurea Sagittariis*. That was the reason for Syagrius' anger. He had chosen to blame the Pallidus Mor for the destruction of the *Sagittariis*. He was acting out of wounded pride again. He was taking the Warlord's fall as a personal insult.

'I will be frank,' Syagrius continued.

'You haven't been until now?' Krezoc asked.

He ignored her. 'Your failures have besmirched the honour of the Pallidus Mor. Such as it was.'

Krezoc didn't know if he meant her failures or those of the entire demi-legio. She decided it didn't matter. The statement was fatuous in either case.

Menas remained silent and impassive. Fleiser was squirming, and kept trying to say something, but the inadequacy of whatever he came up with choked the words before he could utter them. Deyers was vibrating with indignation. He was barely holding back from launching himself across the table and seizing the marshal by the throat. It was likely that the only thing keeping him quiet was the fact that the first punch was Krezoc's to throw, not his. The rest of the guests at the table had stopped talking and were watching the argument. An uncomfortable quiet was falling across the entire hall.

Krezoc's contempt for Syagrius had reached such an intensity that it was almost calming. For the moment, she felt more disgust than anger, and she was actually curious to see where he would take his reasoning. 'How has victory led to dishonour?' she asked.

'Through the pointless losses.'

'Pointless,' Krezoc repeated. 'Marshal, we appear to have very different conceptions of honour.'

'So it would appear. Personally, I see little reason for celebration in this victory.'

'If you think the Pallidus Mor is celebrating, you are greatly mistaken.' Celebration, festivity, revelry – these were foreign concepts to the legio. Victory was not taken for granted, and it was an event to be learned from. So was defeat. Every battle of every campaign was studied afterwards. The Pallidus Mor had long learned to prepare for and expect the worst. The legio's philosophy was one that had been shaped by millennia of long, grinding sieges and drawn-out, exhausting campaigns. There was little room for glory in war. There was, instead, the duty to prepare for the next battle. 'Your accusations mean nothing to me. They are not just wrong, they are nonsensical. Such thoughts within our culture are simply incoherent.'

Syagrius sniffed. 'I have read of the culture of the Pallidus Mor.' He was no less furious, but his tone took on inflections of ostentatious erudition. 'I have even read of your legends. They are full of hardships and those long sieges. The more ancient ones have their share of shameful associations.'

The reference was oblique, almost casual. And it was enough to replace Krezoc's contempt with cold, murderous fury. Many of the tales of the Pallidus Mor's battles during the Great Crusade were fragmentary, and only spoken of within the legio itself. For Syagrius to have encountered those he was alluding to, he would have had to have had someone dig deeply. She felt as if the identity of the Pallidus Mor were being jabbed at by an intruder. Something sacred was being raked open by an iconoclast.

In those legends of the Great Crusade, the Pallidus Mor had fought thankless campaigns by the side of the Iron Warriors. The lesson of the myths was a point of pride for the legio: the wars that had sown the seeds of resentment which had at last blossomed into the treachery of the IV Legion were the wars that had shaped the Pallidus Mor's grim, undeviating loyalty to the Emperor. Syagrius' jab was a deliberate, monstrous misreading of the deep core of the legio's soul.

Krezoc stared at him. It was several seconds before she trusted herself to speak. 'Are you questioning our loyalty to the Father of Mankind?' She managed to sound calm. She spoke slowly, enunciating every syllable with great precision. It was important that Syagrius understand how much depended on his answer to that question. This was the insult she would not permit to pass unanswered.

Deyers looked at Syagrius with undisguised hatred. Fleiser had turned pale with horror. Even Menas had turned to stare at the marshal. It was her look, Krezoc thought, that brought him up short. He seemed to realise he had gone too far if other aristocrats were drawing away from him. 'No,' he said to Krezoc. 'I am saying no such thing. I do not question the Pallidus Mor's loyalty. I question its competence.'

'Our competence? It was your decision, marshal, to chase after mirages. The Imperial Hunters abandoned Gelon to no purpose.'

Syagrius glared at her. 'If the campaign were not over, I would have you charged with insubordination.'

Krezoc shrugged and took a sip of her amasec.

'If yours was a culture of honour,' Syagrius said, 'we would be at the point of a duel.'

'I see no honour in the culture you are championing,' said Krezoc.

Syagrius did not answer. Krezoc met and held his stare. The silence in the hall was complete. It went on and on, filling the air with poison.

Ornastas returned to Saint Kaspha's through the shadows. On his journey to the barracks, he believed that his visibility still meant something, that to be seen was to reinforce the law of the Imperial Creed. He knew better now. His journey had been an illusion. The cancer eating at Creontiades had already won. That was why it had become visible.

Captain Seth had taken him down to a sub-basement of the barracks, and from there to the northern exit of the base. The door was small, and it creaked with disuse when Seth opened it. The alley beyond was free of cultists. They had poured strength into a direct assault on the main gate. They had no need of a siege. They were inside the walls.

'Go,' Seth had said.

'You won't come too?'

'My place is here, with my troops. We'll hold out for as long as we can.'

Ornastas had given in and fled down the alley. He moved through a city erupting in an ecstasy of anger. Many buildings were burning. Riots engulfed the streets. The major arteries were impassable. Ornastas worked his way back by cutting through lanes and abandoned manufactoria. Machines still performed their tasks, adding to the chaos as they went out of control, flooded by unregulated flows of material. Others had been sabotaged. Ruptured forges spread liquid fire across work floors and into the streets. He had to run through complexes in full collapse, but the fighting had moved on from them, and he chose the risk of being crushed and incinerated over having to fight through the mob. All the illusions were gone now. His clerical garb would make him a target of choice, and his mission would fail.

By the time he was a few blocks from Saint Kaspha's, the dawn had fallen to a sudden night. Smoke and ash blanketed the city. Foul chants rose from every quadrant. The heretics shrieked violent praise to their monstrous god, and they spilled the blood of the faithful. The screams of the murdered were drowned out by the triumphant hymns of their killers. Ornastas' ears were full of the din of catastrophe. He thought he could hear a pattern, too. There was more than random, uncontrolled violence at work. The pattern was important. He would have to learn what it was. First, though, he had to survive. And he had to summon help.

He avoided the front entrance of the chapel. The square before it was burning. The smell of cooked flesh made his eyes water. He resisted the urge to charge towards the square, brandishing the staff and hurling anathema at the heretics. Religious anger would only get him killed and serve the purpose of the corruptors.

He circumnavigated the square, doing his best to shut his ears to the chants and the screams. When he reached the narrow alley that ran past the south door, he slowed. A group of about thirty people were gathered around it, trying to get in. They were knocking on the door and shaking it, but they weren't trying to smash it down. Ornastas closed in, thumb ready to depress the stud and send shocks arcing through the crown of the staff.

A man saw him coming and fell to his knees. 'Save us, confessor,' he pleaded. In a moment, all the others were on the ground too. Their hands were outstretched, begging him to bring the salvation of the Emperor to them. He recognised the faces now. He had seen them often enough in his congregations. Their clothes were torn and covered in soot. Many of them were bleeding. They had been workers and low-level administrators. Now they were refugees, seeking sanctuary.

Ornastas was torn between pity and anger. They needed help, but where had their vigilance been when it was most needed? Had none of them heard any whispers? Had none of them fought back when the cultists had begun to move?

'Are you here to hide or fight?' he asked them.

After a few moments, the man who had spoken first said, 'We are here to do as you bid us, confessor.' The others murmured in agreement.

Ornastas saw the first hint of something other than fear in the people before him. That would do for now. He had no direction to give them yet, beyond the need for defiance and faith. He nodded and pushed through them to the door. He unlocked it, let them into the chapel and closed the door tight.

'What would you have us do?' a woman asked.

'Remain quiet,' he said. 'Do not make your presence known to the heretics. Watch the windows, and be ready to move to the crypts when I tell you.' He did not intend to prepare for a siege. They were lucky the chapel had not yet been ransacked. It was only a matter of time before that happened. He and these people would have to be gone before that, unless they chose this place to fight and die. He had no intention of becoming a martyr yet. 'Wait for my return,' he told the faithful.

Before he went to the sacristy to make the call for help, he climbed the spiral staircase of the west tower. Anxiety urged him on, and it took less than fifteen minutes for him to reach the top. He crouched low as he approached the parapet, ducking behind a crenellation so he would not be seen by those below. He looked down into the square.

He had expected slaughter, and he was not wrong. He had feared something worse, too, and that was what had brought him to this vantage point. Below, the massacre confirmed his worst surmises. The people of Creontiades were being killed in accordance with a dark ritual. An enormous pyre, already thirty feet high, rose from the centre of the square. The heretics poured accelerant into the flames to consume the unending supply of victims. The screams of the burning rose and fell like the notes of a monstrous song. Other martyrs were butchered with blades and axes. Their bodies were dragged, leaving lines of blood. The designs formed runes around the pyre. Other lines stretched to the edge of the square and beyond, into the major avenues. Ornastas followed one line of blood with his eyes. It headed off to the north west. It pointed towards the glow of another pyre in the distance. A crimson glow flickered against the building façades. To the north and north east, Ornastas saw more fires. They were coordinated. He began to make out a pattern linking the fires. As it took shape in his mind, lances of red pain shot through his eyes. Cracks of anger spread through his being, like molten cracks of ice. The anger was not his. It was not the anger of righteousness that buoyed him through this day. It was something else. It came from something else. It served a great darkness. If it took him in its grip, it would smash his mind. He would become a thing of rampaging instinct and howling violence. Worst of all, he would still be a priest, only now he would be vowed to the service of the god that sent the anger.

Ornastas pushed himself away from the parapet. He fell to his knees and shut his eyes. He prayed for the souls of the dead, and he prayed to the Emperor for strength. He clutched his staff as though it were the iron of his faith itself. The pain and the anger began to fade as he shook off the sight of the pattern. He leaned on the staff and pulled himself to his feet again. Though he avoided looking too closely at the fires in the darkness, he heard the chanting in a new way. It, too, linked one site of sacrifice to another. Across Creontiades, voices entwined in something worse than heretical worship.

They were calling. They were summoning.

So now he had a much clearer, more terrifying sense of the extent of the threat that faced Katara. He knew the warning he must send.

He descended the stairs as quickly as he could and ran to the sacristy first. He paused before activating the holo-link. It might no longer be functioning. If it was, he did not know who might be monitoring the transmission. He shrugged. He had no other options. He turned it on and began trying to reach his fellow confessors in Deicoon and Therimachus. On his fifth attempt, he got through to Euchenor in the latter. Unlike Vilkur, Euchenor believed him without question. Already, rumours of trouble were reaching the other cities, though they were still only rumours. Ornastas took hope from that.

'There has been no uprising in Therimachus, then?' he asked.

'No, nor in Deicoon, as far as I know.'

Another burst of hope. Perhaps Katara could be saved. The cult seemed to have concentrated its efforts on the capital city first.

'Spread my warning,' Ornastas said. 'Creontiades has fallen. I don't think you will hear from the lord-governor. We need off-world help.'

Euchenor's image nodded. 'We will be heard,' he said. 'I wish you well, old friend.'

'The Emperor is my shield.'

The screen went blank before he finished speaking. At the same moment, a whistling shriek sounded beyond the chapel walls. It seemed to come from the sky. It grew louder by the second. Ornastas burst out of the sacristy, making for the entrance to the crypt. All the refugees had gathered there. Many sobbed and covered their ears. The shriek drew closer. Something was coming down, flying through the atmosphere of Katara, dropping with murderous speed towards the city. Something huge and terrible beyond measure. The people cried out in terror, and it was all Ornastas could do not to join in their scream. His body wanted to collapse in surrender to the threat, but he forced himself to keep going. He reached the door to the crypt. He hauled it open and ushered his desperate flock down ancient stone steps. Before he could follow, the shriek reached its apex. The boom that followed blew in every window in Saint Kaspha's. A maelstrom of stained-glass shards slashed through the chapel. Angry light blazed.

And over the thunder of arrival came the shrieks of more descents. Ornastas hauled the iron door of the crypt shut behind him and raced down into the dark.

# CHAPTER 4

# THE GRAND ALLIANCE

Knocking on the door to his sleeping quarters jerked Albrecht Fleiser awake. He was out of bed and on his feet before he was properly awake. The adrenaline of war still coursed through him. He had barely slept since the nightmare awakening to the coming of the tyranids. He reacted to any interruption now as if devouring jaws were about to snap shut on him.

But it was just a knock. 'Lord-governor?' Gremo, his major domo, called.

'A moment,' Fleiser said. He threw on his uniform. It was always laid out beside his bed now. 'What is it?' he asked a minute later when he opened the door.

'Admiral Menas wishes to meet with you. She is waiting in the briefing chamber.'

Fleiser hoped he hadn't turned pale. *Have they come again?* he wondered. Good news never came in the dead of night. He said nothing, not trusting his voice to keep from croaking. He nodded and made his way down the gilded corridors to the briefing room.

Menas was alone when he entered. The tacticarium tables were dark for the first time since the start of the invasion, the lumen strips dim and the room eerily quiet. Fleiser guessed it was about to come to life again. Menas stood at the head of the main table, her arms crossed, her head lowered in thought. She looked up at Fleiser as he joined her.

'What has happened?'

'A heretical uprising on Katara,' Menas said.

'Ah.' He was glad the room was dark. His relief wouldn't show too clearly. 'The Sixty-Sixth will have to return home immediately.'

'There is more. We have lost communications with the entire Sevasmos System. Before that happened, there were fragmentary reports of landings by a Traitor Titan force.'

'Throne,' Fleiser whispered. He wasn't relieved any longer. As Khania's fall would have threatened Katara, the converse was also true. He swallowed hard and worked to keep his face composed.

'You understand what this means?' said the admiral. 'The Pallidus Mor and the Imperial Hunters are even now receiving orders to deploy to Katara.'

'Campaigning as a single force again? That won't be popular in the ranks. Or with the officers.'

'Quite. And the losses they have suffered here will require a more complete integration on Katara.'

'I see.' He was grateful he was not the one breaking the news to Krezoc or Syagrius. 'What do you want me to do?'

'Be present. I believe the meeting between the marshal and princeps senioris will go more smoothly if they are not alone.'

'I see.' Fleiser had pegged Menas as being in Syagrius' camp at the painful victory celebration. Perhaps she was, yet the natural alliances of class seemed irrelevant now. Though her features were composed into stern impassivity, her eyes betrayed her concern. 'This is not going to be pleasant, is it?' Fleiser said.

'No,' said Menas. 'It is not.'

They faced each other from opposite ends of the principle tacticarium table. Krezoc had arrived a few moments after Syagrius. The table was already alight with hololithic maps of Katara's major cities and surrounding regions. The corner of Krezoc's mouth twitched in sour amusement. Menas and Fleiser had prepared a visual reminder of what was at stake. *They're that sure Syagrius and I would be at each other's throats otherwise,* she thought. *They're wrong.* Deyers was there too, standing by himself opposite the admiral and lord-governor. Another reminder. Krezoc was insulted. She did not need to be recalled to her duty. Even so, the mere sight of Syagrius made her shoulders tense. She tasted something revolting.

Syagrius didn't look any happier to see her. 'We have work to do together,' he said, almost spitting the words.

'Indeed,' said Krezoc. She wished they did not. But her orders were unambiguous. She had rarely received an astropathic communication that was so clear, so little open to interpretation. Krezoc suspected it was given force by the anger of Zarath Mallaheim, Grand Master of the Pallidus Mor. She did not believe he found the humiliating command an easy one to give. The Pallidus Mor were to continue the collaboration with the Imperial Hunters. Given the relative losses, Syagrius would retain command of the joint operations. Krezoc was to extend him every cooperation and respect.

*Meaning I will have to obey.* She already knew what was coming. It was inevitable, given Syagrius' pride. Worse, though, was that it was necessary, following the logic of chains of command and relative size of forces. In terms of competence, it would be a huge, tactical mistake. The fatalism of the Pallidus Mor did not make accepting Syagrius' leadership any easier. It was a demonstrable error. It was a disaster in the making. And there was no way out of the trap it presented.

Syagrius said, 'I have examined the resources we can still field. It is clear to me that a complete integration of our maniples is the way to proceed.'

'I see,' said Krezoc, remaining calm as the nightmare began to unfold. 'Would it not be preferable to preserve the identity of the legios? Bringing crews unfamiliar with each other into the same maniple is risky.' She said nothing about the tensions between the Pallidus Mor and the Imperial Hunters. That was obvious.

'The loss of maniple integrity would be worse, especially when we have the means to restore it.'

Krezoc eyed the marshal, trying to decide if his argument sprang from conviction or vindictiveness. Even from across the length of the table, she could see a vein standing out on his forehead. His words snapped with tension. Emotions warred on his face. He seemed to be swinging back and forth between anger and malicious satisfaction. He hated the thought of the two legios working together as much as she did. But he also relished the authority of his position, and the power it gave him to put her in her place.

'What do you suggest?' Krezoc said. She couldn't bring herself to ask what his *orders* were.

'The Imperial Hunters have the Warlords to lead four complete maniples,' Syagrius said. 'So there will be no integration with those.' He said *integration* as though it meant *contamination*.

*You hate the very thing you are imposing,* Krezoc thought. *How do you intend to have satisfaction? How can you have it both ways?*

She had her answer with Syagrius' next words.

'One of our Reavers and two of our Warhounds will complete your formations. You may, of course, assign them within your ranks as you see fit.' He spoke as if he were acting with impressive largesse.

Krezoc nodded. The son of nobility was treating her as his vassal. She would not do or say anything that would reinforce this image. If he expected her gratitude, he would not receive it. She thought about how to spread three outsider Titans through her demi-legio. No matter what she did, the impact would be painful. *Gloria Vastator*'s maniple had survived the battle of Gelon intact. Preserving its integrity felt simultaneously selfish and imperative. It was one point where she could minimise the havoc Syagrius was imposing on the Pallidus Mor. *Crudelis Mortem*, on the other hand, had nothing left of its escort except two Warhounds. Toven Rheliax would not thank her for placing the Imperial Hunters Reaver and one of the Warhounds with him, but there was little choice. That would leave Merys Drahn of *Fatum Messor* to take on the surviving Reaver from Balzhan's decimated maniple and the other Warhound from the Hunters. There was nothing in this solution that she liked. It was also the least bad configuration she could see.

'Whatever the composition of the individual maniples,' said Syagrius, 'it is the cohesion of the whole that is crucial. The chain of command will be respected. I will tolerate no insubordination.'

Krezoc glared at him. The insult was clear, and she could not respond without making it appear entirely justified. She cursed the fate that had killed Balzhan and spared Syagrius. The marshal stared back at her, inviting her challenge, daring her to make a move against him before witnesses.

She did not trust herself to answer. Anything she said would be either capitulation or thrown gauntlet.

Menas stepped into the silence. 'The Imperial Navy is, of course, ready to assist in the liberation of Katara by whatever means may be required.'

Fleiser joined in. 'Tell me, Marshal Syagrius, have you decided on a landing site yet?' He gestured at the tacticarium table, as if physically pulling the attention of the two officers away from each other.

Krezoc did feel some gratitude now. Menas and Fleiser had redirected the conversation, and she did not have to answer Syagrius. She could preserve that much honour, at least.

'I have,' Syagrius said to Fleiser. 'To the best of our understanding, only Creontiades has fallen. Our strategy will be one of isolation, containment and preservation.'

*Our strategy,* Krezoc thought. *The one I have heard nothing about.*

Syagrius tapped the table. The hololithic representation of Creontiades became brighter. 'The geographic situation of the capital region provides us with an advantage.'

Krezoc agreed, to a point. Three-quarters of Katara's

surface was ocean. It had one main land mass, and much of it was uninhabitable desert. Creontiades was on an island just off the continent's east coast. The Kazani bridge connected it to the mainland. That narrow route would be the enemy's only means of advance. Taking Creontiades first might prove to be the enemy's great mistake. On the other hand, the island also provided the foe with a stronghold. Taking the city back would mean crossing the bridge too.

'We will begin with a landing outside Deicoon,' Syagrius continued.

'Good,' said Krezoc. Deicoon was the smallest of Katara's population centres. It was less than fifty miles across the strait from Creontiades, and so highly vulnerable. It would be the enemy's next target, if it had not fallen already. Therimachus was a fair distance north and west of Deicoon. If the situation was as reports indicated, the third city was not an immediate concern.

'We will take and hold the cities,' Syagrius said, 'then force the enemy to fight the war on our terms.'

Krezoc frowned. Did Syagrius mean to divide the battle group's attention between Deicoon and Therimachus? She started to object, then saw the look on Deyers' face. The captain was pale. His lips were pressed in a determined line. His eyes were flicking back and forth between Krezoc and Syagrius, glinting with hope and concern.

*We are deciding the fate of his home world*, Krezoc thought. She glanced down at the tacticarium table. Perhaps she and the marshal needed this reminder after all. Neither of them knew the situation on the ground yet. She wasn't sure now if her objection was based on something stronger than her feelings of antipathy and distrust towards Syagrius. She had reason to doubt his judgement, but if she opposed him by default, her position was as badly thought out as she believed his to be. Her duty was the salvation of Katara.

She looked at Syagrius, at his hostility and pride, and wondered how conscious he was of their duty. *We are not at war with each other,* she told herself.

She wished she believed that to be true.

The rockcrete expanse of Gelon's space port vibrated. As Lehanna Platen made her way towards the heavy lifter *Foundry's Heritage,* another of the fat-bellied transports launched. It rose on four columns of fire, its thunder turning the air brittle. Ahead, the tanks of the 66th Kataran Spears rolled up the ramps into the *Heritage*'s cargo bay. The roars of their engines turned into crashing echoes when they entered the huge space. Beside the *Heritage,* Pallidus Mor and Imperial Hunters Warhounds were being loaded into another heavy lifter. A group of officers and crews from both legios had gathered at the base of the loading ramp. Platen slowed as she walked past the cluster. Raised voices stopped her.

Two moderati were facing each other. Their comrades had formed a rough circle around them, and were watching each other warily.

'If you're in our maniple, you're in our maniple,' said Sen Narsek, the Pallidus Mor moderati. 'The orders come from the princeps captain.'

'I follow my princeps, not a jumped-up serf,' Velor Balventius snapped. 'You don't understand, do you? I haven't joined your maniple. You're now part of our battle group. We're going to make sure you keep proper discipline this time.'

'This time?'

'We've had enough disasters from your leaders. We want victory on Katara. I know you don't have the same concern.'

Narsek leaned in towards Balventius. His hands were fists. 'You're very free with your insults.'

Balventius snorted. 'How can the truth be an insult? Your marshal led you off a cliff. His death is proof of that.'

Narsek flushed red and took another step forwards. He was a few inches shorter than Balventius, but much more solidly built. 'You will withdraw that–' he began.

Balventius slapped him.

Platen gaped. The crack of the blow sent a ripple through the rest of the crowd. There was a collective intake of breath. When the shock of the act wore off, violence would erupt.

Narsek stared at Balventius, his eyes bulging with rage. The Imperial Hunter regarded him calmly. He had all the self-assurance of an aristocrat who took it as his natural right to strike those he perceived to be his social inferiors. It was inconceivable that he would be struck in return. He looked down his nose at the Pallidus Mor moderati with a tight, pleased smile.

Platen ran forwards. She plunged through the circle of foes as Narsek grabbed Balventius by the collar of his uniform. Narsek pulled his fist back. Platen threw herself between the two men. She broke Narsek's grip and shoved the two moderati back. Balventius staggered, startled and sputtering with outrage that Narsek had dared retaliate.

'Throne, are you all mad?' Platen shouted. She looked back and forth at the men, ready to lunge against the first who made a move. Narsek was a coiled spring.

Balventius was shouting incoherently, but had taken a further step back. He must have realised that he could not win a physical struggle against Narsek. Most of the Pallidus Mor officers Platen had seen looked as if they could handle themselves in combat outside their god-machines. As far as she knew, none of the princeps that had come to Khania were confined to amniotic tanks. They were all able-bodied. They had trained, she suspected, in the expectation of the worst scenarios, and were ready to fight on the battlefield if the fortunes of war pitched them onto it. Balventius looked far less able with his fists. Power was his defence. Authority and high birth were his shield. Narsek recognised neither. He could pummel the Imperial Hunter with ease.

And disaster would follow.

'This is not your concern, tanker,' Balventius said.

His contempt was so clear, Platen was tempted to step aside and let Narsek bloody him. She was almost ready to throw a punch herself. 'Isn't it my concern?' she said. 'Katara is my home. I'm going to defend it, and I'm not going to let a couple of glory hounds put their pride ahead of my world.'

Balventius glared at her. She felt the anger of the Imperial Hunters in the circle shift in her direction.

'Glory hound,' Narsek grunted. He sounded almost amused. 'I've never been accused of that before.'

'Is it refreshing?' Platen asked him.

He grinned, the purple flush leaving his face. 'It makes a change.'

She turned to Balventius. 'Are you going to make me plead?' she said. 'I will if I have to. Katara is more important to me than my pride.' The speech made her feel sick. At this moment, real satisfaction would have involved training *Bastion of Faith*'s cannon on Balventius. But she was speaking the truth. She would swallow her own pride if it meant mollifying this fool and reminding him of his duty.

Balventius shrugged. 'It must be,' he said, as dismissive as ever. At least he wasn't looking at Narsek. He seemed happy enough to shift his disdain in Platen's direction. His nose wrinkled as if he had suddenly become aware of a foul smell. Then he turned and walked away, heading towards the lifter's bay door. The other Imperial Hunters left with him.

'We haven't all forgotten what needs to be done,' Narsek said.

'Good,' said Platen. She didn't look back at the moderati as she started walking again.

Ornastas hesitated only for a second at the intersection of the storm sewers before choosing the left-hand channel. He waded through stinking water a foot deep. The torch he had taken from the crypt of Saint Kaspha's cast a wan cone of light in the darkness. The brickwork of the tunnel glistened, dripping with seepage.

'How do you know the way?' the man at his left asked. His name was Aldemar. He was a worker in the Administratum, monitoring hab construction in a small portion of the western sector of the city. He was pale, and his face was smudged with ash. In the dim light, it looked like shadows were clinging to his skull. The rest of the group following Ornastas had the same look as Aldemar. They were frightened almost to the point of despair. But they hadn't given up yet. Their faith in Ornastas, and through him in the Emperor, kept them going.

'I don't know that this is the right path,' Ornastas said. He had never ventured beyond the crypt himself. 'It's heading west, though. That's where we want to go. Out of the city and across the bridge to the mainland.'

Just behind Aldemar, Velatz asked, 'And then what?' She was a manufactorum serf, blunt and rough-hewn, and one of the most fervent worshippers at Saint Kaspha's.

'Then we fight,' Ornastas said. He risked raising his voice so the entire group would hear. His words boomed and echoed down the tunnel, a shout of defiance. From far above, at ground level, came the sounds of steady, rhythmic impacts, like the tread of something monstrous.

'We'll need weapons,' said Velatz, though it was clear she was not disagreeing with him.

'We'll get them. But we are not unarmed.'

'Aren't we?' Aldemar asked.

'Do you have hands to strike the heretic? Do you have faith in the God-Emperor? Then you are armed,' Ornastas told him.

In the hours since they had left the chapel, he had felt a shift in his flock. There was more than fear present in the citizens now. There was anger too. They were hungry to strike back at the enemy that had taken the city.

Velatz was right, though. They would need weapons.

A few minutes later, there was a sharp rattling overhead. The sounds came closer, dropping down into the sewers. Ornastas stopped and held up a hand. His band waited, silent. They heard voices now, harsh with violent laughter. A hundred yards ahead, an access where the wall curved into the tunnel roof banged open. A group of heretics dropped into the tunnel. They pulled bodies with them. Two still twitched feebly. The others were mutilated corpses. The cultists propped the bodies against the wall, where the victims' blood poured into the muddy water. Shouting and struggling with each other, the heretics tore into the flesh of the dead and the dying. They had hauled their prizes into the storm sewers to devour them away from the greed of other rivals, and even this small group was consumed with competition for the choicest flesh.

Ornastas gave no signal. The rush to attack was spontaneous. The celebrants of Saint Kaspha's shrieked with moral, physical and spiritual revulsion, and they charged at the heretics. The enemy wielded blades. One had a laspistol. It did not matter. A single shot was fired, and then the righteous fell on the unholy. Ornastas and his flock had greater numbers. They also had faith, as he had told them. Ornastas smashed heretic skulls with the iron wings of his staff. The others punched and kicked and clawed. The struggle was ugly. The tunnel walls rang with animal growls. Ornastas shouted prayers, so there would be a voice of faith in the violence, a beacon to guide the faithful and keep them from descending too far into the maelstrom of violence.

He was heeded. When the last of the heretics lay face down in the water, the people did not turn on each other. They seized the weapons of the cultists, then fell to their knees and joined Ornastas in a hymn of martial thanksgiving.

'The Emperor protects,' Ornastas said as they moved on. 'And He provides to those who will fight in His name.'

Some time later, the band reached the end of the journey through the tunnels. The passage they were following reached a huge pool. An underground lake of waste water churned at the edge of channels sloping sharply downwards. Only drowning awaited there.

On the left, a service ladder mounted into the wall rose fifty feet to the ceiling of the chamber. Ornastas led the climb. At the top, the wheel lock of the hatch resisted his efforts to turn it at first, then gave with a metallic screech. Ornastas pushed the hatch open and made his way into open air for the first time since leaving Saint Kaspha's.

It was night. The ecclesiarch and his flock emerged at the edge of Creontiades' outermost wall, in a region of pump stations and power plants. Fires burned on the ramparts. Heretics danced and chanted before them. The revelry of conquest was at its peak. There had been some fighting in the sector. To the right, buildings had been bombed, and the gutted husks of tanks smouldered. Near them, the wall had been smashed. It looked as if something immense had passed through it.

From behind came the sounds of the great treads, loud enough for the vibrations to shake Ornastas' chest.

'Don't look back,' he said. 'Only forwards.'

He broke into a run. The others followed. He made straight for the base of the wall, where the shadows were thickest, then turned right, running hard for the ruins. He did as he had commanded and looked only at his goal. If they were spotted, there was nothing that could be done. So he ran, sprinting for escape and the chance to fight on. A smoky breeze blew in his face. His ears were full of the shouts and thunder of the fallen city. His heart was strong with the Emperor, and he knew he would not fail now. He must not. He was leading what remained of Creontiades' faith.

The heretics on the wall were too caught up in their obscene celebration to spot Ornastas' group. He reached the gap in the defences. Huge chunks of rockcrete lay in a blanket of rubble reaching half a mile into the city. The breach was hundreds of yards wide. Ornastas charged through it. The terrain ahead was rocky. Boulders and jagged outcroppings turned the land into a maze of stone. Some distance to the left, a road had been blasted through the rock. It ran to the city from the bridge and was the only level ground outside the walls. Ornastas kept the road in sight, but led the way into the maze, keeping to the deep shadows of the tallest outcroppings. He kept the torch aimed at the ground. He had to move more slowly now. The footing was treacherous, and he could barely see. The ground sloped upwards gradually as it approached the coast of the island.

Ornastas had the band out of sight of the wall almost immediately. He did not stop to rest for another hour. Only then did he and his followers finally look back towards Creontiades. They had reached an elevation a bit higher than the outer walls, and they had a good view of the city. They saw the fires, the smoke and the flares of the final battles. Most of all, they saw the monsters that had come. The new lords of Creontiades were Titans. They were cruel, spiked, misshapen god-machines. Their armour was a deep crimson. Their war-horns resounded in the night, and they moved with foul majesty, towering horrors bestriding the avenues, walking through hab blocks that happened to be in their way.

Their sight inspired terror that bled the very soul. The people wailed. One man fell to the ground screaming. He curled into a ball and clawed his eyes from their sockets.

'We cannot fight those,' Velatz said. She could barely speak.

'No, but those who can will be coming. When they do,

we will fight with them. We will take back Creontiades. Now turn away,' Ornastas commanded his flock. 'Do not gaze at the unholy.'

He turned away from the sight of the dark colossi. He urged the faithful on. It was important that they keep moving. It was more important that they not dwell on what they had seen. And it was important that he avoid the same mistake. He felt that if he gazed too long on the Traitor Titans, their sublime horror would root him to the spot and turn him into a pillar of salt.

The battle group encountered no opposition when it arrived in orbit over Katara. The transport vessels of traitor legio were empty husks at anchor. They appeared to be captured civilian freighters, twisted into immense tombs by the corruption that had seized them. Enslaved, they had been consumed by their task of delivering the enemy to Katara. Now they were broken, dark, silent shells, their bellies ripped open by the descent of Titans. The Pallidus Mor and the Imperial Hunters had the freedom to land at will, though Krezoc did not like the implications she read in the absence of an enemy fleet. All the traitor forces had reached planetside, and they felt no need for orbital support.

Krezoc found some cause for optimism in the landings at Deicoon. Krezoc was grateful Syagrius had sent the Pallidus Mor down first. That gave her the chance to take the field as she saw fit. The city, by all appearances, had not fallen to the traitors. The banners of the Imperium flew over its walls, the two heads of the aquila glaring a challenge. The city militia and the reserve of the Kataran Spears assembled outside the eastern wall in ceremonial greeting to the legio and the returning 66th. Nevaeh Eukrolas, governor of the city, sent word that she was coming to meet with the commanders of the battle group.

*'That is well,'* Syagrius voxed from the *Currus Venatores* transport when Krezoc informed him. *'Make your arrangements with Governor Eukrolas. I will do the same with Governor Markos at Therimachus.'*

Krezoc suppressed a groan, but not the frustrated slap she gave the arm of her command throne. Her moderati turned to look at her. She did not hide her grimace of anger from them. She should have known better than to see benefit to the Pallidus Mor in the order of deployment. Syagrius had simply used her forces to test the ground. She knew the answer she would receive before she spoke again, but she had to hear the words aloud. She had to make Syagrius articulate his madness. 'We will not be holding Deicoon together, then,' she said.

*'I see no need.'*

'With respect, marshal, the need is to mount our full strength for an attack to retake Creontiades.'

*'By attempting a crossing of the Kazani bridge? Are you that eager for another defeat, princeps?'*

'The traitors will not remain cantoned on that island,' Krezoc said.

*'I agree. They will not. This is why our first task is to secure Deicoon and Therimachus. We will make them impregnable to attack, and let the enemy break himself against the walls of our strength.'*

'Our forces will be divided...' Krezoc began.

*'The cities will be held,'* Syagrius insisted. He ended the transmission.

'Is he a coward?' Konterus asked.

'Therimachus is a suspicious distance from the front,' Vansaak said.

'No,' Krezoc said, as she detached herself from the mechadendrites of the throne and felt the wrench of loss that accompanied every separation from *Gloria Vastator*. 'He is not a coward.' She almost wished he was. His decisions would be easier to anticipate and counter. 'He is misguided. We will win this war all the same.'

She stood for a moment, looking through the armour-glass eyes of the Titan. The Warlord faced east, towards the strait. Though it was midday, the clouds over Creontiades were so black they reflected the glow of the fires in the city. The skyline was a faint smudge on the horizon, but Krezoc thought she could see the movement of huge shapes, and the shadows of the conflagration to come.

## CHAPTER 5

# THE KAZANI STRAIT

The landscape surrounding Deicoon rolled with low, rocky hills and, closer to the city, slag heaps. It was a geology of petrified waves, a panorama of upheaval ground down by erosion, but sharp as exposed bones. It was hard land, and it had shaped its city.

Nevaeh Eukrolas met Krezoc in military uniform. It bore the crossed spears insignia of the Kataran 66th, though her rank was a ceremonial one. Her greeting was bluff, almost boisterous in its presumption of the fellowship of arms. She walked with a brisk, emphatic stride, and Krezoc could well believe that Deicoon's governor had, in her youth, served with the 66th, or at the very least in the militia. That had been a long time ago, though. She was part of the ruling family of Katara. Her brother was lord-governor of the planet, and her cousin ruled in Therimachus. Her path was that of the nobility. Krezoc wasn't sure if her martial bearing ran deeper than nostalgia and self-image. She hoped it did.

They travelled from the gates in Eukrolas' personal transport, a repurposed Chimera whose roof folded back to allow a parade throne and dais to be raised. Krezoc sat beside the throne. Rheliax and Drahn took seats on the dais. They rode through the streets of Deicoon, ostensibly to inspect its defences. They were also on display themselves, exhibits brought to reassure the populace and bolster its morale.

'Have you heard from the lord-governor?' Krezoc asked.

'There's been nothing from Hallard since the uprising began. We assume the palace was one of the first targets to fall.'

'I'm sorry to hear it.'

Eukrolas shrugged. 'Can't be helped. He should have known a cult was growing in power right under his nose. Especially if it was large enough to take over the city.' She clicked her tongue in disgust. 'My brother is my brother, and kin is kin, princeps senioris, but the fact is, vigilance and preparedness were never my brother's strengths. He's a politician, and he's a good one, but there are times when that isn't enough.'

'Such as this one.'

'Precisely. I think you'll find our defences are serious ones.'

Drahn looked back in her seat. 'What we've seen is most impressive,' she said to Eukrolas.

'Glad to hear it. Glad to hear it. We don't do things by halves in Deicoon. If it's supposed to defend, then by the Throne, it had better well defend.'

The walls surrounding the city were almost as thick as they were high, and squat, massive cannon turrets dotted Deicoon. Their guns pointed down the length of the main avenues. These radiated in straight lines from the inner keep, where the region's government was housed, giving the cannons a clear line of fire on anything entering from one of the city's gates.

Deicoon was the most heavily industrialised city on Katara. The route from the east gate took Krezoc and the other princeps past one gigantic manufactorum complex after another. It was like passing through a thunderous, pounding canyon of rockcrete and iron. Clusters of chimneys spewed smoke into the air, blanketing the city with smog. The people of Deicoon thronged the pavements, chanting their governor's name and cheering the princeps. The shouts were raucous and hard. The people, the city and Eukrolas were all carved from the same stone. They were cause for optimism, Krezoc thought.

The keep dominated the centre of Deicoon. It was a massive upthrust of curving ramparts. It was higher than any of the hab blocks. It was a broad-shouldered colossus that guarded each cardinal point of the compass with a macrocannon. The guns were monsters, worthy of void-ship armament. The keep needed to be as big as it was just to support the means of its defence. The range of the cannons would extend far beyond the walls of the city.

The transport drew closer to the keep and fell under the shadow of the east-facing macrocannon. 'Thunderstrike-pattern?' Krezoc asked.

'Yes,' said Eukrolas.

'I see.' Thunderstrikes were older and not as powerful as the Mark VI Mars-pattern macrocannons. They were rarely used on Navy combat vessels any longer, though transports still made use of them. Even if they were lesser armament in void wars, planetside they would be devastating. 'I've rarely seen four guns like those in such proximity on land,' Krezoc said.

'Really?' Eukrolas sounded very pleased.

'Do they see use often?' In the mission briefs, she had seen nothing about civil wars on Katara.

'They haven't been fired for many centuries,' Eukrolas said. 'Their existence is enough. Who's going to be stupid enough to go up against them?'

'Who would have any desire to try?'

'We haven't had political battles since the start of our dynasty,' Eukrolas admitted. 'But we're prepared. Good thing we are, for days like this.'

'True,' said Krezoc.

'My brother didn't understand.' She shook her head. 'The elite have to be strong. The universe doesn't grant any favours. We're ready, he wasn't, and look what happened.'

'The macrocannons wouldn't have helped Creontiades,' Rheliax said. Not if the assault came from within.'

'But they would have helped,' said Eukrolas. 'It isn't just what they can do. It's what they mean. Vigilance. Rigour. If something like them is guarding the distance, that means the rest of the city is doing its duty. You see?'

'What are your troop levels?' Drahn asked.

'Better now the Sixty-Sixth is here. Before, a few companies of the militia and reservists. Plus what the Adeptus Arbites can put in the field.'

'Not much for a city of this size,' said Rheliax.

'It's been enough,' Eukrolas said. She gazed up at the macrocannon as if she had built it herself. 'This is a city of iron, princeps. So is our faith.'

*You haven't been attacked yet,* Krezoc thought. Still, the defences were looking solid. If the keep was properly crewed, all guns fully operational, then the city was as good a stronghold as she could expect. That would give her more freedom of action. 'There has been no sign of cult activity?'

'None. We've taken the warning seriously and we are investigating. So far, nothing. I'm not surprised.'

'Oh?' Eukrolas' utter confidence made Krezoc uneasy.

'Creontiades made itself vulnerable to corruption. All those crystal towers. All that pride in the beautiful. You've never seen it?'

'Only some hololiths on our journey here.'

'It's something to see. The Jewel of Katara!' she announced sarcastically. 'The city as crown!' She shook her head. 'Beauty, pride and weakness. I often think they are the same thing. Don't you agree, Princeps Krezoc?'

'Creontiades was certainly unable to deal with the threat,' Krezoc said, carefully neutral. Eukrolas might be right, but there was a risk that in emphasising the city's weakness, the governor might be underestimating the strength of the enemy.

Eukrolas did not appear to notice the equivocation. 'Deicoon isn't easy prey,' she said. 'I promise you that.'

'I'm glad to hear it.'

The transport arrived at the base of the keep. A squad of honour guard waited before the heavy, adamantine doors. The soldiers' uniforms were similar to the one worn by Eukrolas. They were neither militia nor Kataran 66th, though their insignia shared elements of both. They were yet another force, and Krezoc guessed they were a private army, pledged to the protection of the Eukrolas family. The fifteen-foot-high doors parted with a clanking of gears as the princeps of the Pallidus Mor approached the entrance two steps behind the governor. Krezoc had fallen back to let Eukrolas dominate the arrival, and to snatch a few words in confidence with her fellow officers.

'Well?' she said quietly, as the door finished opening and a cheer went up from the assembled serfs inside the keep.

'Lots of defences,' Rheliax said. 'And the people seem to take what is coming seriously.'

'Though this is based on initial impressions,' Drahn added.

'Those are all we have time for,' Krezoc said. She thought for a moment, eyeing the thickness of the walls as she passed through the opening. The passageway through the wall ran for fifty feet. 'Unless we see something alarming in the keep, I'm going to declare the city as well defended as it can be. That gives us more freedom to act.'

'Will Marshal Syagrius agree?' Drahn asked. She was more inclined to doubt and question than Rheliax. By the standards of the culture of the Pallidus Mor, he was unusually cheerful. She balanced him by being suspicious of every positive development. She had her sense of humour, though. Krezoc was sure Drahn would greet death with a sardonically raised eyebrow.

'The marshal commanded that the city be secured,' Krezoc said. 'It has been. We'll ensure its defences by taking the fight to the enemy.'

'He *really* won't like that,' Drahn said, but she was grinning.

'Good,' said Krezoc.

The bridge over the Kazani Strait was, Ornastas believed, far greater a wonder than even the tallest and most graceful of the spires of Creontiades. It was a gargantuan cantilever structure, spanning a sea in eternal fury. The strait rounded a cape where two powerful ocean currents met. The winds over the bridge never ceased. They warred with each other, shaking the trusses that rose hundreds of feet into the air. The mile-wide span groaned with the strain, yet Ornastas could see no sign of its sway. The iron network of the superstructure was composed of girders so huge the bridge never appeared delicate, even from a distance. It was an arrogant defiance of gravity and storm, reaching for miles across the strait. Below it, the turmoil of the waves crashed against rockcrete supports so massive they seemed more like volcanic cones than the work of human hands. Aquilas with wingspans of hundreds of feet surmounted the apex of each truss. The bridge had stood for millennia, a testament to Imperial power. It was also the most vital artery of Creontiades, the route over which the vast majority of its trade to and from the other cities travelled.

There was no traffic over the bridge now. A few burned shells of vehicles were scattered along its length. The uprising had been so fast, the heretics had sealed the city before there had been a concerted attempt to escape. *We must succeed where others failed,* Ornastas thought. Creontiades was isolated, and the bridge was the way to safety and to continued resistance for Ornastas and his followers. They had made it this far from the city without being found. They were at the edge of a cliff overlooking the cauldron of the strait far below. The waves reached up in their anger, rising fifty feet or more. The bridge was a few hundred yards to the right. Near the start of its span, the heretics were gathering in greater and greater numbers. They came in a chaotic mixture of vehicles, civilian and military. They did not yet venture onto the bridge. Instead, they moved the transports off the road, leaving the way clear. Then they disembarked and clustered in chanting mobs, all facing east, back towards the city. They were waiting for the monsters that would lead the invasion.

'They'll see us when we start to cross,' Velatz said.

'I know.'

Ornastas scanned the terrain between them and the heretics. There were enough outcroppings to provide cover all the way to the bridge, and anchoring walls formed a gateway onto the span. He felt sure he and the citizens he now thought of as his resistance fighters could reach the southern wall undetected. Once they set foot on the road, though, they would be completely exposed. The first cultist to look to the west would see them. They could not cross the bridge that way.

Aldemar had been studying the bridge silently since their arrival. Now he said, 'I think there might be a way.'

'Tell us,' Ornastas said.

'It is dangerous.'

'Every breath we have taken since the uprising began has been dangerous. Show us the way.'

Aldemar pointed to a spot where the truss met the anchor wall. 'Look,' he said. 'Below the lip of the roadway.'

Ornastas squinted. In the failing light of the day, and with the winds whipping his face, it took him a few moments before he could see what Aldemar meant. There was a ledge running the length of the bridge about ten feet below the road. It looked like an access route for construction crews. Ornastas could just make out what must be ladders at strategic points along the span. From this distance, and against the massiveness of the rest of the construction, they resembled threads leading up and down into the trusses.

He wondered if the ledge was as narrow as it appeared to be. If so, it was nothing more than a catwalk. There were no guard rails, and the ledge was completely exposed to the wind. Once over the strait, the gusts would be even more fierce. A blast at the right angle would snatch a person up like a leaf in a storm, and plunge them into the maws of the waves.

'Well done,' Ornastas said to Aldemar.

'Like I said, it's risky.'

'It is also a chance. The only one we have.'

They headed off, a score of insects crouching low and clinging to the edge of the cliff. As they drew nearer to the wall, the edge became more broken, the footing more treacherous. They climbed down, finding a crumbling shelf that followed a jagged path to the base of the first truss. The wind screamed against the cliff face and was strong enough to carry stinging spray. The rocks were wet. Ornastas shuffled sideways, facing the cliff, using his free hand to grab every handhold he could find. Progress was awkward with the staff, and would have been unthinkable without it. This was the icon that had guided the way. It was hope in concrete form. He would hold it high for his followers even under fire from the monsters that were soon to march from Creontiades.

They passed underneath the roadway, entering the shadow of the bridge. There was a gap of about a yard between the shelf and its nearest approach to the catwalk. Ornastas looked down at the drop, fighting vertigo. The modest jump felt like a leap into the void in the buffeting wind. He straightened, faced straight ahead and placed his faith in the God-Emperor.

He jumped. There was a moment of terrible flight, and

then he landed on the iron platform. He stumbled, felt his balance waver. He leaned sharply to the right, banging his shoulder against the metalwork. He winced, but he was steady again. He moved forwards, out of the way, and looked back. One by one, the members of his flock made the leap. He saw his moments of terror and relief reflected in each of their faces. His robes flapping violently in the wind, he stood tall, the staff raised, a sight to keep the faithful strong as they crossed the gap.

Midway through the process, Dessican, another of the manufactorum serfs, misjudged his leap. His foot caught the edge of the catwalk. He slammed down at an angle and slid off the edge. He did not take his eyes off Ornastas. He remained true to the cause to the end, and he did not scream. He fell in utter silence, a stone dropping into the howl of the wind. He vanished into the heaving darkness below.

The next man to jump, an archivist named Runesehn, leapt without pausing. He seemed to rush, as if unwilling to hold back the moment of his fate. He landed safely on the ledge. So did the rest of the party.

Ornastas moved off, staff in his left hand, right hand clutching the girders on his right whenever they were close enough to do so. There were gaps, yards long, where there was a void on both sides of the catwalk. The wind howled around Ornastas, battering and pulling him. His robes tried to become wings, and he placed each step carefully, not lifting one foot until the other felt secure. The span stretched into the gloom of the falling night, and he could not see the other side. The groans of the trusses were deafening. They sounded like a ship about to break apart. Tremors ran through the girders and down the catwalk. The agonised life of the bridge thrummed through Ornastas' frame. And below, the Kazani Strait roared and seethed.

'Confessor!' Velatz had to shout to make herself heard over the wind.

Ornastas paused and looked back. They had come far enough now that the eastern end of the bridge was obscured too. They were in the midst of an iron limbo.

'They're coming!' Velatz said.

She was right. The vibrations were becoming stronger. A few moments later, he saw the glare of scores of headlights in the distance. The heretics were making their run on the bridge.

Something else must be close, then.

Ornastas raised his eyes, and saw what he had feared. There were other lights approaching from on high. They were a dull, crimson glow in the dark, the colour of boiling blood and burning pain. They were towering shadows, and then, as they came on, they became hideous walking mountains. Their silhouettes were distorted by huge, twisting horns and spikes, the metallic growths of corruption. Though they were still some distance from the bridge, it shook with the beat of their footsteps.

*Boom. Boom. Boom.* A slow, relentless drumbeat. The doom of Katara walked, and what foolish pride had led Ornastas to think he could do anything to stop what was coming?

Then, from the west, came another sound. Though miles distant, it was overwhelming, a blast of war and wrath and imperious majesty that forced Ornastas to his knees. He turned again, and there were lights in that distance too. It was too far to make out the beings whose eyes those were, but Ornastas felt their presence. They were monsters too, but sublime ones, leviathans of faith and awe.

The war-horns of the traitors answered the challenge. Then, from the east and from the west, the god-machines closed in on the Kazani Bridge.

'Sound the horns again,' Krezoc ordered.

The roar of the Pallidus Mor shattered the falling night. It triggered vibrations in the Kazani Bridge visible to the naked eye. Then *Gloria Vastator* took its first steps onto the span. The rockcrete of the road cracked under its steps, but the bridge was more than capable of taking the weight of the Warlord. The trusses were not linked over the centre of the bridge, leaving the way clear for even the tallest of the god-machines to cross. The Warhounds and the Reaver of Krezoc's maniple marched ahead. Behind, Rheliax and Drahn had their maniples side by side. The Titans were in close proximity, but the mile width of the span was enough to permit the wedge formation.

'*Our Imperial Hunters brethren are speaking with Syagrius,*' Drahn voxed.

'I would have been surprised if they weren't,' said Krezoc.

'*What are you going to tell him?*' Rheliax asked.

'That we are securing the defence of Deicoon. That is, if he gets through to me.'

She had given orders to her moderati not to respond or acknowledge any transmissions from Syagrius. She had sent a datapack to the marshal just before leaving Deicoon, informing him of the necessity to move on the enemy. She had not communicated with him since. There was no point. There would be consequences, and she accepted them. They would not be as severe as the ones that would come from waiting at Deicoon for the traitors to cross the bridge. 'I seem to be having some technical difficulties with the long-range vox,' she said. 'Maybe you are too.'

Drahn laughed. *'I think we are. We'll just have to leave it to the Hunters to keep the marshal up to date.'*

'Will they follow your orders?' Krezoc asked. That was a real concern.

*'They are following them so far, if under protest,'* said Rheliax.

'That will be good enough,' said Krezoc. She switched channels to address the entire demi-legio. 'Place your shots with care. Do not aim at the bridge. For now, our goal is to keep it intact.'

She looked ahead, to the lights of the approaching enemy. The augur array was showing a force already the equal of hers in size, and more traitors were advancing from Creontiades. The narrowness of the battlefield would mitigate the imbalance a bit, but already she was adjusting her larger strategy. There would be sacrifices on this night, and victory was beyond reach. But she would strike a blow.

'Captain Deyers,' she voxed. 'You may begin.'

Lined up on the eastern edge of the cliff, the tanks and artillery of the Kataran Spears commenced fire. Shells, mortars and rockets streaked across the Kazani Strait. To the north and south of the bridge, on the Creontiades side of the strait, the land bloomed with fire. There was no pause in the barrage. The guns fired at staggered intervals, and however badly hit the regiment had been at Gelon, its armoured ranks were still strong enough that while one portion of the cannons were reloading, others were firing, and the booming, shrieking bombardment became an unceasing thunder.

On the bridge, a swarm of vehicles raced across the span. The heretics surged ahead of their colossal masters like a plague of vermin. Pounding into the lead, the Warhound *Canis Ignem* opened up with its mega-bolter, the controlled spray of fire slamming into the lead vehicles, turning them into rolling balls of wreckage and flame. They collided with each other against the framework of the bridge. The explosions and the mounting pile of tangled metal slowed the cultists down, but many more pressed from behind, forcing their way through the burning wrecks.

Krezoc looked towards the far end of the bridge. She waited for the first glimpse of the enemy Titan lights. In the manifold, her consciousness swam through the data streaming in from the augurs. The machine-spirit fought her restraint. It could sense its foes and it burned with the need to send them to oblivion. She held back, though *Gloria Vastator*'s hate flowed through her soul too at the thought of Traitor Titans. The hate was more pure and more visceral than what the machine-spirit felt for the tyranids. They were a threat to the existence of the Imperium. The xenos had to be eradicated. But treachery inspired something more, something deeper. The mere existence of the fallen legios was an insupportable stain.

The Warlord strained to unleash its full rage. Krezoc held back. The bridge must be preserved if Creontiades were to be retaken. And now that the Pallidus Mor was upon it, its destruction would be disastrous. At least the traitors were showing similar, unusual restraint. They needed the bridge too.

Krezoc sighted her target. Her flesh eyes saw the red of its eyes and maw in the night, and the dim hints of its shape limned by the reflected fire of the Kataran barrage. Behind it came more of its misshapen kin. The traitors advanced, and now Krezoc saw the glint of brass. The sensor arrays scanned the silhouettes. They picked up their markings. They delineated the heads reshaped into the image of death.

'Banelord acquired,' Grevereign intoned. He was so focused on the size of the target, he had not registered its full identity.

Krezoc recognised the enemy. Her fists tightened with hate. 'The traitors are the Iron Skulls,' she announced to the demi-legio. With a name came history, and with the closing distance an even greater, agonised need to turn the foe into heaps of irradiated scrap. Ancient as the Pallidus Mor, the glories the Iron Skulls had once shared with their brethren legios, in the days, ten thousand years past, of the Imperium's great unity, were forgotten, expunged from all records by the fact of their duplicity.

Krezoc's vox buzzed with angry voices and oaths to bring molten justice to the traitors. Krezoc filtered through the transmissions. Some voices were absent. 'Do the Imperial Hunters have anything to say?' she asked Drahn and Rheliax.

'They're acknowledging orders and the receipt of information. Nothing more,' said Rheliax.

'They must not have encountered the Iron Skulls before,' said Drahn.

'They may have,' said Krezoc. 'They just didn't fight them as we had to.'

The Pallidus Mor had clashed with the Iron Skulls more than once. During the Battle of Cruciatus Primus, elements of the Iron Skulls had made a concerted effort to corrupt the Pallidus Mor. The attempt had been an utter failure, but the fact that the traitors had believed the Pallidus Mor might be susceptible was an insupportable insult. They believed that the legio's history of long wars and often unacknowledged sacrifice meant there would be fertile ground for the whispers of the Ruinous Powers. The mere thought was a stain on the honour of the Pallidus Mor. It had to be expunged from the face of the galaxy. Krezoc welcomed the chance to instruct the Iron Skulls further on the magnitude of their mistake. But her hatred for them made it even more difficult to control the fury of *Gloria Vastator*.

'Target is in range,' Grevereign reported. In his voice was the same strain and need to strike that Krezoc felt.

'Hurt it,' Krezoc said.

The volcano cannon fired. The las burned across the span of the Kazani Bridge. It struck the distant shape of the Banelord. The eastern night flared with the warring energies of las and void shields, a struggle more incandescent than the explosions of shells. The enemy stood revealed in all its corrupted might. The ancient work of the forges of Mars had been transformed into a monster from predatory dreams. The form of a Warlord was recognisable, but distorted, with spines along its arms, on its head and running down its back. It had grown a tail that lashed with anger, at the end of which was a cannon. Below the head of the Titan was a gaping maw, from which another gun barrel protruded. The Banelord fired the jaw cannon, a beast breathing fire. The las-beam was a tortured red. It burned and bled the night. Its light was rotten. To see it was to know the universe was cracked and broken, and that behind the fissures of reality there were things that strained to find their way through and bring ruin to all creation.

The dire las struck *Gloria Vastator*'s void shields. As they struggled against it, pushed to the edge of collapse, Krezoc kept the Warlord marching forwards, as if against a hurricane wind. The manifold convulsed with the energy demands of the shields and recoiled from the corrupted touch of the dark blast. The only answer was retaliation.

'Magos,' Krezoc voxed to Thezerin, 'first priority is the volcano cannon. All other weapons systems are on standby. Divert energy as needed. We must fire again.'

*'Understood.'*

The cannon charged up with alacrity, fed by the prayers and rituals of the tech-priest and by the war-rage of the machine-spirit. Krezoc fired again, and was rewarded with a violet-hued blast around the torso of the Banelord. Its shields collapsed, and flame burst from a rent in the armour. The beast's war-horn sounded, and it was the raging cry of a wounded animal, lunging forwards to destroy its tormentor. The bridge shook as the largest Traitor Titans increased their pace.

The distance between the lines of god-machines narrowed, and the intensity of the fire grew. The servants of the God-Emperor and the traitors now all had targets they could assault without blowing up the supports of the bridge. The span was lit by a storm of las. The night turned into a searing maelstrom. *Gloria Vastator* pressed its advantage on the Banelord, and the volcano cannon hit it again before its shields could recharge. The traitor's las punched through the Warlord's defences, but its aim was affected by the hits it had taken. Though the beam lanced through the armour on the left of the torso, it missed vital elements. *Gloria Vastator* walked on.

'Lower,' Krezoc breathed, deep in the fusion of self and moderati and machine. 'Make it fall.'

The next shot struck the Banelord in the left knee. It turned metal molten and severed the lower half of the leg. In mid-step, the Banelord pitched forwards and to Krezoc's right. The monster crashed down, crushing heretics and a Feral Titan beneath it.

The bridge swayed. On the right, the truss nearest the Banelord shrieked. Girders tore free.

*Now comes the true storm*, Krezoc thought.

His flock was terrified. They were in the midst of a war of gods. The night was riven by blinding exchanges of energy. Ornastas could barely think, and he could not hear the shrieks of the frightened over the howl and crack of las. The bridge shook and shook and shook. Flakes of rust and powdered concrete fell like snow on the refugees' heads. But they kept going. He led the way, and they followed. He began to run. The wind still blasted, the waves below reached up in hunger, and the ledge vibrated and swayed with the pounding of the war on the bridge. Ornastas knew the risk of a fall with every step. But he ran, because he knew what the war would bring. He could feel the agony of the bridge growing. He would not die with his flock in futility here. He would not accept that end. His service to the God-Emperor was not done, and nor was that of his followers. There was war here, but it was not one they could fight. Ornastas felt the calling. There was a destiny prepared for his band. They would have a role to play in the struggle for Katara's soul. They just had to live long enough to answer that call.

He ran, and so did they, ducking low even though they were beneath the levels of the battle and beneath the notice of the combatants. The western end of the bridge was in sight at last. They must reach it. Their destiny, whatever its form, waited on the other side of the strait.

From behind came a metallic thunderclap that went on and on, a groaning, booming cataclysm of falling god. The ledge still wavered from side to side, and now it suddenly bucked as the bridge heaved under the impact of an immense body. Metal shrieked. There was a crash of tumbling wreckage.

'Do not look back!' Ornastas shouted. He disobeyed his own command so his followers might see his face even if they could not hear his words. 'Do not look back!' He saw the shattered Titan, and he saw the first of the great wounds in the bridge. Crevasses opened up in the road surface. Huge struts broke away from the superstructure and fell, spinning end over end, into the furious waves. One caught another of the faithful as it dropped. It crushed her, and her corpse plunged from the ledge. Her name was Lankas, and Ornastas marked it. She would be remembered too, for her faith and for her loyalty.

He looked forwards again, and picked up the pace. 'Don't look back,' he said again, to himself this time. His balance wavered. The bridge shook as if taken by an earthquake. He stumbled, clutched at air, then found his footing and ran on.

'The Emperor protects,' he said, and prayed, and pleaded. The end of the run was in sight, but so far, so very far away, and the Kazani Bridge cried out in its agony while the gods hurled thunderbolts at each other. 'The Emperor protects. The Emperor protects.'

The screams of metal grew louder.

And then came more blasts, more terrible than before, huge as the end of days.

*'We can't take them all on,'* Drahn voxed.

More and more Traitor Titans were appearing. They outnumbered the Pallidus Mor already, and still more were showing up on the long-range auspex as they marched from Creontiades.

'I know,' Krezoc said. 'We just need them to think we believe we can.'

*And we have*, she thought. The Iron Skulls were moving onto the bridge at greater speed, rushing their might forwards. Krezoc had feinted a counter-attack, and the enemy had taken the bait.

'Retreat,' she ordered. 'Get off the bridge and draw the traitors onwards.'

She arrested the forwards march of *Gloria Vastator*. The Warlord resisted. The machine-spirit was not satisfied. It wanted more kills, more justice. Krezoc reined it in and took the first step back. She fired again with the volcano cannon, the blast striking a Feral Titan full in the head, shearing away the distorted skull.

The retreat began, and the enemy's massed fire hit home. *Fidelis Venator* loped heavily across the width of the bridge, laying down covering fire for *Canis Ignem* to pull back, and it took two direct hits from Banelord jaw cannons. The stricken god-machine disappeared, melting to slag and then blowing apart. It disintegrated before its processes could go critical, but the explosion blew a hole hundreds of yards across in the surface of the bridge. The ragged armoured infantry of the heretics, charging ahead in the ecstasy of bloodlust, barely slowed for the obstacle. Vehicles swerved to avoid the gap. Some drove straight on to fall into the sea.

Krezoc felt the growing movements of the bridge. Side to side, left and right – they were constant, and they were irreversible. Data streamed into the manifold. Vectors of damage and measures of weakness, the positions of Pallidus Mor maniples and their relative speeds.

*We need to be faster*, she thought.

To the rear, the top of the cliff lit up with a succession of monstrous blasts. The Iron Skulls at the rear, the ones not yet on the bridge, were venting their wrath on the Kataran Spears.

The ledge bucked again, throwing Ornastas into the air. His head spun, his eyes blurred, and for an awful second he had no thought, only the confused expectation of death. Then he landed, hard, twisting his ankle. He skidded to the left, the weight of his staff pulling him to the edge. He lunged forwards with all of his strength. He fell to his knees, but he was still on the catwalk. He rose before Velatz collided with him and ran on, limping.

The western end of the bridge was only a hundred yards away. Land was within reach. The land was burning. Flames roared up into the night. Ruined tanks were falling into sea. Yet it was land. If only... If only...

He had no sense any longer of the maelstrom above. The storm of blasts and coruscating energy was at its height. It could not continue. The catastrophe was playing out on a stage that could no longer support it.

Ornastas ran, ignoring pain, carrying the faithful in his wake. The goal was so close, so close.

*The Emperor protects. The Emperor protects.*

The storm erupted with absolute fury. The bridge jerked with fatal suddenness. It moved to the left.

It kept moving.

Another Warhound died. It was *Nobilis Canem*, one of the Imperial Hunters. Rheliax was reporting major damage to *Crudelis Mortem*. *Gloria Vastator* walked backwards. Krezoc's consciousness swam in the manifold, seeing each step. She was at one with the Titan; its body was her body, and the auspex sensors were eyes that looked behind and forwards at once. She saw everywhere. She saw what she had to do. She saw how many steps remained before *Gloria Vastator* was on land again. The rest of her maniple had obeyed her orders to retreat at speed. Her Warlord was the last one on the bridge.

The void shields were failing. The Iron Skulls concentrated their fire on *Gloria Vastator*. In the background of her consciousness, Thezerin was reporting mounting damage.

The Titan still walked, and its weapons still worked, that was all that mattered.

*Now*, Krezoc thought in the manifold, and the command became *Now!* – a galvanic shout to the moderati, and the roar of the machine-spirit unleashed. Every weapon fired. The target was just in front of the advancing Iron Skulls. The target was the bridge.

Missiles, quake shells, volcano las and mega-bolter rounds struck the roadway and the superstructure. The holocaust swallowed the front ranks of the Iron Skulls and their cultists. Metal ran molten and then vaporised. Rockcrete disintegrated. The trusses exploded into a flight of incandescent spears. On either side of the blasts, the bridge reared upwards as if it would take flight from its pyre. Then it fell, and kept falling, the collapse spreading back along its length. *Gloria Vastator* took another step backwards, and then another. The bridge surface was still solid for the first one, but it was moving with the second. The Warlord's motions were unnatural; the colossus was always steady – that was the nature of its huge mass. The sudden shift, like a ship at sea, was irregular, and it was the sign that time had run out.

The conflagration at the centre began to dim. The trusses collapsed. With the groan of a slain beast, the east and west spans of the bridge dropped forwards.

*Gloria Vastator* took one more step. Its foot crunched down onto the clifftop roadbed. The surface of the bridge fell away just as Krezoc brought the other foot up. If there had been any weight on that leg a second longer, the Warlord would have pitched forwards.

Krezoc held *Gloria Vastator* at the cliff edge and watched the end of the Kazani Bridge. The engineering wonder of Katara died in a cataract of rockcrete, iron and flame. The waves foamed as they swallowed the prey they had battered for so many centuries. Enemy Titans fell with it, vanishing into the depths. Krezoc saw at least five god-machines dropping into the fiery darkness, their war-horns howling despair. On the far side, the rest of the Iron Skulls maintained their bombardment of the west, but the Kataran Spears had pulled back now too. Their work was done. There was nothing more to be gained from this night.

The wreckage fell into the sea and vanished. Not everything disappeared, though. The supports, wonders in their own right whose bases had been constructed on the seabed hundreds of yards below the surface of the waves, projected like broken bones from the cauldron. One of the Banelords had landed against a pillar. It had punched its doomfist into the rockcrete, embedding its arm in the support. It was held there above the waves. Its tail and jaw cannons fired at *Gloria Vastator*. Las burned through the Warlord's struggling shields, and a shell collided with its chest plating. The blow rocked the Titan back. Dark smoke billowed upwards, obscuring Krezoc's view. She cursed, and acquired the target through auspex readings. When *Gloria Vastator* fired in retaliation, a dozen more weapons from the rest of the demi-legio joined it. The Iron Skulls monster lived for only a few seconds before it exploded. Its reactor went critical, and the nuclear blast swept across the Kazani Strait, a sun rising from the waves. A void opened in the sea, where countless tonnes of water had evaporated on the instant. The waves rushed in to fill the void, monstrous in their wrath, and they rose almost as high as the clifftops. The terrible fire dimmed, and when the waves dropped at last, nothing remained above the surface.

# CHAPTER 6

# THE LIGHT OF TRUTH

They clung to the side of the cliff, sheltering in its fissures from the destroying light that filled the strait. Two more of Ornastas' followers died, burned by that infernal dawn. Then came the winds, and the churning of the sea, the waves reaching so high they almost swept the mortals from their perch. At last the wind calmed, and Ornastas led the climb up the cliff, past the twisted, hanging ruins of the bridge, and to level terrain once more.

After the night of fury, the calm over the land seemed like an aftermath, rather than a mere pause in the war. The group moved up the road, beginning the long walk towards Deicoon. Past the approach to the bridge, the land began to rise again, and at the top of the first slope, lines of Leman Russ tanks barred the way. Ornastas shouted a prayer of thanks, and his followers joined him. There were fewer than twenty of them left. They were drenched, numb with cold and shock. Deafened by the war, they had to shout so they could hear their own voices. But they sang to the glory of the Emperor, and they were still singing as they approached the line of the Kataran 66th. His staff raised, Ornastas slowed down, then stopped a dozen yards from the nearest tank. Given the ragged condition he and his flock were in, they might be mistaken for cultists.

They kept up the singing, displaying their loyalty to the God-Emperor, until the commanding officer dismounted from the central Leman Russ and approached. Once more, Ornastas offered his thanks to the Father of Mankind. The Emperor protected. Ornastas knew this man.

'I am glad to see you, Captain Deyers,' he said.

Deyers stared at him for a moment. Between the grime, the blood and the ragged conditions of his robes, Ornastas knew he was barely recognisable. 'Confessor Ornastas?' Deyers asked.

Ornastas smiled and came forwards. 'Yes,' he said.

'How did you get here?'

'We escaped the corruption of Creontiades. We crossed the bridge.'

Deyers' eyes bulged. 'Last night?'

Ornastas nodded. 'It was the Emperor's will.'

'Who are these people with you?'

The answer came to Ornastas with the force of revelation. Whatever identities they had had in Creontiades, those roles had fallen away. They had joined with him to fight the forces of heresy, they had crossed the cauldron of the Kazani Strait, and they had survived the crucible of the night. They were a new thing now, and they deserved a name. 'They are…' he began, then corrected himself. '*We* are the Company of the Bridge.'

Deyers nodded, accepting the plain truth of Ornastas' words. 'What are you planning to do?'

'Fight. In whatever way the Emperor will have us do so.'

'Will you join us here?' Deyers asked.

Ornastas looked beyond the captain and the tanks, up the road to Deicoon. The Titans had departed hours ago and were no longer in sight. He could still feel their presence on the world, though. He could feel this great counterbalance to the evil that had come down upon Creontiades. Where the god-machines were is where his company must go. 'Thank you,' he said to Deyers, 'but we are called to Deicoon.'

Deyers nodded, accepting what Ornastas said without question. Ornastas had not served with the captain, but Deyers was part of his congregation. They shared bonds of mutual respect for the other's skill at his calling. 'I'll see that you have transport there,' he said. 'Is there anything else you need?'

'Better weapons,' said Ornastas, glancing at the collection of crude machetes and hatchets his company carried. 'Rations, if you can spare them.'

'I can do that too,' Deyers said. 'And your company's wounds – you're not above having them seen to?'

Ornastas smiled. 'We are not.'

They dragged him from the cell in which he'd been kept. They marched him down the corridors of the governor's palace. Hallard Eukrolas knew this was the palace because he had not been allowed to leave it since the start of the uprising, but he would not have recognised it. The paintings and tapestries had been burned from the walls. Blood, dried and still fresh, pooled on the floor. Runes had been carved and scorched into every surface. He could not look at the markings without feeling something malign reach into his head.

He was brought out of the tapering spire of the palace into the great square before it. The surviving members of his entourage were there too, as ragged and battered as he was. One of the twisted god-machines of the enemy stood in the centre of the square. It was the size of a Reaver, but so distorted it was no longer a machine. It was a supernatural monster that had emerged from humanity's suppressed nightmares to wound the day.

At the feet of the Titan was a large metallic structure. It was built from wreckage and was a creation of jagged, sheared metal. There was brass in there, too; a lot of it. The structure conveyed both strength and agony. Small cages hung from poles that jutted at odd angles. A rough dais rose from the centre of the metal. On it stood a robed figure. Wailing heretics danced around the dais.

Hallard's captors hauled him and his staff towards the structure. He knew he was going to be sacrificed, but at least, he thought, he would learn who was behind the uprising. He would see the face of the leader, and know who had betrayed him and his world. The figure wore a hood, and did not push it back as Hallard was carried onto the structure and hauled by ropes up to one of the cages. The cultists shoved him inside and locked him in. The cage was too short for him to stand and too narrow for him to sit. He had to crouch, his head and knees brushing against the bars. There were seven more cages, and soon they, too, were filled with sobbing, moaning prisoners.

There was a huge gathering in the great avenues that

stretched out from the square, running between the blackened tombstones that had been the jewels of Creontiades' crown. At first, Hallard had thought this was more of the mob of heretics, larger than his worst imaginings, come to jeer at the sacrifice. Then he saw that, though there were thousands of cultists present, most of the crowd was made up of more prisoners, herded together to this location, and this time.

The figure on the dais came to stand beneath Hallard's cage. It pulled back its hood.

*Now,* Hallard thought. *Show me your face.*

The man looked up.

Hallard had expected revelation. If he was to die, there should be some meaning in death. He should have a target for his last curses. He should be granted the knowledge of who had orchestrated this vast treason.

He was given nothing.

The man had branded and scarred and mutilated his features until he was barely human. He had peeled away all the skin below his eyes, exposing the muscle. He had cut off his nose. A brass plate, shaped into the rune of the stylised skull, was embedded in his scalp. The monster looked at Hallard and laughed. The voice was strange to him too. This was no one he knew. There was no close confederate who had betrayed him. This was someone who had always been invisible to him, and to so many others. He had been beneath notice, and so had done his work without fear of discovery. Now, in his time of glory, his old identity was gone forever.

'Well, lord-governor,' he rasped, his words guttural and malformed as they passed through a lipless mouth. 'Are you ready?'

* * *

The Titans were in the great Viokania forge of Deicoon, midway between the keep and the city walls. As many repairs as could be made quickly were under way. In the keep, Nevaeh Eukrolas received the princeps and moderati of the Pallidus Mor and Imperial Hunters, congratulating them on their victory. Krezoc did not like the hubris that went with the ceremony, but she understood its value to the morale of the crews and of the citizenry, so she accepted its necessity. In the reception hall, Eukrolas and her lieutenants were hosting the Titanicus officers. Krezoc left them there and walked to a communications room a short distance down a corridor from the hall. Eukrolas had given her the use of it and the privacy for the unpleasant conversation she had put off until now.

She contacted Syagrius on the vox.

*'I will have you tried,'* the marshal said without preamble.

'For doing my duty?' Krezoc asked.

*'You abandoned your post.'*

'I protected Deicoon by stymying the enemy's advance.'

*'Your losses–'* Syagrius began.

*You mean* your *losses,* Krezoc thought. She did not believe Syagrius cared for any of the fallen Titans except the Imperial Hunters. 'Our losses were much less severe than those the Iron Skulls suffered. The operation was a success, marshal. I'm sorry that disappoints you.'

Syagrius sputtered something incoherent, then said, *'I suppose we must now consider what to do about Creontiades, since we can no longer approach it.'*

*Which you never meant to do,* Krezoc thought.

*'Since the enemy is contained,'* Syagrius mused, *'orbital bombardment is a possibility.'*

Krezoc was glad Deyers was not present to hear this.

The total destruction of Creontiades would not sound like salvation to him. But there was a grim logic to Syagrius' calculation. If the corruption was stopped there, Katara's losses would be much reduced overall. Even so, Krezoc was reluctant to jump to the most extreme solution immediately. 'There may be an alternative,' she said, doubting that Syagrius would listen.

'*And that would*–' Syagrius began. His voice was drowned out by a blast of static. The disruption went on and on, and Krezoc thought she heard the echoes of screams and chants worming through the white noise. She tried other channels. There was nothing but the rotting static on all of them.

Krezoc ran from the communications chamber. There were shouts coming from the reception hall. She stormed down the hall, ready for battle and fearing the worst.

She was also angry at herself. She was Pallidus Mor. She should have known disaster was coming.

The earth shook. Gantries broke away from the Titans and hurled their work crews to the ground. From his position at the feet of *Gloria Vastator*, Venterras could see through the gates to the forge's work yards. The road on the other side collapsed. A huge cloud of dust rose, billowing into the grounds, obscuring everything in a wash of grey. The tremors continued and the gates fell, jarred loose from the wall. Dark shapes emerged in their hundreds from the crevasse in the road. Las-beams cut through the dust, burning the scrambling enginseers and manufactorum serfs.

The enemy kept pouring out of the fallen road. There were hundreds of them, all converging on the work yards. They were coming for the Titans.

Hoplite and peltast secutarii laid down a broad field of fire with arc lances and galvanic casters. Concussive blasts and bursts of flechettes smashed and tore the attackers. But they kept coming, rushing to overwhelm the defenders with a huge crowd.

<Protector imperative alpha,> Magos Xura Thezerin ordered from within *Gloria Vastator*.

The secutarii responded as if possessing a single, collective mind. Thezerin's doctrina imperative slaved all of their strategy to the overriding purpose of protecting the god-machines. Noospheric links switched their perceptions to binaric omniscience. Venterras experienced the entire battlefield reduced to digital components. The foe was a series of data streams, equations to be solved, then cancelled. The most efficient arc of fire, coordinated relative to that of every other secutarii, appeared before him. His response and his perception were simultaneous. The same was true of all the hoplites and peltasts.

The results were devastating. The heretics ran into a wall of precision destruction. The front wave of the mob went down, not a single attacker making it through the wall of explosions and energy discharges.

As the dust settled, something large and bulky emerged from the crevasse. It looked like a corrupted Onager dunecrawler. A bulbous mass sat atop four spined, insectoid legs. It did not appear to be armed. It crawled forwards slowly, led by a group of cultists fastened to it with long chains. In Venterras' vision, it was an incomplete equation of ones and zeroes. It was a threat, but its nature and scope were undefined. Nevertheless, its presence alone dictated a response, and he aimed his arc lance at the machine.

As it reached the entrance to the yards, secutarii fire converged on the crawler. Energy crackled around its upper mass. Its legs stabbed craters into the rockcrete as it dragged itself forwards like a dying beast. The cultists strained on their chains, pulling it further into the yards. There was still no sign of attack, but its binaric threat vector grew. The flashes and energy bursts circling it became blinding.

It exploded.

The physical blast was not large. It did not reach beyond the ranks of the cultists. Metal shrapnel tore through their ranks, and the fireball incinerated those closest to the device. The other burst went much further. The electromagnetic wave slashed across the work yards. Venterras' binaric perception flared white, then winked out. A shrieking whine filled his senses. His limbs twitched and jerked. Neuro-electronic impulses misfired across his frame. For several seconds, he had no control over his body.

That was enough time for the tide of cultists to crash against the secutarii and bring them to the ground.

From the panoramic windows of the reception hall, Krezoc saw the wounds open in Deicoon. The fissures in the roads were connected, and created a pattern. A menace had risen from the depths of the city to carve huge runes into its face. She turned to glare at Eukrolas. The governor had turned pale. Her mouth was hanging open, aghast.

'You did not look hard enough!' Krezoc snarled at her. 'You did not look *deeply* enough!'

The cult had been here all along. There was no way it had spread here since the battle at the Kazani Bridge. It had lain in wait, concealing itself, eating away at Deicoon from below. Eukrolas had seen no signs at the surface and the heights and, in her pride, believed her city to be strong where Creontiades was weak. Instead, Deicoon's defences were a shell, surrounding putrefaction.

The walls and the guns of the keep meant nothing now. The city could not guard against itself.

Krezoc tapped her vox-bead, trying to reach Venterras. The short-range channels were scrambled too. The same hissing, foul static drilled into her ears until she shut the device off. She could see *Gloria Vastator* from here. In Eukrolas' transport, it had taken only a few minutes to reach the keep from the forge. Now the distance seemed vast.

More roads collapsed. From this height, they seemed to be disgorging swarms of insects. Already, flames and smoke were rising from intersections near the keep.

'We need to reach the Titans,' Krezoc said to Eukrolas. 'With or without your help.'

'You'll have it,' Eukrolas said. Her eyes were narrowed in shame, but her voice was determined. If there was any action by which she could make reparations for her mistake, she would take it.

'Your Chimera is too exposed,' Krezoc said.

'I have others.'

'Good.' She turned to the princeps and moderati standing behind her. 'Let's go.'

They ran from the hall, down the corridor to the grav lifts. Eukrolas' guards were already there, the lifts summoned and waiting for their governor's rapid evacuation. 'The vehicle depot,' Eukrolas told them.

Less than a minute after Krezoc had lost contact with Syagrius, the grav lift dropped down the height of the keep. For the length of the descent, she was blind to the outside world. The handfuls of seconds it took to reach the depot, one stage below the ground-level entrance to the keep, seemed an eternity. She had just seen the entire war change in the same amount of time. It could change again, and for the worse.

The lift doors opened. Krezoc and her officers followed Eukrolas into the depot. There was a faint haze of smoke in the air, leaking in from the fires outside. Eukrolas led the way to an unmodified Chimera. They embarked while one of the guards fired up the engines.

'I'll be with the driver,' Krezoc told Eukrolas. She needed to see. The governor nodded, and Krezoc pulled open the door from the troop hold. She stood behind the driver's seat and watched through the armourglass viewing block as the driver pulled out. The Chimera roared past other armoured carriers where more of Eukrolas' private militia were boarding. The vast, grey space of the hangar rang with the growls of vehicles readying for war.

The Chimera raced down the central space of the depot and up a ramp leading to the streets. A massive plasteel door rose with a harsh grind. It was barely high enough for the Chimera to clear it when the driver tore through the entrance and into the street beyond. He drove straight into flames. The entire block was ablaze. Krezoc could see nothing but fire and collapsing rubble. The heretics had struck with more than numbers. They were armed. She thought of Eukrolas' pride in the strength of the city. Deicoon had weapons as well as walls. Its manufactoria produced armaments in the millions.

Arsenals had been raided, then. The cancer that was taking the city was virulent, and metastasising with blinding speed.

The Chimera rattled over fallen brickwork and shattered rockcrete as it rushed through a tunnel of flame. Krezoc cursed the blazes. She could see nothing of where they were going, or of what might be ahead. The driver veered sharply to the right as a façade came apart on the left, pouring tonnes of rubble into the street. The Chimera skewed violently, and was still swaying when they reached an intersection.

Krezoc registered the flashes on the right with the corner of her eye. In the fraction of a second between the light and the impact, she had time to process what she saw and know what was going to happen. She did not have time to brace herself. The rockets slammed into the side of the Chimera and against the base of its wheels. The combined force of the explosions lifted it and flipped it onto its side. Krezoc hurtled against the bulkhead. The vehicle slid, trailing fire, for fifty yards before a mound of rubble brought it to a shuddering halt.

Blood poured into Krezoc's eyes from a wound in her head. The driver was unconscious. She climbed over the sideways doorway into the troop compartment. One of the Imperial Hunters' moderati had a broken arm, and Rheliax looked badly concussed, barely able to focus his eyes. The others seemed to be battered but were moving well enough. Drahn met Krezoc's gaze as she helped Rheliax to his feet. Krezoc nodded, pressing her lips together in a grim line. They both knew what was coming. They would fight it anyway. They drew their sidearms.

There was pounding against the sides of the Chimera. The rear entrance began to glow in the centre. Someone was cutting through it with a plasma torch. On Krezoc's right, the turret hatch began to turn.

Krezoc raised her plasma pistol. She aimed it at the hatch. She shouted the war-cry of the Pallidus Mor. *'We are the pride of Death!'*

*'The pride of Death!'* her officers echoed.

'For the Emperor!' Krezoc roared and fired the pistol as the hatch opened.

She killed many cultists, denying them access to the hold, before the rear entrance was cut open. Then she, the princeps, the moderati, the governor and the guards hit their attackers with a wide stream of las, plasma and bolt shells. They fought hard. They fought for as long as they could.

They were overwhelmed in less than a minute.

*Are you ready?*

Hallard Eukrolas tried to be. He tried to be ready to die. Could anyone truly be prepared for that moment? He did not think so. Not really. But he braced himself, and he murmured a prayer to the God-Emperor, and he forced himself not to think about the pain that would come with burning alive.

'I am prepared,' he managed to croak out. 'Do your worst.' His crouching position was already agonising. In another few minutes he would be blind with pain. Death would be a release.

But the heretic leader did not leave the platform at the centre of the structure. Around the dais, flames gouted from clusters of gas pipes, but they shot into the air and were not aimed at the prisoners. Not yet.

The heretic turned his lipless smile Hallard's way again. He swept his arm towards the square and the avenues beyond. Hallard followed his gestures, and understood.

The heretic had not asked Hallard if he was ready to die. He had asked if he was ready to *see*.

The spectacle he had been called on to witness began.

Hallard was not ready.

Yet he could not look away, and he could not shut his eyes. Down the wide boulevards, to the limits of his sight, the slaughter began. The cultists turned on their prisoners and butchered them. The howls of terror and fruitless pleas for mercy were a deafening chorus of the damned. Blood filled the streets. It streamed into the square and lapped against the edge of the sacrifice engine. Wherever Hallard turned his head, he saw the same atrocities replicated, and in the end, he understood that it was all a single act, a single monstrosity perpetrated across the city, and though he was forced to witness it, the immense sacrifice was not for his benefit. It was for other eyes. Perhaps it was for the scaled, horned god-machine that presided over the square. Its eyes could see much farther than his. It would see much more of the slaughter. Its head turned back and forth, and it seemed to be surveying the bloodshed, ensuring the sacrifice unfolded as it should.

Then a change came upon the streets of the city, and Hallard understood that even the Titan was not the true object of veneration. It too was a mere witness, a participant in the ritual. The ocean of blood was for still other eyes. And those eyes must have seen, for the cultists were answered. Energy crackled along the streets. It arced across the square and jumped from pole to pole of the iron-and-brass construct. Hallard screamed as the bars of his cage grew hot. He tried to recoil, but there was no room to move, and the floor of the cage was heating up too.

The energy discharges built. Lightning of red and blue and green shot up and down the lines of the immense rune of blood the heretics had created. The air thrummed, and then it screamed. The sky roiled, low clouds of magmatic crimson rushing down as if to feed on the rivers of gore. The earth began to shake, harder and harder. The energy became a blinding, shimmering wall. Hallard could see nothing except the infernal lightning. His cage burned through his clothes. His skin crisped and smoked. And though the agony consumed him and his lungs began to smoulder, his screams were for his soul, and in fear of the wonder that was coming.

The tremors began at the same time that a foul light rose from the direction of Creontiades. Deyers had to lean against the side of *Bastion of Faith* to keep his feet. A hundred yards from the front line of the Kataran 66th, the cliff edge cracked and tumbled into the sea. Across the Kazani Strait, light the colour of flaming blood shot upwards from the distant skyline. The sky twisted, spun, became a vortex and came down to meet the light. Blood in the air, blood in the light, blood in the clouds; all boiling, seething and ravenous.

The tremors grew stronger. Cracks spread outwards from the cliff edge. Deyers climbed onto *Bastion of Faith*. He sat in the turret hatch and voxed the regiment. 'Pull back,' he ordered. 'A hundred yards for now, but be ready to go further.' He muttered a prayer. Ornastas and his company had already departed in two Tauroxes, and Deyers wished the confessor were still here. Deyers needed his strength of faith.

'This isn't an earthquake, is it?' Platen called.

'No. It's something worse.'

It was a thing he had no name for. There were no words, only ancient fears, for the furious, crimson light in Creontiades. It was not of the world, but it was hungry for it, and it was wounding it. The shaking became so violent it almost hurled Deyers from his perch. He held tight to the edges of the hatch and stared across the strait. The clouds were gathering, deepening, turning the day into a bloody night. It seemed as though a titanic maw was about to open in the firmament, one that would come down and devour the world.

Then the world broke. Deyers felt it – a change in the nature of the tremors. There was a snap, and a giving way. Deyers had once broken three ribs in combat. They had fractured at both ends and he had been aware of an awful floating in his body, of objects that had acquired a freedom of motion they should never have had. He felt that same sensation again, only it came from far below. It was the bones of Katara that had broken, were parting, were being reshaped.

A second glow appeared. It came from the depths of the strait. The waves were driven to new heights of frenzy. The glow brightened as the thing came closer to the surface. The water began to boil. Steam rose in vast, writhing curtains. The other side of the strait disappeared. All Deyers could see was the glow in the east and the glow in the water.

Brighter, closer, hotter, whatever was coming was immense. The hideous light stretched across the entire length of the strait, and it was wider than the ruined bridge. It carried those ruins to the surface with it. For several seconds, it seemed the bridge was resurrecting itself.

Smashed superstructure and tumbled supports rose above the waves, then fell away, crumbling and melting, from the surface of the monstrosity below. It came into sight now, climbing higher and higher. It was a causeway of bronze, heated to incandescence in the act of its creation, its glow beginning to cool now but still so bright it hurt Deyers' eyes. At regular intervals and on both sides of its length were towering, twisted pillars, topped with huge skulls. The vacant eyes of the skulls stared westwards, eager for the prey on the mainland.

The causeway climbed until it was level with the clifftops. Where the bridge had been, there was now an even greater expanse of bronze. The waves of the strait, divided from each other, slammed in impotent anger against the metal walls.

The curtains of steam faded. The bronze still glowed. It illuminated the far side of the strait. It reflected off the giant forms in motion. In despair, readying for a battle he knew he could not win, Deyers watched the Titans of the Iron Skulls march in triumph towards the causeway.

# CHAPTER 7
# THE RUN

*Why didn't they kill us?* Krezoc wondered. Though she and her comrades took down many cultists, the heretics fired to disable, except when aiming at the governor and her guard. Eukrolas was slain fighting, as she would have wanted, and Krezoc hoped that salvaged some of her pride in the end, despite the futility of the struggle and the humiliation of the overthrow. When the cultists swarmed into the Chimera, they came to capture the Pallidus Mor, not to kill. *Why?* Krezoc thought as they disarmed her and dragged her from the vehicle. *Why?* she thought as they marched her and the others through the burning streets of Deicoon.

Violence had taken the city, but the battle was not done. Militia and reserve units of the Kataran Spears fought on. The cultists had the greater numbers and the weaponry to make those numbers count against the loyalist forces and the unarmed populace of the city. Krezoc could see how the struggle was going. Deicoon would fall.

But she was not dead. *They want us for something more.* It took her longer than it should have to realise what the enemy wanted from her. Perhaps because the goal was so completely beyond her conception of the possible. It was madness within madness.

The cultists brought the prisoners to the Cathedral of Saint Chirosius. It was on the other side of the ruined street from the Viokania forge yards where the Titans stood, omnipotent giants inert and vulnerable to the vermin that scurried at their feet. Guns prodding her back, her hands tied behind her with brass wire, Krezoc was forced to climb the stone spiral steps of the cathedral's southern tower. It took almost an hour to reach the top. There, a line of crude frameworks, also of brass, had been constructed. Krezoc turned her face from their jagged shapes. They formed the angular, runic skull she had seen emblazoned on the armour of the Iron Skulls god-machines. The cultists cut the bonds on her hands, then fastened her to one of the frameworks, arms spread wide. She was facing *Gloria Vastator*. It was really not that far away. Her spirit tried to fly from the roof of the tower, across the fissured street and into the skull of the Warlord. The machine-spirit was calling to her, distressed that she did not answer. She and the Titan were trapped in their incomplete states. She strained against her bonds. She willed them to snap. Her will felt strong enough to give her true wings. She would give anything to fuse once more with the Warlord. She would…

She stopped, the burning hate replaced by cold fury. She began to understand what the heretics were trying to achieve.

She looked north, to her right. There were more of

the runic frameworks on the peak of the other spire, a hundred feet away. There were still more assembled underneath the huge bells, visible through the tower's gothic windows. They held the secutarii of the Pallidus Mor. There were generators of some kind too, running some kind of disabling current, she guessed, holding the warriors immobilised.

Beside her, Drahn had noticed the secutarii too. 'Why have they been captured too? Why haven't we been killed?' she asked.

Krezoc cast her eyes over the city, at the rising smoke and glint of fires. She thought of the patterns in the streets, and of the true enemy that was directing the actions of the heretics. 'Because,' she said to Drahn, 'the Iron Skulls have unfinished work they wish to complete.'

Carrinas, the princeps of the Imperial Hunter Reaver *Nobilis Arma,* spoke up. 'If they complete it, we have you to thank.'

Drahn snorted. 'I admire your resilience,' she snapped.

'Enough,' Krezoc said. 'Do not help the traitors in their goal.'

Drahn frowned for a moment, then shook her head in disbelief. 'They seek to corrupt us?'

'I believe so.'

'They're going to be very disappointed.'

'Yes,' said Krezoc. But the victory was hollow. She took no comfort in the prospect of an honourable death.

A figure moved to stand between Krezoc and her view of *Gloria Vastator.* The cultist was a tall man. His posture was rigid in spite of the wounds he had inflicted on himself. The left of his body was flayed. Articulated brass plates covered the musculature. His clothes, though torn and debased with bloody runes, had once been those of an officer of the Kataran 66th.

'I am Darroban,' he said. 'I was a colonel. You do not know me?'

Krezoc shook her head.

Darroban shrugged. 'There are some who would remember the name. Perhaps I will see them yet.' His mutilated mouth parted in an angry sneer. 'I have lessons to teach them.'

'I doubt that very much,' Krezoc said.

'Do you? You're wrong. They will look on the weapons we stole so easily from them, and the weapons given to us by the Iron Skulls, and yes, there will be lessons there. I think you will learn things today, too. The same things I learned long ago. When you descend from this tower, you will be sworn to Khorne. You will march to harvest his skulls. You will bring blood for the Blood God.'

Krezoc spat. 'I am not a weak puppet. Now go. I'm sure your masters require you elsewhere, serf.'

Darroban's eyes widened in rage. He took a step forwards, his hand going to the blade at his side. With a visible effort, he stopped himself before he drew.

'That's what I thought,' Krezoc said. 'You aren't even allowed to answer insults.'

'Perhaps not,' Darroban said. He moved back, as if taking himself out of the range of temptation. 'Or perhaps I do not want to deprive myself of the sight of your suffering. Your conversion won't be easy. It won't be stopped, either.'

From the streets below, the sounds of battle and of slaughter rose to embrace the cathedral towers.

* * *

Ornastas rode beside the driver of the lead Taurox. Deyers had dispatched two of the armoured personnel carriers to transport the Company of the Bridge to Deicoon. The walls of the city were just coming into sight, shimmering in the distance, when Ornastas felt a shadow at his neck. He leaned his head out of the narrow window in the passenger door and looked back the way they had come. Crimson light rose to the sky, and the earth roared.

'The enemy has struck again,' he said to the driver, whose name was Folner. 'Can you reach the reserves at Deicoon?'

Folner tried, but got only static on the vox. He shared a concerned look with Ornastas. 'They're blocking our communications,' he said.

'From the strait?'

'I don't think so.' Folner stared at the approaching city with grim apprehension.

Before long, they saw the smoke that did not come from manufactorum chimneys.

'There's fighting going on,' said Folner. 'I'll have to hook up with the reserve units, if I can.'

'Of course,' Ornastas said.

'Will you join us too?'

Ornastas thought that through. The Company of the Bridge would have to become part of something larger if it wanted to hurt the heretics in a meaningful way. But trying to fight alongside the Kataran Spears or even the city militias didn't feel like the correct path. His followers were not trained. They could easily become a hindrance for military personnel. No, their task lay elsewhere.

As they drew closer to Deicoon, the fighting became clear. There were struggles on the walls. Las flashed in the overcast gloom. The air over the city, always an industrial dark brown, was turning black as unholy clouds gathered to answer the summons of the heresy below. There were holes in the wall, and the gates had been blown apart, but from the inside. The husks of vehicles lay at the entrance. Ornastas guessed some loyalist troops had tried to break out of the city to issue a warning and had been stopped at the moment of escape.

In the middle distance, looming above the walls, were the god-machines. In their immobility, Ornastas saw dreadful meaning and urgent mission. 'The Titans,' he said to Folner. 'Can you take us to them?'

'I can try.'

The first of the Iron Skulls Titans was halfway across the causeway when Deyers made his decision. 'Still no answer from Deicoon?' he voxed Halex Rahl in the Chimera *General Lange*. The Chimera held the regiment's long-range communications.

'*Nothing,*' Rahl said. His voice popped and jumped. Transmissions even within the regiment had become rough, though still functional.

'New orders,' Deyers told him. 'We make for Deicoon at all speed.'

He had barely finished speaking when Medina began turning *Bastion of Faith* around. Deyers swallowed the lump of shame he felt in his throat. It felt like he had just commanded the Spears to flee from the advancing enemy. But there was no point in making a stand here. The Iron Skulls would turn the 66th into slag in minutes.

If he was wrestling with the shame of perceived retreat, Deyers knew the rest of the Spears were too. As the tanks backed away from the Kazani Strait and began their run for Deicoon, he spoke to the regiment, hoping enough of his words made it through the static to matter.

'Comrades,' he said, 'we aren't retreating. We're choosing our ground. If we're going to save our world we mustn't just hurl ourselves onto a pyre of futile martyrdom.' They could not take on the Iron Skulls by themselves. That much had to be clear to every trooper of the 66th. 'We must join forces with the Pallidus Mor at Deicoon. A united stand there will matter.' So he needed to believe. But the force of traitor god-machines was still much larger than the Pallidus Mor's portion of the battle group.

When Deyers had finished speaking, Platen called up from her gun seat, 'Aren't we concerned we can't get through to the Pallidus Mor?'

'We are,' Deyers told her. 'So it's all the more important we reach Deicoon.' And do so ahead of the Iron Skulls.

*Bastion of Faith* accelerated. Deyers looked back as the Kataran Spears stormed towards Deicoon, leaving clouds of dust between them and the Kazani Strait. The unnatural causeway still glowed. What looked like an unending stream of monsters marched across it.

For the moment, the gap between the two forces was growing. The Spears were gaining time. It was precious little.

Deyers wondered if they were racing to find there really was no time left at all.

The Tauroxes careened through the streets of Deicoon. The drivers pushed through the struggles at high speed. Ornastas stared towards their target. He registered the thumps of bodies against the grille, the crunching bumps as heretics went under the wheels. The cultists crowded the avenues and rushed the Tauroxes, but the armoured vehicles' velocity was enough to hold them off. If the drivers slowed down at all, that would be enough for the enemy to swarm the transports and catch them in a quagmire of flesh.

Folner stuck to the major thoroughfares. They gave him a bit more room to manoeuvre, and he ploughed a path forwards for the second Taurox. The shapes of the Titans grew larger. Not long now, and they would reach the forge where the god-machines stood immobile.

*Then what?* Ornastas thought. He needed some plan. Something better than disembarking and being slaughtered. If the Titans did not walk, the warriors of the Pallidus Mor were prevented from making them walk. The most likely reason was that they were held captive.

*Is this your goal, then? Is this what you have been called upon to do? To rescue the Pallidus Mor?*

The presumption was enormous. Even if he thought it was true, where would he look?

Ornastas scanned the blackened towers of the city for inspiration. He prayed to the Emperor for guidance.

*We are here to serve You. Show us Your will.*

The Emperor heard. Ornastas' eyes instinctively went to the architecture of faith that was the Cathedral of Saint Chirosius. He saw movement at the top of its towers. He saw the silhouettes of runic crucifixion.

He grabbed Folner by the shoulder and pointed. 'There,' he said. 'Get us there, to the north side of the north tower.'

Folner nodded. If he had doubts about Ornastas' mission, he kept them to himself. He carried on up the current route, then turned sharply into narrower streets. He smashed the Taurox through a group of heretics who had just left the main avenue, and for the first time since their arrival in Deicoon, the road ahead was deserted. The air was sharp with smoke, and the windows of the hab blocks on either side were dark. Ornastas wondered if their inhabitants were hiding, or if the buildings were deserted. If everyone was gone, that raised the dark spectre of where they might be, and what might be happening to them. Ornastas brushed the speculation aside. It was inconsequential. What mattered was the task the Emperor had set before him.

'North side,' Folner repeated.

'Yes. Approach from the east if you can.'

Folner nodded again and did as Ornastas hoped. The streets here remained relatively clear. The struggles were elsewhere, and the few people Ornastas saw were rushing off to join those fights. After a few minutes of careering down narrow alleys, the sides of the Tauroxes grinding against the corners of buildings, Folner and the driver of the second Taurox stopped at the corner of the cathedral's north tower. Ornastas and the Company of the Bridge disembarked.

'We can't wait for you,' Folner said.

'Nor do I expect you to,' Ornastas told him. 'Fight well. The Emperor guides your hand.'

Folner made the sign of the aquila and lowered his head in thanks for the blessing. Then the Tauroxes drove off.

'What are we doing?' Velatz asked.

'There are prisoners on the roofs of the towers,' Ornastas said as he led the company to a small door at the base of the north tower. 'Their position faces the god-machines, and so I believe them to be the officers of the Pallidus Mor.' He reached into his robes and produced a ring of keys. There were doors common to the great churches of Katara that were closed to the general populace but open to all ecclesiarchs of Ornastas' rank. There were commonalities to the architecture of the buildings too, and he made use of those features now. He unlocked the door and ushered his followers inside. He looked back at the street briefly before he shut the door again. No one was following, though that didn't mean they hadn't been seen. He slammed the door and locked it. If someone tried to follow, they would find it difficult.

Beyond the door was a small antechamber that led to a grav lift. It was used by church officials to reach the heights of the cathedral quickly. It had two stops – one at the level of the roof, permitting access to the south tower, and one at the top of the tower. Ornastas pulled down a lever, stiff from lack of use, and the grav lift's heavy wooden doors slid aside. The compartment was small. There was room for only four people at a time.

'We will fight to free the prisoners,' Ornastas told the company. 'This could well be the moment of our sacrifice. If so, let it be a worthy one, as we give our lives to unleash the god-machines against the heretic.'

Solemn nods greeted his words. Many of the faces he saw were pale, clearly frightened, but all were determined. Ornastas looked at the way hands gripped lasrifles. There was no training here. There was only determination and faith. That would be enough. Did the cultists have more military training? Some would. Most would not. 'We have faith, and we have righteousness with us,' Ornastas said. 'That is more than the heretic can say. That is what will make the difference this day.' That, and surprise. 'I will go up with the first group,' he continued. 'There is a chamber similar to this one at the top. We will gather there.'

More nods. More determination. Then the ascent began. The mechanism of the grav lift ground and clanked as the compartment rose. There had been no call to use this access in some time. Most of Ornastas' fellow confessors preferred, like him, to take the stairs, and use the time of the long climbs for contemplation and prayer. Now he murmured his thanks that the grav lift still worked. He hoped the noise would be muffled by the stone, and lost in the wider din of the city's war.

It took almost ten minutes for the entire Company of the Bridge to reach the upper chamber. When all were assembled, Ornastas placed his key in the lock of the outside door. He paused for a moment. He did not know what waited on the other side. He thought about what strategy he could offer. Precious little, except a reminder of the goal. 'Fight to free the prisoners,' he said. 'Free them, and we grow stronger. That is the first priority.' He took a breath. 'May the Father of Mankind strike through us,' he said, then he turned the key and threw open the door.

The Company of the Bridge stormed out of the interior of the north-east crown of the tower's parapet. On the roof, rows of secutarii were fastened to runic scaffolds. They were guarded by a score of heretics. The guards' attention was directed towards the south tower, though. They were confident their prisoners could not break free, and Ornastas saw why before he had taken five steps onto the roof. In the north-west corner, near the main staircase, stood a generator. It was a bloody machine with horns of brass. Cables snaked from it to the scaffolds and down the steps towards the floors beneath the bells. Energy hummed and pulsed along the cables. Its ugly green light coruscated over the iron runes and over the prisoners, the spiralling, arcing energy doing more to hold the secutarii than the physical manacles. The pulses were doing something to disable the machinic augmentations of the prisoners.

'The generator!' Ornastas shouted. He and almost half the company raced for the device while the others turned their fire on the cultists.

The Company of the Bridge had surprise on its side for several beats. The heretics were completely unprepared for an attack. They were hundreds of feet above the fray in the streets, and their prisoners were completely helpless. They reacted slowly. They turned around at the sound of the company's charge, confused, and they fumbled to bring their weapons to bear. The company shot multiple las salvoes before return fire commenced. A dozen bursts hit the generator, burning through its plating and cables. Ornastas brought the charged head of his staff down on the nearest cable. He sent a power surge running both ways down its length. The cable tore free of the scaffold, whipping back and forth like an electrified snake, and then fell, inert.

The roof became a storm of interlacing las-beams. The cultists outnumbered the company and fought back now with wrath. The faithful and the heretic burned and died. Ornastas ducked behind the runic constructions, making his way towards the smoking generator. A few of the secutarii yanked themselves free of their manacles and joined the fight. They were unarmed, but their cybernetic bodies were weapons in themselves. They charged the heretics, battering them and hurling them from the roof of the tower.

Ornastas reached the generator. Misfiring energy burst

from the cable connections. The brass mechanisms were spinning wildly, sparking and spitting fire. Ornastas eyed the control panel. The inscriptions beside the levers were obscene. He did not know how it worked. He suspected there was sorcery infused with its machinery. Beside him, Aldemar and four others trained their rifles at the generator at point-blank range. Ornastas drove the staff into the controls, calling down a curse from the Emperor upon the foulness. An angry flash answered his blow, and a blast sent him flying back. He bounced off scaffolding and landed next to the tower's parapet. The generator was engulfed in flame. The machine shrieked in anger and pain. There was a brilliant flash of curdled, crimson light. Then the generator fell into blackened silence.

The rest of the secutarii had pulled free now. Some gathered up lasrifles from fallen combatants. The battle on the roof turned into a military operation, and then a rout. From below, Ornastas heard more shots. The secutarii held at the next level were freeing themselves now that their prisons no longer had power. Some heretics rushed up the stairs, but they were too late to reinforce their fellow cultists. All they did was run to their own deaths.

The entire struggle lasted less than a minute. Smoke covered the roof, drifting up from the generator and the charred bodies of the fallen. The battle on the lower level ended just as quickly, and the secutarii who had been held there now climbed the stairs to join their brethren. One of the leaders approached Ornastas. He spoke first in an ear-splitting burst of binaric cant, then caught himself and switched to Gothic. His voice was a modulated rumble, designed to be broadcast over the breadth of a field if necessary. 'Hoplite Alpha Venterras,' he said.

'You have our thanks.' He glanced at the dead members of the company. Over a third had been killed. 'Those are not soldiers,' he said.

'Confessor Lehrn Ornastas. And no, they are not. But they have answered the call to war.'

'Their protection is not within our remit.'

'We would not expect it to be.'

Venterras nodded. He turned to face the other tower. If there had been a ceremony under way there, it had been disrupted. Ornastas heard shouts of anger. A few las-shots seared the top of the parapet, but the attack was not organised yet.

'We must get there quickly,' Venterras said.

'We can.' Ornastas told him about the grav lifts. 'There is another in the south tower.'

'Good.' Venterras took the lead going down the stairs. The secutarii formed up into their units, so many gears instantly flowing into a precision military machine. In a chamber just off the cavernous space where the bells hung, their weapons had been stored in heaps. There were scorch marks on the walls and incinerated heretics here, their hands still clutching the weapons they had tried to use for themselves. Venterras bent down and tore one of the lances from a corpse. There was anger in his gesture that made it different from the machine-like grace of his other movements.

When the other secutarii had rearmed themselves, Venterras said to Ornastas, 'Show us the way.'

'I shall.' And the confessor gave thanks that he had, indeed, found the path of his destiny.

The triumph in Darroban's face vanished at the sounds of battle coming from the north tower. Soon he was cursing.

He yelled at the cultists with him to shoot the enemy on the other tower, but there were not enough of them, and even fewer with military training. They could do nothing.

'Your reckoning is coming,' Krezoc called out. 'Not ours. Are you prepared for the cost of heresy? I don't think you are.'

Darroban snarled as he lined up his followers to face the staircase. Most of them were not military, but he was, and he managed to order the cultists into formations that would provide withering fire down the steps. He noticed the door in the south-east corner and put half his rifles covering that position. 'I *am* ready,' he said to Krezoc. 'If I die now, then mine is another skull for the Skull Throne. You are still not prepared for what is coming.'

'I think I would surprise you,' said Krezoc. The warriors of the Pallidus Mor were one with death. They brought it, and they expected it. They never sold their lives cheaply, and they fought to the bitterest of ends, because the unity with death had to be earned.

Darroban snorted. His arrogance was misplaced. The roof of the other tower was empty. Krezoc knew exactly what Darroban was about to fight. So did he, yet he seemed to believe he could fight and win against the secutarii.

When the guardians of the Pallidus Mor burst out of the south-east door, Darroban showed how little he really was prepared. The heretic who had had the patience to prepare so long and so completely to bring about the fall of Deicoon was not ready to fight to hold the moment he had believed was his triumph. The heretics went down before the disciplined fire of the secutarii and the fanatical charge of a group of ragged civilians led by an ecclesiarch. There was no contest, only a slaughter. Darroban was part of the struggle for only a few seconds. He fired two shots from his plasma pistol, then turned and ran for the main stairs. A handful of cultists fled with him. The others were too caught up in their bloodthirst to register what was happening and were cut down by the secutarii.

Venterras freed Krezoc from the scaffold. She stepped briskly away from the rune. It was the festering meaning in its shape that had caused her pain, more than the shackling itself. She ran to the west parapet and looked down at the street and across to the Viokania yards. The ground crawled with heretics, though she saw no organised defence yet. 'They don't know we're free,' she said. She looked at Venterras. 'We need to get down before Darroban.'

'A few of us can,' the alpha hoplite answered. 'Not all.' He pointed back to the other entrance to the roof. 'There is a small grav lift.' There was a minute pause as Venterras' implanted cogitators calculated relative speeds. 'There will be time for two trips before the enemy reaches the street. Eight personnel.'

Krezoc weighed the odds of a smaller force and the benefit of surprise. She shook her head. 'No,' she said. 'Better to attack as a unified force.' She grabbed the nearest lasrifle, cursing the absence of her plasma pistol. 'Let's go.'

It seemed to take an eternity before the princeps, moderati and secutarii had gathered on the cathedral's ground floor. Beyond the doors, the roar of the cultists grew louder and more focused. Darroban had raised the alarm. The enemy was ready. But so was she, this time.

She did not wait for the ecclesiarch's civilians. Their

impact in the concerted assault would be minimal. Ornastas had assured her his followers were pleased to come after, disrupting the cultists in whatever way they could.

Officers and secutarii moved from the tower into the nave of the cathedral. The hoplites formed the front lines, the peltasts the rear. Venterras pushed open the great doors, and the Pallidus Mor charge began.

The fissure in the street was a wide one, but since taking the Viokania yards, the heretics had dropped makeshift bridges of roughly soldered iron slabs over the gap. There was one directly in front of the cathedral, and the Pallidus Mor made for it, running into las-fire and a boiling mob. The secutarii weapons scythed through the cultists. Shock waves from arc lances and blasts from galvanic casters ploughed a bloody path across the street and past the fallen gates of the Viokania forge. Krezoc led her moderati mere steps behind Venterras' hoplites. Venterras had told her of the device that had disabled the secutarii, but there was no sign of another now. Perhaps there had been only one, a bomb assembled for the heretics for this one use, with no expectation of another being needed. *Of course it wouldn't be,* she thought. *We were supposed to have been corrupted before our descent.*

The mob pushed in at the sides of the Pallidus Mor advance. She sent las-shots between the eyes of the attackers. Corpses with burned faces fell, tangling the feet of the cultists behind. A heretic leapt over the falling bodies and managed to grab at her greatcoat. She smashed the man's skull open with the butt of the rifle.

The formations pressed on into the yards. The attacks of the cultists were more disorganised here. They were a frenzied, howling mass, interrupted in the midst of their rituals and caught in the fog of inchoate anger. Krezoc's flesh crawled. The back of her scalp itched from the build-up of sorcerous energies. The ground of the Viokania works was unclean. Already she could see changes in the gantries and machinery of the yards. The metal works were turning into crimson and brass, and the stench of blood filled her nostrils. The thought of what was being attempted against the god-machines enraged her. Something tried to reach into her soul and push her deeper into rage, to turn it into the totality of her being. She refused. Her wrath had a focus and a goal. She had come to kill the unholy and for the salvation of the Titans.

Las and blades and clawed hands came in boiling waves for the Pallidus Mor. The advance slowed, but lost none of its lethal precision. The feet of *Gloria Vastator* came into view. Krezoc's soul burned at the sight. She resisted the urge to charge, roaring, for the Warlord. She glanced to her sides and saw her anger reflected in the eyes of her moderati. There were cultists swarming over the sacred body of the god-machine. The sacrilege could not be allowed to stand. But it must not be fought on its own terms.

'Discipline!' Krezoc shouted. 'Remember who we are!'

Vansaak nodded. '*We are Pallidus Mor!*' she shouted back.

'Let death and fury be as cold as the void!' said Krezoc. She fired the lasgun, one shot after another, precise and metronomic in their rhythm, proving her words as she killed the foe with frozen hate.

Venterras unleashed another shock wave with his arc lance, and there was a momentary clear path to *Gloria Vastator*. The Pallidus Mor warriors paused here, forming lines to hold the foe back while Venterras took his squad with Krezoc and the moderati into the Titan.

When Venterras opened the hatch on the lower right leg, it was all Krezoc could do to hold herself back. Her instincts cried out for her to charge inside the god-machine. The void she felt whenever she was not linked to the Warlord had grown towards agony in the last few hours. She felt the torment of the machine-spirit. The enemy was wounding it in new ways, and it cried out to Krezoc to join with it and smite the foe. She waited, though, and just barely, for the secutarii to enter first. She and her moderati followed in the next breath.

There was a lift inside the leg, and it seemed operational, but Venterras did not take it. He led the squad and officers up the sharp switchbacks of the metal staircase instead, past the colossal pistons and cables thick as tree trunks. Blasphemous runes had been splashed on the interior walls, and Krezoc stared at them, her lips pulled back in a silent snarl. The desecration pushed her to an anger beyond words, but at the same time, she felt a cold, merciless pride. These signs were not enough to corrupt *Gloria Vastator*. They were mere surface blemishes, impotent expressions of the enemy's intent. They could play with their runes and their rituals and their sacrifices. They would not succeed. And they would be punished.

As they climbed closer to the core of the Warlord, Krezoc heard chanting voices. The hoplites raised their shields and readied their lances. The next landing opened into corridors leading to the enginarium sectors of the Titan. The war party headed down towards the power plant. The chanting grew louder. The runes multiplied on the bulkheads. Blood was spattered on the decking.

The secutarii burst into the power plant control chamber. The space was filled with heretics. Magos Thezerin was chained to a wall, a huge skull rune painted behind her. Other tech-priests and serfs of the crew were bound next to her. The servitors of *Gloria Vastator* were motionless, deprived of function. The chanting stung Krezoc's ears. Her mouth filled with the taste of blood. The song of corruption tried to slide its claws into her. She shut it out. The secutarii waded into the heretics with their arc lances, and then Krezoc and her moderati opened fire. She placed her shots carefully. Each burst of las hit flesh, not metal. The searing burns purged the unholy from this sacred place, and she would not cause the Warlord any more harm. It had suffered, but she felt the machine-spirit rejoice in the punishing violence that erupted at its heart. Every component of the Titan had been thrice blessed and anointed with holy oil during its construction, and the sanctity of the god-machine was strong. It had not fallen to the vermin that had infested it. And now it called the righteous to purge its body of the heretic filth.

The cultists reacted with animalistic fury to the attack. Their ritual was ended. Their attempt to enslave *Gloria Vastator* and its crew to their false worship was finished. They leapt at hoplites and crew with rabid madness. Krezoc and her moderati answered with a rage as frozen and controlled. A cultist landed on Grevereign, shoving him back against a bulkhead and dragging his nails down the moderati's face. Vansaak jabbed her rifle's bayonet deep into the cultist's ribs and yanked him away. Grevereign ignored the flaps of skin hanging from his cheeks and put a shot between the eyes of another heretic trying to flank Vansaak. The secutarii laid waste to the bulk of the cultists with swift blows of their arc lances. All the heretics were dead before Krezoc felt even the smallest portion of her anger assuaged.

She turned to Thezerin as Venterras smashed her shackles.

'Can we walk?' Krezoc asked.

'We can,' said Thezerin. 'The most important repairs had taken place before the attack.'

'And the degree of infection?'

'*Gloria Vastator* is strong,' Thezerin said, confirming what Krezoc already knew.

'Then we will walk,' Krezoc said.

There were two more skirmishes with cultists on the way to the Warlord's head. Two of the wretches were trying to pry open the door to the bridge. Thezerin had managed to trigger some of the security mechanisms before being overcome, and the heretics had been denied this prize. Venterras and his squad stepped aside and let Krezoc and the moderati deal with the cultists. Krezoc nodded her thanks to Venterras. This was her sanctum under attack. The privilege of cleansing it belonged to her and her fellow officers. She shot one of the cultists between the eyes, then kicked the corpse out of the way. Vansaak and Grevereign dealt with the other heretic by beating him to death. Their blows were methodical. The crack of each bone was precisely calculated. While the hoplites dragged the bodies away, Krezoc put her eye to the optical recognition plate, and the door opened.

As she sat in her throne and prepared to link to the manifold, Krezoc asked Venterras, 'You will be completing a full sweep?'

'We will, princeps senioris. I will send word when we are ready to disembark and resume ground patrol.'

'Good. Then our initial attack will presume none of our forces are at ground level east of our position.'

'That is correct.'

The secutarii withdrew, and as the last of the mechadendrites plugged into her ports, Krezoc completed the links. With a rush, she and *Gloria Vastator* found each other again. Their fusion was a necessity to human and machine-spirit, and now the full measure of their anger could be unleashed.

But always controlled. Always with the rigour of ice.

The nuclear heartbeat of the Warlord was strong. The power coursed through the god-machine's limbs, and before long Krezoc felt movement return to them. *Gloria Vastator* took a step forwards. The twisted gantries fell away, raining lethal wreckage on the ground below. Krezoc pivoted the torso of the Warlord to the east. She looked down at the swarming, festering insects of the heretics. In the manifold, the Titan's spirit snarled at the vermin that had dared to hold it captive and had spread their unclean touch through its halls. Krezoc felt no tinge of corruption in the machine-spirit. Its loyalty to the Emperor was as fierce as it had ever been, and now there was outrage at what had been attempted. The machine-spirit demanded retribution. So did Krezoc. Was Darroban down there, still fighting to reclaim what he had thought was his? She hoped so.

Retribution began with the volcano cannon.

The Company of the Bridge fought from the relative shelter of the cathedral doorway. The citizen warriors ducked in and out of the walls, sending las bursts into the mass of cultists. It was impossible to miss. There was some return fire, but the focus of the mob was on the Viokania forge. The heretics were desperate to take back the Titans. The company created some confusion at the rear, but no more than that. It didn't matter. The great blow had already been struck. Ornastas' band was smaller than it had been, and more ragged, but also more confident. His followers had had their first victory. They fought because they could, and because they must. And as they fought, they saw the fruit of their labours.

'Look!' Aldemar cried. 'Look!' *Gloria Vastator* had begun to move. Its towering form took a single step, breaking free of the scaffolding as if shattering a prison. The red light of its eyes was the glow of warning. Further back, the other god-machines began to power up. The earth trembled with their first movements.

The right arm of the Warlord took aim at the ground.

'Pull back!' Ornastas warned. He led a rapid retreat down the nave. Some events were too great to be seen up close. The actions of the gods could not be witnessed without cost.

Even so, he looked back.

The blast at short range cut through rockcrete and deep into the ground itself. The yards between *Gloria Vastator* and the gates vanished in the terrible beam. All became fire and molten rockcrete. A wave of sublime fire roared towards the cathedral. The beam itself did not strike the doors, but the flames it unleashed stormed the entrance, reaching and spreading wide. Ornastas took the company towards the rear doors, but he kept looking back, staring through the purging destruction to see the war gods of the Imperium beginning their march and bringing judgement to the heretic.

*We have done this,* Ornastas thought. *We freed the secutarii, and we opened the way.* He didn't say this to his followers. He didn't have to. He saw the pride of that knowledge in every face.

They emerged from the rear doors of the cathedral in time as the volcano cannon fired again and the mega-bolter of the Warlord behind *Gloria Vastator* opened up. The south tower of the cathedral, caught in the edge of the destruction, collapsed, burying the split street in rubble.

Ornastas grieved for the razed cathedral, but it had been defiled by the heretics. A catastrophe had come to Deicoon, and the fire that would now sweep the city would be a purging one.

'What now?' Velatz asked as the company put the cathedral behind them, running down a wide avenue, away from the spreading devastation.

'The Emperor guided us before. He will again,' Ornastas said.

He looked ahead, and felt himself pause. The road sloped downwards in a straight line towards the walls of Deicoon. He saw what was approaching. An army of huge, twisted, corrupt shapes was closing in on the city. At the moment the god-machines of the Emperor at last walked again, the monsters of darkness had come to challenge them.

# CHAPTER 8

# THE GUNS OF DEICOON

The first salvoes of the Iron Skulls smashed through the towers of the city. Gothic spires disintegrated in expanding fireballs. Others toppled, their lower portions severed by furious beams of crimson energy. The city began to fall, a grim harvest before the blade, as the Banelords, Ravagers and Ferals blasted everything that stood between them and the Pallidus Mor.

'Are all maniples walking?' Krezoc voxed. She held her fire for the moment. There were no clear targets yet. Let the Iron Skulls expend their energy on the obstacles for now.

*'We are,'* Drahn and Rheliax answered.

*'The secutarii are on the ground,'* Venterras reported.

'Good.' The ground outside of the Viokania yard was free of cultists. *Gloria Vastator*'s assault had turned it into a desert of melted shapes and jagged glass. Krezoc absorbed the long-range auspex readings. The heat signatures of the Iron Skulls showed the pattern of their deployment.

A contingent somewhat larger than her own forces was spreading out around the walls of the city. It looked like an encircling move, though it seemed to her they were spreading themselves very thin. They were also not moving into the city just yet. She wondered about the delay, but she would use the time it gave her. Meanwhile, a much larger battle group of traitors had left Deicoon behind, and was clearly heading for Therimachus.

Krezoc sent a datapack of the readings streaming to Syagrius and then opened a vox-channel, hailing him. He answered immediately.

'*So much for your having contained the enemy,*' he said.

*If we had concentrated our strength here from the start, this war might already be over,* she thought. She did not say it. This was not the time for a debate. 'Marshal, can you move to intercept? If we can break out of Deicoon, we have the chance to catch the enemy in a pincer move.'

'*Negative. Our post is at Therimachus. We will await the traitors here.*'

'There is a chance the city is already on the verge of falling. The corruption at Deicoon was hidden, but widespread.'

'*We are monitoring the situation closely. We will not be surprised.*'

Again, Krezoc did not rise to the bait. She tried one more time. 'We are letting the enemy divide us with this strategy,' she said. 'And we are remaining on the defensive.'

'*Then defend Deicoon, princeps. You know your duty.*'

The channel shut down. The Pallidus Mor was on its own. Krezoc was not surprised. She had hoped Syagrius would see the new necessities and the opportunities of the situation. He had not. They all might pay for his blindness.

The barrages from the Iron Skulls were coming from four directions now. The city reeled, its towers toppling into the canyon-riven streets. Where buildings had stood, flames and dust and smoke rose to the sky. The cannon blasts from the east, the position closest to the Pallidus Mor, were striking the Viokania yards now. A cannon shell smashed through the remaining tower of the Cathedral of Saint Chirosius. *Gloria Vastator*'s void shields shimmered as they took the impact. Krezoc began the march towards the east gates. If the Iron Skulls saw fit to surround the city, let them. She would hit with a focused strike at one spot.

She hoped they would have time. She thought she saw meaning in the shape of the foe's deployment.

'Maniples,' she voxed, 'assume a wedge formation where possible. Maintain unit coherence. We march to the gates, at speed.'

*'The enemy's strategy makes no sense,'* Drahn said.

'I think it does,' Krezoc said. 'If the heretics have trained crews in control of the keep...'

*'Throne,'* said Drahn.

*'We will–'* Rheliax began. He was cut off by the scream of monstrous ordnance. The shot came from the west, as Krezoc had feared.

The Thunderstrike macrocannons of Deicoon entered the war with a terrible shout. A multi-kilotonne shell burst through the towers between the keep and Viokania. Though walls exploded, and streaks of flame erupted at its passing, nothing it hit was substantial enough to slow it down or trigger its blast. Then it hit the Reaver *Imperio Carnificis*, marching behind Rheliax's *Crudelis Mortem*. The explosion shattered glass for miles around. It lit the forge yards with a blinding, destroying light. The Reaver's shields had just taken a hit from the Traitor Titans in the east. They were straining, and the Thunderstrike shell shattered them. It blew out the Titan's entire midsection. The Reaver stood for a few moments more, as if surprised by the absence in its torso. Then the upper portions of the god-machine collapsed. It fell in on itself, shaking with secondary explosions, flames bursting from its ordnance holds. Princeps Landredd must have lived another moment, his will miraculously linked to the dying manifold and the motive force of the Titan, because *Imperio Carnificis* took one more step, its arms slumping towards the ground, its entire frame rocked with tremors. The fires reached higher, and the Reaver became its own pyre from the legs up. It walked no more. The god-machine fell, internal blasts consuming it. The wreckage that smashed to earth was no longer recognisable as the war engine that had fought through millennia of battles. It was a grandiose ruin. The shattered, burning metal was the broken bones of a fallen giant.

'Forced march!' Krezoc yelled into the vox. There was no space for grief in war. She cauterised the wound left by the death of *Imperio Carnificis*. She crushed the loss beneath the weight of hard necessity. 'Deprive the guns of targets,' she ordered. The range of moment of the macrocannons was limited, and they were not on turrets. Krezoc angled *Gloria Vastator* away from the broad avenue that ran parallel to the forge yards and went directly to the gate. That was in the direct line of fire of the Thunderstrikes. From what she had seen of the keep's armament, the guns did not have a full three hundred and sixty-degree arc of fire.

What they had was bad enough. Another shell screamed into the yards. It missed the last of Rheliax's maniple. It hit the ground, and its sunburst sent a storm of flaming metal and pulverised rockcrete over Deicoon. It left a crater where the forge yards had been.

The strategy of the Iron Skulls was what Krezoc had feared. They were not entering the city, because they did not have to. When she saw another energy beam cut through the skyline from the east, she turned into its path. 'Use the enemy's fire,' she ordered. 'Advance into it. They're trying to force us into the sights of the macrocannons.'

The Pallidus Mor would last longer against the weapons of other Titans than against the Thunderstrikes. But the solution was a poor one. She did not think they would be able to march all the way to the wall without falling victim to a lethal attrition.

They had to take out the guns.

The vox was working again. It had cleared shortly after the rise of the brass causeway. Deyers didn't know if the creation of that ghastly miracle had used up the sorcerous energy that was blocking communications, or if something had happened at Deicoon to kill the interference. It was a small mercy, but he was willing to take any he could get at this point.

The Spears had driven straight into the city. The gates were down, and the Pallidus Mor Titans were beginning to move. The Iron Skulls were closing in, and Deyers' hope of establishing a line of defence with Krezoc's maniples to protect the city had died when the smoke became visible on the horizon. Even if there was something to defend, there would not have been time for the Pallidus Mor and the Spears to join up outside the walls. So he led the regiment into the city, and he did not know the thing it had become. He had left an industrial powerhouse, proud in its loyalty to the Emperor. He had returned to a burning slaughterhouse. Many of the streets were impassable to the tanks, their lengths torn into ragged canyons. Down others, heretics and citizens tore at each other. The cultists had more weapons, and the battles were turning into massacres. Deyers had no choice. The Kataran 66th opened fire, shells and streams of burning promethium gutting the roads ahead. Deyers saw many loyal citizens killed in the waves of destruction he sent before him, and he winced at their sacrifices.

He wasn't the only one. 'Our shells don't discriminate,' said Platen.

'Would the faithful live any longer if we did nothing?' Deyers asked her.

'No,' she admitted. 'Not much.'

'Then it's an act of mercy.' A quick death, not a ritualistic one. *Bastion of Faith* rode up over a heap of masonry and shattered bodies, and roared on through the street. The 66th had barely entered the city, but Deyers was fighting the despair that threatened to clamp its claws around his chest. How had this happened to Deicoon? How had no one seen this coming?

*What is worth saving here?*

He tried to bury the thought. It kept surfacing. The mission on Khania, and all the losses there, had been more than duty to the Imperium. They had been in the name of preserving the home world. Then Katara had called, and every moment between the call and the landing had been torture. But Deyers and his Spears had returned, they had answered the call. And now Katara was falling to pieces before his eyes. Creontiades was lost, Deicoon was aflame, and how long before Therimachus suffered the same fate?

*What are we saving?*

He had to make himself believe there was something worth fighting for here. *Hook up with the Pallidus Mor. Defeat the Iron Skulls. Then take the city back.*

The barrage from the traitor god-machines began, and with it the levelling of Deicoon. Everything over fifty feet in height was suddenly a target. The skyline began to topple, hurling immense masses to the ground, crushing the struggling insects below. Then there was the shriek and crack of monstrous thunder. Searing annihilation erupted from the Viokania yards. Blinded by the fireball, Deyers feared for several seconds that the Pallidus Mor had been destroyed. The towering shapes of the god-machines emerged from the flames, and then there was another blast, just as immense.

'Thunderstrikes!' Platen yelled, awed.

Deyers had grown to know the shape of those guns as a characteristic of Deicoon's cityscape. He had never imagined he would witness them fire.

The crossfire of destruction became clear to him. The Titans were the target, and the city would be levelled completely to get at them.

'Rahl,' Deyers voxed the communications officer, 'can you raise Princeps Krezoc?'

*'Trying, captain.'* Rahl came back on the line a moment later. *'I have her, sir.'*

*'Captain Deyers,'* Krezoc said. *'The macrocannons must be silenced.'*

'Agreed. How can we assist?' Then, remembering, he added, 'The keep is void-shielded.'

More infernal beams from the Iron Skulls shot across the city above him. A flight of missiles followed. Before his eyes, the gothic spires of Deicoon became a landslide of rockcrete. Thick dust clouds, tinged red by fire, rolled down the streets and over the lines of tanks.

'*I know,*' said Krezoc. '*We need to split their focus. Even a small distraction might be sufficient. If the Iron Skulls remain outside the walls, your regiment will not be in their sights. Close in on the keep, Captain Deyers. Do what you can.*'

'We will, princeps,' he said.

He could not hear his own answer over the city-shaking boom of another macrocannon shell. More followed, too quickly to be from the same gun.

'What are they doing?' Platen yelled.

'They're firing all the guns,' Deyers said. Whether they had targets or not, the heretics were unleashing Deicoon's greatest strength against itself. They were going to destroy the city with its own defence.

'Turn west,' Deyers called to Medina. 'Get us to the keep as fast as possible.' He thought through the geography of the city for a moment. 'Head for the Avenue of the Holy Vigilant.' It ran parallel to the shattered thoroughfare leading from the gate. It had not collapsed, and it was wide enough that the rubble of buildings might not block it entirely.

Medina acknowledged.

Two intersections later, the Spears were turning onto Holy Vigilant. The dust was so thick, Deyers could barely see two blocks ahead, but the surface of the street was still intact this far. Thousands of silhouettes fought savagely in the choking air. There was room here for the tanks to advance four abreast.

'Full speed,' Deyers ordered the regiment, and a mechanised wall rolled up the slope of the avenue, crushing anyone who did not flee beneath its treads. The blurred shapes of a mob rushed the Leman Russ lines. Cannon shells and turret bolters tore them apart. Deyers spotted a massive crowd gathering outside a chapel not far ahead. The building had been desecrated with runes, and smoke roiled from its gutted interior. 'Platen,' he said, 'the chapel. Drop it on them.' *Bastion of Faith*'s battle cannon roared. The shell hit the façade just above and to the right of the doorway. The explosion destroyed the building's structural integrity. The front half of the chapel collapsed, the façade toppling into the street and the roof following in a slide of rubble. Hundreds died, and the mob scattered from the fall. The wreckage reached across half the street. New clouds of dust and smoke made the air even harder to breathe.

*Is this salvation?* Deyers wondered as the tanks manoeuvred around the ruin of the chapel, grinding more bodies into the pavement. *All we have left is the razing of our own cities. Is this salvation?*

He didn't feel like anything was being saved. Katara was dropping into an abyss of darkness and flame, and all he could do was bring more darkness, and more flame.

The regiment rode on, heading for the keep, spreading destruction at street level while the air above screamed with the energy beams and the flight of monstrous shells. The keep came into view at the top of the Avenue of the Holy Vigilant, its shape an indistinct mass of black in the dust. There were flickers of brighter visibility when attacks from the Pallidus Mor struck void shields, and then bright flashes from the barrels of the macrocannons. A shadow moved, like the hand of a sundial. It pointed down the avenue at the Spears.

'I think we've been spotted!' Platen called.

'Medina!' Deyers shouted. 'Faster!'

The command was pointless. There was no way to get beneath the gun's arc before it fired. The Thunderstrike flashed. The limbo howled. The shell hit the road towards the rear lines of the regiment. Deyers whirled in the hatch and looked back at the immense fireball. Tiny objects that had been Leman Russ tanks hurtled over the broken roofs of the city.

The heat baked the skin of Deyers' face. Blocks away from the centre of the strike, but still within the area of the blast, a promethium reservoir exploded. In the space before another shot from the macrocannon, a firestorm engulfed entire square miles of the city. Its rage kept spreading, manufactorum complexes going off in a chain reaction, the destruction reaching out with blazing hands to consume more and more and more of the city, and the street, and the regiment outlined by the hungry flames.

There would be no evasion. There was nothing left to do but fire.

The Company of the Bridge struggled through streets choked with smoke and rubble and death. Directions became vague. The dust clouds turned the city into a red twilight. It was hard to breathe, and Ornastas' eyes watered from the stinging grit. He kept his bearings from the slopes. As long as he was going downhill, he was heading towards the walls.

Three times since the battle at the cathedral he had

been asked what the company must do next. Three times, explosions nearby had prevented him from answering. It was all he could do to speak without coughing now, but for the fourth time he made the effort. The company had to have a mission, and its members had to know there was one. 'We will leave the city,' Ornastas shouted. 'Our mission here is complete. We are called elsewhere now. We march to Therimachus. There we will be guided again. Be certain of that.' He managed to get through the speech before he bent over, coughing as if he would expel his lungs. His chest grated when he breathed. Velatz and Aldemar stood beside him, ready to help, coughing too. Ornastas held himself up with both hands clutching his staff. Then he nodded and walked on.

They journeyed through a confusion of shapes and struggles. The flames of the city mounted higher and higher at the same time as more and more of its towers came tumbling down. Ornastas could see nothing beyond the next intersection. Phantoms clawed at each other in the clouds of grey and brown and red. The roads the company travelled were narrow, away from the grumbling roar of tanks and the colossal explosions unleashed by Titans and macrocannons. The route went over and between heaps of rubble, and into clusters of fighting. Cultists lunged out of the dust fog, their silhouettes suddenly becoming clear, shadowed features turning into snarling masks. The company gunned down the ones who came near. Firefights impeded the progress of the march. The battles were short, and though the company took some casualties, it kept moving.

It also began to grow.

Ornastas called to the faithful of Deicoon. He held his staff high through every battered street and while crossing every field of rubble. Though his coughing grew worse, he shouted prayers to the God-Emperor. He cursed the faithless who had turned from the true path. He praised the loyal and the faithful, and those willing to die for the Imperial Creed. 'Join us!' he cried. 'Join us! We are the Company of the Bridge! We have fought since Creontiades, and we will fight until Katara is once again in the light of the Emperor!' Another coughing fit silenced him. He spat out a wad of black phlegm, breathed raggedly, and repeated his exhortations.

Individuals and small groups of citizens worked their way through the crimson-and-grey murk to join him. They came cautiously, the movements of their shadows pious and hopeful. The warriors of the company were able to distinguish them from the cultists, and not kill them as they drew near. The train of marchers behind Ornastas grew longer. A few enforcers of the Adeptus Arbites, those who had lost all their comrades, became part of the company. They added their combat skills to the grouping's strengths. One, a brutally scarred, greying veteran named Brennet, walked near the front, just behind Velatz and Aldemar, stepping forwards to support Ornastas when breathing became just too hard and he started to sag. Brennet did not try to lead, though. None of them did. They seemed to recognise they had become part of something other than a military formation. The company fought for Katara and the Emperor, but it was a movement. It was the rejection of corruption. It was the light of the Kataran spirit that refused to be extinguished.

This truth was visible in the range of citizens who joined. Few had training. They came from the undercity, where they had fought, and then hidden from, the rising cult. They came from the manufactoria. They came from the towers of administration and wealth. They were the people of Deicoon who said *no* to the heresy, and *no* to defeat. They were the people who were desperate not for survival, but for the chance to do their duty to world and Emperor, who asked for nothing more than to show their faith to the last of their breath.

They came, and they marched, and many died, but they died with pride. Ornastas' voice grew hoarse. His lungs felt like ragged bellows. But he kept up the call, and the people sang with him, spreading his words, calling to still more. The Company of the Bridge grew and grew, and it snaked its way through the erupting city to the walls and the land and the destiny beyond.

Terrible cannon fire sounded. Not far behind, entire sectors of the city disappeared in a wall of flame. Ornastas did not look back. He clung to the hope that there might still be a way forwards.

Krezoc pivoted as soon as *Gloria Vastator*'s shields started taking hits from Iron Skulls fire. She angled the Warlord's trajectory towards the keep, in a line with the traitor's aim. Its thunderous steps leaned left, then right. The Titan was too immense to duck and weave, but the sinuous course Krezoc established took the Pallidus Mor in and out of the partial shelter of the city's rapidly vanishing towers. The pall of dust and smoke was so thick, line-of-sight targeting was impossible. Visibility was next to zero. Even auspex-controlled fire was being affected by blooms of heat from the explosions and conflagrations raging in all directions. As Krezoc had surmised, the Iron Skulls were not really shooting at the Pallidus Mor any longer. Their barrage was intended to push her forces into the arc of the Thunderstrikes.

'Princeps Rheliax,' she voxed. 'Cover our rear flank. Concentrate your fire towards the wall. Give the traitors something to think about.' Any interference at all with the enemy's salvoes would provide that much more time to manoeuvre towards the keep.

*'Acknowledged,'* said Rheliax. *'And I'm sending my Warhounds forwards.'*

'Good.' Until the keep was within reach, the smaller Titans were the most vulnerable and the least able to act.

*Gloria Vastator* strode onwards through the burning murk. The streams of energy and shells hit on all sides. More of Deicoon exploded with every step. Soon Krezoc could see the keep above the broken skyline before her. Her maniple and Drahn's began their barrage. 'Missile launches,' Krezoc ordered. 'Don't give them a clear line back to us yet.'

Flights of Apocalypse missiles streaked from the launchers of multiple god-machines. The missiles hammered the keep's shields, a chain of explosions illuminating the gloom. The energy sphere surrounding the building flickered and pulsed with angry violet light. A moment later, the Thunderstrike on the near side of the keep fired, but it was aiming to the left of the Pallidus Mor formation. The shot angled downwards into an avenue and set off a colossal chain reaction. An answering barrage rose from the street. The tanks of the Kataran 66th were invisible to Krezoc, hidden by the slumping, burning masses of rockcrete. Their cannon fire seemed pathetically small next to what they were fighting. The blasts barely strained the void shield.

But the tanks had drawn the attention of the enemy inside the keep. They were the visible target. And the window of opportunity opened for Krezoc.

'Full force,' she commanded. 'Take down those shields. Warhounds, advance at speed. Get under the guns.'

The Thunderstrike hurled another shell at the Spears, its terrible devastation a blow at the wrong enemy. *Gloria Vastator*'s main armament fired at the same time as that of *Fatum Messor* and of the Reavers. The Warhounds of two maniples closed in on the keep, sheltered from the Iron Skulls' barrage by their smaller size and the bulk of the greater Titans. Volcano and quake cannons, macro-gatling blasters and plasma annihilators hit the keep with a fury that was the match of its destructive power. The traitors within had the weaponry to engage in an orbital bombardment from the centre of the city, but they struck out in all directions. What hit them was disciplined anger. It overwhelmed the void shields in an instant. Their death-cry was a violet sun, the shock wave racing out across the entire city.

The Thunderstrike cannon tracked towards the Titans as far as it could go. It fired. The shell went wide of Krezoc's formations, but only just. The blast washed over the god-machines, straining their shields. Missiles rained in from the east. On the vox, Rheliax cursed as *Crudelis Mortem* rocked under the hits. The ground under *Gloria Vastator*'s left foot gave way, collapsing into the tunnels, pipes and drainage systems of the undercity. Gas mains erupted, sending sheets of fire up the god-machine's flank. Krezoc leaned unconsciously in the throne, her body sympathetically compensating for the Warlord's precarious balance. She sensed the collapse as it began and brought the leg up and forwards. The manifold sent urgent demands to the enginarium plant. Krezoc felt Thezerin's immediate energy redirects, the arms of the Titan jerking to the right to compensate for the precarious balance. *Gloria Vastator* remained upright, and when the left foot came down again, the ground held.

The Pallidus Mor hit the keep with the next round of the barrage. Even without the shields, the walls were twenty-feet-thick reinforced rockcrete and armour plating. Nevaeh Eukrolas' pride in Deicoon's incorruptibility had been misplaced. Her pride in the formidable defences had not been. The keep, built and reinforced by generations of the Eukrolas dynasty against an enemy never really expected to arrive, withstood the hit. Where many other redoubts would have vanished, blown to rock fragments and vaporised metal, it remained standing, though portions of the wall sagged and flames burst from the windows. The fortress was burning, but it still fought. The Thunderstrike appeared to have survived the blast too, though smoke rose from the length of its barrel.

The bombardment from the Kataran Spears continued, the shells pockmarking the façade of the keep. The intensity of the fire was encouraging. The regiment had not been destroyed.

'Captain Deyers,' Krezoc voxed. 'You troops have done what was needed. Withdraw now. Put distance between yourselves and the keep.'

*'Because the enemy is going to target us again?'*

'No, because of what we are going to do to the enemy.' She switched channel and ordered the secutarii to pull back and take cover as well. *Gloria Vastator* led the advance again, two more steps in the time it took the traitor forces to reload the monstrous macrocannon. The enemy was slower, struggling for control as the damage to the interior spread. And now the Warhounds, hunting as a pack, reached their prey. They were too close for the Thunderstrike to fire downwards at them, though still far enough away from what Krezoc planned to unleash. A stream of fire from plasma blastguns and Vulcan mega-bolters struck upwards, hitting the barrel and the base of the cannon.

'Aim for the centre mass of the keep,' Krezoc commanded the rest of the Titans.

Still another cataclysmic barrage slammed into the structure. It blew open the walls. A hurricane of fire and plasma stormed through the fortress.

In their rage and in their foolishness, the traitors fired again.

The barrel of the Thunderstrike was warped and punctured. The shell exploded inside the gun. The entire east face of the keep blew up. The fireball reached out and within. Destruction struck the most well-protected core of the building. For a few seconds, titanic blasts shook the structure but it kept them contained. Then all the shells of its arsenal went up.

Protective filters dropped over the armourglass eyes of *Gloria Vastator*. Krezoc still winced at the light. The detonation was colossal, a blinding tribute to the might of the Pallidus Mor. The fireball banished the gloom of the city. It etched Deicoon's broken lines onto the eyes, leaving the dazzling negative of a city. It was as if a volcano had erupted in Deicoon, and had done so with such violence that its cone was blasted apart. The keep ceased to exist. The centre of the city, for blocks around the structure, shot high into the air in a thunderous column, a mushroom cloud of dust that roiled with lightning in its head.

The crater left behind was a mile wide.

The barrage from the Iron Skulls faltered. The devastation was so huge, perhaps they did not know whose victory they beheld.

'Now we march for the gates,' Krezoc voxed her demi-legio. 'Now we bring this battle to the Iron Skulls.'

## CHAPTER 9

# FLAMES AND ASHES

Governor Pheon Markos of Therimachus, cousin to Nevaeh and Hallard Eukrolas, now sole representative of the Eukrolas clan and by default lord-governor of Katara, was already in his bunker. Syagrius had come, at the governor's request, to meet him at the palace, which stood on the highest of the city's four hills, in the north west of the hive. Syagrius had expected to meet with Markos where they had spoken before, in the governor's quarters. Markos had received the marshal, when the Imperial Hunters had first arrived at Therimachus, in a handsomely appointed study. The chamber's twenty-foot vaulted window looked to the south east, over the enormous expanse of Katara's largest population centre. The study was the space of a man who was a scholar at least as much as he was an administrator. The walls were lined with chronicles of Katara and exegetical texts. Markos served Syagrius an excellent vintage of amasec. The two men had discussed the conduct of the war in an atmosphere of calm and mature thought. Syagrius had come away from his meeting impressed.

He was not impressed now. Instead of taking him and the officious, sweating major domo hundreds of feet up into the clearer air of the hive, the grav lift descended five hundred feet beneath the foundations of the palace. It deposited them outside an immense vault door of reinforced adamantium plate.

The major domo placed his hand on an identity plate next to the door, stood still for a retinal scan and spoke into a vox-speaker, announcing Syagrius. After a pause, the door rolled aside into the granite and rockcrete walls. On the other side of the doorway was a guard chamber. The officers wore the uniforms of the Eukrolas family's private militia. On the other side of the chamber was an even larger vault door. The sergeant and the major domo repeated the identification procedures, and when this door too opened, Syagrius entered a corridor that was disproportionately low for the imposing portal that covered it. The major domo led him into the bunker proper. The space was much more cramped than Markos' study. There were shelves of books here too, but the governor's desk was functional rather than ornate. All of one wall was given over to a shrine to the Emperor. Syagrius guessed many prayers had been offered to it over the last few hours.

In the centre of the chamber was a tacticarium table. Markos was pacing back and forth before it, on the far side from Syagrius. His eyes flickered between the marshal and the hololithic display. 'Thank you for coming, Marshal Syagrius,' he said. He spoke rapidly, and with a faint tremor. He was sweating. His fingers tap-tap-tapped the edge of the table as he paced. He did not look like the academically inclined aristocrat who had welcomed Syagrius to Therimachus.

Behind Syagrius, the massive door rolled shut once more with a reverberating boom. Markos did not relax in the slightest.

'How can I be of service, governor?' Syagrius asked. He was about to ask why Markos was down in the bunker, then decided not to. The answer was obvious. The man was terrified. Confronting him with his cowardice would not be useful at this moment.

Markos waved at the display. 'I'm trying to get a full understanding of our situation,' he said. 'I want to know where we stand.'

Syagrius stepped up to the tacticarium table. Markos' information was correct. The map showed Therimachus, Deicoon and Creontiades, and the regions between them. Therimachus appeared in considerable detail, despite the scale. The other two cities were red smears, as if they no longer existed. There was a bright patch in the centre of Deicoon, designating the massive heat bloom that had been detected there a short time before. Runes and arrows indicated the position and movements of Imperial and enemy forces. 'Your data appears to be up to date,' Syagrius said.

'I know it is,' Markos said. 'But I want to know what it *means.*'

'I don't follow.'

The governor stopped pacing. He stared at Syagrius with wounded, fearful eyes. 'Marshal, is Katara lost?'

Syagrius stiffened. 'Of course not. The mere question is offensive.'

'I'm sorry, marshal. I don't question the courage and skill of the Imperial Hunters. But it's the numbers. I can't put aside the numbers.'

Syagrius said nothing. He waited for Markos to go on, cursing that the man had zeroed in on the very thing that had been troubling him too.

Markos pointed to the bright spot in Deicoon. 'That explosion...' he began.

'It was caused by the Pallidus Mor,' Syagrius said. 'That was a blow against the enemy.'

'Oh. Oh, good. So they're still in the fight?'

'Yes.'

'Are they on their way to reinforce us?'

Syagrius kept himself from grimacing at Markos' lack of faith. 'I have sent word to Princeps Senioris Krezoc to make for Therimachus when possible. The Pallidus Mor is still engaged in combat, however.' He shouldn't have to point this out. The estimated numbers were there in glowing numbers on the table. The precise dispositions in Deicoon were unknown, however. Syagrius knew Krezoc was fighting. He knew the situation was far from resolved. Beyond that, there were too many unknowns about who or what might march from Deicoon to Therimachus.

Markos was nodding to himself like a nervous rodent. 'I see. I see. And the main force of the Iron Skulls is heading our way.'

'Yes.'

'And the road...'

'Yes, the road is no longer passable.' He was growing tired of confirming what Markos already knew. The highway from Deicoon ran along the coast. In orbit, the *Currus Venatores* had picked up geological deformations occurring in the wake of the Iron Skulls. Behind the enemy and Deicoon, the tremors had opened fault lines deep into the mainland. Canyons now ran from the strait to the coastal mountain chain that separated the two cities. They had swallowed large sections of the road. Nothing was going to come by that route. The terrain west was even more mountainous. It would take weeks to make such a crossing. In between the two main chains, offering an illusion of an easier path between the cities, was a wide desert plain that was a virtual lake of promethium.

The tacticarium table had covered the region of the plain with another red glow. Markos pointed to it now. 'Is it true about the Klivanos Plain?'

'Yes.'

As far as the *Currus Venatores*' auspex array had been able to tell, the main battle group of the Iron Skulls had launched a sustained barrage of missiles into the plain as they were moving beyond Deicoon. The rockets had flown over the horizon from the Iron Skulls' position, and fallen over a wide area of the Klivanos. The explosions had ignited the promethium, creating a sea of fire that already covered thousands of square miles and was still growing. The ground of the Klivanos would have been treacherous in the best of circumstances. There would be nothing coming that way now.

'So,' said Markos, 'and I say this with no disrespect intended, but your orders notwithstanding, there can be no possible reinforcements from the Pallidus Mor. Deicoon is cut off.'

It was. 'The force the Iron Skulls left there will not be reaching us either,' he pointed out. He sounded like he was on the defensive, and he became irritated with both himself and Markos.

'But the size of the contingent that is marching on Therimachus is larger than yours, isn't it?'

'War is not reducible to numbers,' Syagrius said.

'No. No, it isn't.'

Markos did not sound reassured. He started pacing again, now looking as if he was summoning the courage to say what was on his mind. Still walking, he said, 'Forgive me, marshal, but war isn't reducible to opposing armies, either. There is also the battleground, and what is contested, which are sometimes the same thing, but not always. I do not question your war expertise, but I do know Katara, and my city, and their history, and the landscape. When it comes to defence, Therimachus is not Deicoon. It is not even Creontiades. Therimachus' greatest periods of growth came centuries after there had been any wars on Katara. Their memories are longer in Deicoon. That branch of the family made sure of that. But here...' He stopped and waved his hand over the hololithic representation of Therimachus.

Syagrius began to understand what Markos was driving at. There was nothing the governor was saying that Syagrius did not already know. The tactical situation of Therimachus was obvious. The hive had expanded beyond its walls so many times over the centuries that new ones had stopped being built. There was no point. So the city was a gigantic sprawl over the landscape. It was not a city that would ever be besieged because it could not be defended in the traditional sense. What Markos needed was to know that Syagrius understood this. And he needed to know what the marshal planned to do.

'We are not waiting for the enemy to arrive at Therimachus,' Syagrius said, only just holding his temper. He did not worry if he sounded condescending. 'We will march out to meet the Iron Skulls and destroy them before they arrive here.' He doubted he could make things any clearer than that.

'I see.' Markos had stopped pacing again, and was staring down at the table disconsolately.

'You'll be returning to your quarters in the palace?'

The morale of the populace was not normally Syagrius' concern. It mattered more now, though. The question about cult activity hovered unspoken in the air between them. There had been no sign of heresy in the city. There hadn't been in Deicoon either. The Adeptus Arbites and Markos' security forces were taking their investigations even deeper than before. But in a population of so many tens of millions, covering so wide an area and so many levels above and below ground, the task was immense. That nothing had been found meant little. So Syagrius wanted to see Markos visible and confident. He wanted the population of Therimachus under control.

'No,' said Markos, very quietly. 'I will not.'

'May I ask why?'

The man's refusal was insulting.

'I said I knew the history of my city, marshal. That matters too.'

'Why?'

'Because Therimachus has always been taken. It is the indefensible city. In this world's ancient past, in every war of conquest, the city fell to the invader. It accepted the new rule, and so survived. That is not an option this time. If we fall, marshal, and we will, then we are doomed.'

Syagrius snorted. 'I could have told you that.' He leaned over the table towards Markos. 'Leave this bunker. Get back to doing the business of governing instead of hiding like the coward you are. Do your duty or I'll shoot you myself.'

He spun on his heel and strode out of the bunker. He looked back when he was in the guard chamber. Markos was standing quite still, and watching him with deep sorrow. He gave no sign that he was going to obey. Then the massive door rolled shut again, sealing the small man inside.

*'The marshal wants us in Therimachus?'* Drahn voxed.

'So it would seem,' said Krezoc.

A line of rocket blasts stitched up the height of the building to the right of *Gloria Vastator*. The hab tower collapsed, its lower floors imploding and the upper half falling forwards in a disintegrating heap. Krezoc pulled the Warlord back a step. 'Volcano,' she said to Grevereign. The worst of the rubble avalanche landed in front of the Titan. Large chunks of rockcrete bounced off the adamantium hull as the weapon powered up. Krezoc pivoted *Gloria Vastator* and fired the cannon. The beam slashed through the deep, gritty obscurity of the dust and smoke. It struck the Banelord that had toppled the building at the joint of its left arm and torso. Krezoc was rewarded with the flash of overloaded void shields.

*'That's nice,'* Rheliax said. *'How does he expect us to get there?'*

'He didn't say.'

Krezoc followed up with a flight of Apocalypse missiles and a prolonged burst from the mega-bolter. More blasts hit the traitor's arm and joint. The arm blew up. A comet of flame roared up the limb. Internal explosions turned it into a twisted wreckage, and it hung downwards, a useless weight dragging on the Titan's movement. 'First we have to get out of Deicoon.'

The Iron Skulls had closed in before the fireball of the keep's destruction had dissipated. Krezoc had led the Pallidus Mor in a march east to escape the encircling movement. She had no intention of retreating from the city. She would not leave until the last of the traitors present was reduced to slag. But she was no longer going to fight this war on the enemy's terms.

The demi-legio was less than a mile away from the wall. Two Banelords and a number of smaller Titans were in the near vicinity. Harrying fire came from the enemy approaching from the other directions, but those traitors were still too far off to bring their numbers to bear effectively.

The Banelord's shoulder racks sent streaks of missiles against *Gloria Vastator*. The Warlord shook with the pounding impacts. Krezoc walked forwards, deeper into a new dust cloud, and made a temporary shield out of the building shells on her right. *Canis Ignem* and *Canis Vindictae* shot forwards near the Banelord's feet and strafed the monster with mega-bolter shells. The beast did not turn to fight them, but it hesitated for a moment between targets, giving Krezoc the few moments she needed. The traitor's Ferals lunged over the rubble at the Warlord, their nuisance fire exploding against its legs, and blowing up the street where the secutarii and cultists fought. Krezoc had expected them and ignored them. Makthal in *Tempestas Deorem* hit one with the Reaver's power fist, crushing the Feral's flank. The traitor turned, limping, into a second hit from the fist.

'Ready,' Grevereign and Vansaak told Krezoc at the same moment. And she knew, already. Their eagerness had spiked their vital signs in the manifold, and Krezoc had felt the deep energy thrum that indicated both of *Gloria Vastator*'s primary weapons were prepared to fire again.

The quake cannon fired a beat before the volcano cannon. The Banelord's shields were trying to come back online, but the Warhound assault was enough to disrupt them. The Mori shell struck the traitor's torso on the right. The explosion set off tremors in the earth that even Krezoc registered. The Banelord rocked back and to the side, in time to take the second volcano las hit. The energy beam sheared through the weakened armour. The Banelord's arm fell off, blowing up as it hit the ground. The Titan staggered forwards, a machine of pain and anger now. Energy discharges crackled from its shoulders, blue lightning flashes reaching far into the dusty air. Its carapace launchers flared again. The missile flights were erratic. They came down wide, the hits scattering over Krezoc's maniple. The Banelord's targeting was damaged. The foulness inside the machine was hurt, perhaps dying. Its corrupted war-horn issued a raging howl. It walked into the ruins of the hab block between it and *Gloria Vastator*. It waded into rockcrete that slumped down further against its legs, slowing its charge. The monster seemed to waver.

'Quake cannon, lower torso,' Krezoc said. Her words and her will, Vansaak's will and *Gloria Vastator*'s actions fused. There was no distinction between them. Krezoc spoke, and the shell struck the target, hitting deep into armour. The explosion was as much inside the Banelord as outside. The monster trembled, its war-horn turning to a disbelieving wail, and fell.

To the left, *Crudelis Mortem* and *Fatum Messor* had the second Banelord in a crossfire. It struck back wildly. A coruscating energy beam hit *Crudelis Mortem*'s head. Rheliax grunted in pain on the vox, but his Warlord kept hitting the traitor machine. Drahn drew more of its fire towards *Fatum Messor*. The two Warlords began to circle the Banelord. It was a slow, majestic dance of war, and it was an inevitable execution. Plasma blasts and massive shelling took the enemy apart.

The Ravager and Feral Titans had lost their leaders. They tried to rally, closing together to concentrate all of their firepower on *Gloria Vastator*, now closest to the wall.

'They're forming a pack,' Vansaak said.

'They should know better,' said Krezoc, pleased that they did not.

In the flame and dust that swirled and roared over all of Deicoon, targets were harder to zero in on. To the naked eye, the city was a phantasmagoria of explosions and hulking shadows. Many of these shadows moved, but they might only be buildings surrendering to their deaths and crumbling to earth. Titans moved between and through the ruins. What seemed to be a tower might suddenly reveal itself as a god-machine. The firestorms were generating their own winds, and the dust whirled itself into blasting cyclones. The chaos of the city made auspex readings suspect. There were heat blooms everywhere, concealing the enemies from each other. The actual battles between the Titans were taking place at what was almost point-blank range.

If the lesser Iron Skulls had kept apart, strafing targets of opportunity and avoiding direct confrontations with the organised maniples of the Pallidus Mor, they might have survived until the arrival of the rest of the force. By grouping into a pack, they showed themselves and made themselves vulnerable.

Krezoc made out the pack half a mile ahead, just before the ruins of the wall. 'Target acquired,' she said, and sent a flight of Apocalypse missiles to light the way for the other Warlords.

*'I see them,'* said Rheliax.

*'Confirmed,'* Drahn added.

'Take out the road in front of them,' she told Grevereign. To the rest of her maniple, she said, 'Target at will.'

Volcano las-beams cut the street open. The fissure gaped wide, molten, a sudden abyss of fire going down into the smouldering undercity. Two Ferals, rushing forwards, could not arrest their momentum and tumbled into the gorge. Upended, they were helpless. The Pallidus Mor barrage hammered down on the others. The battered regiment of the Kataran Spears, moving at the feet of the Titans, gave their own measure of punishment to the traitors. Ravagers and the other Ferals, realising their error, fought back with the full measure of their ferocity. For almost a minute, the eastern edge of Deicoon was brilliantly lit by the fury of las, plasma, missiles and shells converging on a single, contained area, and lashing out from the same point. A snarling, soiled dawn broke in the city, strobing and throbbing with the endless percussion of the explosions. The dawn became a howling brightness as reactors went critical and ruptured god-machines became their own annihilating pyres.

Then the day died once more, fading back to the crimson-and-black storms, and what remained before the Pallidus Mor was a heaving, boiling pit. Much more of the road had fallen in during the battle. Krezoc had been forced to march *Gloria Vastator* back several paces as the fissure had lengthened and widened, sucking down buildings and Titans. The destruction in the undercity, begun by whatever force it was that had been granted to the heretics for their uprising, had continued and escalated since. As above, so below. What Krezoc could see of the undercity looked like the interior of a volcanic cone. Combustible gas and liquids flowed like lava. Layers were collapsing upon layers, forcing everything further and further down. Already the pit was hundreds of feet deep.

*'We have a bit of a detour to make,'* Rheliax voxed.

'When we leave,' Krezoc answered. 'And we aren't going yet.'

The rest of the Iron Skulls were much closer. As the firestorms had increased, the long-distance barrages had diminished in intensity and accuracy. The traitors had no more of an idea of where their targets were than did the Pallidus Mor. But they were close now. The shadows were falling across the auspex data streaming through the manifold. The positions were still vague. Even the precise composition of the force was hard to scry. It was larger than the Pallidus Mor.

*And this is a splinter of the main force,* she thought. The Iron Skulls had mustered a colossal showing for this invasion.

She took *Gloria Vastator* back another few steps from the pit as more of the edges crumbled in. Tremors continued. A web of cracks spread over the avenue, racing outwards until they vanished from sight in the murk.

'Head south,' she voxed to the demi-legio and to the Spears. 'Face west, towards the centre. The moment of our stand approaches.'

'*What is our strategy?*' Drahn asked.

'To send the enemy to perdition.'

Krezoc rotated *Gloria Vastator*'s torso on its axis. Its guns pointed upslope, ready for the enemy to appear. The Warlord moved south, away from the pit, its ponderous steps shaking the fragile being of the city. Deicoon's strength had always been a shell, and everything hollow was coming to its end.

The Spears drove between the feet of giants. Coughing, Deyers lowered himself down through the turret and closed the hatch for a moment. He wiped the dust from his eyes and breathed the dank but comparatively clean air of the tank for a few breaths.

'What is she planning?' Platen asked.

'I don't know,' said Deyers. He could see no course ahead except one form or another of annihilation. He could not keep the despair at bay. The victory over the first detachment of Iron Skulls did nothing to hold it back. What he retained from the fall of the enemy Titans was the vision of the city destroying itself from within. There was nothing in Deicoon except destruction. He had no fear of death or sacrifice. He would follow his duty to the end. He would have the Spears follow Krezoc's lead. She had earned that on Khania. And yet the burning storm of Deicoon filled his mind and soul.

He could hear echoes of that destroying wind in Platen's voice. The Spears had all come to save Katara, and there was less and less left to save.

Krezoc's voice came over the vox. '*Enemy in sight. Prepare for massed fire. Captain Deyers, I suggest you continue to pull your forces back.*'

'We will not abandon the fight,' he said.

*'I am not asking you to. You will engage as you see fit, of course. But I strongly urge you to pull back. We all will presently. We are leaving Deicoon. You must too.'*

'I understand, princeps,' he said, only he didn't. He was confused. He did as she said, however. 'Guns on the enemy and fire at will,' he voxed. 'And make for the walls at all speed. We're getting out.' The road to the gate was destroyed, but so much of the wall was now down that it would not be difficult to break out of the city.

'That sounds like a retreat,' said Platen.

'Somehow it isn't,' Deyers said, dreading the truth.

'Here they come!' Platen shouted, all her focus now on taking down the overwhelming foe.

Deyers opened the hatch and climbed out into the suffocating dust again. Uphill from his position, the monstrous giants had appeared. Their distorted shapes were made even more terrible in the half-light of the shrouded firestorm. They were tall as death, twisted as nightmares. The city shook with their tread. The spined, horned masses rocked back and forth as they advanced. They were the unholy given form. They seemed to have sprung from the underworld of lost mythologies. They rose up from the burning city, and their armour of crimson and black made them things of flame and shadow. The towering Banelords were escorted by the foothills of the Reavers and Ferals. The Iron Skulls approached in a cluster, a new city of blood and brass marching through the death throes of Deicoon. Opposing them, the god-machines of the Pallidus Mor were no less awe-inspiring, but fewer in number.

The guns of the Kataran 66th opened up against the nightmare invaders. The shelling seemed pitiful to Deyers, a child's ignored cry.

Then the Titans of both sides unleashed their wrath, and the world began to come apart.

The Company of the Bridge was more than a thousand strong by the time it crossed the wall and moved out onto the rocky terrain beyond Deicoon. The ground was trembling with greater and greater violence. Ornastas kept marching, looking back all the while, until the company reached a zone of jumbled boulders and dry gullies. Immense energy discharges from the city cast jagged shadows over the ground.

Ornastas hesitated. His initial impulse had been to march for Therimachus, but the distance involved now sank in. The company had neither transport nor supplies.

*How do you plan on getting there?* he wondered.

An inner voice said, *Wait.*

It said, *Witness.*

'Take cover!' Ornastas called to his followers. He coughed again, but not as violently as before. The air was a little cleaner here.

'Are we fighting?' Velatz asked, puzzled.

'We are watching!' Ornastas announced. 'We pause here to see the history of Katara unfold, and learn what our role in its next chapter will be!'

He led by example. He chose a boulder the size of a Chimera and stood with his hand against its side, ready to duck behind the rock when the need arose. He looked towards Deicoon and felt the overwhelming event approach. He needed guidance, and it was coming. Once again, he would see destiny take form. When it did, the Emperor would speak to his soul, and he would know what path he should take.

The war in the city hurt his eyes with the brilliance of devastation. He was already moving his lips in a prayer of thanks when a cracking boom, deep and fatal, announced the moment of destiny.

The foul energy burst against *Gloria Vastator*. The barrage was unending, concentrated, an explosion of violence from mad gods. Krezoc felt the pain of the Warlord. Its shields could not withstand so massive an assault. Thezerin channelled power to the forward shields, bringing them back online almost as quickly as they went down. They pulsed in and out of existence with the stutter of an arrhythmic heart. The energy to power or destroy a city burst into life and imploded a moment later, disrupted by forces even stronger. The enemy attacks reached deeper and deeper into the being of the god-machine, burning through plating, crackling along power lines. In the manifold, Krezoc felt the wounds to the body of the Warlord. Severed power cables were burned nerves. Burst conduits were cut veins. *Gloria Vastator*'s pain was her pain. Its anger was her anger. Her determination was the machine-spirit's.

She did not let the growing damage distract her from the objective. She kept to her target, and demanded the same of every princeps in the demi-legio. No matter how ferociously the instinct of the machine-spirit tried to bring the weapons to bear on the Iron Skulls, she used nothing except the mega-bolter to fire directly on the Traitor Titans.

Everything else smashed Deicoon in a vast swath before the Iron Skulls.

In the region of the barrage, cultists still fought with loyal civilians. The struggles were pointless, the combatants on both sides doomed to be crushed or burned by the disintegrating city. They were invisible to Krezoc, except in brief glimpses when the wind cleared the dust for a moment. There was no meaning in those battles any more. They were violence that fed itself. It raged for its own sake.

Krezoc could have rationalised the death she brought as a mercy. She did not. She accepted that she was killing the innocent and the loyal along with the heretic. She took on the cost to her soul. And she did what was necessary. This, too, was the culture of the Pallidus Mor. The road to victory was bloody. To travel it meant leaving behind the hopes of forgiveness. To travel it well, and not be among the corrupt, meant seeing the cost. It meant knowing the harm done. It meant never turning away from the ugliness she unleashed.

It meant never blinking.

If Deicoon could have been saved, Krezoc would have given her life to do it. But it was doomed, and so Deicoon must give its life for the greater cause of the salvation of Katara.

Every primary weapon of the demi-legio hit the same region of ground. Citizens and heretics vaporised along with the hollowed-out shells of manufactoria. No structure survived beyond the first seconds of the bombardment. Rockcrete and bedrock melted. A fist with the impact of an asteroid shattered the crust of the city.

For seconds that lasted an eternity, the Iron Skulls battered the Pallidus Mor, and the Pallidus Mor punished the earth onto which the Skulls advanced. The seconds were the time of Krezoc's gamble. She wagered the Titans under her command were stronger than the surface of the city.

She won.

The great pit opened, a maw gaping wide to swallow

Deicoon. The bombarded region fell away suddenly, taking three Iron Skulls at once. Millions of tonnes of stone, rockcrete and corrupted metal plummeted, crushing all below, smashing into levels, many of which were already on the verge of collapsing themselves. The city fell and fell and fell, the depths of the plunge increasing as the maw widened.

'Keep firing,' Krezoc commanded. 'Send everything to the core of this planet!'

Somewhere to the right, there was the devastating blast of another god-machine dying. The blast shook the other Titans, overloaded void shields and sent dangerous tremors through the ground.

*'We may fall with the enemy,'* Drahn said.

'We will not,' said Krezoc. She would not allow it.

The chain reaction set in. The great plunge was so sudden, so absolute, Krezoc grunted in unwanted awe. The entire slope between the Pallidus Mor and the crater that had been the keep disappeared. The Iron Skulls dropped into the darkness of flame. Explosions gouted from the maw. Fountains of burning gas reached upwards like the hands of a drowning man. Volcano las and quake shells followed the traitors down. The torrent of destruction turned the abyss into an erupting crater. A Titan exploded. The blast was nuclear, and in the confined quarters of the pit it annihilated everything that might have slowed the fall. It punched all the way through the depths of the undercity and deeper into the crust of Katara.

'Keep firing,' Krezoc said again. 'Keep firing. We do not stop until there is nothing left of them.'

The monsters of the Iron Skulls landed on each other. Some fell hundreds of feet and shattered their limbs with the impact of their own mass. They were prone. They collided with each other. Many still blasted upwards with their weapons. Rockets rose from the pit and arced down onto the Pallidus Mor.

These were the attacks of desperation. They were last gasps. What Krezoc had begun could not be arrested.

Fortress-destroying las melted the earth. Shells blew the wounds of the crust wide. Now direct fire on the Iron Skulls was useful. Tangled, damaged, enraged beasts hurled their rage up at their executioners. Distorted limbs emerged from dark seas of flame to blast violet lightning one last time. Uncontrolled bursts ushered the end closer. Metal skeletons wrestled against the formation of their grave. Each explosive death pushed the fall deeper.

Deicoon's roots went down far. So very far, it was as if their construction were nothing more than a foreshadowing of the form of their annihilation. The holocaust cracked through the crust until the even greater heat of the mantle rose to meet it.

The greatest explosion came then. The true eruption. The pit became a caldera. *Gloria Vastator* ceased fire as the wall of magma and incandescent clouds roared to the sky.

# CHAPTER 10

# THE CALL OF THE HUNTING HORN

As the god-machines manoeuvred into formation, Syagrius had the luxury of time to survey the landscape that would host the coming battle. Beyond the trailing edge of Therimachus were rolling hills. The road from Deicoon came in from the east, rounding the coastal mountains. The south was forested. The region had been relatively untouched by the rapacious industry of Katara. Further south was the Klivanos Plain. Despite the richness of the promethium reserve, the region was too volatile to permit extraction. In the distance, visible above the trees, were the remains of the last attempt, two centuries old, to exploit its resources. The charred, twisted tops of derricks looked like the fossil remains of a leviathan caught by the ferocity of the Klivanos.

Syagrius had seen the glow of flame geysers in the plain since his arrival in Therimachus. Now, though, what he saw looked more like curtains of fire, an incendiary aurora rising from the earth instead of descending from the sky. The burn had reached the edge of the forest and was spreading quickly.

Syagrius looked south through the armourglass eyes of *Augustus Secutor*. He grimaced at the obvious symbolism of the conflagration. Katara was aflame. He had come to lead its liberation. Instead, more and more of the world was being consumed. The fire of war was licking at the edges of Therimachus now. The green of the hills to the east and of the threatened forest to the south felt like the last untouched region of Katara, just as Therimachus was the last city. Now the Iron Skulls were close. So was the judgement of his strategy on the planet.

Syagrius did not believe in doubt. It was a poison, the creator of battlefield paralysis. He had been a stranger to it from youth. Upon his early induction into the Collegia Titanica, he had consciously ground even its trace beneath his boot heel. His refusal of doubt had served him well. He had the victories to prove it. Many had been hard won. There had been sacrifices. But there had never been any reason for doubt.

Not until Khanid. The initial battle against the tyranids had disturbed him. He had pursued a return to unblemished pride in the second phase of the campaign. He remained convinced the near-disaster at Gelon had been Balzhan's fault. He was just as convinced his strategy on Katara was correct. Land at the cities. Hold them. Defeat the traitors when they rose to the bait.

The campaign was sound. There were no doubts. There was only certainty.

Only the fire was spreading. And there was something in his chest, a sharp knot he could not banish.

Rekorus said, 'I have Princeps Krezoc, marshal.' The moderati had been attempting to make vox-contact with Krezoc since the preparations for the march had begun.

'Patch her through,' Syagrius said. He made the conversation private.

'*Marshal*,' said Krezoc. There was a lot of noise in the reception, as if the flames were burning the very ether.

'What is your status?' Syagrius asked her.

'*We have defeated the enemy at Deicoon.*'

There was no triumph in her statement. Only exhaustion, and a determination so dark Syagrius could almost see it.

'I congratulate you, princeps.' The words tasted of sawdust. He spat them out as quickly as he could.

'*How are you faring at Therimachus?*' Krezoc asked.

'The enemy is not yet in sight, but will be soon.' Syagrius paused for a moment. 'Your orders stand. You are to make for Therimachus with all due haste.' He said this because he had to. He had given the orders once. Rescinding them was not an option, even when he knew obeying them was impossible.

'*I understand, marshal,*' Krezoc said. The same bleak determination as before. She did not question the orders. She did not raise questions about his strategy. She did not suggest that it had gone awry. But as flat as her tone was, through the hisses and pops of the voxmission Syagrius thought he heard a deeper meaning to what she said. *I understand, marshal.* What did she think she understood. That disaster was inevitable?

He shut his eyes for a moment and shook his head once. *Disaster.* There was no reason to think of that eventuality. Krezoc's cold voice must be more insidious than he had thought, for it to imply such a thing. She had…

*Stop it.*

He opened his eyes. He looked down the road ahead, to where it curved shortly before the horizon to disappear behind the shoulder of the mountains. Now of all times, he must see clearly. There was no room for illusion.

'Will you come?' There was relief in the honesty of the question.

*'The road has been cut,'* she said.

'Yes, it has.'

Silence. Then Krezoc said, *'The Pallidus Mor will walk on Therimachus, marshal.'*

She did not say how. She did not say when they could arrive. Those were not answers she could give. He did not ask them of her.

*'What of the heretics, marshal?'* Krezoc asked. *'Did the cult reach Therimachus?'*

'It is not a threat,' Syagrius said.

*'We thought the same in Deicoon. I let my guard down. I was wrong to do so.'*

'We learned from that,' Syagrius told her. He surprised himself by not saying *your error*. Berating Krezoc was pointless. He had no energy for it. He felt himself suspended in a sphere of stilled time. Outside its confines, war and an avalanche of consequences waited. Within, he floated in an atmosphere of rarefied clarity. It was important that he not squander the crystalline moments. Antagonising Krezoc would be a waste. 'The enforcers looked hard. They found some pockets of cultists. They were disorganised, easily purged. The heresy did not have time to take root here.'

*'Good,'* said Krezoc. *'And what was planned here was disrupted. Perhaps we will be spared further surprises.'*

'I agree.'

'Marshal,' Trovalis said, 'auspex readings of large movements.'

'Thank you, moderati.' To Krezoc, he said, 'Our moment has come.'

*'Fight well, marshal.'*

'We shall. And we will look for you when you join us.'

*'See that you do.'*

It was the closest he had come to a friendly exchange with Krezoc.

When he ended the conversation, Syagrius saw Rekorus looking at him.

The younger man raised an eyebrow. 'Are they on their way?' he asked.

'They are.'

'When will they get here?'

'When they do. Until then, the glory is ours alone.'

Rekorus grinned, recognising a hard truth rather than vainglory in Syagrius' answer. 'So much the better,' he said, answering in kind.

Syagrius opened a command channel to the entire demi-legio. 'Imperial Hunters,' he said, 'our moment has come at last on Katara. Our prey approaches. Let us fall on its neck. Let us cover the land with its blood. We hunted well on Khania. I am honoured now to lead you on our greatest hunt yet. Sound the horns, comrades! Let the foe tremble before our coming!'

He finished speaking, and the war-horns of every Titan in the demi-legio blasted. The sound was colossal. It was immense, and it was hungry. It roared over the landscape and bounced against the mountainsides. It was a fanfare of gods, so loud it would have been heard by every citizen of Therimachus, no matter how deep underground they might be.

*Do you hear us, you coward?* Syagrius thought, picturing Markos in his bunker. The governor had refused to emerge. He was issuing commands to the militia from his hole in the ground. Coming from such a man, his directions were not orders. They were miserable pleas.

'Sound the horns again!' Syagrius called. 'Tell the enemy we are here! Announce our coming! Let all of Katara know that the Imperial Hunters walk!'

The maniples were in formation, and with the second blast, the colossal majesty of the Imperial Hunters began to march. The wind was blowing from the north, pulled towards the firestorms of the promethium plain. The banners of the Imperial Hunters streamed in the gusts, snapping proudly. *Augustus Secutor* strode forwards. With each footfall, Syagrius felt his mark etched more deeply on the face and history of the world. The Warlords leading the four maniples marched in synchrony. They left Therimachus behind. They walked over the hills, giants of eternal magnificence. The formation stretched over a line miles wide. Syagrius smiled at the thought of any foe that thought to pass through the spaces between the Titans. Markos was distressed that Therimachus did not have a wall. He was wrong. The Imperial Hunters were that wall, and the wall moved. It marched across the land, and it would grind anything that tried to break through it to dust.

The horns sounded again, warning and exulting. Here was strength and here was pride. Here was the most august of powers. Dark clouds scudded overhead, but they could do nothing to dim the lustre of the Imperial Hunters. The legio's colours were the green of the Imperium's glory, the white of purity and the red of nobility. The icon of its banner was the claw of the predator, but it was also a sun bursting above the field. The Imperial Hunters were the sun of every world on whose surface they marched. And they carried in their weapons the fury of a star.

Yet again, the war-horns shouted.

*Here we are*, Syagrius thought. *Will you face us? Do you dare?*

The answer came, first with a countering roar of war-horns. This sound was deeper, cacophonous, a braying howl of anger issuing from ulcerous, deformed throats. The layered madness of the echoes had not faded when the Iron Skulls appeared. Massive figures of rage thundered out from behind the mountainside and made for Therimachus.

Anger and majesty closed with each other.

Ornastas gazed up at *Gloria Vastator*. It stood astride a ridge only a few hundred yards away from where the Company of the Bridge had gathered. The head of the Titan was almost lost to his sight in the blowing ash. The Warlord, and the other giants that stood with it, faced away from the city. They had done with it.

So his duty was clear.

'We're going back in,' Ornastas said.

'To what?' Brennet objected. He had been staring at the caldera of Deicoon. Now he looked at Ornastas in disbelief.

Ornastas understood his doubts. Lava still fountained from its centre. It poured in torrents down the ruined streets, its angry glow slowly dimming to black as it spread out into the land beyond. The air here, beyond the reach of the eruption, was thick with ash, and harder to breathe than it had been in the centre of Deicoon.

'We will go back,' Ornastas told him, 'because we are called.' He raised his voice as much as he could, though he was rasping and coughing again. The rumble of the city's collapse continued, thunder cracked in the ash cloud, and the wind howled. Only those standing nearest Ornastas could hear him. He climbed on top of a nearby boulder, making himself as visible as possible to the company, and he gestured with his staff as he spoke, pointing back towards the city. Those who could not hear him would see him, he hoped, and they would understand something of what he was urging them to do. He would have to rely on word of what he said spreading. He had no doubt it would be shared by those closest to him.

'But there's nothing left,' Brennet objected.

'Isn't there? Look to the ruins. Look to the broken ramparts. Do you see what I see?'

What was left of Deicoon was a smouldering ring. Not a single building had been left intact. Their shells stabbed upwards, hollow and fractured. The wall was slumping rubble, the heaps separated by wide gaps. The city reminded Ornastas of the shattered teeth of a lower jaw surrounding a fiery maw. Just visible through the billows of smoke and the sheets of fire that roared through Deicoon, figures struggled. They had taken refuge from the lava atop the mounds of wreckage, and they fought there. Some ran in the streets, fleeing the molten judgement, and they did battle there, too. All who were still alive in Deicoon were locked in combat. The daemonic Titans had been destroyed, and the god-machines of the Pallidus Mor had gathered outside the city. They would be leaving soon. Their battle here had ended, and Therimachus had need of them. But Deicoon was more than its pyre. The city bled. The city fought.

'The war in Deicoon is not over,' Ornastas said. 'We must not turn away from it. Who will be its champions and its guardians if not us?'

Brennet looked uncertain. 'What will we champion? Soon there won't be anything left.'

'There will be,' Ornastas said, his confidence absolute. 'We will wait a short while, but then we will return. There will be a Deicoon to save. Already there is a Deicoon to avenge.' He pointed again, this time to figures struggling on the side of a fallen hab block. 'The heretic must be destroyed.' Somewhere in the fire and ash, he thought, there were leaders of the cult. He prayed some had survived the devastation so he might punish them himself.

Brennet turned his head to watch the fight, and when he looked back at Ornastas, the confessor saw renewed determination in the face of the enforcer.

'Deicoon calls us back,' Ornastas told him. 'Will you answer?'

'I will,' said Brennet. 'I will!'

*'Will you answer?'* Ornastas shouted to the company.

*'We will!'* the people chanted back as he bent over double, coughing up black phlegm. *'We will! We will! We will!'*

Ornastas refused to wait. With the fervour of the company resounding, he climbed over the boulder and took the first symbolic steps back towards Deicoon. The radiant heat of the lava felt like a benediction.

Krezoc met with the other princeps, the secutarii alphas and Deyers at the base of *Gloria Vastator*'s right leg. The massive limb and the ridge behind it provided enough shelter from Deicoon's storm for them to talk without having to shout.

'News from Therimachus?' Deyers asked. The captain's face was pinched. His left cheek twitched from strain.

'Marshal Syagrius is leading the Imperial Hunters into combat against the Iron Skulls,' said Krezoc. 'Our orders are to join him.'

Deyers blinked. 'Meaning he doesn't favour his chances.'

The other officers were silent for a moment. Then Carrinas said, 'I will not stand for any insults to the marshal, or to the honour of the Imperial Hunters.'

Deyers stared at him, then shook his head. 'I meant no insult.' There was something dead in his voice. He seemed to have moved into a kind of blankness beyond despair.

'The marshal's valour on the battlefield is second to none,' Krezoc said carefully. That, at least, was true. She cursed his strategy, but she could not fault his courage. 'We have defeated the enemy here. Of course we should make for Therimachus.'

'As fast as possible,' Deyers said.

'Are you in the habit of taking your time on the way to a battle, captain?'

Deyers shook his head.

'What is it that is really on your mind?' Krezoc asked.

Deyers looked towards the conflagration of Deicoon, then back at Krezoc. 'Have we come to save Katara or destroy it?' he said.

'We have come to do our duty,' she told him, her tone full of iron and ice. 'We are here to destroy the enemy. If we do not, there is no salvation possible for Katara.'

Deyers nodded, but said nothing.

'Are the Kataran Spears ready to do their duty?' Krezoc insisted.

'They are,' Deyers said. There was still no real hope in his eyes.

Drahn said, 'I can't dispute the need to reach Therimachus with all speed, but how do we get there with the road gone?'

'Heading west isn't an option, is it?' said Rheliax.

'No,' Deyers said. 'It would take weeks.'

'Then how do we get there?' Drahn said, frustrated.

Movement to the right caught Krezoc's eye. She turned to look. The ecclesiarch who had freed the secutarii at the Cathedral of Saint Chirosius was climbing over the rocks and walking towards Deicoon. His civilian warriors, over a thousand strong now, followed him. He leaned into the wind-blown ash and held his staff high and angled at the burning walls. He was leading a charge to battle. He was taking his followers into the flames because that was where they must go to fight their holy war.

Krezoc continued to turn until she faced north. The ridge blocked her view of Deicoon. She could see the angry glow of the eruption colouring the sky. That was where Ornastas was heading. She thought about another fire, larger yet.

Krezoc turned back to the other officers. 'We must walk through the flames,' she said.

Rheliax stared at her. Drahn began to grin at the audacious madness of what Krezoc proposed.

'Will we reach Therimachus in time?' said Deyers. There was hardly any expression, and even less hope, in his voice.

Krezoc noticed he did not ask what route she meant to take. Perhaps he guessed. Perhaps he was beyond caring. 'We will not be expected,' she said.

His grimace told her that he understood he could hope for nothing more.

The Banelord struggled in the crossfire of Syagrius' maniple. The Traitor Titan had advanced at its full, lumbering speed, its strides outpacing its smaller escorts. It came on, lured by the challenge of *Augustus Secutor*'s war-horn, answering with its own blasting howls of rage. Syagrius made his Warlord the single focus of the Banelord's attack by hammering the traitor's shields with mega-bolter and Apocalypse missiles. The beast hit back with a punishing barrage of shells. Its right arm was a power fist, crackling with corrupt energy, already reaching forwards in hunger for *Augustus Secutor*. Syagrius walked the Warlord back a few slow paces, drawing the Banelord in further. The traitor stormed past the positions of the Reaver and Warhounds of the maniple. They opened fire on its back and flanks. The Banelord took two more steps before reacting, and now it was assailed by a steady assault.

The monster's horn became a roar of anger and pain. Its tail-mounted energy cannon whipped around, firing at all of its attackers in turn.

Syagrius took *Augustus Secutor* in a lateral movement around the Banelord. 'Keep circling it,' he ordered. 'Destroy it in the net of our fire.'

The Banelord's shielding flared with angry light. In the manifold, Syagrius and the Warlord's machine-spirit recoiled from the auspex readings of the foe. The energy that surrounded the traitor was wrong. It defied spectrographic analysis, overpowering the sensors with nonsense. To the auspex, this was no recognisable power, though it bore some of the signatures of warp taint. Syagrius saw sorcery, not technology. The Titan's behaviour was too much like a living thing. It was hard to imagine the actions of a crew within. The image came to Syagrius of no crew at all. The thought was repulsive. He wanted the Titan purged from existence.

The Banelord's shields collapsed entirely for a few instants. The Warhound *Triumphum Cane*'s turbolaser and mega-bolter shots converged on the same point on the Banelord's right leg, in the gap where the two armour plates met at the knee. There was a burst of flame and smoke from the interior of the limb. The Banelord staggered. Its right leg seemed to lock rigid. It pivoted on the limb, leaning dangerously forwards. For a moment, Syagrius thought the Titan would topple. Instead, its grasped at its foes with its power claw. Its tail was straight out, giving balance to its huge mass. As it spun, the Banelord gained just enough reach. *Triumphum Cane* came within its grasp. The claw snapped over the Warhound's turbolaser. It crushed the barrel. The weapon exploded. The Banelord dragged the Titan through the fireball. It straightened, and with its horn blaring, it lifted the Warhound into the air, then hurled it to the ground. It followed through with a blow from the claw. Eldritch fire bloomed as the claw punched through the midsection of the Warhound.

Syagrius restrained the fire of *Augustus Secutor* during the seconds the traitor held *Triumphum Cane* close. The Reaver *Aurea Exterminatore* and the Warhound *Sacra Canis* kept up an assault on its rear and flank. They seemed to be causing damage. More smoke rose from the rents in the Banelord's armour, but the focus of the machine, or the things that controlled it, was the victim at hand.

When Syagrius saw the power claw slam through

*Triumphum Cane*'s armour, he knew the crew of the Warhound was dead. 'Cavellus,' he voxed the princeps. There was no answer, and the reason for restraint vanished. 'Firing,' he warned the other two crews. They were a safe distance away, hundreds of yards from the Banelord. Still, they needed to be prepared. 'Sunfury,' Syagrius said, and Moderati Rekorus echoed. The gun hurled its annihilating blast at the Banelord. The rage of a sun struck it in the chest even as the rest of the maniple collapsed its shields yet again. Armour melted. Explosions rocked the entire body of the traitor.

'Las,' Syagrius said, and Moderati Trovalis said, 'Las.' And the las turret fired with the explosions of the Sunfury still bright. The glare had not yet faded from Syagrius' eyes.

The huge lascannon mounted on *Augustus Secutor*'s left arm hit the Banelord's claw and chest with a long burst. The Banelord could not get its shields up against the onslaught. It fired back at Syagrius, and a shell of enormous magnitude slammed into the lower torso of the Warlord.

'*Marshal,*' Magos Prendivian voxed him a moment later, '*we have serious damage in the–*'

'Not now,' Syagrius snarled and cut him off.

The turret hit the Banelord again and again. The traitor's movements became erratic. The god-machine swerved as if drunk. Its fire went wild.

Warlord, Reaver and Warhound continued to circle it. The beast lashed out, carving huge furrows through the earth. Coruscating energy beams struck the Imperial Hunters, but the monster was surrounded, wounded, doomed. Feral Titans closed in, their supporting fire against the Hunters too little and too late to aid their master. *Augustus*

*Secutor* fired the Sunfury again. The plasma explosion disintegrated the power conduits running from the Banelord's back and feeding into its skull. The protective cowling melted. The full force of the blast tore the monster's skull loose from its moorings. The head dangled upside down, hanging on by half-molten shielding and shredding cables. The immense body spun again, its legs stamping craters open on the ground, uncontrolled energy arcing from the cowling. Guns misfired. The tail whipped back and forth, its cannon shooting at the sky. Abruptly, the energy vanished. The war-horn issued a long, mourning, hateful wail that cut off sharply. The huge figure of the Banelord was motionless, its limbs splayed. Then it fell, shaking the ground, crushing the remains of *Triumphum Cane*.

Syagrius turned the las turret to the right, training its volleys on one of the approaching Ferals, driving it back. The remaining Warhound and Reaver of his maniple formed up on *Augustus Secutor* once more. The three Titans fired together on the Banelord's escorts, pounding one to burning slag and sending the other's reactor critical. Another nuclear fireball erupted over the battlefield, and its light was cleansing for Syagrius' soul. The Feral had been quite close, and radiation warnings sounded through the decks of the Warlord, but he ignored them. He revelled in the enormous death of the foe, and in the fire that burned all traces of the unclean thing from Katara.

The light was so bright and vast, it seemed that it should swallow all of the enemy in its embrace. It could not. The world-encompassing light was due solely to Syagrius' relative proximity to the explosion. The battle for Therimachus unfolded over miles upon miles of landscape.

But the spectacle of the Feral's demise was a satisfying one. Syagrius' heart swelled with the ecstasy of triumph.

'See them fall!' Syagrius voxed to the demi-legio. The fireball was still the only thing he could see. 'Hold the line, Hunters! Hold the line!'

*'We cannot, marshal,'* Lukretus voxed from *Primum Victor*. *'The line is broken.'*

The fireball faded with his triumph. His vision had narrowed to the immediacy of the fight with the Banelord. He looked at the wider scene now, and he absorbed the full influx of positioning and tactical data in the manifold. The line formation the Imperial Hunters had used to march towards the Iron Skulls was like a moving fortress wall. Each maniple was a strongpoint, and the distance between the maniples could be covered by interlocking fire of devastating intensity. The Iron Skulls showed little discipline in their formations. They could hardly be said to have formations at all. Syagrius intended to roll the wall over the enemy, cutting the traitors apart with a machine created from the collective strength of the demi-legio.

The Iron Skulls attacked with numbers and with rage. The horde of corrupted Titans marched over the land, a monstrous battering ram smashing against the Imperial Hunters' wall. The hills beyond Therimachus were turning into a cratered, smoking graveyard of god-machines. Imperial Hunters and Iron Skulls alike were destroyed. Some of the Titans were still upright. Too massive to fall, they were burning monuments of metal.

And Lukretus was right. The Iron Skulls were breaking through the line. They kept coming, hurling mass and firepower at the maniples. The discipline of the Imperial Hunters was not enough. There were half again as many traitors as there were Hunters. Their attack was not unthinking, Syagrius realised. The Titans towered over the landscape, so there were no defensive positions, and there was no high ground. If ferocity was the soul of the Iron Skulls, it was also the strategy that used the relative strengths of the forces to their advantage. One of the Banelords and clusters of Ravagers had crossed the line. Then they turned back, attacking from a new front.

The shape of the battlefield was changing. The Imperial Hunters were about to be surrounded.

*Change the strategy,* Syagrius thought. *Change it now before it's too late. This is a mistake.*

'Tighten formations,' he voxed. *Make a fist,* he thought. *Batter the traitor with it.* Concentration of force. That was what was needed now. 'Lukretus,' he said, 'can you–'

Light, again, the awful, obliterating flash of a Titan's power plant going critical. A much bigger explosion, this time, from further away yet far more devastating. *Primum Victor* dead, the scream of its machine-spirit a brief but staggering wound through the manifolds of every Titan of the demi-legio. And the blast was so colossal that it killed two more Titans of Lukretus' maniple. The dying roars of the god-machines struck Syagrius' consciousness in the manifold at the same time as their crews shouted their agony and despairing anger over the vox.

A massive hole opened up in the line. The Iron Skulls marched through it and rounded on the other maniples. Syagrius saw what was happening. There was no time now to create the fist. Lukretus had held the centre point of the line. With *Primum Victor* gone, the other maniples were isolated. They were going to be surrounded and cut down one by one.

Syagrius confronted the inevitability of defeat. He tried to deny it. He failed. The knowledge, certain and shameful, entered his heart and its cold flame withered his soul.

Shells hit *Augustus Secutor* from the front and the left flank. The second attack came from the direction of *Primum Victor*'s position. Ahead, another Banelord advanced, its tail cannon already firing again. Syagrius took his Warlord to the right. He struck out at the two foes, he and his moderati fighting as a single, raging, desperate entity. They launched a flight of Apocalypse missiles to the left, trying to hold back the other attacker long enough to deal with the closer one to the fore. The rest of the maniple took on the streams of fire coming from other Iron Skulls.

Plasma annihilator and las turret blazed again. *Fall, damn you, fall,* Syagrius thought. He willed the Banelord to die under his first salvo.

It did not.

'I don't like this symmetry,' Rekorus said, his voice rasping with strain. *Augustus Secutor* had killed the first Banelord in a crossfire. Now the same trap closed around it.

'Nor do I,' Syagrius said. 'So we'll break it. Forwards, full speed.' He would ram the foe if he had to.

The enemy on the left emerged from the firestorm created by the destruction of *Primum Victor*. It was another Banelord. Tail and left arm cannons blazed. Flights of missiles blackened the air. They hit at the same time as the forward enemy's salvo. The traitors walked through the counter fire of *Magnificum Virum* and *Arma Dominus*. The double barrage hit *Augustus Secutor*. Rockets slammed down on the Warlord's cowling. Warp-tainted light erupted before Syagrius' eyes. The void shields imploded.

An enormous projectile hit the Warlord's right leg. Worse than the damage data that rushed into the manifold was the awful sense of *looseness* that Syagrius felt when he had his god-machine take another step. It seemed his own right leg wanted to fall off. *Augustus Secutor* walked, but the grinding of the worsening injury sent vibrations through its entire hull. The Warlord's gait was awkward. It listed to the right.

*How many more steps?* Syagrius wondered. *Let there be enough. Throne, let there be enough.*

*'The shields...'* Magos Prendivian voxed.

'I know,' Syagrius snapped.

*'We might not get them back.'*

'Get them back. Do it *now!*' The energy readings of the two Banelords were spiking. Another barrage was imminent.

*Augustus Secutor* and the forward Banelord were only a few hundred yards apart. Black smoke billowed from the cracked armour plating of the traitor. It came on with the dark cloud of its wounds surrounding it. Infernal energy arced up and down its limbs and torso. The eyes in its horned head blazed the crimson of hate. Its power claw opened and closed like a hungry maw.

Syagrius leaned forwards, pulling at the mechadendrites, as if he could reach the traitor faster. Fires were breaking out in the conduits and halls of the Titan. His second body was bleeding, but he would preserve its honour. He would smash the trap. He was an Imperial Hunter, and he would turn the Iron Skulls back into prey once more.

The air outside the Warlord flickered as the void shields came back up. They were weak. They were enough for more time. 'Everything,' Syagrius breathed, and below his throne, and in their carapace compartments, the moderati echoed him. *'Everything,'* they said, and *Augustus Secutor* blasted the Banelord with its entire arsenal. The Iron Skull unleashed its fury at the same time. The Titans walked into a maelstrom of energy, shells, las and missiles. Katara vanished from Syagrius' senses, swallowed by the cataclysm. His jaw was rigid with his scream of defiance and pain. There was nothing except fire and blood. *Augustus Secutor* walked through a holocaust, and it was burning; its flesh was being flayed from its body. Armour plating buckled. Electrical surges exploded throughout its systems. The machine-spirit's pain flashed down the mechadendrites. Rekorus went into a seizure. White agony burst in Syagrius' head. His sense of the god-machine's body receded. A fatal numbness crept into his limbs. He clung to consciousness and to his grip on the Warlord with the determination that came with a final act.

The storm ended. Syagrius saw the world once more. *Augustus Secutor* and the Banelord were within a few steps of each other. The Iron Skull was wreathed in flames. The cannon of its left arm was a ruin, the barrel exploded by the Warlord's plasma blast. It had to drag its right leg forwards. But its wrath was undiminished, and its power claw heaved back in preparation for the great blow.

'Hit it again!' Syagrius shouted. 'Everything! Again!' He tasted blood in his mouth. He was shouting at himself more than the moderati, and he was demanding the impossible. The Sunfury's drain on the Warlord's power plant was enormous. The las turret sustained its steady burst of fire. The other weapons could not fire again. Not just yet.

But he needed them now.

'Everything,' Syagrius gasped, and then the other Banelord hit *Augustus Secutor*'s flank with another barrage. There were no shields this time to mitigate the damage at all. The left half of Syagrius' body felt as if it were on fire. The plasma annihilator died before it could recharge. Syagrius tried to move the Warlord forwards. He could not. The right leg moved, still loose, still grinding. But the left was immobile.

'Magos,' he yelled for Prendivian.

There was no answer.

The Banelord took one more step. Its war-horn sounded a call of blood triumph. It brought the power claw down. The blow was savage and devastating. The claw flashed as it struck. It punched through the upper left torso of *Augustus Secutor*. The Banelord thrust upwards with the claw, and it came out the top of the cowling, ruptured hydraulics trailing from its grip. It ripped the Apocalypse launcher from the carapace, and hurled it into the distance. The Warlord's left flank was motionless. Syagrius went numb on that side of his body. He could not lift his arm from its rest on the throne. He felt half his face sag.

'We are not dead yet!' he shouted. The defiance felt empty. His lips could not form the words properly. There was smoke in the compartment. Rekorus was unresponsive. Trovalis grunted in acknowledgement, and that was all.

Syagrius saw the lie at the centre of his words. He could still control the las turret, and he fired point-blank at the Banelord.

There were voices on the vox. They came to Syagrius from a great distance, echoes from the other Titans of the Imperial Hunters. There were still two Warlords, weren't there? Did he hear their princeps calling to him? Or did the scratching sounds come from *Aurea Exterminator* and *Sacra Canis*? Where were the Reaver and the Warhound? His senses in the manifold were confused. His awareness was swamped by the anguish of the machine-spirit. *Augustus Secutor* demanded satisfaction for its injuries. Its pride required the utter destruction of its foe. But it could barely move. Its strength had been taken from it. It howled at the edge of madness.

The las turret fired, and the burst lasted less than a second. The second Banelord reached *Augustus Secutor*. It hammered the back of the Warlord with its power claw. Once, twice, the tolling of a terminal bell, and with the third blow it drove through plating and into the heart of the god-machine. Syagrius' chest exploded with pain. *Augustus Secutor*'s war-horn blasted one more time. It sounded across the battlefield and the roofs of Therimachus. It was a call for vengeance, a roar against fate, and it was a cry of final despair. Then the Warlord's power shut down. The manifold blinked out of existence. The sudden blankness threw him fully into the flesh world. The mechadendrites, inert, became chains imprisoning him upon the throne. Trovalis was screaming. His eyes had rolled back, and blood poured from his ears.

Syagrius flailed in his throne. His right fist pounded against the rest. He managed to jerk free of the mechadendrites and fell, bloody, to the deck. He looked up through the eyes of the Titan for the last time. He wanted to speak, to spit at the foe, to die unbowed. The sounds that came from his lips were not words. They were unformed moans.

He saw the Banelord reach out with its claw once again. It stabbed into *Augustus Secutor* below the skull. Sawing vibrations shook the deck beneath him. Metal shrieked until he shrieked too, in a futile attempt to blot out the noise. Then there was movement. He was rising, and the skull of the Warlord was tilting forwards.

The Banelord had decapitated its foe. It held the skull aloft in its power claw. Syagrius rolled forwards and fell against the armourglass window. He stared down into the boiling red of the Banelord's eyes.

The power claw began to close. The walls pushed in on Syagrius. In his last moments, when all pride was gone and he had nothing left except his helpless anger and despair, words crept in on his consciousness. They were as lethal as the tonnes of metal coming to crush his body, and more terrible yet because they came to devour his soul. They were fiery as brass.

*Skulls for the skull throne.*

# CHAPTER 11
# THE KLIVANOS CROSSING

Vansaak descended from *Gloria Vastator* and approached Krezoc while she was starting to outline how the demi-legio would approach Therimachus. Krezoc saw her waiting to one side and acknowledged her with a nod. 'You have something to report, moderati?' she asked.

'Grave news from Therimachus,' said Vansaak. She stepped forwards. '*Augustus Secutor* has fallen. Marshal Syagrius is dead.'

No one said anything at first. Krezoc waited, letting the implications sink in, giving all present the chance to process what had happened for themselves. 'Any word of the battle?'

'It is not going well.' She paused for a moment, then said, 'The Iron Skulls will take Therimachus.'

'How soon?'

'Unknown. But they will. I was speaking with Princeps Spinther of *Magnificum Virum*. There are two Warlords left, and they are badly damaged. The outcome,' she carefully avoided saying *defeat*, 'is not in doubt.'

'I see. Contact Princeps Spinther again. Tell him we are coming. We will be there by sunset tomorrow.'

Deyers gaped. He started to say something, but checked himself, waiting for Vansaak to depart. Krezoc fixed him with a stare, warning him to hold his tongue for now. Then she turned to the princeps of the Imperial Hunters, Carrinas of the Reaver *Nobilis Arma* and the two Warhound officers.

'We mourn with you in your loss,' she told them. 'Marshal Syagrius was a great warrior. There can be no doubt that he took many of the enemy down with him.'

Carrinas nodded his thanks. The other two said nothing. Their faces were riven by grief and anger. Krezoc thought she saw resentment there, too. That was natural. With Syagrius' death, she was the senior officer of the battle group, and its leadership fell to her. The Imperial Hunters had been resentful additions to her demi-legio, arrogant in the presumption of their superiority. It had seemed to Krezoc that they saw it as their role to somehow monitor the Pallidus Mor, to make sure Syagrius' orders were carried out, and to report back when they were not. Now they had lost their commander. They had been part of the bloody victories at the Kazani bridge and at Deicoon, and now learned that their parent legio was going down to defeat. Krezoc had no intention of taking advantage of the power shift as long as they did not force her to. They had followed her orders this far, though. She trusted they would continue to do so. This was the moment, then, to show what respect she could for Syagrius.

*You were a fool,* she thought. *Why did you think this strategy was the correct one?*

Then she saw Deyers' expression again, and she understood. Syagrius had answered the same call the Kataran Spears had. He had come to destroy the enemy, but also to preserve Katara. Perhaps he had heard the plea for aid more clearly than she had.

*If he did,* she thought, *that was the mistake.* The depth of the corruption saw to that. If salvation was possible, it was only through destruction. She was tasked with the defeat of the Iron Skulls. If Katara was reduced to a cinder in the struggle, she would mourn for the world, but she would not shirk from doing whatever was necessary, no matter how painful.

Still addressing Carrinas, Krezoc said, 'I know your first thought is for your comrades at Therimachus. The route I propose is the fastest way of reaching them.' *If any are alive by then,* she thought but did not add.

'We appreciate that,' Carrinas said.

'But the Klivanos Plain…' said Deyers.

'There is no other route,' Krezoc said. 'We take this path, or there is no point.'

'What point? The crossing is impossible.'

'No. Crossing the chasm that has been created in the coastal highway is impossible. Traversing the plain is possible.'

'Unpleasant, though,' Rheliax said with grim humour. 'This will be a war in itself.'

'True,' Krezoc said. 'And the land will be the enemy. But we can defeat it.'

Deyers was shaking his head. 'In Titans, maybe. In tanks… Princeps Krezoc, I'm doubtful.'

'Not certain, though?' Before he could answer, she went on. 'I know exactly what I'm proposing, captain. I know what it means to all our forces. Yes, the Titan crews will be above the worst of the flames. Yes, your troops will be closer. Then there is the stability of the ground. What do you think will happen to a Titan if the crust gives way?' When Deyers was silent, Krezoc turned her head to take in all the officers before her. 'Princeps Rheliax is absolutely correct. This will be a war. We will have losses. It is also a battle as necessary as any of the others we have fought.'

'We must,' Carrinas said, grief underlying his urgency.

'There is another consideration,' said Venterras.

'Yes,' the Peltast Alpha Trigerrix added. 'Crossing on foot will not be possible.'

Krezoc nodded. There were environments that even the augmented, armoured secutarii could not survive. The readings sent down from the *Nuntius Mortis* showed conditions worthy of a death world. 'We won't be needing infantry support during the crossing itself,' she said. 'The secutarii will be transported. Alpha Venterras, Alpha Trigerrix, I will ask that you divide your forces between those who will travel in the Titans and those who will accompany the Sixty-Sixth.' She glanced at Deyers. 'The mutual aid could prove useful, wouldn't you say, captain?'

'It could,' he conceded, clearly not convinced that Krezoc hadn't ordered mass suicide.

'Good,' Krezoc said, seizing on the letter of his words and ignoring their spirit. 'Then we should begin.'

The Company of the Bridge did not venture far into the city. As yet, that was impossible. The streets were deep in lava. The individual firestorms had coalesced into a single hurricane of fire that consumed most of the sectors surrounding the caldera. Ornastas took his troops to the wall. There was a battle to be won there, and that was good enough, for now. This was the start, the beachhead. Here was where the reclaiming of Deicoon would begin.

They had climbed the nearest portion of the ruined wall. It was a heap of broken rockcrete a few hundred yards long. It was wide, and the top was like a sea of stone, with waves of rubble cresting in storm. Hundreds of figures fought each other along its length. The battle was as savage as it was primitive. There were no firearms. The combatants attacked each other with chunks of rockcrete and rebar, and with their bare hands. At first, Ornastas had trouble telling the difference between heretic and loyalist, and that disturbed him. If there was only chaos in the battle, if it had degenerated to the point where violence fuelled violence and there was no goal except blood, then he had been wrong to come back.

All the people here were in rags, and all were bloody. Ornastas paused at the top of the slope. He raised his arms, holding back his troops. *Father of Mankind*, he thought, *do not abandon this city. Do not abandon this world. We fight for you still. Show me the way.* And he saw there were still differences. The heretics bore ritual scars. Many of them had icons of brass or necklaces of skulls around their necks. The people who fought them screamed in anger, but Ornastas could also see fear and determination on their faces. They had not fallen yet.

He lowered his arms and sent his followers into the fray. 'See the enemy!' he shouted. 'Know them by the signs of their heresy!' Then he rushed to join the struggle.

Within seconds, he knew he had made the right choice. The Company of the Bridge was greeted by an energised roar from the beleaguered faithful. He waded deeper into the maelstrom, smashing his staff from side to side, crushing ribs and dealing out paralysing electrical shocks. Every breath was pain, ash scraping his lungs. But every step was another small victory, another step down the path of holy service to the God-Emperor. He fought in swirling clouds of smoke and stinging ashfall. In the wavering light, crimson slashed with streaks of black, the faithful and the heretics more than a few yards away from him became indistinguishable silhouettes, the conflict reduced to abstract shapes, a murderous dance of violence and retribution. Because that, he knew, was the essence of the struggle. The heretics fought for the bloodshed alone. Through it, they were engaged in an unholy communion with their dark god. The faithful refused to be sacrifices. They refused to surrender their city. They refused to abandon the God-Emperor.

In their adamantine stand, Ornastas found the wellspring of hope. It would have been easy to despair. That so many citizens of Katara had been corrupted was dishonour greater than any Ornastas had seen in his life. He could not pretend they were invaders. The sickness had grown beneath the surface of the cities, and it had called the Iron Skulls to Katara. The reckoning for the people's sins was long from complete. But the corruption was *not* complete. There were people left to fight the heretic. And they would triumph. He would see to that.

A cultist leapt for his throat. Ornastas reared back and caught the man in the neck with his staff. The man fell. Ornastas held him in place, jabbing the staff into the wretch's chest. The heretic squirmed like the insect he was. Wracking coughs shook Ornastas' frame and his grip on the staff weakened. A figure ran at him through the smoke. It became a woman, her face covered in blood, her clothes flaking from burns. She held a block of rockcrete over her head with both hands. Ornastas tensed, but could not stop coughing. The woman brought the block down on the cultist's head, crushing it to pulp. Crouching, she looked up at Ornastas. 'Confessor,' she rasped, 'you bring the light of the Emperor with you.' She smiled, and tears streaked the blood on her face. Then she seized another piece of rubble and took off into battle again.

There was a large slab a few yards to Ornastas' right. It was canted, its side angled sharply upwards. Ornastas ran to the slab and scrambled up. Balanced on the edge, he looked down at the battle before him. The Company of the Bridge had turned the tide decisively. The heretics were in retreat. The army of the faithful had grown again. Something almost like order had come to the broken wall. The crowd before him moved with focus, not madness. The people were renewed with hope. As they took down the remaining heretics, Ornastas heard prayers and chants.

The coughing fit passed. He gave thanks for the reclamation he saw before him. In another few moments, this portion of the wall, this broken piece of the city, would belong to the light of the Emperor once more.

A war-horn sounded, its overwhelming blast a second gale that blanketed the city. Ornastas hunched, then stood tall in the colossal cry, ecstatic in the strength of the servants of the Emperor. After the war-horn came the long thunder of Titans on the march, the hum and roar of their power plants punctuated by the concussive tremors of their footsteps. The Pallidus Mor had begun its march. Ornastas craned his head back to take in the walking mountain of *Gloria Vastator*. The blast of its war-horn felt like a salute, and he took a knee before the god-machine. The captured hill of rubble erupted in cheers. The Company of the Bridge, grown even larger, celebrated the Titans. The people stood atop ruins, breathing ash, their skin baking in the heat of the lava-filled streets, and they knew joy in this moment. They were ready for sacrifice, complete and total sacrifice, in the cause of the holy war. They drew strength and courage from the immensity of the god-machines. A city of war walked before them, and it too was heading to sacrifice. Ornastas didn't know what conditions held at Therimachus. Nor did his followers. But they had all seen the size of the traitor battle group.

Katara might be doomed. The victory Ornastas felt now might be brief. The journey into flames might be nothing more than a journey onto a funeral pyre. If that were so, then he would die with a glad heart, because he marched for the Emperor.

He did not believe Katara would fall. He had too much faith for that.

He watched the Pallidus Mor move off until the demi-legio was lost in the swirl of the ashfall. Then he lowered his eyes from the heavens of the gods to the ground and the task before him. He turned around, scanning the chunks of wall on either side of the rampart the company had taken. *Take the wall*, he thought. *Create a ring of purity around the city, and then move in.*

Across a gap a hundred yards wide, there was another tumbled mass, larger than the one where Ornastas stood. Portions of a manufactorum complex had collapsed against the wall, creating an irregular plateau of rubble. A large gathering had appeared on its surface. The figures were motionless, facing towards Ornastas and his company. They were too far away from him to make out any details. He didn't need to. Their anger thrummed across the intervening space. One silhouette stood out at the head of the crowd, separate from the others.

A leader.

*You*, Ornastas thought. *You are the one. You will be held responsible.*

'Look,' Ornastas shouted to the company. 'Look!' He pointed with this staff. 'There! He faces us! There is the betrayer of Deicoon!'

There was nothing else he needed to say. Everyone felt the call as he did. Shouts and prayers and song melding into a thunder of faith, the Company of the Bridge charged down from the hill, racing to war and to justice.

*'Look on the walls,'* Krezoc's voice said over the vox. She was speaking to the entire battle group.

Deyers did as she asked. As *Bastion of Faith* rumbled past Deicoon's broken defences, he saw the ecclesiarch's improvised army in combat, overwhelming cultists and adding to its ranks. The people were mad, he thought. They had escaped the destruction of the city only to plunge back into it. There was nothing to save. *Why are they throwing their lives away?*

*'There is our model,'* Krezoc said. *'They march into the fire. Knowingly. They do it because they must. We will do the same.'*

'How can they do it knowingly if they're mad?' Deyers muttered.

'Your presumption is incorrect, captain,' Venterras said. He was riding with the Leman Russ and had chosen, for the time being, to sit on its hull. He crouched on the turret behind Deyers' hatch as he spoke. 'They are not mad.'

Not taking his eyes from the wall, Deyers said, 'Aren't they?'

'Look,' was all Venterras said.

The patchwork army was victorious. They controlled their ruin. They seemed to be bowing now towards the passing battle group.

'That is a first victory,' Venterras said. 'It will not be the last.'

*Won't it?* Deyers thought. He said, 'So we hope.' He turned to keep watching. He kept his eyes on the ecclesiarch's crusaders until they vanished in the distance. 'Is their example the best we can hope for?' he asked Venterras. 'To fight for what has already been destroyed?'

The secutarii regarded him without expression. Deyers felt like he was speaking to a machine more than a human being. With no change in his inflection, Venterras said, 'If that is what we must do, will you refuse to do it?'

'Of course not,' Deyers snapped. He looked forwards again. The Titans were leading the march. As the battle group swung around the perimeter of Deicoon, Deyers was able to make out the glow of the fires on the Klivanos Plain. There were mountains ahead, and a wide cleft between the east and west chains. The Pallidus Mor marched towards the gap and the red aurora beyond. 'Is it wrong for me to wish to save my world?'

'Is this not what we are engaged upon?'

'I don't know,' said Deyers. He waved back at Deicoon. 'I don't know that we saved anything there. I don't know that a suicidal run to a battle that is already lost is serving a useful purpose.'

'I did not hear you propose an alternative course of action.'

'No,' Deyers admitted. *Because there isn't one,* he thought. Even so, he resented the prospect of a useless death for himself and his troops.

Machine-like though Venterras was, he seemed to read Deyers' thoughts. 'There is no other way, captain,' he said. 'If we took weeks to arrive at Therimachus, that would be futile. This strategy is the only valid one.'

'Then we must follow it,' Deyers said, without enthusiasm.

He had done his best to sound committed to the plan when he had explained it to the regiment. Either he was too transparent or the scale of the folly was too apparent. There had been no mutiny, but the unhappiness of the Spears was palpable. Deyers looked back at the column of tanks following *Bastion of Faith*. He wondered how many of their number would reach the far side of the Klivanos Plain.

The battle group moved through the wide pass. The mountains rose up on either side of the tanks. Midway through, the ground, which had been rising steadily since Deicoon, began to drop again. Two hours later, the cleft ended suddenly, and the hell of the Klivanos stretched ahead.

The plain was wide and long. The crossing would be hundreds of miles long. Deyers could see no more than a mile ahead, sometimes less. Fire roared over the plain in sheets. Geysers of burning promethium vomited flame to the heavens. Wherever Deyers looked, he saw fire. Smoke choked the sky, turning the late afternoon into full night. The terrain was a rocky crust that Deyers did not trust for a second. It looked brittle, a shell covering an inferno. It was webbed with cracks glowing an angry red. Warring winds roared across the plain, creating cyclones of fire where they collided. Huge lakes of promethium burned like suns. Their flames, hundreds of feet high, waved back and forth in the hurricane winds of their own creation. The breath of the Klivanos blew into Deyers' face. His eyes dried instantly. When he breathed, his lungs shrivelled in his chest.

There was no obvious way forwards. There were gaps between the burning fountains, but they were filled without warning by huge billows of flame roaring in from the lakes. Deyers bit back a howl of despair. This was madness. The crossing was doomed before it began. The tormented, screaming landscape became all of Katara for him. It was the entire world, consumed by holocaust, a hell of rock and flame. There could be no salvation here. There was only death.

This was the end of hope.

'How can we cross this?' he said. His body was numb with horror.

'We cross it inside,' said Venterras. The secutarii straightened up. He stood over Deyers, waiting for him to descend through the hatch.

Deyers nodded. He climbed down the ladder. Venterras followed and sealed the hatch. Inside, Platen looked ashen. There would be nothing for her to shoot here. She and Deyers would be helpless to govern their fate during the crossing. Medina, at least, would be active.

'Follow the Titans,' Deyers told Medina. 'Let them find the route of solid ground.'

'Yes, captain.' He didn't sound any happier than Platen looked.

Deyers braced himself against a bulkhead. He thought it already felt warm. The engine idled while Medina waited for the Pallidus Mor to begin its advance. Beyond that low growl, outside the hull, Deyers listened to the greater rumble of the Titans, the muffled howl of the wind and the endless, thrumming bellow of the flames.

Then Medina engaged the gears. There was a jerk, and *Bastion of Faith* led the regiment into the inferno.

*Gloria Vastator* took the lead. 'We are the symbol,' Krezoc said to her moderati. 'We are the hope, for all behind us, that the Klivanos can be crossed.'

'Unless we fall,' said Grevereign.

'Was that meant to be funny?' Vansaak asked.

'I'm not sure,' Grevereign admitted.

'It is,' Krezoc said dryly. 'It's also true. If we fall, Princeps Drahn and Rheliax will take up the role.'

'And the Pallidus Mor will cross,' Grevereign said, not joking now.

Krezoc nodded. The fatalism of the Pallidus Mor was not defeatism. It was the acceptance of the worst as the cost of victory.

Her consciousness filled with the single task of walking through flames as high as the Warlord's legs. Freed of the need to operate the weapons, the wills of the moderati majoris and, in their carapace pods, the moderati minoris, bolstered hers. She had an even more heightened awareness of the Titan's body. She felt it more keenly than she did her own. Her control over its every movement was acute. She knew exactly what speed she must assign to each step so she could place the foot on the uncertain ground with the maximum of care. Magos Thezerin directed the entire auspex array to the analysis of the terrain's stability, reading the ground for micro-tremors and heat blooms suggestive of a thin crust.

Though they moved with the maximum care and precision of control, every step was a gamble, and every completed stride a victory. Yet the Warlord's gait was smooth. The pauses between strides were minute. The data flowed through the manifold into Krezoc's single-minded awareness, and though her decisions were made on a rational basis, they happened with the speed of instinct.

*Gloria Vastator* waded through the sea of flame. The fires roared around its hull. They wreathed the pillars of its legs. The Titan stepped over geysers, and the fountains raged upwards, burning the legio banners. The ground cracked. It sank under the god-machine's tread. It did not collapse. The Warlord moved further and further onto the plain. Soon, Krezoc had to depend almost entirely on the auspex. Outside *Gloria Vastator*'s head, she could see nothing except the waves and vortices of the conflagration. Storms of flame raged against the Titan, grasping upwards for its head. The ground was almost invisible. Now and then the orange tide would part long enough to reveal the wounds below. The terrain resembled an expanse of scabs broken by fresh injuries. *Gloria Vastator* blazed the trail. The rest of the Pallidus Mor followed in its footsteps. Nothing was taken for granted. The crews of every god-machine subjected the ground to the same analysis.

But the land was the enemy. The land was treacherous. The land shifted.

*Canis Gladio*, in Rheliax's maniple, was the last of the Titans ahead of the Kataran 66th. The Warhound followed the path of *Crudelis Mortem*. Deyers had crowded in behind Medina's seat, peering through the driver's viewing block at the burning plain, and when the collapse began, his brain had trouble processing what he was seeing. The Warhound canted suddenly to the left. Its leg sank into the ground. A colossal fireball rose around it, and then it dropped out of sight. A wave of promethium washed outwards from where the Titan had been. Medina braked. There was no way to evade the wave. The wall of liquid fire rushed at *Bastion of Faith*. It hit, and Deyers saw nothing but fire. The tank shook with the impact. It slid to one side. The heat inside, already intolerable, increased. When the wave exhausted its force, there was a deep, continuous, ominous cracking, loud enough to be heard through the hull.

The Leman Russ was drenched with promethium. Flames licked over the viewing block. There was nothing to see. Medina could not move forwards. And the cracking was growing louder. Deyers lunged for the hatch.

'Captain?' said Platen.

'No choice,' Deyers said. He could feel the warmth of the wheel through his gloves as he turned it. 'We have to see where to go.' He took a deep breath, held it and opened the hatch.

The heat was so intense he almost let his breath out. A shallow stream of fire ran by the Leman Russ and down the line of the regiment, licking halfway up the tanks' hulls. Ahead, there was a heaving lake where *Canis Gladio* had stood. The ground was crumbling at the edges, cracks spreading wider and wider, reaching out to the other Titans beyond and to the Spears. The Warhound's mega-bolter arm thrust up from the lake for a moment, then vanished beneath the surface. More waves splashed ashore, thrown outwards by explosions in the depths.

Deyers looked left and right. There was a wider stretch

of ground between the new lake and the nearest geyser on the right. And still the crust was breaking off and falling into the burn. The searing wind gusted against Deyers' face, and a roiling cloud of flame, fifty feet high, rushed off the pit towards him. He half fell down the ladder, slamming the hatch after him as he dropped.

'Right!' he shouted to Medina. 'Go right, then ahead. Can you see yet?'

'Clearing a bit,' said Medina. 'I can see a dark patch.'

'That's it. Head for that and swing around the collapse.'

*And pray to the Emperor the ground holds.*

The reports of losses filtered into Krezoc's consciousness. They were unwelcome distractions from her focus on finding *Gloria Vastator*'s path, but they could not be ignored. The Klivanos Plain laid siege to the battle group. It was a war of attrition. The flames and the treason of the earth ate away at the column. It sought to halt their progress. Krezoc's responsibility was to see that the march did not stop. She had known the losses would come. She had prepared herself for them, as she did for any campaign.

But this was different. The enemy could not be destroyed. It could not be conquered. There was no retaliation possible. Morale was as much a casualty as flesh and metal. *Canis Gladio* was the first to die. Its destruction took a toll on the Kataran 66th. Most of the regiment made it past the lake of fire, but a second collapse, triggered by the first, linked the lake to the geyser as the last of the heavy armour passed. Two Leman Russes and a Basilisk artillery tank sank into the fire.

Hours later, the ground became even more porous. It broke apart, part sand, an incinerating marsh. *Gloria*

*Vastator*'s feet sank into ten feet and more of promethium. The auspex readings were a confusion of heat. There was no clear path. Krezoc marched the Warlord forwards, risking greater depths. Burning waves radiated outwards from its legs.

'The Spears can't cross this,' she said to her moderati. 'They need a route.' She could not seek one. That would draw too much of her focus away from her Titan's steps. Grevereign and Vansaak, though, could look, if only briefly.

'On the right,' Grevereign said after a minute. 'Five hundred yards away. Looks like a ridge. It might be more solid.'

'Good. Relay the data back to Captain Deyers.' *Gloria Vastator* marched on through flames that reached almost as high as its head. In the manifold, Krezoc registered the steady stream of heat readings and accumulations of minor damage. Thezerin knew better than to report on their status and the risks they were taking. There was no choice but to walk, descending further and further into the crucible of the plain.

Krezoc lost track of time. It was night now. Beyond that, she had little sense of how long the battle group had been amidst the flames, or how far there was to go. What she knew was the necessity to march, and not to stop, for any reason.

From the ridge through the marsh, Deyers voxed and pleaded with her to wait. '*Our tanks are getting bogged down in marshy ground,*' he said. '*If the Pallidus Mor gets much further ahead, we will lose sight of our path.*'

'Is the column blocked by the trapped vehicles?'

'*No. They're towards the rear. The ground was in bad shape for them.*'

'Can you free them?'

*'Without being able to get out of our tanks, I don't think we can.'*

'Leave them.'

*'Princeps…'*

'Rescue the crews if you can, but we do not stop. Neither do you. To stop is to die, captain.'

*'If the crews leave their vehicles…'*

'That is their only choice. I am not being cruel. This is our situation. Keep moving, captain. Keep us in sight or get left behind. That is your choice.'

Because really, she knew, there was no choice at all. She had to make Deyers understand this too. When he started to protest again, she cut the link. A few minutes later, she voxed Rheliax. 'Are the Spears moving?'

*'They are.'*

'Good.' Deyers had received her message.

Onwards, through fire, onwards on ground that sank and erupted and cracked. Onwards, through a world in eternal cry. *Gloria Vastator* marched through the destruction, its pace relentless. The erupting plain battered it with wind and fire, and could not slow its advance.

Krezoc did not see the trap when it came. It was too well hidden by the flames. *Gloria Vastator* was moving through another erupting swamp. The Warlord's left leg came down. It sank through ten feet of promethium to the soft ground below, as Krezoc expected. Then the ground was a shell over a cavern, and it gave way. The leg dropped thirty feet. The Warlord leaned suddenly to the left. It came to rest at a sharp angle, almost toppling over. The lake of fire rushed to fill the cavern. Flames embraced the Titan's torso as though it were a burning log.

Krezoc gasped. The immobilisation of the Warlord hit her like a shock maul. Pain flared behind her eyes. She bore down on her focus and read every detail of the damage and what movement was possible before pulling back to consider what must be done.

'Maniple!' she shouted into the vox. 'Cease advance! All units, go around us. Princeps Drahn, the lead is yours.' She waited for the acknowledgments, dreading that the cave-in might catch the Reaver and Warhounds following on *Gloria Vastator*'s heels, drowning them in the depths of the promethium. She breathed more easily when she received confirmation of the escort pulling back.

*'How can we assist?'* Drahn asked.

'By moving on,' Krezoc said. 'Do not approach us. Do not risk multiplying losses.' The brutal arithmetic she had forced Deyers to follow applied to her Titan as well.

She consulted with Thezerin. 'Magos, you concur that free movement is possible only with the right arm and carapace turrets?'

*'I do, princeps. We have no leverage for the legs. The left arm has limited range before the barrel falls beneath the surface of the promethium.'*

Krezoc thought for a moment. 'Extrapolate consequences of the following course of action,' she said, and sent a datapack to the tech-priest.

Thezerin responded almost immediately. *'Extrapolation is equivalent to speculation in this instance, princeps. The available data is insufficient to make qualified predictions.'*

'Speculate, then.'

*'Unnecessary. No other course of action is open to us.'*

'I agree. Thank you, magos.' Choice, she thought, was a rare luxury for the Pallidus Mor. Over and over and over again, in the legio's history, the apparently hard decision had not really been a decision at all.

She voxed Drahn again. 'Give us a very wide berth,' she said. 'There will be weapons fire.'

*'The Omnissiah guide your aim,'* said Drahn. *Gloria Vastator* jerked and settled closer to the burning surface.

'If the ground gives way any more…' Vansaak began.

'I know,' said Krezoc. 'We're about to find out if it will.' She turned to Grevereign. 'Moderati,' she said, 'we are going to bring the fight to the enemy.'

Grevereign turned around to look back and up at her from his throne. 'The enemy will be very displeased, I think.'

'I'm counting on it.'

'The Belicosa at this range?' Vansaak said.

'The Vulcan is on the wrong side,' Krezoc said. 'It can't reach the targeted zone, and the Apocalypse missiles lack the precision. Moderati Grevereign, are you ready?'

'I am. Weapon charged.'

Krezoc rotated the volcano cannon's turret until the barrel was almost parallel with the Titan's right leg. She kept enough of an angle that it was still aiming forwards, enough that the proximity of the blast would be within the tolerances of the Warlord's armour. Thezerin was still streaming auspex data to her through the manifold. The tech-priest isolated what information she could about the state of the ground beneath the shallow lake of promethium. Krezoc adjusted her aim again. She looked at the wall of flame through the armourglass eyes of the Titan, and braced herself, gripping hard on the arms of her throne.

The gun fired. The las vaporised the promethium. It

melted the ground beneath, instantly creating a new cavern where none had been before. Molten rock and liquid flame fell into the new pit. The explosion pushed out for hundreds of yards from *Gloria Vastator*'s epicentre. The entire subsurface trembled and dropped. In the midst of searing light, in an all-consuming eruption of its own creation, the Warlord dropped further onto shifting rubble. It righted itself as it sank further into the flames. When it stopped moving, it was almost up to its chest in the fire. Krezoc angled the turrets upwards during the descent, and the barrels were still above the level of the promethium.

*'Interior fires,'* Thezerin warned. *'The breaches are happening faster than the crews can seal them.'*

'Then we must rise above,' Krezoc said.

The Warlord was in the depression. It could not walk out of it. The Vulcan mega-bolter was free now. Krezoc linked with Haziad in his carapace pod and aimed the gun down at a shallow angle and forward of *Gloria Vastator*. She triggered a sustained burst. The shells punched through the lake, into the ground beneath it. Krezoc moved the Vulcan up and down, directing the fire to shape the land. The auspex reports exploded as the shells cut a swath through the fire, their blasts momentarily exposing more of the ground to the sensors. Thezerin took the data, and now she could extrapolate. She refined the information, sent it to Krezoc, and Krezoc used it to control the barrage. She turned destruction into creation. She hammered the plain into submission, forcing it to mirror her will. When she ceased fire, she had created a rough slope leading up to the higher ground beyond the burning lake.

With a blast of its war-horn, *Gloria Vastator* walked again. Its march was slow, the rubble beneath its tread constantly shifting. But there were no pauses, and the god-machine rose from the burning tomb, shedding cataracts of flame. With the inexorability of a mountain chain thrust upwards by the collision of tectonic plates, it climbed the slope, the ascending conqueror. When it reached the level ground, Krezoc sounded the war-horn again. The answering cries of the rest of the Pallidus Mor welcomed its victory.

Krezoc took *Gloria Vastator* forwards on as direct a path as she could. The arc Drahn had led the demi-legio on to avoid the devastation the volcano cannon unleashed in the subsurface was so wide that the Warlord caught up with the battle group in less than an hour. Drahn slowed the pace of *Fatum Messor*, giving Krezoc the chance to move up once more to the front of the column.

The battle group continued its march to the north. Dawn came, though there was no sign of it through the fire and smoke. The cycles of night and day had no meaning over the Klivanos Plain. It roared in an eternal twilight of red and black. Its attacks were unceasing. It sought to retaliate for its defeat by *Gloria Vastator*. More tanks became bogged down and had to be abandoned. The rage of the plain eroded the armour of the god-machines. Flames found their way inside hulls. The Warhounds, lower and much closer to the fury of the conflagrations, suffered the most. Their gaits became more difficult, each step harder won.

The second day was ending when the ground at last began to slope upwards again. The change was gradual but real. The surface became more solid, less treacherous. The encircling mountain chains slowly came into sight again, though the distance between them was much greater than at the southern entrance to the Klivanos. The fires raged on for mile after mile ahead of the Pallidus

Mor. The nature of the burn began to change. The auspex reported the difference before Krezoc could see it. The firestorm consumed forest, not promethium.

In the hour before sunset, the battle group left the plain behind and entered the trees. Krezoc increased the pace. The god-machines flattened the burning timber. Their passage left behind a firebreak hundreds of yards wide. The Kataran Spears charged down its centre. The tanks with dozer blades moved to the fore, clearing the charred and crushed trunks from the path of the column.

The heat was as intense as over the plain. The temperatures inside the vehicles was intolerable. The reports of unaugmented troops succumbing mounted. But vox-chatter increased too. Krezoc no longer had to second-guess each step, and she listened to the voices of the battle group. From the Kataran Spears, she heard the beginnings of hope. The embers of morale were flaring once more. The plain was beaten. It howled in impotent fury, bereft of further prey. It had injured many of the Titans, but claimed only one of them.

'Moderati, you may resume normal duties,' Krezoc said. *Gloria Vastator*'s weapons powered up. The auspex array scanned the distance for the war the Pallidus Mor had come to find. Distorted echoes of the conflict worked their way through the sheets of flame. They became stronger and more distinct.

The Warlord passed through a final wall of flames. Dark, guttering remnants of the forest gave way to the hills outside Therimachus. Brush fires swept over the grasses. Other flames, from other causes, billowed up from the distant city. The great blaze that had spread from the Klivanos parted like curtains, revealing the hell of war unleashed across the land.

'Sound the charge,' Krezoc commanded the Pallidus Mor. 'Let the traitors know we have come, and bring their reckoning.'

The war-horns of every god-machine howled, and the giants of cold, unwavering death thundered onto the battlefield.

## CHAPTER 12

# THE LAST CITY

Pheon Markos heard the war-horns in his bunker. The sound was too colossal. No being, above or below ground, could avoid hearing it. It carried down the grav lift shaft. Markos jerked away from the tacticarium table and looked up at the ceiling, as if he could see to the surface and know whether he could dare hope again.

There was nothing for him to see. There was plenty to hear, though. There were other sounds that made their way down through the earth to him. Those noises had been coming long before the war-horns. They were the thunder of the breaking of his city. The thunder ran deep. It was massive. It had begun with a few concussions, and very quickly had become almost continuous, a cracking rumble of explosions, impacts, energy discharges and building collapses. The walls and ceiling of the bunker vibrated from the force of the destruction.

Markos looked back at the tacticarium table. He had

watched its display constantly since he had come to the bunker. His eyes ached from the strain. He had barely slept or eaten in the last few days. His obsession was futile. He knew it, but he could not fight it. He despised himself for his cowardice, but he could not fight that, either. His cousins were all dead. So were their cities. He did not have the courage to stand up to the end now it had come for him and Therimachus too.

He watched the war as he hid from it. He watched the clear icons of the Imperial Hunters fall one by one to the larger, less-detailed mass that was the Iron Skulls. He watched as the display on the table became more vague, more approximate, as the chaos of battle engulfed the land and the sensors feeding data to the bunker were overwhelmed or destroyed. Since the Iron Skulls had entered the city, the display had become a hololithic scream. The murder of Therimachus was a smear of overlapping glows. He couldn't make out anything now except catastrophe.

The walls shook again. So did the floor. Markos gripped the table to keep from falling. He hissed through his teeth, clenching them with as much resentment as fear. It wasn't fair. Therimachus was faithful to the Emperor. The heretics had not corrupted the city. Markos had searched for the cult, and he had uprooted it. Therimachus had done its part, and it counted for nothing. He had even warned Marshal Syagrius about the vulnerability of the city. None of his efforts mattered. The Imperial Hunters were defeated. The Iron Skulls were in the city, and the butchery had begun.

The vox-unit to the right of the table buzzed for his attention. It was Sorren, the captain of his honour guard, asking to be admitted to the vault. Markos tapped the control pad attached to the vox, and the massive door rolled back. Sorren entered. 'Governor,' he said, 'I have concerns about the integrity of the refuge.'

Markos began to laugh. Events were reaching the stage where laughter was the only response left to their bitterness. 'What, captain?' he said. 'You mean we won't survive in the long run?'

Sorren grimaced. 'I can't speak to that long run, governor.'

'I think you can. I think all of us can.' Markos glanced upwards again in answer to a swell in the thunder. 'We both know how this ends.'

'We must fight until that end,' said Sorren.

'Or fight to hold it off,' the governor muttered. He shook his head. 'The game is rigged, captain. I'm not playing any longer. We did our part. The Collegia Titanica failed to do theirs. If the war wants me, it will have to come and get me here.' The vault trembled again. Dust fell from the ceiling. 'The bunker was built to withstand war in the city. This will be the safest place to be until the end.'

Sorren nodded, but hesitated before leaving. He looked like he had something else he wanted to say.

'Speak freely, captain,' Markos said. He wasn't about to take offence at anything now. There was no point.

'Governor,' Sorren said, 'is reaching the end what you really wish?'

The question stopped Markos cold. The answers he had thought he knew flew away from him. He thought about what the end would be. Everything he had sworn to serve on Katara destroyed. Dying like vermin in his place of concealment. Cowering in the dark that would surely come, hearing the final poundings of the city's death.

*Is this how you want to die?* That was what Sorren was truly asking.

*I don't want to die at all,* Markos thought. He had done his best for the city. It wasn't fair that he should have to die for the mistakes of others. He had tried to look his death in the face. He found he was afraid. Sealed in the vault, he could pretend, just for a little while longer, that the end, *his* end, was not imminent.

Sorren had broken his illusion.

*You don't want to die, but you will. And soon. So choose your end.*

He thought for a few moments longer. At last, he reached the truth about himself. He was simply too frightened. 'We will remain here,' he said. He was forcing Sorren and the rest of the detachment of the guard to meet the same end with him. Markos knew what he was doing to the man's sense of honour. He hated himself for it. He hated the thought of dying alone even more.

He decided he would leave the door open between the vault and the guard chamber. At least for now.

'I understand,' Sorren said.

If he did, Markos thought, then he was doing a commendable job of keeping the contempt from his voice. Markos doubted he would have been able to do the same, had their positions been reversed.

Sorren walked out of the vault. Markos started to return to the tacticarium table. He took only three steps before the punishment for his cowardice came.

The vault was directly under the governor's palace. A massive barrage hit the building. The thunder above was no longer distant. Markos froze as the roar of explosions went from muffled to acute. The shells seemed to be hitting just above his head. He crouched instinctively. The sound of stone and rockcrete cracking raced towards his heart. He gasped in terror. The impacts kept coming. The thunder and the shattering drew nearer. Markos dropped to his knees. Judgement was descending through the earth to find him.

It arrived. He stared up at the ceiling, and this time there was something to see. The ceiling split in two. Rubble crashed through it. Half the vault collapsed, burying the tacticarium table and the sleeping quarters beneath the weight of the destroyed foundations.

Sorren grabbed Markos under the arm, lifted him to his feet and dragged him from the vault. 'We have to leave, governor!' he shouted.

Markos found his footing again as they crossed the guard chamber. 'How can we get out?' It was his sole thought, sole hope, sole desire. And he didn't believe it was possible. *Trapped, trapped, trapped, trapped*, went the idiot chorus in his head. He was on the knife edge of hysteria.

Sorren didn't answer. He released Markos' arm as the other guards formed up behind them, and ran forwards to the grav lift. The power to the bunker was still on for the moment, but flickering. Sorren opened the door beside the lift. An iron staircase spiralled up a second shaft. 'Quickly,' the captain said, and started up.

Markos hesitated at the doorway. The lumen strips on the sides of the shaft were frequent enough to light the stairs, but the five-hundred-foot ascent was dark with shadows. 'Is this safe?' he asked. The question was stupid, but he had to ask it. He could not contain his fear.

'There is no choice,' Sorren said. His last words were

drowned out by the roar of more of the palace foundations being blown apart by explosives and compacting down on themselves. Vibrations rang through the stairs.

Sorren climbed, and Markos followed.

The spiral was endless. After the first few twists, Markos lost all sense of distance. He was in a limb of dark iron. The bombardments continued, shaking the walls. Cracks webbed their way down the shaft. Markos expected the stairs to tear away from the walls at any moment, throwing him down into the black. His instinct at each tremor was to curl into a ball, close his eyes and wish the world away. But Sorren was moving fast, and so were the guards behind. The pressure kept him moving. So did the terror of being alone.

The higher up the stairs they went, the closer they came to the thunder. It grew sharper and louder. There were no pauses, merely shifts where it seemed to vent its fury at a distance before returning with a vengeance. Markos felt as if he were rising into the centre of a final storm, the one that was unmaking Katara, and he would emerge to a shattered world, its fragments spinning off to the night of the void.

The tremors were violent by the end. A rain of rockcrete chips fell in the shaft, pattering on Markos' hair and shoulders. Dust crusted his eyes. A large chunk bounced back and forth down the stairs and cut his cheek as it passed. His lungs protested. He could barely lift his legs. He would have fallen, but the adrenaline in his veins pushed him on.

At the top of the stairs, a tunnel ran left and right. The left headed towards the heart of the palace. A fall of rubble blocked it barely twenty feet from where Markos stood.

Sorren turned right, pounding down the passage towards the outer wall of the palace. The lumen strips were out here, but there was light ahead. It was irregular, dark red, shifting and flickering. The tunnel was filling with smoke.

Markos followed Sorren closely. Everyone was moving more slowly now, coughing from dust, smoke and exhaustion. The light became more intense. They ran through a red glow, but there was no sign of the exit. The smoke was so thick, Markos could see virtually nothing past the figure of the captain.

Sorren stopped suddenly. Markos almost ran into him. They had arrived at the base of another collapse. Above them was the source of the red light. The roof of the tunnel had been torn open by the cave-in. The flames of Therimachus roared outside and sent their angry light into the shadows.

Sorren signalled for Markos to wait. He climbed the heap of rubble cautiously and scanned the world outside. His shoulders sagged. He looked down, and Markos saw something of his own despair now mirrored in the captain's face. Markos worked his way up. His terror, sustained so long, was giving way to a numbness that spread out to his limbs from his soul. The blunting sensation was a relief. So was the prospect of the open air after the vertical tomb of the shaft.

He reached the top just ahead of the other guards. They sheltered beside a vertical fragment of wall a few paces to the right and downhill from the tunnel roof. The palace had been built upon the highest of many hills of Therimachus, in the western sector of the city. Markos looked down to the south and east, at Katara's last, fatal wound. Huge monsters walked the streets, unleashing madness and flame with weapons that seemed to be the products of sorcery more than technology. They were vast nightmares. Horned, tailed and spined, their eyes burning with hate, they were something other than machines. They were distortions, horrors that should not exist but which imposed their reality upon the world through their very mass and violence. They had spread their force widely through the city. They were everywhere, and where they walked, they spread ruin.

Buildings fell. The wide avenues became seas of flame. Wherever he looked, Markos saw Therimachus savaged, and there was no hope at all. In the distance, near the outskirts, battles seared the night. There were still some Imperial Hunters fighting the traitors, but they were very few. Their efforts meant nothing now.

Markos watched, and his numbness grew thicker, filling his skull. There was nothing he could do. There was nowhere to go. Even Sorren looked slumped, deprived of purpose. They could watch the end take Therimachus. When it came for them, they could run, grasping for those last few pointless seconds of life. As he watched, a new pain cut through the numbness. The Iron Skulls laid waste to the city along definite lines. Something was being enacted. Something was being shaped. About a mile down the slope, where a chapel had once stood, there was now a vast wasteland. It was not empty. It was full of people, a huge crowd of refugees milling there, running from the fires. More and more citizens were pouring into the streets nearby. Already, Markos thought he was looking at a hundred thousand packed into a relatively small area.

Animals herded into a pen, in preparation for the slaughter.

Or perhaps the sacrifice.

And the movements of the Titans cut even more deeply into Markos' spirit. An act more terrible than simple destruction was taking form.

Then a furious roar sounded over the city. It was the cry of many war-horns sounding at once. Markos grabbed the wall to keep from falling. The destroyers of Therimachus ceased their march. Their guns fell silent as they turned, all of them, to face the south east. The blast of the horns went on and on. It was a challenge, and it was the sound of pure, holy, incandescent fury. It served notice to the traitors of punishment. It was as if a scythe blade of unforgiving, skeletal purity swept over the entire city. It burned with unforgiving cold and scoured the numbness from Marcos, cutting him down to the marrow. He saw the night with a new clarity. His unworthiness pierced him to the core. He saw that the Iron Skulls were not the only ones who must be judged.

'The Pallidus Mor has come,' Markos said. It was not hope he and Sorren exchanged in their looks. It was more like the exchange of one fate for another, perhaps a more fitting one. He and the guards watched for the sight of the legio's coming, beyond the city, beyond the suddenly intensifying skirmishes with the Imperial Hunters.

The Iron Skulls began to move again. Half of their number converged as they lumbered towards the edge of the city. The others turned once more to the murder of Therimachus.

Sorren took a pair of magnoculars from one of the guards. 'How did they get here?' he said.

Markos shook his head. They were coming from the direction of the Klivanos Plain, but he had seen its conflagration in hololithic form. They could not have crossed that inferno.

'I see them,' said Sorren. He moved the lenses down slightly. 'There are tanks with them. The Spears are here too.'

They left the ruined wall. They did so with no thought or discussion. Something more profound than instinct pushed them to head down the slope. Markos barely realised what he was doing, at first. The fear had not left him. Nor had the despair. His city was dying, and soon he would be too. But those truths were background. All he thought of now was to reach the 66th. He did not think about how he and the guards could hope to cross that distance. He did not think about getting past the Iron Skulls. There was only the goal, to fly to Katara's warriors, and not to the shadow of the uncaring gods that marched with them.

There were two wars for Therimachus. The only path left for Markos was to become part of the one that was still human. The one where Katara was a name to defend.

He wasn't running towards hope. He was running towards what remained of his home.

On the plateau of rubble at the edge of Deicoon, the righteous and the heretic clashed. For the first time in the war, in a city that was already destroyed, the struggle was an equal contest. The heretics did not have the advantage of surprise, numbers or weaponry. Thousands of cultists fought with the thousands of the Company of the Bridge. Both forces attacked with a mixture of improvised hand weapons and lasrifles. On the uneven, jumbled surface of the rubble, they tore into each other. The heretics attacked with a hunger for naked violence. The company fought with the anger of a people whose world had been betrayed and with the strength that came with their unwavering faith in the God-Emperor.

Ornastas kept his eye on the leader of the cultists as he led the charge from the company's reclaimed portion of the wall. He sensed the other man's focus on him. The heretics fired down on the company, but they did not have the guns to hold Ornastas' followers off the rubble. The company roared up the hill, shouting praise to the Emperor, and slammed into the cultists. The righteous were a great wave, and they forced the heretics back. Ornastas swung his staff like a scythe. Snarling wretches fell before him. His breath came in wrenching, ragged gulps, but purpose kept him moving hard and fast. He was clearing his path to reach the leader.

His nemesis had the same idea. His need to confront Ornastas seemed to be as strong as the confessor's. The tumbled base of a tower rose in the midst of the rubble, and both men made for its prominence, fighting their way through the close-quarter battles and the storm of ash. As they drew nearer to their goal, Ornastas started to make out some details of the man's face. The darkness and the debris-filled air made identification difficult, but Ornastas realised he had seen him before, at a distance. He had been on the Cathedral of Saint Chirosius.

The man shouted orders, and the last dozen yards between Ornastas and the tower were clear. The heretics got out of his way. He grunted. Their leader wanted the duel. Ornastas took what amounted to an invitation. He covered the ground at a run, risking a broken ankle on the shattered surface. He vaulted over a chunk of rockcrete like a man half his age. Destiny gave him strength and speed. He scrambled up the ruined tower as easily as if it were a flight of stairs.

The peak was rounded, with jagged fragments of stone jutting out across its twenty-foot span. He strode onto it at the same time as his opponent. They advanced towards each other. Ornastas held his staff with both hands, ready to swing. The other carried the symbol of his imagined office. It must have been fashioned before the uprising had begun, because it had been constructed with some care. It was a brass spear topped with the skull rune.

They did not rush to attack one another. Ornastas stared at the man, feeling recognition forming at the back of his mind. The heretic was studying him just as fixedly.

They stopped a few paces from each other. They were both coughing from the exertion and the ash. The heretic spoke first. 'Lehrn Ornastas,' he said.

Ornastas frowned. The voice, rasping through the wounds to the throat, was familiar. There was something about the bone structure of the skull that he knew, too, but the mutilations were too extensive. He could not see past the muscle and brass plate to the mask of normality the wretch had once worn.

'Darroban,' the man said.

Ornastas caught his breath. Another name from the past, another officer from his days in the Kataran Spears. They had not been close, but Ornastas knew him. Darroban had led well, though his brutality against the enemies of the Imperium had often seemed motivated by enjoyment rather than duty. He nodded once, acknowledging that he remembered the name. 'You seem proud of your dishonour,' he said.

Darroban snorted. 'Is that supposed to bait me? Yes, I'm proud. I'm proud of what I have done in the service of the Blood God. I'm proud of what is coming.'

'What is coming?' Ornastas asked. This was their moment to speak, to come to full clarity. Each man wanted the other to understand what was happening. Ornastas was conscious of his own vanity, and he accepted it. He would have the traitor know the extent of his crimes, and of his failure, and feel the force of the Emperor's judgement.

'Slaughter,' Darroban said. 'Slaughter so vast that it tears asunder this false dream of reality.' His hands tightened on his spear as he spoke. He was preaching. 'Katara has been chosen. The ritual began in Creontiades. It will be completed at Therimachus. When it is done, the armies of the Skull Throne will flood Katara. A storm is coming. Katara will be its centre.' Darroban looked up to an invisible sky. 'The maelstrom will take system after system. It will be a spiral of blood, Ornastas. You will not see it, but I want you to imagine it. I want you to take this knowledge to your doom.'

'It will never happen,' Ornastas said. 'It has already failed.' He gestured to the cauldron of Deicoon. 'You may have begun a ritual here. It was not completed.'

Darroban shrugged. 'Therimachus will be enough.'

'It will fail there too, just as you have failed. Do you think your god will reward you?'

'I already have my reward,' Darroban said. 'And what of your failure? The war turns at Therimachus, not here. Nothing you can do here matters.'

'Not to the war,' said Ornastas. 'But what I do here matters. I stand for the honour of Katara, heretic. I stand for the Emperor. As for you…'

'As for me, I will take your skull for Khorne.'

They stared at each other in silence for a moment, wrestling with the uncomfortable truths of wounded pride. They had come to the tower as chieftains, proud of their importance. *We don't matter*, Ornastas thought. Darroban was right. The war was elsewhere. It had left them both behind. The survival or death of either man would make no difference to Katara's fate. Darroban had aimed true in telling Ornastas what was planned for Katara. Ornastas' soul bled at the thought that he was helpless to affect his world's fate.

*We don't matter*, he thought again. *Not yet.* Therimachus would not fall. The ritual would not be completed. And when the Iron Skulls were purged from Katara, then the reclamation would begin. Deicoon would matter again. This battle would have meaning.

He saw uncertainty, determination and anger move across Darroban's bloody features. The warlock was wrestling with the same sense of futility.

Ornastas felt a dark gratitude. He and Darroban needed each other in this battle. Each was the other's guarantor of meaning. A leader to destroy, a symbol of triumph in the midst of burning ruin.

And so they raised the symbols of their gods, and attacked.

*'They really don't want us in the city,'* Drahn observed.

The Pallidus Mor was almost within effective range of the enemy. The auspex readings showed the Iron Skulls had formed up at the outskirts to Therimachus, creating a mechanised wall between the Pallidus Mor and the hive. Slightly to the north of the barrier, the last contingent of the Imperial Hunters was engaged with another splinter of the traitors. The Iron Skulls had decided that their goals within Therimachus superseded committing everything to finishing off the foe.

'They don't want us in,' Krezoc agreed, 'and they want to finish their task. They're playing for time. Which means they're worried we can stop them.'

*'From doing what?'* Rheliax wondered.

'From completing another ritual. Can't you feel it?'

Though the hills and towers of Therimachus prevented Krezoc from getting a general sense of the city's layout, she could see enough. The lines of destruction were not random. As in Deicoon, sorcerous energy was building. She felt its pressure in the back of her eyes. The Titan's machine-spirit snarled as the force that had tried to corrupt it once crept forwards again. A potential was growing. Soon all it would need was sufficient blood to ignite a terrible becoming.

*'Disruption, then,'* said Drahn.

'Focused charge on their line,' Krezoc said. 'Maintain a spread for the initial attack. Force them to divide their fire. We will converge our fire on the centre. Close up as we approach, and break through them. We must snap their spine here.

'Secutarii,' she continued, 'the traitors don't have their infantry here. You are not escorts now. Attack where and how you can.'

The secutarii travelling in the Titans had disembarked as soon as the battle group had emerged from the burning forest. They had a nimbleness and flexibility of attack that could be of use now. She paused for a moment. 'Captain Deyers, you are with us?'

*'We are.'* Anger gave his voice life again.

Krezoc hoped he wasn't expecting to save the city. The path ahead of her was clear, and it burned.

'Very well,' Krezoc said. 'Pallidus Mor!' she voxed to the demi-legio. 'We are the pride of Death!'

*'The pride of Death!'* the princeps shouted back over the vox.

'The pride of Death!' Vansaak and Grevereign cried.

The war-horns blasted again, this time in concert with the unified barrage launched by every god-machine. The giants of the Pallidus Mor marched across the cratered wastes before Therimachus. The Iron Skulls laid down a wide bombardment, raising a curtain of fire across the fields. Energy blasts tore the earth open and strained void shields with a force that would consume armies. The Pallidus Mor's fire zeroed in on the Banelord that raged at the centre of the formation. Hundreds of missiles flew against the monster. Multiple volcano las-beams, quake shells and Sunfury plasma blasts hit the traitor at once. The assault was colossal. No single Titan could withstand the massed fire of twelve others. It survived several seconds, its war-horn shrieking like a maddened beast. The Banelord actually advanced several steps into the barrage, in defiance of its fate, before it disintegrated. Its final explosion was subnuclear, though that was enough to damage the smaller Titans on either side of it. The Pallidus Mor turned its fire to the left, and the Ravager it struck vaporised even more quickly than the Banelord.

The victories were quick, but costly. The entire demi-legio weathered the Iron Skulls' bombardment. *Gloria Vastator*'s shields failed once, and a shell punctured its right upper torso. The movement of the right arm was hampered.

Thezerin dispatched repair servitors and rerouted what controls she could. Krezoc and Grevereign could still aim the volcano cannon, but its responses were sluggish, delayed.

In Drahn's maniple, the Reaver *Terribilis Ossa* ceased all communications. It stood motionless in the field between two craters, smoke rising through the eyes of its skull. It had taken a direct hit to the head. The Titan might be salvaged, but its crew, princeps and moderati had been incinerated. It was nothing more than a tomb now, a monument to a battle that had barely begun.

The Iron Skulls moved to compensate for the gap in their lines as another Ravager turned into a sudden, bloody sunrise. The distance between the two forces shrank, and the Pallidus Mor began its convergence. The fire between the Titans became more concentrated, a collision of devastation that turned the intervening space into the heart of a supernova. The Iron Skulls moved back and forth on their line, directing their warp-tainted holocaust at the approaching wedge of the Pallidus Mor. Traitor and Imperial god-machines vanished from sight of each other as the conflagration spread, screaming, over dozens of square miles. Portions of the land before Therimachus turned molten. At the very centre of the crossfire, a cauldron of lava roiled, hungry to swallow the combatants.

Krezoc navigated and aimed by auspex readings again. Her eyes could see nothing but the flare of void shields and the endlessly renewed flash of explosions. *Gloria Vastator* was marching through the sun. She took it through by being a thing of the manifold, her thoughts fused with the machine-spirit, reading the enemy signatures and signals of collapsing, melting ground as if the data were fed directly into her senses. She turned, altered the Warlord's aim and course as the battlefield shifted and sank. She maintained enough of her identity to read the broader picture of the war. She maintained the strategy of the attack. The surviving Imperial Hunters, energised, managed to move their struggle closer to the edges of the Iron Skulls' line, turning two battles into one, forcing the traitors to battle on two fronts. Therimachus burned, but the fire that closed in was all-consuming. If it moved into the city, it would raze even its shadows.

'The Spears are making their move,' Vansaak said.

Krezoc picked up the signals of the regiment and the secutarii riding their hulls. They were racing ahead of the Pallidus Mor advance on the left flank, risking the cataclysm of shells and las as they arced around to come for the edges of the Iron Skulls' formation. They were tiny components of the huge machine she had thrown into motion.

Vansaak felt the same sense of perspective. 'Are they beneath notice?' she asked.

When Krezoc answered, her bodily voice felt distant from her consciousness and slow to respond. 'I hope they are,' she said. She needed the Iron Skulls to ignore the threat. The battle for the gates of Therimachus was approaching a state of devastating balance. She needed the equilibrium to tip.

Even a small stone could start a rockslide.

The Kataran 66th had returned to an inferno. Deyers' life was a journey from flame to flame. Deicoon, Klivanos, Therimachus – it was all a continuum of fire. He rode with *Bastion of Faith*'s hatch open this time. The firestorm that threatened his regiment now was very different from the one on the plain. Its intensity was more focused, and more overwhelming. The air was thick with the smoke that rose from the land in the aftermath of the Imperial Hunters' lost battle. It came too from the burning city. But he could still breathe. And if the flames of the struggle between the Iron Skulls and the Pallidus Mor swept over the Spears, there would be no taking shelter inside the tank. *Bastion of Faith* would melt to slag in moments.

The armoured column skirted the edge of the battle. The god-machines tore Katara apart between them. They were dark leviathans with blazing eyes, burning the night with the anger of their guns. Deyers felt his world turn brittle on his right. Immensities were warring with each other, their thunderous steps grinding Katara to cinders and dust. Ahead, Therimachus blazed. Flames silhouetted its skyline. Towers burst and fell under the continued onslaught of the other Iron Skulls. Death moved in colossal shapes through the pulsing crimson glow.

Therimachus was the goal. Though its wounds were grievous, there was a city there still. Katara could make a last stand. There was something of its civilisation, culture and soul yet to save. Between Deyers and the goal was the line of the Iron Skulls. He could keep swinging south, go completely around the traitors while they were engaged with the Pallidus Mor, and head straight into the city. But the giants that remained there would make short work of the 66th. He didn't trust Krezoc's strategy. It was predicated entirely on destroying the enemy, not on preserving the city. Syagrius had promised preservation, though, and failed. The only path now was Krezoc's, so he would follow it. And pray.

He glanced up at Venterras. The alpha hoplite was riding the outside of the turret. Two more of his squad were crouched on the hull. The secutarii were unreadable in their helms. They were motionless, armoured statues of mechanical calm. Their eagerness to be at war came through in a constant, low thrum. They were war machines primed for combat. Deyers wondered if they were capable of doubt. If they were, it was not on this day, or in this battle.

Medina turned the Leman Russ towards the north west, driving towards the southernmost of the Iron Skulls. The Titan was a Feral, small next to its brothers, immense to the human on the ground. It hunched forwards, its back humped and lined with jagged plates. Its tail ended in a spiked club that crackled with dark energy. It whipped angrily back and forth as the Feral stalked along the line, firing mega-bolter rounds and blasts from what must once have been a turbolaser destructor, but which now fired tainted beams of cancerous intensity. A few hundred yards beyond the Feral was another of its kind. The two twisted god-machines behaved like pack animals, their cannon fire the snapping jaws of predators seeking to bring down much larger prey but unable to advance closer without marching into the incandescent apocalypse.

Venterras crouched a little lower. He was a wound spring, seconds before launching himself into the war. The vox-speakers in his helm emitted a short, squealing burst of binaric. The other two secutarii answered in the same fashion. Deyers sensed an entire battle plan presented, refined and confirmed in seconds. Then Venterras turned to Deyers. 'The first of the traitors is ours,' he said.

'We can support you,' Deyers said.

'No. We will be in the way of your guns. If you take the

second, our coordinated efforts will be more efficient. Do you agree, captain?'

Deyers nodded. He voxed Medina. 'Make a run for the second Feral.'

The blaze Therimachus cast silhouetted the first Iron Skull and cast its shadow forwards. The lead tanks of the column entered the shadow. The Feral did not react except to turn back towards the north, narrowly missing a stream of mega-bolter fire from the Pallidus Mor. Then the Spears were within range for the secutarii. The Leman Russ formation came in close, risking the Feral's trampling feet, directly underneath its extended cannon arms, too near for it to shoot down unless it backed up towards the city.

The secutarii leapt off the tanks. The entire contingent of hoplite and peltast squads charged over the churned mud and stone, flowing with the brutal grace of a single machine. Platen turned *Bastion of Faith*'s cannon towards the Titan but held fire. The Feral ignored the column. The Spears passed through its shadow, ants before a giant. The vibrations of its footsteps rattled the hull. The concussions of bursts of fire hammered at Deyers' ears. The thud-thud-thud-thud of the fire rattled the bones of his chest. This close, he could see the distorted nature of the Feral even more clearly. He recoiled, body and soul. Its armour looked like reptilian scales. Foul icons writhed in his peripheral vision. When he looked up at the lunging head, he expected it to open, revealing a giant maw. Its taint was so pervasive, its shadow crawled over Deyers' flesh like an oil slick.

The Leman Russ roared past the Titan, into the space between it and the second target. The secutarii reached the feet of the Iron Skull.

With a snarling blast of its war-horn, the other Feral turned away from the Pallidus Mor and trained its weapons on the 66th. A line of explosions walked towards the tanks.

Venterras mag-locked his shield to his back and leapt onto the toes of the Feral's right leg. The moment he made contact, the monster reacted, as if he walked on skin instead of metal. Its hunched form lurched down. It jerked back and forth, a beast trying to see its tiny enemies. It took two long steps backwards. He tried to magnetise himself to the moving foot, but his boots began to slip. They could not hold on to the transformed substance. He staggered forwards and jumped up to the plate of the leg. His right hand found a hold on the shifting, overlapping scales. He stabbed up with his arc lance, triggering a blast at the same time. The lance forced a small crack in the armour. It held the blade enough for Venterras to avoid being shaken off when the foot slammed down to the ground again. More hoplites had joined him on the foot, while others had begun to climb the left leg.

On Khania, he had ascended *Gloria Vastator* to cleanse it of xenos filth. Now he was climbing again. This god-machine was lesser, and more foul. Before, the mission was defensive. Now he was on the offence. The symmetry had meaning. Difference and repetition were interlocked teeth of adjoining gears. The machinery of fate was clear to him, and with it the hand of the Omnissiah. He was privileged to experience a fragment of the divine mechanism. He gave thanks, and shot upwards.

The peltasts moved to circle the monster, harassing it with kinetic hammer-shots from their galvanic casters.

They placed their shots with machinic precision, the supersonic masses punching into the armour just above the hoplites' positions, creating more handholds. They ran hard to keep pace with the Feral's retreat.

It moved faster. It brought them into range of its guns. Its mega-bolter chewed up the ground. Shells overwhelmed kyropatris fields, shattering bodies and armour, turning them into pulped masses of ceramite and bone splinters. The peltasts scattered to either side of the fire, and ran harder.

<The window is limited,> Trigerrix signalled to Venterras.

<Acknowledged.> Venterras moved quickly from handhold to scale, propelling himself up towards the Titan's knee. He calculated the vectors of the Feral's movements, its cannon fire, the speed of the peltasts and the rate of the hoplite climb. The results were dark, but they could not account for all variables. The Omnissiah knew all, and this was the one path open to serve Him. The variables Venterras could not see would determine the true solution to the equation.

He had faith.

His faith was rewarded.

A turbolaser from the Pallidus Mor cut across the night and struck the Feral's torso. The traitor's shields held, barely. It reared up and sidestepped. It fired back into the dark, giving the peltasts a brief reprieve.

Even seconds mattered.

The hoplites reached the knees before the Feral could exterminate the peltasts. There were no massive plates at the joint, and the armour was weaker here. Trigerrix coordinated one more hammer-shot barrage just before Venterras reached the target. The shots struck a single location on each joint, cracking open the rippling, distorted, adamantine flesh of the Titan. The repeated blasts left smoking holes just big enough for the hoplites to pass through, one at a time, to the interior of the machine.

Venterras pushed his way through the rent in the armour. He entered a realm that was all the more monstrous for just being recognisable as a Titan's interior. But everything was tainted. The machinic had been fused with the flesh. Pistons were indistinguishable from bones. Cables were veins. Musculature covered the walls, and the pulse of the power plant was the beat of an infernal heart. Acidic slime coated the surfaces. It poured down Venterras' armour, sizzling and gnawing at its surface. Light the colour of blood and throbbing anger rose and fell.

Venterras was inside an abomination. This was a mockery of the purity of the machine. It was a perversion of every tenet of the Omnissiah. The machine here had been plunged into the deepest corruption of the flesh. The machine was infused with the instincts and irrationality of the unthinking beast. The metallic had become porous, its nature indeterminate.

And there were voices. They whispered and shrieked and echoed. They were a choir of damnation, oozing from the walls, falling down the squelching shaft of the leg and twisting about the bones. Their words, chanted and snarled, were beyond human understanding and beyond human articulation. No mouth with a single tongue could pronounce those syllables. The voices clamoured for Venterras to listen, to know them, to understand them, to embrace a totality of anger. To become the machine that raged, and so fall into the damnation that was the worst of the flesh.

<Purge it,> he said, but the purity of binaric was distorted as he spoke. A parasitic code attached itself to the cant. Venterras switched to flesh speak, and his commands were clearer. 'Banish the monster from the sight of the Omnissiah! The machinic is pure!'

He and his squad attacked in concert. They stabbed arc lances into the thick of the nexus where the huge bone pistons met. They sawed through sinew and iron, shocking the muscle with repeated jolts of electricity. The voices screamed their outrage. Blood spouted from severed hydraulics. Shimmering faces, contorted with rage, formed in the tissues and spat acid and hate at the hoplites. Venterras' kyropatris field flashed an angry blue. It could not keep all the foul liquid out. Tinged with the madness of the warp, it fell on him and sought the seams of his armour and the weakness of his soul.

The movement inside the leg was violent as the Feral stamped back and forth, trying to shake off the attackers stabbing it from within. The space rose and fell, the angle shifting to change walls into floor and then back again. Venterras dug into the roaring mass of the joint, driving his arc lance deeper, charring his way through cabling and sinew. Gravity tried to pull him away. The shaking battered the hoplites. The flesh of a wall came away and swallowed two of his comrades, crushing them beneath tonnes of suppurating, hungry metal.

Metal parted. Choking smoke blackened the shaft. Blood and obsidian ichor spurted against the attackers. The voices screamed, and so did the foul material of the Titan's being.

A greater roar of anger than any before boomed. It climbed the octaves of outrage and pain, and then the movement of the shaft stopped. Ichor-spewing cables snapped and whirled like electrocuted serpents. Immense bone gears spun uselessly against each other, spitting out shrapnel. Dark flames licked up and down the walls.

'Withdraw,' Venterras ordered, and he followed the surviving squad members through the rent and out into the air once more. The Feral's legs were motionless, frozen at awkward angles. The torso rotated back and forth on its axis, as if it might somehow force movement back into its limbs. Hoplites were scrambling out of the left joint too, and climbing down the leg as fast as they could. Internal fires burst from the wounds, and the war-horn of the Feral blasted its helpless anger.

Venterras slid down the leg, grabbing handholds just long enough to slow his descent to a speed he could survive. The ground below was shattered, a smoking upheaval of shell impacts. He saw very few peltasts. Trigerrix was still there, though, her binaric acknowledgement of his emergence greeting him with welcome purity.

The Feral fired at the ground and into the night. There was no discipline to the shots. Whether crew or god-machine was the guiding intelligence of the monster, the Titan now reacted with unreasoning, chaotic wrath. It was fighting fate, but its paralysis doomed it.

The Pallidus Mor barrage arrived as Venterras hit the ground. A hail of shells flew, streaming fire, into the upper portions of the Feral. It fired its guns one more time, and then it came apart, the blasts from the shells setting off a greater explosion from the inside. Its cannons flew cartwheeling into the night, its torso parted like the blossoms of a dark flower. The head disappeared in a fireball.

The legs began to buckle as Venterras pounded away

from them. He looked up at the blooming explosion. For a moment, the fireball shaped itself into a maw howling in agony. Then the voices were still.

Medina swerved *Bastion of Faith* over the broken ground. The tank responded with a surprising nimbleness. Deyers hung on to the hatch to keep from being thrown out. The stream of huge bolter rounds from the Feral passed over his head. The impacts hurled geysers of mud and stone skywards. *Heart of Creontiades* jerked to the right, also evading the attack. *General Passevas* was not as lucky. The cannon fire cut the Leman Russ in half.

The Feral backed up again, but its earlier manoeuvres to keep the 66th in its range no longer served it as well. The Spears had it surrounded. They pressed in, a spiral noose closing around the Iron Skull. It had shattered and melted several tanks on their approach. Now it could target only a few at a time.

'Stay close,' Deyers voxed. 'And keep the lines ragged! Don't give it a cluster of targets.'

Battle, demolisher and vanquisher cannon shells slammed into the Titan on all sides. Its void shields collapsed again, and a plasma destroyer blast hit its cowling. The Feral jerked forwards in a stumble. Smoke billowed out of a score of rents in its armour. It was a giant at bay. It was more terrible than any one of its attackers, but it could not take out the entire swarm of tanks that hemmed it in. Every time it fired, it destroyed another Leman Russ, another Basilisk, another Manticore. Deyers' regiment eroded. It was a shadow of the force he had led to Khania. But it fought on, and he would see it fight to the end of Katara's last stand.

And he would bring this monster down.

Platen fired the battle cannon again. The shell hit a growing wound in the Feral's midsection. The effect was greater than the explosion. The Titan shuddered as if stabbed in the heart. Its arms jerked, their aim uncertain. It marched forwards now, its movements a shuddering, running lunge for freedom.

'Back!' Deyers ordered. 'Keep it surrounded!'

As if scenting blood, the Spears' bombardment enveloped the Iron Skull. Plasma and shells burst against it without a pause, a score of daggers striking its front and flanks and back and head, exploding against its legs in mid-stride. Twin fountains of flame, majestic as solar flares, jetted from the Titan's chest and back. The flames met above its head. It staggered two more steps, cannons firing madly in one final, lethal burst. This time *Heart of Creontiades* was not as lucky. It died with its victim, erupting as the Feral fell. The monster's shadow stretched ahead of it. Medina pushed *Bastion of Faith*'s engine to its limits, racing against the collapse. The Feral crashed to earth. Dust clouds rolled over the retreating tanks, then sank back, covering the inert mass of the Titan.

The Leman Russ was heading north, towards the howling intensity of the central clash. Deyers shielded his eyes. He could barely make out the shapes of any of the god-machines. They were so close to one another now. Two collective fists of unimaginable power were smashing against each other.

'Slow down,' Deyers told Medina. To the surviving tanks he voxed, 'Form up.' The Spears and the secutarii had completed their missions.

'What now?' Platen called up.

Deyers looked towards Therimachus, then at the holocaust to the north. If the Pallidus Mor broke the Iron Skulls' line, a new phase of the battle could begin. He saw an opportunity. Even though to look at Therimachus was to feel the approaching culmination of a horror he could not name, he saw a chance of hope. It was frail as a fading dream. He had to seize it now before it vanished in the terrible waking of the night.

'Princeps Krezoc,' he voxed. 'At your signal, we will begin to draw the enemy out of the city.'

He didn't expect an answer. He acted as if he had received one, and that it confirmed his strategy. *Lure them back to the plains,* he thought. *Spare Therimachus and finish this in the wastes.* 'Make for the city,' he told Medina, and the gathering line of tanks began its turn east.

But Krezoc did answer. *'Attack at will,'* she said. *'But you will not draw them out.'*

'Are you forbidding–'

*'I am stating, captain,'* she snapped. *'The Iron Skulls will not follow. Attack. Bombard them. Hit them with everything. Disrupt their ritual. That is all.'*

Hope frayed and vanished. Krezoc would have him turn his guns on the city. She would have him destroy, not save.

He hesitated.

'Captain?' Platen asked.

Then, from the north, nuclear flashes, five of them. Deyers fell back, blinded, as the shock waves seized the regiment in their jaws.

# CHAPTER 13

# SALVATION'S PYRE

*Tempestas Deorem*. The Imperial Hunter *Canis Imperio*. Two of the Iron Skulls' Ravagers. A traitor Banelord. Their power plants went supercritical at virtually the same moment, but Princeps Makthal's Reaver was the first. It was the trigger, and Makthal was granted the boon of realising what was about to happen and the moments to knowingly speak his last.

'*We are the pride of Death,*' he voxed to Krezoc, a farewell and a warning.

That was the end of mercy. Krezoc did not have time to acknowledge the farewell. Though she heard the warning, there was nothing to be done to prepare.

She had known from the start what might happen. She had done the cold arithmetic of nuclear explosions in close quarters. She had known it was probable. She had known the possible cost. And she accepted it.

They might even purchase a victory. *Tempestas Deorem*

exploded, triggering the chain reaction. The cataclysm enveloped both forces. There was no escape, no shelter. The god-machines would survive, or they would not. A simple binary. One or zero.

And so she marched *Gloria Vastator* through the fire, to encounter the one or the zero. The five blasts came in the time it took for the god-machine to take a single step. The adamantine shutters slammed down over the eyes of the Warlord, blocking out the destroying light. The manifold was a scream of data, an overload flare that almost blinded all her senses. Her mind swam through fire, yet the deaths of the Titans were so immense that she knew and felt each new explosion, each new apocalypse that led to the next. A single step, because there was no choice. There was only, as ever, the fate of the Pallidus Mor to walk through the flames, and so *Gloria Vastator* walked. It took that step, into the enemy and through annihilation.

The moment of the blasts passed and became the time of the fireballs, and *Gloria Vastator* had not become zero.

The binary was resolved. Now the damage warning klaxons sounded, and the damage reports flooded in through the manifold. Radiation spiked, and kept spiking. The Warlord led the demi-legio through a crucible that only destroyed. It embraced the Pallidus Mor and the Iron Skulls, and tried to melt them down to ore. Krezoc pushed the knowledge of the fires racing through the god-machine to the back of her mind. She shut out the klaxons. They were the concern of Thezerin. Even the radiation levels were irrelevant. They would kill her or not, but right now, she still felt the linked wills of her moderati, and she could make the Titan walk, and she could make it fight. No other truth mattered.

The guns were charged. The shutters withdrew from the armourglass. The killing light had passed, but the world beyond the Warlord was nothing but the rage of the fireballs. *Gloria Vastator* was moving from the core of a star towards its surface. And there was a target, little more than a vague mass registered by the overwhelmed auspex array. Krezoc's body was the Warlord. Its pain was hers. The machine-spirit's fury was hers. She and god-machine were fused into transcendent unity. She snarled, low in her throat, and in the midst of flame unleashed still more. The volcano cannon fired at the same moment the Banelord came into view through the holocaust. The las-beam hit point-blank. *Gloria Vastator* walked its own inferno, a burning juggernaut ramming into the Iron Skull. The traitor's arms jerked mindlessly, their fire going wild. The Belicosa's las-beams melted the Banelord's head. It stretched and liquefied, a waxen death mask that ran down the monster's torso. *Gloria Vastator* struck the standing corpse and hurled it to the ground. Her snarl turning into a roar, her flesh riven by the searing agony of the god-machine, her spirit exalted by the Warlord's annihilation of its foe.

Forwards, then, forwards through the firestorm that at last was fading, through the shattered line of the Iron Skulls. The traitors had only lost one Titan to the chain reaction, but with *Gloria Vastator*'s kill, all the Banelords of the barrier had fallen. The Irons Skulls that survived the blasts were lesser, and were more badly damaged than the engines still marching with Krezoc's battle group. The Pallidus Mor advanced through them, a blade heated to red slicing through weakened metal.

Forwards still, through the thickened night of dust and smoke, and then Therimachus lay before Krezoc. The near suburbs were gone, scraped from the earth by the nuclear vortex. After a mile or so, the stumps of buildings burned. Further on, in the heart of the city, the Iron Skulls drew their great rune in blood and flame.

The extent of *Gloria Vastator*'s injuries became clear as Krezoc tried to increase the pace of the march. Its right leg resisted her commands, dragging forwards with great reluctance. Looseness pervaded the Warlord's body. Her will seemed to take longer to reach its limbs. She felt its struggle as groans of data in the manifold. There was silence from Thezerin, though. The magos understood the priorities of the battle. Krezoc cursed the wounds and ignored them, forcing the machine on.

For the first few steps into the outer ruins of Therimachus, Krezoc concentrated on the enemy Titans. They no longer outnumbered the battle group, but these god-machines were strong. If they had suffered in the struggle with the Imperial Hunters, they showed little sign in their movements and their weapons fire. Krezoc guessed that the Hunters had managed to kill every Iron Skull they had wounded. If so, Syagrius' small victory was even more pyrrhic. He had left a strong enemy behind. The traitors had not deviated from their task. They showed no interest in the apocalypse on the south-eastern fringe of the city, nor in the fall of their brothers. Krezoc plotted targeting solutions, and then the implications of the Iron Skulls' single-minded focus sank in.

'Banelord in the north quadrant,' Vansaak said. 'Acquired.'

'No,' Krezoc said. 'There isn't time.'

Vansaak and Grevereign's confusion thrummed through the manifold.

'Their task is almost done,' Krezoc said. She looked hard

at the city and not just the enemy now, and the danger hit her with soul-withering force. Reality over Therimachus was turning brittle. The air flickered, like a stutter in the world. Near the top of the hill where the governor's palace had been, two Ravagers faced each other across a distance of about a mile and were pouring their fire onto the ground between them. There were few buildings there. Instead, there were wide avenues and squares. Krezoc could easily guess what was being burned and what the source of the clouds of black smoke was. The sacrifice was reaching its climax. The ritual was about to bear fruit.

The veil of the materium trembled. Immense hunger pressed against the other side, eager for its release.

The totality of the battlefield clicked into place for Krezoc. Only a few, miserably frail seconds remained before the veil was rent. She saw the precision in the destruction the Iron Skulls had caused in the city. She saw the machinery of the ritual.

And where there was precision, there was another sort of frailty.

Markos had thrown himself down on instinct at the first flash. So had his guards. He huddled next to a low mound of rubble, his eyes squeezed shut against the light, his hands over his ears in a futile effort to blot out the thunder of the explosions. His ears and nose were bleeding when he rose, his head stuffed and ringing. His skin burned from the passage of the hurricane wind.

Five mushroom clouds blotted out the sky to the south east. They were darkening pillars, disappearing into the night as the furnace of the blasts faded. The massive shapes of the Pallidus Mor, outlined by fires guttering on their armour and lit by the flashes of void shields struggling for stability, marched from the site of the blasts. Iron Skulls fell before them, the defensive line becoming a new ruin. Further to the south, Markos could still see the lights of the Kataran Spears. Something of the regiment had survived. He stumbled after Sorren, barely seeing the dying city around him. He lost sight of the 66th as he ran downhill, taller wreckage blocking his view. He saw them in his mind. They were the goal.

Sorren led the way through back lanes, fleeing the Iron Skulls and their butchery. The massacre of the herded civilians began, and the smell of burned flesh filled Markos' nostrils. The ashes of the martyred population spread over Therimachus.

The flickering began. Markos could not run straight. Vertigo assailed him. Though his feet drummed against rockcrete, the broken road seemed insubstantial as vapour. Everything he could see had thinned, become a membrane stretched to the last point before tearing.

'What...' he gasped. *What is happening?* he tried to cry, but he had no breath.

Then he was thrown to the ground again. From the south east came the shriek of a new bombardment. Before the city could tear, it began to shake.

Ornastas blocked another blow from Darroban. His muscles retained enough of their old training that he could counter the heretic's spear jabs with his staff. But Darroban was faster and stronger. He had been in combat for decades longer. He attacked relentlessly, shouting promises of blood to his new god. Ornastas managed a few jabs in the first moments of the duel, ones that Darroban knocked aside with easy contempt.

Adrenaline and zealotry kept Ornastas alive. He blocked another thrust from Darroban that would have pierced his neck. He hadn't stopped all the blows, and he could feel Darroban taking him down one small wound at a time. His arms and flanks were bleeding. A deep cut on his forehead threatened to blind him as blood dripped down his face. One of his ribs was broken. He was choking on phlegm and dust, and breathing was an agony.

He would not go down. He would not let his service to the Emperor and to Katara end at the hands of this wretch.

Ornastas half staggered back, narrowly avoiding an overhand strike from Darroban. 'You're weak,' he taunted.

Darroban hesitated, surprised and amused. He circled Ornastas, looking for another opening. *'I'm* weak!' He laughed.

It was hard to talk with the thickness in his throat. Ornastas spat. 'Weak,' he repeated. 'A weak fight. Cutting your foe down a piece at a time. A coward's strategy.'

He didn't expect Darroban to react to the taunts. They were too transparent. He used them to gain a few seconds to breathe, that was all. To his surprise, Darroban's mutilated features contorted in a furious snarl and he threw himself forwards, flailing rapid, wild blows with his spear. Darroban's rage made him reckless. Ornastas backed up over the uneven rockcrete, countering the strikes. Darroban reared back, left himself open, and Ornastas slammed the shock head of his staff against the heretic's chest. The jolt only enraged Darroban further. He leaned into the staff and swung his spear sideways.

The blade struck Ornastas in the side of the head. It sliced his face to the bone. The impact was stunning. He stumbled to the right, tripped over a chunk of rockcrete and started to fall forwards, and so saved his life. The movement brought him closer to Darroban as the heretic brought the spear down again. Instead of the blade splitting Ornastas' skull, the shaft hit his crown, driving him to his knees.

Ornastas hissed, seeing double. He raised his staff to block the next blow.

It did not come.

Darroban howled. He dropped his spear and clutched his head. He weaved away from Ornastas, moving unconsciously towards the drop from the ruined tower. He screamed, clawing at his face. Long strips of muscle came off, caught in his jagged nails. He faced north west, his scream unending, spiralling up and down a scale of madness.

Leaning on his staff, Ornastas made it to his feet. He realised Darroban's shrieks led a choir. Across the plateau of rubble, the cultists had stopped fighting. They were all screaming, all facing in the same direction. Ornastas followed the line of Darroban's tormented gaze. He could see nothing past Deicoon's eruptions. As he stared, though, and the thousands screamed, an intimation of a huge event came to him. He felt it as a trembling of the spirit, as if the sublimely terrible was just beyond the horizon.

The ripples of the great event reached Deicoon. The tremors threw Ornastas off his feet. The burning city shook with mounting violence. The lava fountains surged higher. Ornastas clung to the rubble as it bucked. He stared in awe as the high mountainsides, glowing dimly in the reflected light of the leaping flames, cracked, crumbled and began to slide.

\* \* \*

'The target is the rune,' Krezoc commanded the battle group. 'Full bombardment. Fire until nothing is left.'

'*Princeps!*' The voice was Deyers', shouting in horror.

'Fire,' said Krezoc. 'Fire or lose Katara.'

*Bastion of Faith* had weathered the shock wave and the killing wind that had followed. Not all the tanks of the regiment had. Some had burned. Others had been upended by a giant's hand. Deyers had been slow taking shelter, and his skin was charred. The regiment still existed, though, and it was ready to move into the city.

Then Krezoc issued the order.

Deyers hesitated. He looked back and forth between the Pallidus Mor and the Iron Skulls at work in Therimachus. The Titans blurred together. They were all bent on the annihilation of the final city.

The guns of the Spears were aimed at the Iron Skulls.

Krezoc said to target the rune. To bombard the city itself.

*Fire or lose Katara.*

The seconds fell away. He could not give the order.

The Pallidus Mor unleashed the totality of its might on Therimachus. Flights of missiles that reduced square miles of hive blocks to dust, las that melted the greatest fortifications, shells that shattered the earth, plasma bursts that vaporised entire divisions – they fell on the wounded city, striking the molten lines of the colossal rune. Deyers stared in horror as the darkness exploded with the light of the murder of hope.

Towers burst to shrapnel or collapsed into seething flame. Chasms ripped open, pulling entire blocks into the abyss. Manufactoria erupted, chaining fireballs and sending floods of ignited promethium roaring through the narrow canyons of the streets. The Iron Skulls turned in fury as the lines of the rune extended, crossed, disintegrated. The pattern being carved into the face of Therimachus was torn apart.

It did not die easily.

The air over the city seemed to tie itself into a knot. Deyers gasped, lightning pain striking him behind the eyes. He saw the reality of the city bend and twist. Then the potential that had been building, that power that had come to the very edge of manifesting as a thing with a name and a will, descended at once into uncontrolled chaos. The materium and the warp collided and warred. The reality of Therimachus turned molten, and the eruption seized the entire city. Therimachus broke up into slabs floating on magma, like ice floes on an ocean in storm. Some were only a few hundred yards long, some were a mile or more.

The magma heaved in waves a hundred feet high. The stone rafts of the city reared up and down, leviathans in agony. Slabs broke apart and disappeared beneath the crimson waves. Two massive rafts hurtled towards collision. The rockcrete prow of one hit the flank of another like a ramming void ship. It rode over the centre of its victim, the underbelly of glowing bedrock scraping the skyline flat. As it passed over, it tilted the other slab onto its side, and then over. The needles of hab blocks and cathedrals pointed to the side and then down. The first slab kept going, pushed by the fury of the waves. Its prow angled higher and higher, and at last it paused, a vertical island a mile high. The impossible moment stretched. Walls collapsed and buildings tumbled over each other, falling like pebbles down the surface of the slab. There were Iron Skulls on the vertical blocks, a Feral and a Ravager, and they dropped, figures that suddenly seemed small, down the face of the slab towards the red ocean. The slab trembled and then it sank, straight down, a plunge into the depthless molten sea.

The earth outside Therimachus trembled, the trauma of the upheaval reaching across the continent. Crevasses split the hills outside the city and raced for the mountain chains. The peaks swayed and broke. The tremors shook the Spears. A Wyvern to Deyers' left disappeared into a sudden fissure. Medina backed *Bastion of Faith* away from the widening gap. The tank jerked forwards a dozen yards, and then the ground beneath it disintegrated. The treads spun, seeking a grip on breaking gravel.

Deyers gripped the hatch, riding the torment of the earth. The crackling, rumbling thunder of Therimachus swallowed all other sound. He stared at the upheaval, his soul riven like his world.

Somewhere, at a great distance, Platen was shouting to him. But he no longer had any orders to give.

'What is the condition of *Ferrum Salvator*?' Krezoc asked.

Aboard the *Nuntius Mortis*, Tech-Priest Thassanis said, *'The primary systems are operational. There remains much to do.'*

'Send it down,' said Krezoc. She sent Thassanis a datapack with coordinates a short distance from the edge of the magma sea.

Thassanis knew better than to object. Even so, he asked, *'But who will be its princeps?'* Left unsaid was the enormity of the task facing any soul who hoped to replace Balzhan.

'No one, unless the Omnissiah wills it,' Krezoc said.

But the shifting equations of the war demanded the unthinkable.

Krezoc ended contact with the *Nuntius Mortis* and led the impossible charge into Therimachus. She took *Gloria Vastator* into a landscape possessed by madness. The advance was mad, but necessary. The war was far from finished. When reality lashed out and the city broke, Iron Skulls died. But more still walked the heaving slabs. They were not making for the edge of the city. They were manoeuvring into the beginning of a circular formation. They were trying to regain the reins of the unleashed energy.

Extermination was the only road to victory.

*Gloria Vastator* stepped across a magmatic strait and onto one of the larger slabs. The Warlord shouldered aside gutted hab blocks. They crumbled to the streets. At the very edge of her awareness, Krezoc registered the presence of panicked crowds. Millions had died in Therimachus, but there were millions more who lived to experience the terror of their city's final catastrophe. The assault Krezoc led would kill many of them.

The knowledge settled into the back of her mind. It would remain there, buried by the necessity of the battlefield, and if she survived, if there was an aftermath to this conflict, she would deal with it then. She would confront the costs she had exacted from others. But now it was a distraction, as were the fleeing hordes.

Her focus, cold as the void, zeroed on the Traitor Titans in her range.

The Pallidus Mor stormed Therimachus. The maniples attacked together, the reduced demi-legio forming a wedge that sent out a hail of rockets, shells and energy before it. The Ravager at the far end of the slab exploded before it could turn and counter the attack. The other Iron Skulls abandoned their attempt to salvage the ritual and returned fire. Their circle converged. The fist of the Pallidus Mor moved towards the grasping claw of the Iron Skulls.

The semblance of strategy on both sides lasted less than a minute. Massed fire shattered god-machines, and when another Iron Skulls Ravager went nuclear, the slabs broke up into smaller islands. The magma's convulsions became more and more violent, the unleashed, raging force still unspent. The waves surged higher. More slabs upended and sank. The god-machines walked on surfaces that heaved up and down at ever more violent angles. Formations came apart as lava forced itself up through the plates and split.

The monsters of war fought each other on the back of a dying world.

Markos clung to the tangle of metal wreckage and screamed. The land tilted higher and higher. He looked up and saw the molten waves reaching for him. The immense feet of the Warlord dug the pavement of the avenue, pushing a barrier of rubble before them as the god-machine's stance slipped. Then the slab fell back. His perspective whirled. The bleeding land slipped out of the sky again.

Markos tried to work his way deeper into the wreckage. He looked around for Sorren. The captain was a few feet away, holding tight to another spur of iron. His mask of determination had fallen away. His face mirrored Markos' terror.

The other guards were dead, crushed beneath falling buildings. Markos tried to catch sight of the Kataran 66th. He failed. He didn't know where to look any longer. The ground spun as it rode the waves. There was no north, no south. There was only fire and the coming of the end.

'What do we do?' Markos shouted at Sorren. Any answer, any purpose would suffice. Any meaning at all. But not this. Not this death. This was worse than being buried in the vault. *'What do we do?'* This was beyond defeat, beyond disaster.

Sorren didn't answer. But his gaze sharpened on Markos, as if suddenly remembering that the governor was still there. Sorren stood up, his movements jerking, unnatural. He pointed.

Markos turned his head. There were only more ruins and flames in the direction Sorren indicated. That darkness would take them away from the god-machines, though. That would have to be enough.

Markos rose, then hunched as the Warlord and two Ravagers exchanged fire. The blasts of crossing las cracked the night with furious day. Monstrous shells struck the Warlord. The Titan withstood the hits, but the force of the explosions transmitted itself to the surface. Cracks chased each other across the floating slab, and it began to split again. The fissures glowed red, then the lava leapt through, jetting from a severed artery. The Warlord walked forwards. Its heavy tread smashed the weakening surface. The fissures behind the Titan widened, and the slab came apart. It split, and split, and split again. Markos tightened his grip on the iron. He was on an islet of rockcrete less than a hundred feet across. It spun on the sea of magma. It rocked violently, tossed by the towering waves. The heat came for him. His skin began to crisp. His vision was a vortex of fire and destruction.

Sorren fell back into the wreckage. A spike pierced his

chest. He jerked once, blood spurting from his mouth, and was still.

Markos was alone. Abandoned, he screamed at the universe. Around him, all form of meaning hurled itself into the flames. His life and death were nothing, just another splinter in the galaxy's endless howl of pain.

His fragment of the city rose towards the crest of a magma wave. The climb was too steep. The slab tilted past the vertical. Markos caught one last, upended sight of the god-machines wreaking destruction on each other and the world. Then the slab fell on the wave, delivering him to the darkness and the agony.

'Banelord to the right,' Vansaak said. 'Crossing over.'

'Apocalypse salvo,' Krezoc voxed Konterus. 'Hold it off.' She gave only a fraction of her attention to the missiles. She left the attack to the moderati minoris. The priority was *Gloria Vastator*'s struggle with a second Banelord directly ahead. The battle had reduced the size of the slab by half. Krezoc divided the Warlord's fire between the Iron Skull and the ground at its feet. Volcano las-beams slashed into the traitor's shields at the level of its head. Quake shells shook the earth. The Banelord fought back in kind. The rockcrete raft cracked. It rocked high and low. *Gloria Vastator*'s internal gyros tilted to the extreme. Krezoc felt a machinic form of vertigo as the Warlord turned top-heavy and came close to toppling, first forwards, then back.

The Banelord's tail cannon launched a shell that struck at the same moment an initial blast from the new arrival overloaded the void shields. The blast rocked the length of the torso. The controls became even more sluggish. The change was instantaneous. Krezoc grimaced in pain. *Gloria Vastator*'s motor functions were being severed.

To the right, the night flashed with fury.

*'We're down!'* Drahn voxed. *'Right leg severed by two slabs. Took two of the bastards first.'*

Krezoc walked the Warlord to the right, shifting with a new tilt of the island. 'Can you retreat?' she asked Drahn. The commander asking the question was detached, barely linked to the warrior fighting to kill two opponents.

Drahn's laughter was sardonic. *'Drag ourselves to firm ground? Perhaps.'*

'Do it.'

*'My weapons systems are operational. We can provide support.'*

Belicosa and Mori, simultaneous shots at the right foot of the Banelord, in the wake of a steady mega-bolter stream to strain the Iron Skull's shields. 'Save *Fatum Messor*,' Krezoc ordered. She was running the cold arithmetic again, comparing the remnants of both forces. Drahn's position was isolated. Her salvoes would be of limited use. Better to preserve something. *Fatum Messor* was not far from the edge of the city.

*Gloria Vastator* had gone much further in, and the slab was drifting further and further still.

The las and shells hit. The beam melted halfway through the leg where it joined the foot. The leg buckled and the ground gave way. The Banelord sank on one side into lava. The impact of its torso smashed the weakening surface. Fissures multiplied, and the forward third of the slab broke into pieces. The Banelord fell backwards into the waves.

Krezoc turned *Gloria Vastator* on its waist axis the moment she saw the disintegration of the slab, turning the Vulcan onto the other Banelord, unleashing another Apocalypse flight while the Belicosa recharged and another shell was loaded into the Mori's chamber. The Warlord's void shields blazed under the traitor's energy assault. Crimson, warp-tainted plasma burned through the defences and melted the front armour.

The primary weapons readied. Her will gave the order to fire again. In the same moment, she registered a flood of vox-bursts and auspex reports. The shape of the battle changed second to second, and the equations reduced to a single solution.

The war had turned into a chaos of skirmishes and duels, determined by the chance of the city's immolation. Slabs broke up, capsized and sank. The names of princeps and god-machines disappeared from the feed to the manifold. Enemy signals vanished too. Krezoc's situational awareness stripped the confusion of the battlefield to the essential vectors. The Banelord before her, and one other, engaged by *Crudelis Mortem*. That fight was to the west, about the same distance from the shore of the magma ocean.

Krezoc aimed the volcano las and quake shells low again. But the ground held, and so did the Banelord's defences. It closed in, firing again. A smaller slab ground against *Gloria Vastator*'s, and two Ravagers marched off it, joining the battle.

Second to second, the changes.

*Hold them off, hold them off*, Krezoc thought. The god-machine stepped backwards and its carapace weapons sent missiles and mega-bolter shells into the path of the Ravagers. The Banelord's plasma bursts cut deeper into armour. Krezoc felt the Warlord's movements slipping away from her grip. The machine-spirit roared, its coherence eroding.

Second to second...

'Rheliax,' Krezoc voxed as the weapons readied again, rising to aim at the Banelord's upper body and head. 'Status.'

He never answered. Instead, the west exploded. *Fatum Messor* died, its final cry annihilating the entire sector of Therimachus, the shock wave and heat sending the ocean into new paroxysms. Waves built upon waves, rage upon rage, and a two-hundred-foot monster crested to the west, swallowing the floating rafts of the city as it roared eastwards.

Second to second...

The first Banelord was doomed when Krezoc turned from it. It was falling to molten depths. There was no recovery possible. It died, but in its last burst of anger, its tail whipped above the waves and blasted *Gloria Vastator*'s back.

The Warlord fired its primary weapons. The advancing Banelord stopped in its tracks. Flame burst from its chest and fissured carapace. But the light of its eyes blazed undimmed. The Ravagers caught the Warlord in a plasma crossfire. Its void shields struggled, fading and surging erratically. Krezoc still shut out the damage warnings, but there was one she could not ignore. The radiation levels throughout the god-machine were climbing rapidly, even in the brief moments when it was not being hit.

The pain of the machine-spirit was so intense that her body arched, mirroring its agony.

'Thezerin,' she voxed.

'*Rupture in the power plant,*' the magos said, confirming what she knew. '*It is past containment.*'

'How long do we have?'

*'Minutes. Perhaps less.'*

'Can you accelerate it?' Krezoc had come to the final equation. She worked through the variables and the constants in an instant. She saw the inevitable, and she saw the path to the end of the war.

*'I can.'* Thezerin did not ask why.

'Do. And reach the head if you can.'

Weapons powering up again. More salvoes smashing the Ravagers. The one on *Gloria Vastator*'s left flank slowed, its left arm exploding. The Warlord took its final steps towards the Banelord. Krezoc writhed with the effort of trying to move the god-machine's legs. Grevereign and Vansaak's bodies trembled with the same pain. Krezoc fought through it to vox the moderati minoris. 'Abandon your posts,' she said. 'Make for the head. Evacuation is imminent.'

*'Negative,'* Konterus said. *'The fire is outside my pod.'*

*'My route is blocked too,'* said Haziad.

*'It has been an honour to serve with you.'* Konterus spoke with the proud fatalism of the legio.

*'Glory to the Omnissiah,'* said Haziad.

'Your duty will be remembered,' Krezoc said.

The moderati had the luxury of making farewells. That made them unusually fortunate.

Less than a hundred yards separated *Gloria Vastator* and the Banelord. The traitor's power claw snapped open and closed. Monstrous, sorcerous light built up in a corona around the claw.

'Brace for emergency launch,' Krezoc told Vansaak and Grevereign. The manifold registered the power plant's intensifying crisis. Energy slipped its reins. The chain reaction began. She saw the precise second of the end approach. She saw how long she could give Thezerin. Her awareness split evenly between *Gloria Vastator*'s final blows and the count towards zero. For the Warlord, the binary could no longer resolve into the *one*.

There was no grief yet. There was no room for it. There was no anticipation of pain when all was agony. Rather, there was the supremacy of cold fury. Krezoc joined with the Warlord's machine-spirit as it gave vent to its full wrath, hurling itself forwards to take down its final prey. Krezoc sounded the war-horn with the last blast of the weapons. *Gloria Vastator* roared, indomitable, undefeated. The barrage blew open the traitor's front armour. Burning promethium and ichor poured down the Titan, but it only came on faster, as if enraged by pain.

There was no energy left for the weapons. *Gloria Vastator* took one more step and then stopped, motionless on the heaving slab of city. The Ravagers hit it again, scavengers closing in on the fallen apex predator.

The monster wave came closer.

The Banelord arrived, its war-horn taunting, triumphant. It raised the claw.

The door to the command pod slid open to admit Thezerin. She closed it again and sealed it fully three seconds before Krezoc's deadline passed.

'Launch,' Krezoc said.

Explosive bolts severed the head's connection from the body of *Gloria Vastator*. Its rockets fired, and it shot upwards, arcing to the preset coordinates. Krezoc gasped. The manifold vanished. Void swamped her. She was barely conscious of the G-forces of the climb and the bone-shaking rattle of the engines. The pain of the separation went deeper than any physical sensation.

The mechadendrites still held her to the throne, but they were linked to nothing. Her mouth was open in a tendon-straining silent howl. Through the eyes of the head, as the slab rode up the towering wave, she had a last glimpse of *Gloria Vastator*, motionless, its massiveness standing its ground to the last.

Then they were out of sight. All she could see was the wave.

And then there was the light.

The void behind Krezoc's eyes shattered. She fell through its savage fragments, and they bled her. The pain of every separation from *Gloria Vastator* she had ever experienced was devoured by the greatest agony. Since she had become princeps over half a century before, the irreducible constant of her life had been the existence of the Warlord. Now it was gone. The pole star of her existence winked out.

*Far away, in another reality, the faint awareness of the blast, so huge it decapitated the wave, evaporating magma, disintegrating the raft of the city, the Warlord taking its killers to oblivion with it.*

The shards of absence stabbed into her being, shredding it, pulling every sense of self into bloody tatters. Meaninglessness engulfed her. She fell into endless cold.

*No.*

There was duty still.

She was Pallidus Mor, and for the Pallidus Mor, there was never release from pain or duty. In the end, they were always the same. In the void, there was cold, the cold of death, and it was her birthright and her strength. She seized it, made it ice, and made the ice the foundation of her being once more.

She dragged air into her lungs and gave voice to her pain. One long howl of grief, her entire soul issuing bloodily from her lungs. Then she opened her eyes to the world and to necessity.

The head of *Gloria Vastator* sailed over the Kataran 66th. It came in at a hard angle towards the ground. Retro-rockets fired a single blast just before impact, and the pod came down with a jarring crash.

Krezoc rose from her throne the instant motion stopped. She detached the inert mechadendrites. Her moderati were stirring, too, their eyes hollowed out. 'Keep moving,' she told them. *Keep ahead of the despair.*

Thezerin opened the door and they jumped out of the head to the ground. Tremors almost threw them off their feet. The long death of Therimachus continued to shake the land. Half a mile to the south stood a dark colossus. The walls of its drop coffin surrounded *Ferrum Salvator*.

Krezoc looked back towards the city. The explosion of *Gloria Vastator* had destroyed the rogue wave unleashed by the death of *Crudelis Mortem*. The ocean's upheaval was more violent than ever, but there was no more combat on the few slabs of the city that remained. Near the edge of the sea, what was left of the battle group had gathered. Krezoc made out the silhouettes of one Reaver and two Warhounds. Coming ashore, the rockcrete raft it rode washed inland by the waves pushed out by the great blasts, was the last Banelord. It was wreathed in flame and glowed with red corruption. If Rheliax had managed to damage the traitor, it showed no sign of its injuries. It strode ashore, the god of the battlefield, walking into the Pallidus Mor's barrage, contemptuous of its dwarfed foes.

Krezoc spoke into her vox-bead as she led the run towards *Ferrum Salvator*. 'Pull back,' she ordered. 'Keep the enemy busy, but do not engage directly.'

She ran faster over the trembling ground. Cracks snaked through the stone. She leapt over widening gaps. Vansaak, Grevereign and Thezerin kept pace.

'Your course of action presents considerable risk of failure and death,' Thezerin said, the electronic voice as flat and affectless as if she had been walking.

'It is this or defeat,' Krezoc answered.

She kept her eyes on the goal. The thunder of battle to the rear had nothing to do with her. She did not look back until they were at the feet of *Ferrum Salvator*. When she did, she saw the Banelord was making directly for Balzhan's Warlord. It fired to the left and right, disdainfully annihilating tanks and blowing the right arm off *Nobilis Arma*. The intelligence guiding its path recognised the last possible threat on the field. It would reach *Ferrum Salvator* in a matter of minutes.

From the exterior, the Warlord was dark as a sepulchre. But the power plant was running, and the interior glowed the sombre red of the god-machine's slumber. As they took the grav lift up the right leg, Krezoc wrestled with the conflicting sensations of familiarity and alienation.

'You were moderati here, weren't you?' Vansaak asked.

'I was,' said Krezoc. So long ago now, and the road of her return was paved with loss.

They left Thezerin in the operations centre. A crew of serfs and servitors awaited her there, sent down from the *Nuntius Mortis*. It was her task to awaken the machine-spirit fully. Thezerin paused at the threshold to a second grav lift, the one that would take princeps and moderati to the

Warlord's head. 'The machine-spirit will resist,' she said. 'It is injured. It is bereaved.'

'So am I,' Krezoc said, and the doors closed.

They reached the head. Krezoc paused before the throne. Balzhan's throne. For a moment, the decades fell away, and her instincts rebelled at the trespass she was about to commit. Her place was in the throne that Vansaak was about to occupy. Her responsibility was the Mori quake cannon. *Ferrum Salvator*, mightier and more ancient even than *Gloria Vastator*, was not hers.

Except it would have to be.

She sat in the throne, bracing herself. 'I will begin alone,' she told Vansaak and Grevereign. 'Wait for my signal.'

The figure of the Banelord was drawing closer. It left a wake of explosions and burning wreckage. It might turn its weapons on *Ferrum Salvator* at any moment.

Mechadendrites extended from the back of the throne. They plugged into Krezoc's ports.

She plunged into the manifold, and into the howling, raging outrage and grief of the machine-spirit. Its loss surrounded her, it battered her, it was a tempest to level mountains. She was an invader, and she would be destroyed.

*Remember me!* Krezoc commanded. *Ferrum Salvator* had known her once. It must again. *Remember me!* She poured her memories into the manifold, memories of her service in the Warlord, of the battles fought, of its corridors, of the jerk of recoil from the Mori, of her fusion of wills with Balzhan.

The machine-spirit circled her mind, uncertain. It yanked away when she tried to seize the reins. It was too consumed by its grief. It was hollowed, bereft of meaning and purpose. The winds of sorrow caught Krezoc in their anguished spiral.

She opened herself up to them. She met *Ferrum Salvator*'s loss with her own.

*We are the same. We are the bereaved. Let our grief become vengeance.*

The raw wound of *Gloria Vastator*'s end bled in torrents. Its psychic artery was severed, and her pain was a storm in its own right. The vortices of princeps and machine-spirit met. They fused.

A new pain began. Krezoc had joined with a god-machine with no ceremony, no preparation. *Ferrum Salvator* recognised her and their losses were the bridge. If it had not, the link would have been fatal. As it was, the bioelectric feedback jolted her body hard enough to make her spine crack. Her teeth clamped tight, slicing through her tongue. She felt as if blood were boiling inside her skull.

She held to the ice of duty and the necessity of sacrifice, and worked her way back to awareness of the outside world. She held it and the manifold in her will. Less than a second had passed since the mechadendrites had linked her to the god-machine.

'Now!' she shouted to the moderati. 'Do it now!' They had run out of time. The Banelord had turned its attention away from the distractions. It brought its tail and right arm cannons to bear. The barrels glowed as they charged. *Ferrum Salvator*'s void shields flickered into being. It took its first step as its arms began to rise. Moving the Warlord was pain. Krezoc felt as though she were pushing a marble statue uphill. Vansaak's will was in the manifold, assisting. So was Grevereign's. But they were distant, the connections rough, irregular like slipping gears. Without moderati minoris, she could barely touch the carapace weapons.

The Banelord fired. *Ferrum Salvator* marched into its barrage. The burning impact focused the anger of the machine-spirit. It hungered for the death of the Iron Skull. It would make the traitor pay for its new pain and for the totality of its grief. Krezoc barely had to command the Titan to walk. The weapons slipped into her control, eager for retribution.

'Charged,' Grevereign said.

'Loaded,' said Vansaak.

*End this now,* Krezoc thought. Her consciousness was spread thin throughout the Titan. The effort of keeping the machine-spirit from descending into the rage of insanity was shredding her. She had the weapons now. On the carapace, the Apocalypse missiles and plasma blastguns responded to her commands. Their aim was rough. It didn't need to be precise.

*End it.*

Fury tore the night in two. Krezoc's fury. The godmachine's fury. Fury shaped by loss, directed by ice. *Ferrum Salvator* was death. It had surged from its tomb to send the traitor to the dark. Four weapons drilled into the Banelord at the same point. It had shrugged off the attacks of the smaller Titans, but the minor damage mattered now. Its shields collapsed. The centre of its armour split wide. Burning plasma roiled from its midsection.

It did not stop. It marched on, weapons firing again, its power claw reaching forwards.

*End it.*

*Ferrum Salvator*'s war-horn thundered over the blasted landscape, answering the Banelord's challenge. The

Warlord moved through the energy and shells of the Iron Skull, mounting damage merely a goad. It blasted the traitor again. A Titan could not stumble, but its movements jerked. It was no longer a juggernaut. Even so, it came on.

The god-machines slammed together in their wrath. The Banelord's claw seized the volcano cannon. It began to crush the barrel. Explosions rippled down the gun's length.

*End it!*

Krezoc was *Ferrum Salvator*. Its body was hers. She reached forwards. Her arm was a quake cannon. She plunged it into the heart of the Iron Skull. She fired.

She was Pallidus Mor. She was the scythe of the Omnissiah. She was death itself, and before her judgement of bone, the enemy's form shattered.

# EPILOGUE

# REDEMPTION'S ASHES

The Company of the Bridge began the executions while the mountains still swayed and fell. As the world cracked, Ornastas smashed Darroban's skull. Then he and his followers began a methodical extermination. The heretics could not fight back. A thousand died in the first minute. Soon the plateau of rubble was clear of their foulness. The faithful of the company moved on, as far and wide into Deicoon as they could, killing with blade and club and rifle. The streets of the city that were not red with lava were red with blood. Ornastas did not know if Katara would survive the next hour, but the world's fate did not change his duty.

Katara did not end. At last, the ground calmed. Aftershocks still toppled buildings, and the day was hidden by ash and smoke and dust. But the war was over. His lungs burning, his breath coming in gasps, Ornastas led the company in hymns of thanks as they purged the ruins of Deicoon.

The executions went on for days. They were not done yet when the new landings began. Regiments of the Death Korps of Krieg came to Katara, bringing with them the judgement of the Imperium. Creontiades was razed. Therimachus was gone. Deicoon would be rebuilt, after a fashion. The world's heresy had been too widespread. The resistance was enough to spare Katara from being subject to Exterminatus, but that was all.

Katara would became a penal world.

Ornastas gave thanks for this judgement too. He saw its righteousness. His internment was punishment for the mistakes he had made. His life was a reward for his small efforts in the war. He wept with gratitude.

He saw Deyers once, early in the construction of the cell blocks at Deicoon. There was no thanks in the former captain's eyes. There was regret, bitterness, failure, hopelessness. They were assigned to the same detail for a few days. Ornastas tried to speak to him, but Deyers did not respond. He did not see Deyers speak to anyone. He toiled in silence, a man who had died at Therimachus, but for his failures was denied the rest of oblivion.

Carrinas approached Krezoc and Drahn in the loading bay of the lifter shortly before it was scheduled to launch. It had taken weeks to establish the most primitive space port in the region between Therimachus and the Klivanos Plain. The god-machines were as they had been at the end of the battle. No repairs were possible on Katara. *Fatum Messor* and *Ferrum Salvator* were secured in their immense bays. Their injuries were profound. So were those of their princeps. Krezoc saw that Carrinas favoured his right arm, mirroring the wound his Reaver had taken.

'We will be returning to the *Currus Venatores* within the hour,' Carrinas said.

Krezoc nodded. 'Then we shall consider the battle group dissolved.'

'Yes.' The Imperial Hunter seemed to feel he should add something, but the words did not come.

'Yes,' Krezoc said to him, showing she understood. The two legios had been reduced to fragments. She suspected the brutal victory was harder for the Imperial Hunters to accept than the Pallidus Mor. Carrinas looked like a man unsure if pride had a place in his existence any longer.

After a moment, Krezoc said, 'In the end, we all fought as we had to.'

'We did,' said Carrinas. And then, because there was nothing more to say, he saluted and left.

'As we had to,' Drahn repeated as they turned back to their contemplation of the god-machines.

'As always,' Krezoc said. That was their creed, their culture, their fate.

She remained in the bay when the lifter rose from Katara's surface. She had no interest in the shell of the world she was leaving behind. In her mind, she turned her back on the graveyard of comrades, and on the tomb of *Gloria Vastator*. She could gain nothing regarding the pain of the past. She looked instead at *Ferrum Salvator*. It was her future. It was her task.

She shook off the pointless luxury of grief. She had room only for the cold necessities to come.

# ABOUT THE AUTHOR

**David Annandale** is the author of the Horus Heresy novels *Ruinstorm* and *The Damnation of Pythos*, and the Primarchs novel *Roboute Guilliman: Lord of Ultramar*. He has also written *Warlord: Fury of the God-Machine*, the Yarrick series, several stories involving the Grey Knights, including *Warden of the Blade* and *Castellan*, as well as *The Last Wall*, *The Hunt for Vulkan* and *Watchers in Death* for The Beast Arises. For Space Marine Battles he has written *The Death of Antagonis* and *Overfiend*. He is a prolific writer of short fiction set in The Horus Heresy, Warhammer 40,000 and Age of Sigmar universes. David lectures at a Canadian university, on subjects ranging from English literature to horror films and video games.

# YOUR NEXT READ

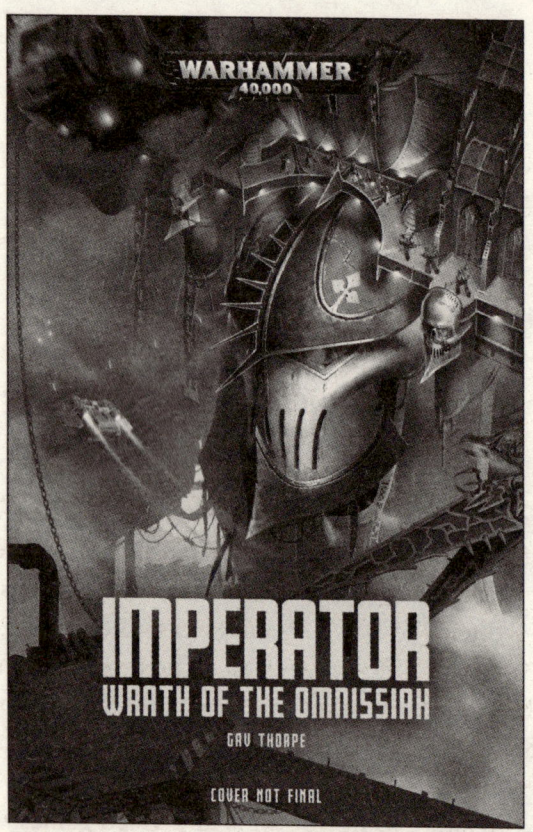

An extract from
IMPERATOR: WRATH OF THE OMNISSIAH
by Gav Thorpe

Find this title, and many others, on **blacklibrary.com**

The command module dominated the inside of the Imperator Titan's head. Two massive eye-like screens relayed realtime feeds from thousands of augurs across the war engine, creating a complex representation of the surroundings in both visual and noospheric frameworks. Exasas not only saw the doors of the barge's hangar as a human would, but knew exactly the composition of the metal and the weight and torsion values, as well as a welter of data on atmospheric pressure, temperature and other tertiary readings. It was the closest ve could come to feeling as the Titan felt without the benefit of the mind impulse units to organically share the sensation.

The princeps senioris' main command throne sat on a dais towards the back of the chamber, looking down at the three moderati positions. Each was a reclining chair beneath a tangle of cables that would connect to the incumbent's MIU systems. On the left, Moderatus Haili controlled the energies of the plasma annihilator; the twinned position on the right for the hellstorm cannon was the seat of Moderatus Rasdia. The two of them made for their couches, handing their interface helms to the tech-priests attending each station.

Moderatus Gevren was stationed between them, responsible for the activation and monitoring of the rest of the *Casus Belli*'s considerable arsenal – main battery, defence laser, anti-aircraft systems and point defence weaponry.

In most Titans the moderati were in sole control of their armaments, but the guns of the *Casus Belli* were too large for a single moderatus to control – or in the case of Gevren, too numerous. They were aided by gunnery teams with the weapons themselves, mostly slaved servitors that acted as extensions of the moderatus' will, each team overseen by a trio of tech-priests to ensure their continued operation.

Between the princeps senioris' throne and the moderati, and along the outer walls of the chamber to either side, the tech-priests addressed their panels and interfaces. The noosphere crackled with their intent, linking their minds even as dataports and mechadendrites connected them physically with the Omnissiah's greatest warrior.

Exasas' position was just behind the moderatus prime, from which ve could link into the noosphere signals related to the skitarii systems and personnel. Connecting to the cogitators, ve felt the company of warriors settling into their barracks chambers within the two leg-citadels, and several more platoons likewise preparing for departure in the battle stations of the akropoliz.

Ve could feel the skitarii as a homogeneous force, or relay part of vis strategic consciousness into one of a hundred and forty-two separate organisms via their noospheric cortical weaves. In a split second the magos dominus could switch to the individual view of a particular warrior – ve picked one on a whim and watched the faces of the three soldiers opposite through vis chosen receptacle's eyes. At the same time, cyclical simulators tracked other battle-pertinent datafeeds, for the moment semi-dormant and reliant on the last orbital data uploads ve had taken just before boarding.

Little had changed and the princeps senioris' assessment

that there was only a small probability of infantry engagement remained accurate. Their mission was to break the heretek lines defending a citadel and break into the mountain passes, spearheading the full battle group. It was an overwhelming use of force, mounted not only to sweep aside the barriers to the advances of the Astra Militarum and other skitarii armies, but also to demonstrate the folly of further resistance to the will of the Omnissiah.

Exasas played back vis memory-store of the prime dominus' instruction, passing it through vis thoughts and into the minds of vis subordinates.

Exasas [broad trans/concept/loop]: <Az Khalak will burn by nightfall.>

A tremor ran through the noosphere, a throb of intent that channelled into every datafeed. Exasas turned one of vis sensory inputs to the princeps senioris and saw that she wore her helm, its MIU cables linking her to the essence of the behemoth she would guide into battle.

Sharing her thoughts, made whole by the metaphorical sacrifice of her consciousness, *Casus Belli* started to rise from its slumber. The leading edge of a powerful wave of awareness touched upon the noosphere and digital systems flickered into wakefulness, caressing Exasas' sensory inputs. Ve heard a sigh from Iealona's parted lips, grunts and murmurs emanating from the moderati as they were joined to the machine spirit.

Exasas could not comprehend how it might feel to be one with the god-machine. Ve could interpret the millions of data-signals and extrapolate sensory curves for eternity and still not *know* what it was like to share physicality with the might of the Imperator. Only Iealona and her predecessors had shared that singular, glorious experience.

A visual feed highlighted a glint of amber light on the head of the bone cane leaning against the side of the command throne. While monitoring the other developments, Exasas allowed a portion of vis thoughts to consider the implications. Princeps senioris, and to a lesser extent moderati, had shortened lifespans due to their connections with the immortal spirits of the Titans. For the Machine God's warriors to live, their mortal components had to shed a little of their span. Even as her frail body was failing, the princeps senioris was able to clad her thoughts in the armour and power of the Imperator. She could not escape her mortality – in fact she hastened it – but in the time she had, she could share the body and thoughts of an immortal.

As an exchange, it was not without merit.

The noosphere flared with reports and counter-signals, confirming the readings of the plasma reactor, the online status of motivation and balance systems and the networking of the mind impulse units with the moderati and princeps senioris.

Exasas sent vis own confirmations, having spared a moment to check that all skitarii personnel were aboard and at their stations.

Awoken, the spirit of *Casus Belli* yearned to be free of the confines of the barge. With a final flurry of data exchanges, the tech-priests allowed the reactor to come to full power and the MIU to flow unhindered between the circuits of the Imperator and the synapses of its princeps senioris.

*Casus Belli* lived.